THE SAD

THE SADDLE CLUB SUPER COLLECTION

BONNIE BRYANT

THE SADDLE CLUB

HORSE CRAZY

BONNIE BRYANT

A BANTAM BOOK®
TORONTO • NEW YORK • LONDON • SYDNEY • AUCKLAND

For Marilyn E. Marlow

". . . AND THAT'S *FINAL,* Stephanie!" The words echoed in Stevie Lake's ear long after her mother had closed her bedroom door. She knew her mother meant what she had said. When Mrs. Lake's mind was made up, she was every bit as stubborn as her daughter.

Stevie flopped onto her bed. "I hate it when she calls me Stephanie," she grumbled. Her cat, Madonna, settled down at the foot of the bed. Absentmindedly, Stevie stroked the cat. She had some serious thinking to do.

Her parents had told her in no uncertain terms that if she didn't improve her grades, she wasn't going on the horseback riding camp-out next month. Unless Stevie proved she was a responsible student, her parents certainly weren't going to pay for this treat.

"Treat" was an understatement, Stevie thought. The Mountain Trail Overnight was the grand finale of the year. She'd been talking about it for months with her friends at the Pine Hollow Stables, especially her best friend, Carole Hanson. They'd even already decided what to pack! There was no way she was going to miss that camp-out. She just *had* to go.

Stevie sighed. She knew she could do well in school when she put her mind to it. She wasn't dumb, she was just more interested in having fun than doing schoolwork. Math did give her a bit of a problem, though. It was Stevie's bad luck that she had a math project on decimals and percentages due in three weeks for the quarter term grades—right before the overnight trip. There was no way she could do a math project good enough to improve her grade.

Possibilities raced through her mind. She considered basing her project on her younger brother Michael's guppies. She could count how many more appeared in the tank each day. Too boring, she decided.

She could do some work for her dad's business that had to do with decimals and percentages. But then, Stevie considered the consequences if she made a mistake for her father. So, that was out, along with the guppies.

It seemed hopeless. Suddenly Stevie realized that her mother hadn't said she couldn't go on the overnight trip if her grades didn't improve. She had just said that Stevie's parents woudn't *pay* for it.

If her parents wouldn't pay for it, Stevie could pay for it herself! Stevie had a few dollars in her frequently raided piggy bank, but definitely not nearly enough to pay for the overnight trip. Her allowance was usually gone a few days after she got it. Her twin brother, Alex, said the problem was that there were too many days in a week for Stevie's allowance. Stevie knew she couldn't do anything about that, so that meant saving up for the trip was out.

But she could *earn* money for the trip, Stevie thought excitedly. There must be a zillion things people needed to have done that they'd pay her to do. She'd never tried to earn money before, but lots of other kids did it, so it couldn't be too difficult.

Stevie's active imagination began working. She could see herself helping people carry groceries from the store. She could walk dogs. She could baby-sit. She could help her friends with household chores they didn't want to do. She could water plants for people on vacation. The possibilities seemed endless.

She was roused from her thoughts by Madonna's insistent meows at the bedroom door. Stevie hopped off the bed and opened the door for Madonna. The cat zipped out of Stevie's room and set off down the hall, swishing her tail disdainfully. Stevie, suddenly cheerful now that she had a plan, went down to the kitchen to help her mother with lunch. For as soon as lunch was over, it would be time to get ready for her riding class. And that was definitely something to be happy about. Besides, Carole would be sure to have more ideas for money-making schemes.

Things were definitely looking up.

CAROLE HANSON WAS already at Pine Hollow Stables. Her father, a Marine Corps colonel stationed at Quantico, near Washington, D.C., had afternoon duty that day. He could only bring Carole to Pine Hollow in the morning. He had apologized for dropping her off at her riding class two hours early, but Carole assured him that she didn't mind at all. She loved every minute she spent there. It was just about perfect.

Carole loved the stable area where Pine Hollow's twenty-five horses lived. The stable area was U-shaped, with the horses' stalls in double rows on the long sides of the U. The short side of the U housed saddles and bridles in the tack room, equipment such as grooming aids and pitchforks in the equipment room, and grain and a few bales of hay in the feed room. Carole could spend hours going from stall to stall, patting the horses, chatting with them. She could, that is, except for one thing: Max Regnery.

Max owned the stable, which had been passed down from his grandfather to his father, and then to him. On the surface, Max seemed sort of relaxed and laid-back, but it was well-known among the riders that idleness bothered Max. Carole was welcome to hang around the stable—as long as she was doing something useful.

Today, she was cleaning tack. She had a saddle on the stand in front of her and she applied the saddle soap with a damp sponge and rubbed it gently in circles. She admired the shine the soap brought out in the worn leather.

Like Stevie, Carole Hanson was twelve years old. She was a slender girl, with an intense look in her dark brown eyes. Her wavy black hair usually fell loosely to her shoulders, but when she rode in a horse show, she made a single braid in the back and pinned it up. Carole was totally committed to horses and planned to own her own stable when she grew up.

Even though her friend Stevie hadn't gotten to the stable yet, she wasn't alone. While Carole worked, she chatted with Max's mother, affectionately known as Mrs. Reg.

"Dad just kept apologizing to me today about having to bring me here so early. These days he's always telling me he's sorry about something. . . ."

"Well, perhaps he is, Carole," Mrs. Reg said gently.

Carole thought about that for a minute. It was true that her father had been sorry, and really sad, ever since her mother had died six months earlier from cancer. So had she. They both missed her very much.

"But it's more than sad, Mrs. Reg," Carole said.

"I know that. I think your father does, too. But I think what he's sorry about is that he can't be both a mother and a father to you."

"But that's silly," Carole protested. "I don't expect him to be."

"Try telling that to him," Mrs. Reg said.

Carole buffed the saddle for a few minutes, considering how she might assure her father that he wasn't letting her down.

"Mrs. Reg," she said finally. The kind woman looked over at her. "Have you ever heard the expression, 'Tell it to the Marines'?" Carole asked wryly.

Mrs. Reg laughed and nodded. "Okay, then, you'll just have to wait. He'll learn, Carole, he'll learn."

Carole picked up the clean saddle and carried it over to its rack. Then she reached for the bridle, which hung on the bracket above the saddle rack.

"When you finish that bridle, I need you in the ring," Max called brusquely as he strutted past the tack-room door. He was leading Patch, a black-and-white pinto, toward the indoor ring. Carole paused to watch. Max and the horse were followed by a girl who looked familiar to Carole, and a woman who appeared to be the girl's mother. The girl was slight, with wavy brown hair and a little ski-jump nose, which was sprinkled with freckles. She had a look most people would call cute, but her eyes seemed to see beyond the surface. One glance and Carole could tell she was smart.

Carole suddenly remembered the girl's name. It was Lisa Atwood. She went to the same school Carole attended, Willow Creek Junior High School, but she was a grade ahead of Carole. Carole had barely recognized her, though. At school, Lisa had the confident look of a straight-A student—which she was. Honors Day at the junior high was really more like Lisa Atwood Day. But here, at the stable, Lisa looked decidedly uncomfortable. Carole decided to finish soaping the bridle quickly so she could see what was up.

LISA RELUCTANTLY FOLLOWED her mother into the riding ring. She felt like a fifth wheel. Mrs. Atwood was having a lively conversation with Mr. Regnery about horsemanship. She was telling him about this wonderful rider who had so much natural talent, but just a bit of schooling, who wanted to be his student. She told him about the rider's devotion to the sport and the hours spent reading about equitation.

"In fact," Mrs. Atwood said, "just the last time she rode in a show, she got a blue ribbon."

With a start, Lisa realized her mother was talking about her. *She* was supposed to be this naturally skilled, intensely interested rider. The show her mother was talking about had been a pony ride at the zoo when she was four years old. *All* the kids who didn't cry had gotten blue ribbons!

Lisa sighed. The thing that Lisa was the best at was school. But it seemed that her mother wanted her to be the best at absolutely everything else. Lisa took ballet class on Mondays, painting on Wednesdays, tennis on Fridays, and now seemed to be fated to go riding on Saturdays and Tuesdays. She didn't really *mind* this frenzy of activity, but it seemed a little ridiculous to her.

And sometimes, like now, she felt a little embarrassed. She and her mother had spent hours last weekend at the riding store, purchasing the outfit she now wore. Lisa was in riding breeches, with shiny black leather boots up to her knees. She had on a white cotton shirt and a necktie. (Mrs. Atwood had insisted on buying a tie with horses on it. She wouldn't even let Lisa borrow a striped one from her brother.) Lisa was also wearing a black jacket, slightly flared at the hips. On her head, she had a black velvet-covered hard hat. To complete the outfit, Lisa carried a pair of brown leather riding gloves. She may have looked ready to enter the ring at New York's famous Madison Square Garden, but she felt like an imposter, dressed for Halloween.

Max Regnery waited quietly while Mrs. Atwood continued her one-sided discussion about Lisa. He held Patch's reins with his right hand. Lisa stood to his left. While Mrs. Atwood chatted, Max turned toward Lisa.

Lisa was sure he thought she was weird. She felt her face reddening. And then, while Max was nodding sagely at Mrs. Atwood, he winked at Lisa.

He knew! He knew her mother was stretching the truth. And that was all right with him. When Mrs. Atwood finally stopped talking, Max turned to Lisa.

"Have you done much riding, Lisa?" he asked.

"Just ponies at the zoo, and once at day camp. I mean, I know how to walk and how to stop the horse," she said, ignoring her mother's glare.

"Okay, then, we'll see what you learned at the zoo," he said. Then he showed her how to mount Patch and, within seconds, she was on the horse.

"Good," Max said approvingly. She felt wonderful. Being in the saddle was okay, but what was wonderful was that this man didn't take her mother's silliness seriously, and he didn't mind that she really didn't know much about horses. Lisa felt more relaxed than she had since they'd arrived. Maybe riding wouldn't be so bad, after all.

Just then, a girl entered the ring. She was wearing riding breeches and high boots like Lisa's, but they had long ago lost the sheen of newness. Somehow, this tall slender girl looked comfortable in her riding clothes—not costumed, the way Lisa felt.

"Lisa," Max said, "I'd like to introduce you to Carole Hanson." He pointed to the girl. "Once our young riders are past the introductory level, they're grouped more by age than skill. You'll be in Carole's class so I thought you should meet now."

"We already know each other, Max," Carole said. "We go to the same school."

Lisa looked at her in surprise, then recognized the seventh-grader. At school, Carole always seemed to be disorganized, papers flying around, pencils trailing from her book bag. But here at the stable, Carole seemed completely at ease and full of confidence. Lisa found her very likable—the kind of girl she'd like to have for a friend. Maybe horseback riding would be fun after all. Somehow, Carole's confidence was contagious and Lisa caught it.

"Okay, now, show us your stuff," Max said. "Begin with a walk."

Lisa took the single reins in her hands and nudged Patch with her heels. The horse began walking. It was a slow, rambling pace, comfortable and natural. After she'd circled the ring three times, Max asked her to trot. She didn't know how to make a horse trot, but it seemed that Patch understood the word, for he immediately began a bouncy trot. Almost instinctively, Lisa began rising and sitting with the horse's pace, more to get away from the bouncing saddle than anything.

"Good, good," Max said. "Now walk again." The horse slowed to a walk. It didn't seem particularly extraordinary to Lisa, but she could see that her mother was beaming with pride.

Just at that moment, another girl came through the door from the outside into the indoor ring, letting the door slam loudly behind her.

Patch, like all horses, had a long memory for things that spooked him. Fireworks spooked Patch, and even though he couldn't see any flash of light, a sudden loud noise was just as bad. At the instant the door slammed, Patch took off with Lisa aboard.

First, Patch bucked. Lisa grabbed the front of the saddle with her right hand and held on for dear life. At least when Patch started galloping, she had a good grip. At first, Lisa was afraid she would fall off, and then, she began hoping she would. Patch tore around the ring so fast, Lisa could barely tell where she was. Walls, doors, people, all merged into a blur. There seemed to be no way to control the horse.

She heard Max calling to her, telling her to relax—or was he saying it to Patch? It didn't matter. Neither of them was relaxed. Patch kept circling the ring and Lisa kept holding on. And the pounding of the horse's hooves continued in a very fast-one-two-three beat. It was like a waltz at top speed.

Lisa could waltz. She'd taken ballroom dancing for three years. She began to sway with the horse, shifting her weight in the saddle with the rocking of the pace.

Now; instead of feeling like a helpless sack of flour, she was riding! She was in control. Lisa let go of the saddle and put gentle pressure on the reins. Instantly, Patch responded, slowing his pace. Apparently, he was no longer spooked and was ready to behave. He switched to a trot. She pulled the reins again, and the trot changed to a walk. Lisa brought him over to where her mother and Max stood with Carole. Her mother was white-faced. Carole's look was one of frank admiration. Whoever it was who had slammed the door was nowhere in sight.

Max reached up to help Lisa dismount from Patch. "That must have been some zoo!" Max said.

MAX DISMISSED THE girls, asking Carole to show Lisa around. Lisa followed her and Patch back to the stall area while Max and Mrs. Atwood talked before the class.

The Class. It would be Lisa's first class and she wasn't sure she liked the idea of it. She was still feeling a strange mixture of fear and pride from her ride on Patch.

"What made him go crazy like that?" Lisa asked.

Carole glanced around uneasily and then shrugged. "Most horses *do* have things that frighten them, which you try to avoid. Some don't like dogs. Some jump when they see something waving. Patch doesn't like loud noises. See, when something scares a horse, he remembers it for a long time—especially if it happened when he was young. They may learn in the meantime that the thing *isn't* dangerous, but they still never forget that fear from long ago."

Although it was odd, it made some sense. After all, even though Lisa was confident that she'd handled Patch well when he'd run away with her, she knew it would take her a long time to forget how scared she'd been. Perhaps she had something in common with these big animals after all. But if everybody knew Patch was afraid of loud noises, why would someone have slammed the door and caused her such trouble? Lisa was too shy to ask and Carole didn't offer an explanation.

While they walked Patch to his stall, Lisa looked around her. There were stalls on either side of the long skylit passageway. Each stall had a window on the outside with a door-gate three-quarters high—just high enough for the horses to look over. The horses watched Lisa and Carole passing them with Patch.

"Horses are curious animals. They like to be able to see what's going on," Carole said. "That's why stalls always have windows and doors the horses can see over."

Carole slid open the door to Patch's stall and led him in. She handed Lisa the reins to hold while she loosened the girth on the saddle. Lisa looked in Patch's eyes, expecting to see some resentment. There was none. The horse's dark eyes seemed almost sleepy and certainly contented. Lisa patted Patch's soft nose tentatively.

"You'll be riding him in class," Carole explained.

"It's easier to leave the tack on him, and he doesn't mind, as long as he can get some water." Carole checked to be sure there was fresh water. She slipped a halter over his bridle and snapped ties on either side of the halter so he couldn't roll in his stall and tangle his tack. Then she patted Patch on the neck and the two girls left the stall, sliding the door closed and locking it behind them. Lisa noticed that the stall had a standard sliding latch as well as a key chain-type clip.

"Is that really necessary?" Lisa asked.

"Just watch," Carole said. As if on cue, Patch stuck his head out over the top of his door and began nuzzling the sliding latch. Within seconds, the horse had grasped the bolt and was working at it. "Horses are natural door openers. Never give one a chance—he'll take it, and you'll be in big trouble. Okay, next stop is the tack room."

Just then, a nearby stall door slid closed and was latched. Carole tried to lead Lisa past the girl who had emerged from the stall, but the girl's look was commanding.

"Lisa Atwood, this is Veronica diAngelo," Carole said, introducing her to the pretty girl with smooth black hair. "She's the—"

Veronica interrupted Carole. "So *you're* the new student!" she said.

It surprised Lisa that anybody knew she was there. She didn't know what to say to Veronica, so she just stood there awkwardly while Veronica's eyes took her in. It took only a few seconds. Lisa felt as if she were being analyzed by some twenty-third-century ultrabeam. When Veronica's smile warmed from automatic to sincere, Lisa knew she'd passed. She didn't know why.

"How's Cobalt?" Carole asked, gesturing toward the horse behind Veronica. Lisa turned to look. Even with her untrained eye, she knew this regal-looking horse was special. His shiny coat was coal-black. His bright eyes sparkled and his head nodded invitingly. Carole walked over and rubbed his forehead affectionately.

"He's fine, as you can see," Veronica said offhandedly. "Would you like to exercise him tomorrow?" Carole nodded eagerly. "Good. Then let's talk after class to make arrangements." There was something almost threatening in Veronica's voice, Lisa thought, but she couldn't imagine why that would be. Carole seemed so nice. Veronica turned to Lisa. "I'll see you in class," Veronica said, and walked off.

The girls continued along the hallway toward the tack room. As they progressed, they met some of the other students, but it all happened so fast, Lisa couldn't remember any of their names until Stevie Lake came running up to them.

"Carole!" she cried. "I've got to talk to you!"

Carole grinned at her irrepressible friend. "This is

Stevie Lake," she told Lisa. "And Stevie, meet Lisa Atwood, who's joining our class."

"Oh, right, the new girl," Stevie said. Lisa wondered how she had known. Could she have been the one—

"What's so exciting?" Carole asked Stevie, interrupting Lisa's thoughts. Stevie jumped right into a long explanation about her parents and her grades at school. Lisa realized that she knew the Lakes. They lived in her neighborhood—at the nicest end of it. They had a big house on the corner with a pool in the back yard.

She'd seen Stevie around, but she'd never met her. Stevie went to a private girls' school in the neighboring town. Because Lisa knew their house, and knew that Stevie went to the exclusive school, she knew the Lakes were fairly wealthy, but she never could have guessed it by looking at Stevie. Stevie was wearing an old, worn pair of jeans and some cowboy boots that looked as if they'd seen better days—*lots* of them. Stevie caught her eye. Embarrassed, Lisa looked away. She realized she'd been looking at Stevie almost the same way Veronica had looked at her. She didn't want to be rude to Stevie. In fact, Lisa thought Stevie was funny and seemed like a lot of fun.

"I think I'll *die* if I can't go on the trip!" Stevie exclaimed. "I mean, I've already chosen the jeans I'm taking and I've been having dreams about campfires and mountain trails for months! Right? You have, too." Carole nodded. "So, anyway, I've got this scheme—I know, I *always* have a scheme, right? But this one'll work. It'll make me a fortune. I'll never have to do another math project as long as I *live*!" Then, without taking a breath, Stevie switched gears. "Look, I'll tell you all about everything later," Stevie went on. "I've got to groom Comanche before class. Welcome to Pine Hollow, Lisa. You're going to love it. This place is just full of traditions." And before Lisa could ask her what she meant, Stevie disappeared into one of the stalls. Lisa laughed to herself. She'd like to be Stevie's friend, but if it meant following crazy conversations like that, it could be exhausting!

"Is she always like that?" Lisa asked.

"Always," Carole assured her, smiling broadly.

But somebody like Stevie could be the kind of person who would slam a door when Patch was in the ring. What kind of friend was *that*?

"Coming?" Carole asked Lisa. "Tack room's this way." Obediently, Lisa followed her to the end of the corridor.

The first thing Lisa noticed in the tack room was that it appeared to be very disorganized. Endless tangles of leather straps hung on the wall, and saddles seemed to be everywhere. The second thing she noticed was the smell. The rich, pungent leather smell mingled with the earthy smell of the horses themselves. She breathed deeply.

"It's great, isn't it?" Carole asked her.

Lisa nodded, smiling. "But how do you know what tack to take for each horse?" she asked.

"Oh, it's all completely organized," Carole assured her. "You just have to get used to the system. Also, in here are hard hats for riders who don't have their own like you do." Carole pointed to a large wall where about forty black velvet-covered hard hats of all different sizes hung on nails. Lisa stared at the wall for a second. Carole did a double take.

The hats weren't just hanging on the wall. They were, in fact, carefully arranged so that they spelled "MTO!" Carole burst out laughing.

"What's that?" Lisa asked.

"That's Stevie," Carole said as if it were an answer to the question. "What I mean is that Stevie did it. She's always doing fun things like that. She thinks that the hat wall is a sort of message board, too. Anyway, MTO stands for Mountain Trail Overnight, which is an overnight horseback trip next month. You'll hear more about it soon. Stevie's excited about it already. Actually, so am I."

Lisa wondered if she'd be able to go on such a trip. Would she want to? Would her mother *let* her go? It seemed odd to Lisa to realize that only a half an hour ago, she was dreading climbing on a horse, and now, after one hair-raising ride, she was already thinking about an overnight trail ride. But she didn't have much of a chance to think about it anymore. Carole was all business on her tour of the tack room.

Carole showed Lisa the tack she had soaped earlier, which they would now put on Delilah, the horse Carole would ride in class.

"Delilah—that's a funny name." Lisa laughed.

"Wait'll you see her," Carole said, leading her back out to the row of stalls. This hall was on the other leg of the U from where Patch was stalled. Delilah, it turned out, was a luscious creamy palomino with a long silvery mane. Her name really fit her. She *looked* like a flirt. But she didn't act like one. She was clearly a high-strung creature and nervous around strangers. It didn't seem to bother Carole, though. She patiently went about her business.

In the next fifteen minutes, Carole showed Lisa how to put a bridle and a saddle on a horse. It seemed impossibly complicated to Lisa.

"I'm never going to remember the difference between the crownpiece and the headband—to say nothing of the cheek strap and the throatlatch!" she groaned.

"Oh, sure you are," Carole consoled her. "See, you already know their names. That's half the battle. Besides, the horses are pretty used to this process so they don't make a fuss. As long as you need help, one of us will give it to you. Then, when you don't need help anymore, you'll be able to give it to another new student."

"Oh, I don't know about that."

"It's one of the traditions around here, Lisa," Carole told her patiently. "We all help out. We help the stable and we help each other. It's a good way to learn. And, it helps keep the costs down."

"Oh, it's not that I *wouldn't* help another girl," Lisa said quickly. "It's just that I don't know if I'll ever be able to live up to that tradition!"

That was the second time Lisa had heard the word *tradition*. She had the feeling she would hear it often at Pine Hollow. But she did wonder how far one had to go to help other riders. Lisa was almost certain Carole knew who had slammed the door and frightened Patch. Why was she being so closemouthed about it? Who was *she* helping?

"You almost done in there?" Stevie Lake asked, peering into Delilah's stall, interrupting Lisa's thoughts.

"Almost," Carole said. "But do me a favor, huh? Can you get Patch ready for class and bring him to the mounting area for Lisa?"

"Sure," Stevie said agreeably.

Stevie left and Carole showed Lisa how to tighten the horse's girth—the "belt" that held the saddle in place. Delilah didn't like it at all. First, she'd take in a big breath so that when she let it out, the saddle was too loose. Then, she'd step away from Carole or bob her big head up and down. She even got Lisa cornered in her stall. Lisa was frightened, but Carole took it all in stride. As many times as Delilah tried to cause trouble, Carole spoke sharply to her and proceeded to tighten the girth. After six tries, the job was done.

It reminded Lisa of what it was like to look after her little cousins, ages two and four. She didn't much like doing that.

Finally, Carole led Delilah and Lisa to the mounting block in the outdoor ring. Patch was fastened to the fence, waiting for Lisa. She eyed him uneasily, but he seemed unconcerned. Lisa decided she should be, too—until she realized that she and Carole were practically the last ones ready for class. Max was across the ring, helping one student tighten the girth on her horse. Everybody else was looking at them. Lisa really didn't want everybody to watch her get back on the horse, but there was no way around it. She looked to Carole for instruction.

"Okay, here's what you do," Carole said. "First, see that horseshoe nailed on the wall?" Lisa saw it and nodded. "Well, that's one of our traditions here. It's the good-luck horseshoe. You have to touch it with your right hand before you mount your horse. Nobody has ever been badly hurt at Pine Hollow and the tradition is that it's because of the good-luck horseshoe." With that, Carole brushed the worn horseshoe with her right hand. Then, smoothly, she swept onto Delilah.

It was such a simple motion, done so gracefully, Lisa thought. She could do it, too. Mimicking Carole's gesture, she touched the horseshoe. Then, she held the reins in her left hand and prepared to mount, uncomfortably aware of the eyes that stared at her.

Something was wrong. She raised her left leg to where the stirrup ought to have been and tried to lift herself up, but it didn't work. Because there wasn't any stirrup there. Nothing to step on, nothing to hold her foot. She tried jumping up, but the horse was too high. She tried pulling herself up by the saddle, but that didn't work either because she couldn't get a good grip. She stared helplessly at the impossible task, tears welling in her eyes.

That was when she heard the first spurt of laughter. Through the blurry tears of frustration, she looked at the girls in the class around her. Each seemed to be smirking, some giggling, and one, openly laughing. Lisa's eyes met Stevie's. Stevie tried to control her laughter to meet Lisa's stare with mock seriousness. But her mirth bubbled over and she tried to smother her giggles by putting her hand over her mouth.

Lisa was beginning to get the feeling that there were some traditions at Pine Hollow that she wasn't going to like at all.

"NOW, LISA," MAX called firmly from the center of the ring, "I want you to sit more forward in the saddle. Tighten up on your reins. Don't *lean* forward. Relax your calf muscles. Heels down!"

Lisa tried, but following five directions at once wasn't easy.

"Shoulders back! And don't point your toes out. But relax those muscles!"

Make that eight directions at once. Lisa sighed. Things seemed to have gone from bad to worse ever since Carole had helped her replace her stirrups and she'd mounted Patch. She'd never make it as a rider and she didn't think she'd want to. In fact, she'd never wanted to. It was her mother who wanted her to ride.

Lisa decided that her mother could take the lessons from then on.

At last, Max focused his attention on someone else. Lisa could relax now that she was out of the spotlight. She looked around at the six other riders in the ring. Besides Carole and Veronica, there were Polly Giacomin, Betsy Cavanaugh, Meg Durham, and, of course, Stevie Lake.

Lisa could still feel the pain of Stevie's laughter after she'd intentionally left the stirrups off Patch. Lisa thought the kind of girl who would play such a mean trick on her was also the kind of girl who would slam a door when Patch was in the ring. After all, Carole and Stevie were good friends, so that explained why Carole wouldn't tell Lisa that Stevie had caused Patch to run wild. Lisa promised herself that she'd get even with Stevie. She had no idea how, or when, but she knew the time would come, and she'd be ready when it did.

"Okay, now, pair up!" Max called to all the riders. That meant that they were to begin riding two by two.

"Isn't this just the *most* fun?" Betsy asked Lisa as she brought her horse next to Lisa and Patch. "I love horses!" Lisa really couldn't think of an answer so she stared straight ahead.

"Good, Lisa. Much better," Max said. She liked the compliment, but Lisa had no more idea of what she was doing right than of what she'd been doing wrong.

* * *

USUALLY, STEVIE HATED it when Max had the class walk and then trot two by two. It meant the end of the class was near and she'd have to stop riding soon. But today, she didn't care so much because her mind was filled with plans. Before class, she'd talked to one of her neighbors about earning money and she had her first assignment: pool cleaning.

Also, she had to tell Carole about her plan. Carole could be flighty about some things, but when it came to horseback riding, she was all business. Earning money for horseback riding was part of that business. Stevie was counting on her help.

At Max's instruction, the horses began trotting. Class was almost over. All that was left was the soda whip—another of Pine Hollow's traditions. On the last trip around the ring, each rider grabbed a riding whip from a bucket. The rider who got the whip with the bottle cap attached to it was in charge of getting sodas for the rest of the class and her partner was in charge of putting her horse away.

"Hey, it's my turn for the soda whip!" Stevie called out as she grabbed at one of the whips in the bucket. No luck. It was just a whip. "Oh, drat!" Stevie said. The other girls in the class laughed.

"How come you want it today?" Carole asked her.

"I've got a job to do—remember I told you about how I've got to earn money?"

Carole nodded her head, but Stevie thought she looked doubtful. Stevie would show her that she could stick with *this* project!

In the end, it turned out that Lisa got the soda whip. Disappointed, Stevie dismounted and led Comanche back to his stall while Carole explained to Lisa what she'd have to do.

Lisa groaned inwardly, but she wasn't going to let Carole—or anybody else—think she was a bad sport. She readily relinquished Patch to Betsy and headed for the tack room, where there was a small locker area and the refrigerator.

Lisa was alone. All the other riders were with their horses. Mothers, fathers, and sitters waited in the office, which was in a separate building on the stable grounds. Suddenly, much sooner than she had expected, Lisa had her chance to get even with Stevie.

Usually, Lisa could shrug off something like this afternoon's incidents and maybe even laugh a little bit, too. But this time she just couldn't. She remembered vividly her terror as Patch tore around the ring. She could still hear Stevie's laughter and see the smirks from the other riders when Stevie had left off her stirrups. She could still feel the embarrassment.

There, on the floor, was a pair of sneakers belonging to Stevie Lake. Her initials were written all over them and there was nobody else in the class whose initials were S.L. So, before Lisa opened the refrigerator to get seven sodas, she took a minute—just a minute—to tie knots in Stevie's shoelaces.

When Lisa was younger, she'd been in the scouts—one activity which she had loved—and she'd learned every kind of knot there was. She did them all in Stevie's laces. Of course, Stevie would know who had done it. Lisa was the only one with the opportunity. But that didn't matter, because Stevie would also know she deserved it. A practical joker had to be prepared for retaliation.

Quickly, Lisa did her work, rendering Stevie's shoelaces useless for hours, unless she'd been a scout, too. As soon as she was done, Lisa grabbed seven sodas from the well-stocked refrigerator and delivered them to the riders who were untacking the horses. She was far away from the tack room when she heard Stevie's first yelp.

CAROLE WAS CLOSEST to the tack room when Stevie began screaming. She ran to find out what had happened. She found her friend standing in her socks with a pair of sneakers in her hand. The laces of the sneakers were all tied in an incredible set of knots, impossible to untie—and making it impossible even to separate the sneakers from each other.

"I don't believe this! And when I'm in such a hurry!" she wailed when she saw Carole. "Look at this mess! I can't go anywhere! And I can't wear my boots when I'm doing my job!"

Carole was used to Stevie's mood swings. She could be all sunshine one instant and thunderclouds the next. But the thunderclouds usually disappeared as quickly as they came. This time, they didn't. Stevie had told Carole about the job she was going to do. Carole had rarely seen her so eager to work. And now, at the very least, she was going to be late. This thundercloud wasn't going to disappear quickly.

Stevie went on howling about the knots. Within a few seconds, all of the riders were in the tack room, watching Stevie's temper display. Carole glanced at the girls. Most looked embarrassed at Stevie's outburst. A few looked sympathetic. Veronica stood by one door, masking a smile. Carole would have expected that.

Then Lisa appeared at the door. One look at her face and Carole knew she'd done it. Stevie, glaring at the onlookers, spotted Lisa at the same time. Her face had "guilty" written all over it.

Carole knew that Stevie could dish it out, but she didn't like to take it. It wouldn't occur to Stevie that Lisa hadn't liked the stirrup trick any more than Stevie was enjoying the shoelace trick. All Stevie would think of was that she had something important to do and she was going to be late because of this dumb joke. She began yelling at Lisa.

Lisa would have been perfectly happy to disappear into the ground. She hated being yelled at—almost as much as she'd hated being made a fool of without her stirrups. If she could have taken back the knotted laces, she would have—*if* Stevie also could have taken back the slammed door and the stirrup trick. While Stevie ranted, Lisa stood still. Then, when Stevie turned her attention to unknotting, Lisa turned on her heel and walked to the office, where her mother was waiting to drive her home.

Lisa slumped in the far corner of the front seat of the car. "I'm not going back there again, Mom. I don't want to learn to ride. I don't want to see those girls ever again. I don't want to ride another horse. I don't want to tighten saddle girths, slip bits into mouths, relax my calf muscles, look straight ahead, heels down, toes pointed in, shoulders back, forward in the saddle. Ever."

"Oh, darling, isn't it exciting?" Mrs. Atwood asked, almost breathlessly. "Max is such a dear and the horses are so nice. I'm just certain you'll be a wonderful rider, Lisa. Your father and I will be so proud of you. And, imagine—Veronica diAngelo is in your riding class. You will be her friend, won't you, dear?"

Had her mother heard her? Lisa wondered. Or, had she once again only spoken her doubts and her unhappiness to herself?

"You're so *quiet*, Lisa," her mother said, answering

that question for Lisa. "You *did* have a good time, didn't you, honey?"

Lisa knew that once again, she would just do what her parents wanted her to do. Once again, she'd be their good little girl, no matter what *she* wanted to do. Besides, her mother had made an interesting point. Veronica diAngelo *did* seem to want to be her friend. So, perhaps she could be Veronica's friend and ignore Carole and Stevie altogether.

For a moment, Lisa forgot about Carole and Stevie and thought about her gentle horse, Patch. All during class, Patch had been very sweet-natured, as if he understood her ignorance. In spite of herself, she had to admit that being on a horse was nice. It made her feel tall and powerful. And, much as she disliked Max telling her eight things to do at once, she'd loved it when he'd complimented her.

All right, she sighed to herself. She'd go again on Tuesday to the next class—and then she'd see. . . .

"CAROLE, CAN I borrow money for a phone call?" Stevie asked, hopping over to Carole on her one sneakered foot. She held the other sneaker, still hopelessly knotted, in her left hand.

"Sure," Carole said, reaching into her pocket for change. "What's up?"

"Well, I'm going to be late for my job. I'm supposed to vacuum the O'Mearas' pool. I thought I'd ask my brother Chad to do it for me. They've got a daughter I think Chad has a crush on. He'll like that. Then, I can go over to the shopping center and put a notice on that bulletin board. Good idea?"

"Sure," Carole said, though it seemed to her that Stevie would make more money by *doing* a job than by advertising for one. "Then I'll walk over there with you. I can get the bus from there."

"Great," Stevie said. "We can hang out for a while."

"Well, okay, but how's that going to earn you any money?" Carole teased. Stevie just shrugged.

After Stevie made her phone call and finished unknotting her lace, the girls walked the half-mile to Willow Creek's modest shopping center. Willow Creek was a small town about a half-hour drive from Washington, where most of the people, Stevie's parents included, worked. Since they were so close to the big city, they didn't have much of a shopping center. It had a variety store, a supermarket, two pharmacies, a jewelry store, an electronics store, a sporting goods store, a Tastee Delight ice cream parlor (TD's, as it was called by the junior high school kids who hung out there), and three shoe stores. It wasn't exactly a major shopping mall, but it was within walking distance of the stable *and* Stevie's house. Carole and Stevie had both spent a lot of time hanging out there after riding classes, especially since Carole's bus stopped there.

"I can't believe what that new girl, Lisa, did to me," Stevie said as they walked together to the shopping center.

"And what about what you did to her?" Carole asked.

"What I did to *her* was funny," Stevie said defensively.

"Funny to you, maybe, but not to her."

"Well, maybe, but playing a joke on a new kid is sort of a Pine Hollow tradition—"

"One I think we could do without," Carole interrupted. "Besides, didn't you hear what happened to her when Max was testing her?"

"No, what? Did she get some dirt on that fashion-model outfit she was wearing?"

"No, but she could have—or worse. She was on Patch and somebody slammed the door and—"

Stevie knew what happened when a door was slammed near Patch. "Oh, no! Patch took off? Who would do such a stupid thing? Did she fall hard?" Stevie asked.

"No. It was amazing. She stayed on!"

"No wonder Max let her into our class," Stevie said. For a moment she felt badly about her stirrup joke—until she remembered how angry she'd been about her shoelaces. And then they got to the shopping center and everything else was forgotten. Carole trailed Stevie into the supermarket and waited while she filled out a card for the bulletin board announcing she would do "odd jobs." She posted it with a pushpin. "Now, let's go to TD's," she said.

"First I want to stop at Sights 'n' Sounds. I think it'll be fun if I can get Dad a golden oldies tape—you know, stuff from the sixties when he and Mom were dating. I was teasing him about that stuff the other day. It turns out when he was in high school, he really wanted to be a rock star. He sang for me. I think it's a good thing he went into the Marine Corps instead!"

Giggling, the girls went into the electronics store together. Carole took a long time choosing a tape, trying to find one with the songs her father had been singing. While she riffled through the tapes, Stevie hung out near the counter, reading promotional material on televisions and stereos. Then she found a contest she could enter. First prize was a trip for two to Hawaii. She thought that would be fun. She was quickly lost in a dreamy image of herself riding bareback along the beaches of Hawaii at sunset, a handsome boy on the horse next to her. She wore exotic flowers in her hair. By the time she'd filled out the contest blank, she had put an imaginary lei around her neck and she could practically smell the sweet tropical blossoms.

"I'll take this one, please," Carole said, handing a cassette to the check-out woman. It brought Stevie right back to Willow Creek. A little disappointed to find herself so far from her tropical paradise, she shoved the contest entry slip into the cardboard box by the cash register and then waited by the door for Carole. A chocolate-dipped ice-cream cone would taste good—since she couldn't go to the luau she'd just daydreamed about.

* * *

CAROLE TOOK THE tape and stuffed her change into her pocket, following Stevie to TD's. Stevie paid for her cone and headed toward the outside tables behind the shop. Carole had to wait for her sundae and then dropped most of her change on the ground. Then she nearly dropped her ice cream while she picked up her money.

Stevie reappeared at the front of the shop in time to help Carole collect all her belongings.

"Sometimes I don't know how you make it through a day without me," Stevie teased.

"I wonder the same thing myself," Carole said, laughing at her own disorganization. "And I'll never make it through the MTO without you, so you'd better tell me more about this new business venture of yours."

As if on cue, Stevie was off and running—way off, as far as Carole could tell. Stevie was a great friend and all that, but her attention span was notably short. Carole didn't see how in the world Stevie could focus on earning money long enough to make the fifty dollars she'd need for this trip—particularly if she expected to do pool cleaning and garden work like hedge clipping! Stevie didn't know the first thing about hard work.

"Stevie!" Carole said when she'd finished. "Are you for real?"

"Sure am," Stevie said positively. "This is a new me, Carole."

"I don't want a new you. I liked the old one just fine. But wouldn't it be easier if you just got the old you to do a math project?"

"You know what kind of grade you get for counting guppies?" Stevie challenged. Carole had no idea what she was talking about. She stared blankly at Stevie. "C. That's what you get for guppies. And a C won't do me any good. I need at least a B-plus, preferably an A. So that's why I'm earning money."

"But what if you don't make enough to go on the MTO?" Carole asked. "You'd miss three wonderful days and nights of riding on a gorgeous mountain trail. We've been planning them for—"

"You don't think I can do it, do you?" Stevie was genuinely hurt.

"Well, it's not that," Carole protested. "It's just that . . ." Carole didn't know what to say. She didn't really believe Stevie could make fifty dollars cleaning pools and clipping hedges in three weeks. And, if she spent all of her time *trying* to earn the fifty dollars, she'd never have time to do a math project; and if she didn't do a math project *and* didn't make fifty dollars, she definitely wouldn't go on the trip.

Carole and Stevie had been talking about that weekend trip for months. It was the most important event of the year. It was what riding was *really* about. They had practically had their clothes packed for weeks! Now it seemed that their plans were falling apart and there was absolutely nothing Carole could do about it.

Carole took a bite of her sundae, but its gooey sweetness didn't make her feel any better. Stevie didn't seem to notice anything was wrong. She just began listing all the wonderful things she could do for people—for money.

". . . walk dogs, water plants, deliver newspapers, put up wallpaper, paint . . ."

Paint and wallpaper? Carole thought to herself. At this rate, Stevie would never make it to the MTO!

Lisa stared uncomfortably at Pepper, the horse she was to ride in class that day, her second riding lesson. She held his bridle in her right hand, but she really had no idea how to put it on him, and while she looked at it and tried to figure out how it went, she only seemed to manage to get the straps more tangled.

"Hi, Lisa," Veronica greeted her over the stall door, walking toward her own horse's stall. Maybe Veronica could remind her what to do.

"Can you help me with this thing?" Lisa began. "I mean Carole showed me all about it on Saturday, but it's so complicated—"

"Sure," Veronica said agreeably. But instead of coming into the stall to help Lisa herself, she called down the stable's hallway, "Oh, Red! The new girl here,

Lisa, needs some help. Can you saddle Pepper for her?"

A man, perhaps twenty, emerged from a stall at the end of the hall. He had a pitchfork in his hand. He'd obviously been cleaning out one of the stalls. He didn't say anything to Veronica—he just glared at her. But he also nodded and put down his pitchfork. As soon as he began walking toward Lisa, Veronica continued into Cobalt's stall.

Lisa watched carefully as the guy—who introduced himself as Red O'Malley—put the tack on Pepper. It seemed so easy when he did it.

"If I'd have had to do this myself, class would be over by the time I'd be done," Lisa joked.

Red glanced at her. "You want to learn?" he asked, almost surprised.

"Well, sure," she said. "Isn't that what we're here to do?"

"I guess so," he said. He began to explain the parts of the bridle and the saddle to her, showing her how to put them on and fasten them securely. She'd heard it before, but she knew she'd have to hear it all several times more before she could do it herself.

"Thanks," she said, honestly grateful to him, as he helped her bring Pepper to the ring.

"Good luck," he told her as he left for the stalls.

Lisa brushed the good-luck horseshoe with her hand and mounted Pepper.

"Well done," Max said, handing her a riding crop.

She glowed a little bit at Max's compliment, but tried not to show it. Sedately, she began walking Pepper around the ring while the other girls finished tacking up and mounting.

Riding Pepper felt both strange and familiar, but not unpleasant. Lisa felt secure at a walk. It was a comfortable pace. She'd learned how to make her horse turn to the right or left; by moving the right or left rein away from the horse's neck you could turn his head in the direction you wanted to go. It surprised her a little when the horse, who, after all, had so much experience, followed her directions; she was so new at riding. But he did. If she held her hands still and sat down in the saddle with her back straight, he stopped. If she applied gentle pressure with her calves, he started again. Pepper did what she told him to do. It really worked! The horse was actually following her instructions. Lisa smiled to herself. She was riding.

CAROLE TIGHTENED DELILAH'S girth and led her to the mounting area. "I've got a job!" Stevie called to her, her eyes dancing with excitement. She was already in the ring, circling at a walk on Comanche.

Carole breathed a sigh of relief. If Stevie had a job, that meant she really might be able to earn the money to go on the trip. Maybe, just maybe, it would work out.

"What's the job?" Carole asked while she slipped her foot into the stirrup and lifted herself up.

"It's for one of my neighbors," Stevie said. "He's had a drainage problem with his gutters. He's asked me to clean them for him."

Stevie cleaning gutters?

Carole swung her right leg over the saddle and sat down on Delilah. She checked her stirrup length, and when she was satisfied it was correct, she pressed on the horse's sides with her legs and Delilah moved forward.

As soon as she could feel the horse's movement under her, Carole was transported. She was doing something she loved doing, but it wasn't just that. When she was on a horse, she was in a world where *she* was in control. Carole couldn't control Stevie any more than she could control her father—or than she could have controlled her mother's illness—but she could control Delilah. It was something they enjoyed together. And while she was riding, she didn't have to think of the funny picture of her friend Stevie cleaning gutters. Stevie probably didn't even know where the gutters were on a house!

Then class began.

"OKAY NOW, PAIR up!" Max called for the girls to ride in twos for their final rounds in the ring that day. Lisa had been concentrating so hard in class that she was nearly exhausted, but there *was* something wonderful about it.

"Oh, good!" Veronica said with delight in her

voice. "I'm your partner." She urged her horse up toward Lisa's and their horses trotted together. Lisa was having trouble keeping her horse at a steady trot. Pepper kept wanting to walk.

"Here's how you do it," Veronica said. "You tap him just behind your leg with your whip. It's what I do with Cobalt. It makes him keep going."

Lisa didn't like the idea of using a whip on Pepper, but Max had assured her that it didn't hurt the horse. He told her that a whip should be used to reinforce an instruction the horse already knew he was supposed to follow. Lisa tapped Pepper with the whip. He began trotting at the same pace as Cobalt.

Veronica leaned over toward Lisa while they trotted together. "Isn't some of this stuff just so boring?" Veronica asked.

To Lisa the class was hard, confusing, uncomfortable, difficult, and a little frightening. It wasn't boring at all. But it was lonely. She wanted to make friends at the stable. She liked Carole; she'd like to be her friend, but then she'd have to be Stevie's friend, too, and it wasn't likely Stevie would ever want to be hers. It seemed that the only person at the whole stable who wanted to talk to her was Veronica, the very girl her mother wanted her to become friends with. It was very tempting just to agree with Veronica. She was about to when Max spoke sharply to them.

"You girls can chatter all you want while you're having your sodas. Lisa, perhaps you don't know it, but our rule is that there is no talking during class."

Lisa felt her face flush.

"I'm the one who was talking, Max," Veronica volunteered.

Max's lips formed a thin line, but he said nothing to Veronica. He just continued with his instructions to the class. "Now, we'll finish our exercise for today with figure eights. Carole, you and Polly please lead off across the ring. . . ."

When the class was over Lisa just wanted to remove Pepper's tack and go home. She didn't want to talk with anybody over sodas in the tack room. She hoped her mother was waiting outside so she could go right home and escape to her homework.

"Here's your soda, Lisa," Veronica said, handing it to her. "Meg got the soda whip, but I thought you'd like to have yours right away. You looked thirsty to me."

"Thanks," Lisa said automatically, accepting the cold can. She took a drink. It did taste good to her. "And thanks, too, for telling Max you were talking. How come he didn't get mad? I thought he was all set to blow up at me."

"Oh, there are ways to manage Max," Veronica said airily. "Say, would you like to come to my house on Saturday after class? Maybe stay for dinner? I can talk my mother into letting us order a pizza—with *everything.*"

"Uh, sure," Lisa answered automatically. At least she was making a friend—one her mother would approve of—even if it wasn't the one she wanted. Then she realized that by agreeing to go to Veronica's after class on Saturday, she was agreeing to go to another class. Her mother would like that, too. Deep down, she wondered how *she* felt about becoming friends with Veronica, the girl who "managed" Max and ordered the stable boy around. But maybe a friend like that was better than no friend at all. Maybe.

CAROLE TOOK HER time untacking Delilah. She'd been hoping to have time to visit with Stevie, but Stevie had dashed out, spilling her soda as she went, as soon as she'd untacked her horse. Carole had to wait for her dad and he'd be at least another half-hour. She decided to groom Delilah, who was stalled next to Pepper.

Carole didn't mean to overhear the conversation between Lisa and Veronica, but the walls were only boards and there was open space at the top.

To Carole, Veronica was the most stuck-up person she'd ever known. And she liked to collect admirers. It sounded like Lisa was being recruited for the collection. That was too bad, too, because Carole thought Lisa was nice as well as smart. Maybe, Carole thought, if she hadn't been so busy with the horses and if Stevie hadn't been so busy with her jobs, they would have invited Lisa to TD's with them. That would have been nice. But it was too late for that now.

Carole picked up the brush and began working from the top of Delilah's neck, brushing vigorously. The last thing she heard was Veronica' whiny voice. "Tell your mother you're coming to my house and you'll be home about, oh, ten o'clock on Saturday."

That meant that from the end of class until it was time to go home, Lisa would be with Veronica for almost seven hours. Carole was glad she wasn't the one who was going to Veronica's. She wouldn't want to spend that much time with Veronica—ever!

LISA FELT REALLY good right after class on Saturday. Max had worked with her a lot during class. At first, it seemed like he was picking on her, but then, as she listened to him, she realized that he was trying to help her—and that if she listened to him, it would work.

They were working on a posting trot. Lisa had to rise and sit with the beat of the horse's hooves. Two things about it were difficult. The first was sensing the beat. The second was keeping her balance. But Max was patient and she was learning. Even Patch, whom she was riding again today, seemed to have patience with her.

"He's in a better mood today than when I rode him before," she said to Max.

"Why do you say that?" he asked.

"Because he's easier to ride today."

"Maybe," was all that Max said. "Okay, now up, down, up, down, up, down . . ."

Lisa tried her hardest to follow his instructions, and by the end of the lesson, she actually thought she had a good idea of what she needed to do.

"Now, instead of standing straight up, swing your hips forward and up—yes! That's it! Very *good*, Lisa. Nice job!"

Lisa could hardly believe it. She'd gotten a real compliment from Max. She had enjoyed the lesson and—although she hated to admit it to herself—she was really having fun riding. Another nice thing that happened was that Max kept telling Stevie to keep her mind on her riding. Lisa was still smarting from Stevie's trick. They hadn't spoken to each other since the first lesson. That was okay with Lisa.

Not only were all these nice things happening, but Lisa was making friends, too. Or at least one. This was the day she would go to Veronica's house.

Her mother had been somewhat horrified by the idea of Lisa returning home as late as ten o'clock, but when Lisa reminded her she'd be at *Veronica's*, Mrs. Atwood agreed.

As soon as class was over, however, things began going a little sour for Lisa. And then they went straight downhill from there. While she was still untacking Patch in his stall, Veronica appeared.

"Aren't you done *yet*? I don't want to keep my mother waiting," Veronica told her. Lisa squirmed at the idea of keeping Mrs. diAngelo waiting. She tried to hurry, but the more she tried, the more trouble she had with the tack.

"I've got the bridle all tangled and I can't loosen the girth," she complained.

"Here, I'll help you," Veronica said, sighing. She finished the job quickly, though she made it clear she wasn't happy about having to do Lisa's work for her. Then, as they carried the tack back to the tack room, Polly Giacomin came up to Veronica. She barely seemed to notice that Lisa was standing next to Veronica.

"Uh, hi, Veronica," she said. "My birthday's this week and I'm going to have a party. A magician is coming, too. Would you like to come?"

Lisa thought it was rude of Polly to invite Veronica to a party right in front of her, even if they weren't friends. After all, what were telephones for? But before she had a chance to feel really hurt, Veronica raised one eyebrow and stared at Polly with a blank look of surprise. "I'm busy," she told her.

"It's Friday afternoon," Polly said, apparently realizing too late that Veronica meant she'd be busy *whenever* Polly had a party. Polly looked down at the ground as her face turned red in embarrassment. She turned and walked away.

"Imagine that," Veronica said to Lisa. "Polly Giacomin thinks I'd go to her party. A *magician!*" She laughed out loud. "Polly probably expects her friends to wear paper hats, too! Is she for real?"

Lisa stared at Veronica uncertainly. She loved to see magic shows. A birthday party with a magician seemed pretty neat to her. Lisa couldn't figure out why Veronica objected to a magic show, but she had the distinct impression that arguing about it—or even asking about it—wouldn't help her friendship with Veronica in the least. She laid the saddle on its rack in the tack room and put the bridle on the bracket. "Come on, let's go meet your mother," she said.

Veronica looked out the window toward the parking area. "I don't think she's here yet," she said.

Lisa decided not to remind Veronica that she'd been rushing her for her mother's sake only a few minutes ago. Right then it seemed to her that about the worst thing that could happen would be if Veronica were to give *her* the same glare she'd given Polly Giacomin. Lisa kept quiet.

Mrs. diAngelo came to pick the girls up twenty minutes late. She was driving a Mercedes, and there were two large dogs in the back seat, tracking mud on the leather upholstery. Veronica jumped in the front seat, leaving Lisa to sit in the rear with the dogs. Lisa liked dogs okay, but these Labrador retrievers didn't seem to like her. They certainly weren't being very friendly. She spent the entire trip to Veronica's house trying to get enough space on the seat to sit. Neither Veronica nor her mother paid any attention to her problem. They were locked in battle in the front seat on the subject of a new pair of breeches for Veronica.

"Did you see *hers*, Mom?" Veronica said, pointing to Lisa in the rear. Mrs. diAngelo looked at Lisa in the mirror. "That's the kind I want—only in hunter green."

"Those won't suit you at all," Mrs. diAngelo said firmly. As she went on to describe exactly what was wrong with Lisa's riding pants, Lisa squirmed. She couldn't wait until the ride was over. By the time they arrived at the diAngelo house, Veronica and her mother weren't speaking to each other. But Lisa suspected Veronica would wear her mother down eventually.

Lisa couldn't imagine arguing with her mother until she wore her down. And she didn't think she'd like to have a mother who could be worn down like that. Even more important, she couldn't imagine taking up an argument with her mother in front of a guest.

The diAngelo house was grander than anything Lisa had ever seen, except in movies or on guided tours. It was a big old white colonial house, with a two-story portico in the front. The center of the house was three stories high. The wings were each two stories. The whole house was surrounded by perfectly trimmed bushes and glorious shade trees carefully spaced in the acres of lush grass, all set against a background of rolling Virginia hills. Behind the house, Lisa spotted a swimming pool, a garden shed that was larger than most garages she'd seen, and a guest house as big as her own home.

She swallowed deeply and closed her eyes to see if the house would disappear. When she opened them, the house was still there and Veronica was staring at her.

"Come on, Lisa. We don't have all day."

The dogs tumbled out of the car in front of Lisa, running into the beautiful house with their muddy feet. The girls followed them in.

The rest of the day was mostly a blur to Lisa. She had lived all her life in nice middle-class neighborhoods and nice middle-class homes. Veronica had apparently spent her life living in a palace. Lisa had a lot to learn about living in luxury, but Veronica knew it all. She knew how to get the maid to deliver a snack to their room. She knew how to get the gardener to vacuum three leaves off the bottom of the pool before they swam. She knew how to get the chauffeur to go for the pizza even after her mother had said the girls would eat whatever the cook made that night.

Lisa shook her head in amazement. No wonder Veronica had known how to order Red O'Malley to saddle Pepper for her. And actually, come to think of it, she seemed to have a good idea of how to order Lisa around. She never asked Lisa what they would do next. She *told* her. Lisa didn't mind too much because most of it was new to her, but there was a part of it that made her uncomfortable.

After they'd finished their pizza, Veronica made another announcement.

"Mom stopped at the shopping center to pick up a prescription before riding class and I snuck into Sights 'n' Sounds and rented this neat horror movie she wouldn't let me see. We'll watch it now." Veronica slipped the tape into the VCR in her room, which was connected up to her television.

Lisa looked at Veronica's clock radio and saw that it was eight-thirty. If she watched the movie, she'd never be able to be home by ten. Besides that, she didn't want to watch a horror movie, whether Mrs. diAngelo permitted it or not.

"I think it's time for me to go home," Lisa said.

"Home!" Veronica said, as if the very idea were a personal insult to her.

"Well, it's getting late, and I don't want Mom to have to come out after ten. She'd be annoyed, you know?"

"Don't be ridiculous!" Veronica said. "Your mother doesn't have to come here. We can have the chauffeur drive you home. It's no trouble at all."

Though Lisa wasn't crazy about the idea of a chauffeur driving her, it would solve one problem. She knew that if her mother had a chance of being invited into the diAngelo house, she'd want the grand tour of absolutely every inch of the mansion.

Veronica pushed the start button on her remote control, piling the pillows from her sofa on the floor to watch the movie in comfort.

"I think I'd better go home now," Lisa said firmly. Veronica gave her a dark look. Lisa felt cornered. "That pizza was a bit much, you know. I think it was the sausage. My stomach feels a little funny."

"I'll have the chauffeur get the car now," Veronica said, reaching for the intercom on her telephone.

CAROLE CARRIED A large bowl of fluffy, salty, buttery popcorn into the living room with one hand. The other hand held two cans of soda, precariously balanced, and two napkins.

"Ten hut!" she said sternly.

Her father, who had been stretched out on the sofa, jumped to attention. "I knew I smelled something wonderful," he told her, helping her unload the sodas.

"Well, it's quarter of nine and I know that *Casablanca* is on at nine. It's no fun watching a movie without buttered popcorn—and since *you* made dinner, I thought it was my turn for popcorn."

"There's still a front-row seat available, too," Colonel Hanson said, pulling a lounge chair up near the sofa, which he'd claimed for himself. Carole slid a small table between them and put the bowl on it. She had just settled into her seat when the phone rang.

"I'll get it, honey," said the colonel. "I want to get the salt anyway."

"Okay," Carole agreed, digging into the popcorn, which was salty enough for her taste.

Carole didn't know who was on the phone, but her father was chatting so agreeably that she suspected it was Stevie. The first time the two of them had met, they'd discovered their mutual passion for old jokes. Some of them were pretty corny but Stevie and Colonel Hanson seemed to love them.

Carole heard her father roar with laughter. "That's a good one. I'd forgotten that!" he said.

Carole stood up and walked into the kitchen, where her father was talking on the wall phone.

"Come on, Dad. Let *me* talk to Stevie."

"My daughter is pushing me around again, Stevie," he joked into the phone. "Next time we talk, though, I'm going to tell you the one about the gorilla on the golf course. Can't wait, can you?" he said before relinquishing the phone to Carole.

"Hi," Carole said. "What's up?"

"Oh, I'm just exhausted," Stevie said matter-of-factly. "I spent the whole afternoon after riding class going from door to door in my neighborhood, giving everybody fliers I had copied so they could tell me if they have work for me to do. Nobody did. They all just wanted to invite me in for cookies. Remind me next time not to accept cookies from Mrs. Crocker. She makes these health-food things and they're disgusting."

Carole laughed. Stevie then told her about the dogs who had chased her and about some people who were really rude to her. She told about one house that smelled funny and it turned out they were just putting up new wallpaper and did Carole know how funny new wallpaper smelled? She told Carole everything that had gone on. But there was one thing that hadn't gone on at all. Nobody had asked her to do any work.

"No luck, huh?" Carole asked.

"Oh, they'll call me eventually," Stevie assured her.

"But will 'eventually' be soon enough for the MTO?"

"Of course it will," Stevie snapped.

Stevie's moodiness was sometimes more than Carole could take. "What makes you think that?" Carole shot back. And then, wary of Stevie's fiery temper, she spoke quietly. "You know, you've really got me worried," Carole said. "The MTO is just two weeks from now and you're going to have a hard time earning so much money so quickly. I mean, what kind of jobs have you been offered so far? Cleaning pools, cleaning gutters? You can't do those things, can you?"

"No way," Stevie said. "I ended up giving both of those jobs to my brothers."

"But Stevie—" Carole began.

"Don't worry about me, Carole," Stevie said. She said it with such assurance that Carole was tempted to believe her. Did Stevie have something up her sleeve?

"To tell you the truth, I think it's *me* I'm worried about," Carole confessed. "I really hate the idea of going on that trip without you. Can you actually imagine me and Veronica and maybe that new girl, Lisa, on the camp-out? I'll spend the entire three days telling Veronica to take care of Cobalt herself."

"But you won't let her, will you?"

"No, of course I won't. She hasn't got the first idea of how to take care of that beautiful horse of hers. Cobalt would be better off living in the wild than with Veronica."

"Why don't you talk her into letting him run free and then you can capture him and own him yourself," Stevie suggested.

"*That's* the most sensible thing you've said tonight. And it doesn't make any sense either," Carole teased.

"Thanks, pal. I'm going to sit here now and wait for my customers to swamp me with calls. You go watch that movie with your father. Oh, and ask him for me: What's handsome and purple and says 'Play it again, Sam'? Bye!"

Carole hung up the phone and returned to the living room, where the movie was just beginning. Carole asked her father the riddle. He chuckled.

"What's the answer?" she asked him.

"Humphrey Bogrape," he told her.

Carole laughed, but it didn't make her feel any better about Stevie's chances of earning enough money.

"ARE YOU THE young boy who is looking for chores to do?" the voice on the phone asked. The phone had rung right after Stevie had hung up with Carole.

"Yes," Stevie answered. She didn't want to disagree with a potential customer.

"Well, the beds under my hedges need cleaning. Can you rake them out for me?"

Gardening work like that was hot, sweaty, and unpleasant. Stevie didn't even like to rake leaves in the cool weather in the fall.

"I'll pay two-fifty an hour," the woman continued.

"Sure," Stevie said eagerly.

"Monday at four o'clock?"

"I'll be there," she promised. She took the woman's name and address and then hung up.

Raking out from under hedges was not only difficult, but was a job for a small person who could crouch easily to reach the hard places—a younger person, perhaps one who was trying to save up money for a fifty-gallon fish tank. Someone just like her younger brother.

"Michael!" Stevie called upstairs.

Her nine-year-old brother appeared on the landing. "Yeah?" he asked suspiciously.

"Want to make some money?"

Michael smiled broadly, nodding.

The phone rang again. "Is this Stevie Lake?" a man asked when she answered. "I need someone to help me clean out my attic," he began. Stevie knew it was a perfect job for her twin brother, Alex.

Stevie made the arrangements and gave Alex all the information. By the time she'd finished with that, the phone rang again. She couldn't believe it. She had begun to think that walking around the neighborhood had been a dumb waste of time, but it seemed that a lot of people had work they wanted done. Stevie was nearly ecstatic.

The phone kept ringing all day Sunday, too. One woman wanted somebody to dig worms for her six-year-old son to use for fishing. Another needed somebody to till her vegetable patch for planting. Mrs. Ziegler wanted somebody to sit for the twins Wednesday afternoon. It seemed that everybody in the world had something they didn't want to do themselves. Stevie could understand that. After all, she didn't want to do her math project.

On Sunday night, practically exhausted from making plans on the telephone all day long, she fell into bed and closed her eyes. In her dreams, Stevie was riding Comanche proudly along the wooded trail, sleeping bag fastened to the back of the saddle. Only Stevie, Carole, and Max were on the trail, though. Everybody else was back in town: They were an army of kids doing loads and loads of chores for Stevie's neighbors. Stevie smiled contentedly in her sleep.

THERE WAS NO riding class on Monday, but Carole had called Veronica on Sunday to remind her that she'd promised Carole she could exercise Cobalt after school. Veronica had forgotten completely. Carole wasn't surprised. It wasn't so much the promise to Carole she'd forgotten; it was Cobalt who had slipped her mind again. But she readily agreed that Carole could do the job. Carole had the school bus drop her off by the shopping center and she got to Pine Hollow by three-thirty.

The outdoor ring was empty, so she'd be able to work with the beautiful Thoroughbred in the large exercise area. Smiling to herself, she entered his stall. He nickered and nuzzled her shoulder when she put her arm around his shiny, silky black neck.

"Poor old boy," she whispered into Cobalt's ear.

"Your problem is that you're too pretty. If you weren't so good-looking, Mr. diAngelo would never have bought you and you'd never belong to Veronica. You'd belong to somebody who would really care about you."

Not that Veronica didn't care about Cobalt, exactly. She cared about him in the same way she cared about her friends. They were part of a collection to her, things that made her feel more important just because they were hers.

Cobalt was a Thoroughbred stallion. Mr. diAngelo had paid a lot of money for him. But Cobalt wasn't the right kind of horse for Veronica. His personality didn't mesh with hers at all, though Carole wondered briefly if anybody's personality could mesh with Veronica's. Cobalt was high-strung and powerful. Veronica needed a horse she could control, and she couldn't control him. She was constantly fighting with him. Carole knew that it couldn't be much more fun for Veronica than it was for Cobalt, but she felt sorrier for Cobalt than she did for Veronica.

She slipped on his saddle and bridle and within a few minutes had led him out into the ring. Max was there training a new bay, which he had just bought as a school horse. He smiled broadly when he saw Carole and Cobalt.

"I always like to see you riding that horse, you know," he said.

"And I always like to ride him," Carole said. "I keep hoping that if I can ride him enough, he'll develop some confidence in people."

Max shook his head a little sadly. "He's a fine horse, and always will be. Veronica can't change that. But she can damage him as a riding horse. I mean, look at this one I'm on, Diablo. He was named that because of his short pointy ears." Carole looked at the ears and laughed. They did look a little devilish. "Anyway, this is a nice horse and he's gentle enough for most of the new riders. But his mouth is a little tough."

Carole knew what that meant. If a horse needed very strong signals with a bit to follow commands, he had a tough mouth. If a slight signal was followed, the horse had a soft mouth.

"Cobalt has a soft mouth. Every time I see Veronica tug at her reins, or ride on them, yanking away, I think about that soft mouth and how much it must hurt."

"No wonder he's so jumpy when Veronica's riding him," Carole said.

"But not with you," Max assured her.

Carole knew that was true and she was proud of it. Cobalt responded to the slightest pressure with the reins. In fact, he usually responded just to the pressure of her legs on his sides. Sometimes, it seemed to Carole that Cobalt could practically read her mind.

"Let's see how smart you and that horse really are,"

Max challenged her. "It'll give me a chance to test Diablo, too. I'll lead you on a figure around the ring. See if you can follow it."

Carole loved challenges like that. She was sure Cobalt would be up to it, too. Most riding classes were for the students. With a lot of work, and cooperation from the horses they rode, they could learn the basics of riding, and most students were perfectly content with that. Once the rider was schooled, however, the rider's goal became teaching the horses good manners and good form. This was known as dressage. In dressage competitions, it was the horse as much as the rider who was judged.

Max wanted to test Diablo and he wanted to give Carole a chance to have Cobalt show off his stuff. As a Thoroughbred, he was fast. Thoroughbreds were bred for racing. But Carole knew that Cobalt was smart, too, and she was eager for the challenge.

Max led off. He cantered Diablo down the center of the ring, turning him left at the corner. Then he began a figure eight crossing in the center of the ring. As he passed the center of the X, he changed leads, meaning that Diablo's gait switched from one lead leg to the other when he switched directions. A horse always had to lead with his inside leg on a circle, since all his weight was being thrown in that direction as he leaned into the turn. When the circle changed directions, as in a figure eight, the lead went from one side to the other.

With Max on board, the transition was smooth, barely noticeable. Max brought Diablo down to a walk and took him over to the side of the ring, making room for Carole.

With nearly invisible leg signals from Carole, Cobalt sprang into a balanced canter down the center of the ring. Carole swung Cobalt to the left and began her figure eight. As if he'd known all his life how to do it, Cobalt switched leads at the X both times they went through it.

"Beautiful, Carole, beautiful," Max said.

Carole knew it wasn't she who deserved the compliment. It was Cobalt.

Max worked with Carole and Cobalt for more than an hour, teaching both of them good habits and good manners. Never once did Cobalt try to take the bit or get fussy. He seemed as content to follow Carole's instructions as Carole was to give them.

"That's all for today," Max said. "You two have put in a lot of hard work. Time for a cooldown for both of you and a nice grooming—for Cobalt, that is!"

Carole dismounted and walked Cobalt in circles around the ring until he was cool enough for his grooming. She took him back to his stall and removed his tack. Then she brought the grooming tools back from the tack room.

Grooming a horse took a long time, but Carole didn't mind. When she groomed Cobalt, she thought he was the most beautiful horse in the world. She cross-tied him in his stall and began the job by cleaning out his hooves with a hoof pick. Next, she worked with a currycomb and then a brush all over his body, brushing out dust and sweat. She also used a comb and brush on his mane and tail. Then she used a damp sponge to smooth his coat and make it shiny. Finally, she put a blanket on him to protect his coat and to keep him warm in the cool spring evening that was coming.

When she was all done with that, she took a sugar lump from her pocket and gave it to him. Usually, Carole didn't like to give horses treats. They were better off eating their regular meals, and besides, a horse that got treats often began to expect treats all the time. Carole had seen horses who just wanted treats and would nip at their riders. It was a very bad habit horses developed sometimes.

But with Cobalt, it was different. He seldom got treats from Veronica, so he didn't expect them. He liked the sugar lumps Carole gave him, and the carrots she sometimes brought, but he always kept his good manners—at least with her. Veronica, however, often complained about how naughty he could be. Carole didn't think Cobalt was the one who was misbehaving at those times.

She gave Cobalt one final hug and left Pine Hollow to catch the bus for home at the shopping center.

When she owned her own stable some day, Carole decided, she wouldn't let in any owners who didn't take really good care of their horses, no matter how important the people thought they were.

"OH, IS *THIS* your house?" Veronica asked on Saturday afternoon as Lisa's mother drove them up the short driveway. Suddenly, Lisa was sure it was going to be a very long day.

The two girls retreated to Lisa's room. Mrs. Atwood said something about bringing milk and homemade marshmallow krispies in a few minutes. Lisa was glad her mother didn't see Veronica grimace.

Lisa liked her bedroom and she always had. It suited her very well. The walls were papered in pink flowers on a white background. She had a pink-and-white lounge chair covered in a fabric that matched the bedspread on her four-poster bed. She had a well-loved collection of stuffed animals by her pillow. On the far wall, next to her closet, was a small vanity with a large mirror. On the wall near the windows was the desk where she did her homework. There were two bookshelves containing her favorite books and some games and toys. There was a small rag rug near the bed. The rest of the floor was covered with wide wooden boards, which gleamed in the sunshine that streamed in every morning. As far as Lisa was concerned, it had everything she needed.

But she could see right away that for Veronica's taste it was missing a few things. There was no bedside telephone. No sofa. No television. No VCR. No stereo tape deck. No intercom to call the servants.

Veronica claimed the lounge chair. Lisa lay down on her stomach on her bed, facing Veronica. "I don't have a lot of the things you do," Lisa began apologetically.

"Where'd you get your breeches?" Veronica asked, ignoring Lisa's apology. Apparently, she and her mother were still arguing about riding pants.

"Mom and I went shopping at The Saddlery," Lisa said.

"Oh," Veronica said. It was just a sound like any other sound, but the way Veronica said it, it meant more than *oh*. It meant that Veronica bought her riding clothes at the fancier riding store at the West End Mall. It meant that even though Veronica had admired Lisa's pants, she wouldn't get a pair like them *because* they came from the less exclusive shop. Did it also mean that Veronica didn't really want to be friends with somebody who had to shop at The Saddlery?

Lisa began wondering about the type of girl who would make judgments about her friends based on where they bought their riding clothes. Just then, Mrs. Atwood came in with the milk and cookies. That time, Lisa knew her mother saw Veronica's grimace.

It was going to be a very long afternoon.

"STEVIE, ARE YOU working on your homework?" her mother called up the stairs.

Stevie didn't like to lie, but she didn't want to say no. She hated the idea of her mother coming into her room for a lecture right then. She compromised. "What else is a Saturday afternoon for?" she yelled, as if that were an answer. Her mother stayed downstairs.

Besides, in a way, she was working on her homework—her math project "substitute." All three of her brothers were in her room—and in on the conspiracy.

"Chad," she began, starting with her older brother. Chad was fourteen and very interested in girls. The only way she could get him to take any of the jobs she'd been flooded with was to promise that there were cute girls on the premises. "There's a lady on Granite Street who needs her grass cut this afternoon. Her name's Richman. I think she's Janet's mother."

"Oh, yeah, Janet," he said somewhat dreamily. "I'll do it."

"I knew you would," Stevie said, chuckling. "Alex, you want a dog-walking job?"

"As long as it's not a toy poodle or some other sissy kind of dog."

"I don't know what kind of dog it is. Just do it, will you?" she asked, a little annoyed. Quickly, her twin agreed.

"Michael, you did such a good job last week on those beds under the hedges that the lady wants you back for her flower beds."

"That lady kept calling me Stevie, you know, and I don't like to be called Stevie."

"Sure, she thinks I'm a boy. But she pays two-fifty an hour and that's two bucks clear for you." Stevie was very good at matching needs and skills—or greeds and skills, she thought to herself, laughing.

"I'll take it," Michael agreed.

"Okay, then, what are you all waiting for?" Stevie asked her brothers. "Go on, do your work."

They shuffled out of her room, but she barely saw them go. She had to make notes on her pad about which jobs had been filled and who was doing them. Just as she finished, the phone rang again.

"Stevie," a girl whined. "It's Polly. I can't do that baby-sitting job on Wednesday. I have an orthodontist appointment—"

"I'll call Mrs. Ziegler and see if it's okay for you to

take the twins to your orthodontist," Stevie said, thinking fast.

"No way!" Polly said. "They're little monsters! They'd probably kill the fish in Dr. Mellman's fish tank. Get somebody else."

"Okay," Stevie agreed and then hung up. But *who*? She decided to try the new girl in her riding class. After all, she lived pretty near the Zieglers. Maybe that meant she knew how awful the twins were, Stevie thought, pausing while she reached for the phone. Before she could make up her mind, the phone rang again.

"Is this Stevie? Would you like a job helping me take all the stuff out of my basement? It flooded in those rains last week and everything needs to be dried, you see . . ."

"YOU JUST WOULDN'T believe all the calls I'm getting," Stevie told Carole on the phone later that night. "I mean, my ear is sore—"

"Stevie, just exactly what *did* you put on that flier you handed out?" Carole asked. Their town was full of kids who wanted jobs to do, and she couldn't understand why everybody was calling Stevie.

"Oh, I suppose it was kind of a hard sell," Stevie said vaguely. Whenever Stevie got vague, she was trying to cover something up.

"'Hard sell'?"

"Yeah, sort of."

"Like what, specifically?" Carole said.

"Want me to read it to you?" Stevie asked.

"Yes, I'm dying to know what you said," Carole shot back.

"Okay, here goes." Stevie sighed. "It says 'I'm desperate for money! Please hire me to do odd jobs for you. Nothing is too big or too small for me. I'll do any kind of honest work. I must have cash immediately to put a shelter over my head and food on my plate! Signed, A Starving Twelve-Year-Old. Call 555-7823 and ask for Stevie.' "

"Stevie, I don't believe you! Haven't you heard about truth-in-advertising laws?"

"Well, it's sort of true. I mean, I'm earning the money to pay for the tent and the food on the camping trip, aren't I? And it's working, isn't it? I mean, I've had dozens of calls—uh, say, would you groom Cobalt on Monday?"

"Well, sure, I'll always groom Cobalt, but—"

"Uh, thanks. Listen, Carole, I've got to go. See you," she said, and hung up before Carole could ask her why *she* was finding somebody to groom Cobalt. Carole decided that Stevie had agreed to do it for the Original Lazy Bones, Miss V. diAngelo, but had gotten a paying job for the same time. Well, if that were going to help Stevie be able to go on the trip, then Carole was glad to do it. Besides, she was always glad for a chance to groom Cobalt.

But Carole was still uneasy about her friend's project as she got ready to go to sleep.

LISA LAY BACK in bed, watching the half-moon in the clear sky outside her window. The moon was reflected in her vanity mirror—two half-moons a quarter of a million miles apart. If she could put them together, would she have a full moon? Perhaps the halves wouldn't match. These days, it seemed to her a lot of halves didn't match.

Even though she had thought she would hate riding, now that she was doing it, she loved it. She had been wrong about that half. She had thought she wouldn't ever be any good at it, but Max had praised her today. Max didn't lavish praise on anybody. She knew that she'd worked hard and deserved it.

She had thought that it would be fun to be Veronica diAngelo's friend. But being a friend to Veronica didn't mean having Veronica be a friend to her. Those were two halves that didn't match at all.

Lisa was beginning to realize—no, if she wanted to be honest with herself, she'd have to admit that the signs had been there ever since Veronica had summoned Red O'Malley to help her—that Veronica was a very selfish person. She may have been willing to share her VCR and her parents' chauffeur with Lisa, but she didn't seem to be able to share herself. She wasn't much of a friend, Lisa decided finally.

Riding was something you did with other people. Riding classes were for groups, not individuals. A horseback camp-out would be really neat—if she had a friend to share it with. But Veronica would have a hard time sharing that, too, Lisa knew. It would be horrible, just horrible, if she couldn't be friends with anybody at riding class, but that seemed to be the case. And if that were true, she'd have to give up riding. Her mother wouldn't mind now, not after she'd seen how rude Veronica could be—the "great" Veronica diAngelo. The *rich* Veronica diAngelo was more like it, since that seemed to be the single most important thing as far as Veronica was concerned.

Lisa closed her eyes for just a few minutes. When she opened them again, the moon had set. The sky was dark except for the soft sparkle of a few stars. The mirror on her vanity was completely dark.

LISA STOOD CAUTIOUSLY next to Pepper in his stall. It was Tuesday, time for her next riding class. She was still feeling torn about her riding lessons. It was one thing to have fun with horses, another to have fun with friends, and it didn't seem to her any more likely that the two things would happen together at Pine Hollow Stables than it had while she was trying to get to sleep on Saturday night. She was probably going to quit. She'd just about made up her mind when her mother had loaded her into the car to come to this lesson. Now she was sure. This would be her last.

She was uncomfortably aware of Veronica in Cobalt's stall next to Pepper's. Veronica was having a hard time with her Thoroughbred and, as Lisa listened, it seemed that the horse was having a hard time with his owner. There was a loud thump when Veronica swung the saddle onto Cobalt's back—and a second thump just as loud when the saddle hit the ground. Lisa knew that if you threw a saddle onto a horse's back, he was likely to object. And she couldn't say she blamed him!

"You dumb horse," Veronica whined. "I'll have to get Red to saddle you. Red! Where are you?" she called. There was no answer. Lisa had seen Red in the tack room and knew he could hear Veronica perfectly well. It didn't really surprise her that Red was ignoring Veronica's call. She decided to do the same.

Lisa smoothed the saddle pad onto Pepper's back and then gently swung the saddle up onto the dappled gray horse. He shifted his weight from one side to the other, but he remained standing still. Then, just as Red had showed her, she checked the pad for wrinkles and then lifted the saddle forward over the end of the mane so she could slide it back into place, brushing Pepper's coat in the right direction. She had learned that if she didn't do that, she'd end up with the saddle too far back and she'd be tilted forward when she tried to ride.

The front of the saddle had to be at the horse's withers. When she first heard the word, Lisa thought withers sounded like something shriveled, but Red had told her it was just the name for the slight bump in a horse's back at the top of his shoulders.

When she was sure the saddle was in the right place, she reached for the girth.

At that moment, Lisa heard Carole's voice. "You want some help?"

Lisa was about to say yes, then realized that Carole wasn't talking to her. She was talking to Veronica, who eagerly said yes.

"That stupid, lazy Red! He won't give me any help and I'm sure he's not taking proper care of my beautiful horse," Veronica said petulantly.

Carole didn't answer that. She began talking to Cobalt. "There, there, boy," she said soothingly. Lisa could hear her patting the horse's neck. He nickered gently in response. Carole continued talking to him while she tacked him up. There were no thumps and bumps this time. It was as if the horse understood her. When the bridle had been secured, Carole spoke to Veronica. Perhaps because she couldn't see her—only hear her—Lisa was particularly aware of the change in Carole's voice when she spoke to Veronica. The assurance was gone. The gentleness was missing. Carole, the totally assured Carole, was apparently uncomfortable talking to Veronica.

"I really had a good ride on Cobalt the other day. Max and I were working on things with him in the ring. I—"

"I hope you didn't tire him out, Carole," Veronica spoke sharply.

"No, I didn't. I just rode him for an hour for exercise, but I was wondering if I could—"

"Carole," Veronica spoke again, this time more sharply. Lisa was surprised that Carole could be spoken to this way, but Veronica seemed to have the upper hand. "You haven't . . . "

"Look, Veronica, don't talk to me like that. I didn't tell anybody, not even Max, that you slammed the door and scared Patch. If you want to add Lisa to your collection, it's okay with me, but I think she's too smart for you."

"Collection?" Veronica said, as if she didn't understand the word. "I'm sure Lisa's smart, but we really don't have anything in common. She's not even a good rider," Veronica said smugly.

"Good rider?" Carole echoed. Then, suddenly on the offensive, she challenged Veronica. "What would you know about that?"

There was a moment of silence before Veronica spoke again. "Listen, Carole, if you'd like to ride Cobalt again on Thursday, it's okay with me. Just don't get him too tired this time, okay?"

The next sound Lisa heard was the clunking of Cobalt's hooves as Veronica led him to the mounting block. Lisa ducked below the edge of the wooden wall of the stall so that neither girl would know she'd been there.

Her hands felt clammy. It was humiliating to hear herself discussed that way. An addition to a collection? Nothing in common? Not even a good rider? What was she? Some kind of toy to be played around with? Just who did Veronica diAngelo think she was? *She thinks she's the daughter of Willow Creek's richest resident, that's who she thinks she is,* Lisa answered her own question.

And then the tears came. Once they started, there seemed to be no way to stop them. She sniffled and tried to wipe them away and she stifled the cries she wanted to make. There was no way in the world she would ever, *ever* let that awful girl Veronica know she'd hurt her. No way!

"Pepper, you okay?" Carole's voice came toward the stall. "Say, what's up, boy? Your gear on okay? I'll check it for you," she said. And then the stall door slid open and Carole stepped in. There was no place for Lisa to hide from her. As soon as Carole saw her, she knew what had happened. The look on her face confirmed it.

"You heard that, huh?" Carole asked.

Lisa nodded.

"Better now than later," she said matter-of-factly. "Veronica's a rotten person. You shouldn't believe anything she ever says about anybody—good or bad."

Sitting on the straw in the stall, Lisa drew her legs up to her chest and put her forehead on her knees. The last few tears dropped onto the straw. When her crying stopped, she looked up at Carole, who had put on the bridle and was patting Pepper.

"What about *you*?" she asked. "When do *you* tell the truth?"

"Me?" Carole looked at her, puzzled.

"Yes, *you*. You knew all along that it was Veronica who slammed the door the day I was riding Patch, didn't you?"

"Well, yes, but—"

"But what? Why didn't you tell me?"

"What difference would it have made?" Carole asked.

"It would have kept me from thinking I could be her friend. I would have known right away that she was a jerk—"

"Everybody knows that," Carole said.

"Well, I didn't; I'm new. Anyway, it would have kept me from blaming Stevie," Lisa told her.

"You thought *Stevie* did that?" Carole asked, astonished. Lisa nodded. "Oh, boy," Carole shook her head. "Stevie does jokes, all right—like the dumb thing with your stirrups—but she'd never, and I mean *never*, do something dangerous like slamming a door when Patch was around." Carole paused. "I guess you deserve an explanation," she said. "The reason I didn't tell you it was Veronica was because if I had, she wouldn't have let me ride Cobalt. He's the most wonderful horse in the world, and I couldn't give him up. I'm really sorry if it hurt you, though."

Lisa stared at her, astonished. Before she could speak, though, the loudspeaker in the stable area crackled. "Time to assemble for class," Mrs. Reg's voice announced.

"Oh, no!" Carole squealed. "I have to tack up Delilah. Say, you want to go over to the shopping center after class, maybe get some ice cream at TD's?"

"Uh, sure," Lisa said uncertainly.

LISA WAS RELIEVED when class began. When she was trying to figure out how to tack up a horse or make sense out of her classmates, everything was a hopeless muddle. But when Max was running the class, it was very clear what she had to do. She had to do exactly what Max told her. And when she did what Max told her to do, Pepper did what she wanted him to do.

All the horses were lined up to trot around the outdoor ring when Stevie arrived.

"We're proud to have you join us, Miss Lake," Max said. Some of the girls giggled, but Lisa could tell from the tone of his voice that he wasn't being funny. He took riding very seriously and didn't like to have any disruptions in his class. A student coming in late was a disruption. So was talking. So was not paying attention. Max didn't seem to care if you didn't know things, or if you'd forgotten how to do something. The important thing was for you to try as hard as you could. If you were late, or talking, or not paying attention, you weren't trying.

"I'm sorry, Max. There was something I had to take care of and it made me late. I promise—"

"It won't happen again?"

"Yes, Max. It won't happen again," she said, and then mounted Comanche. She joined the end of the trotting line.

Max had them working at keeping the distance between their horses the same. Lisa found it very hard to do. Pepper liked to trot and he liked to trot quickly. He seemed to have a natural competitive spirit, always wanting to catch up to and pass the horse in front of him.

Lisa was riding behind Polly Giacomin. Her horse, Nero, was an old stable horse. He'd taken so many classes he knew the routines better than Max. In fact, he'd learned them the same way Max had. They'd both been trained by Max's father. Nero seemed to know exactly how slowly he could go and get away with it. Lisa was becoming exhausted trying to get Pepper to go more slowly, and wished Polly would get Nero going a little faster.

Usually, Max would have been after both of them, urging Polly to "trot on," and telling Lisa to control her horse. Both of them certainly deserved warnings today. But Max's attention was focused on Stevie.

"Stevie, use your legs to even your horse's pace. Stevie! Your diagonals! Come on, now, you missed the beginning of the class, you've got to catch up. I won't have you slacking off!"

Stevie just nodded. Lisa cringed a little bit for her, surprised to find herself feeling sorry for Stevie Lake.

Maybe she was more relieved that Max wasn't watching her so closely this time.

"Stevie Lake! There's a phone call for you," Mrs. Reg announced over the loudspeaker. "It seems to be very important. Please come to the office."

"Uh, Max, could I please be excused to go to the phone?" Stevie asked politely.

Max glowered in silence while Stevie led Comanche to the gate of the ring.

STEVIE WAS HAVING a horrible day. Two of the people she'd gotten jobs for this afternoon hadn't shown up. Right before she had left home, there had been the two furious phone calls. She'd only had time to make a few calls, looking for replacements, and ended up leaving a desperate note for Alex before she'd had to run over to Pine Hollow. And then she'd been late.

"Hello," she said warily into the phone.

"Stevie, it's Alex. I got the note and there is no way I'm going to go shopping with old Mrs. Ramsey. She's a crabby lady and —"

"Alex, I'm desperate!" Stevie wailed over the phone. "Sid Jackson said he'd do it and then he ratted out. Mrs. Ramsey just needs somebody to go along and help her read the labels and stuff and then carry things home for her."

"*No* way," Alex said.

"She's a poor old woman, can barely see; she just needs a helping hand for an hour or so."

"No way."

"I'll pay you the full five dollars," she said, her voice dripping with temptation.

There was silence for just a moment. Alex sighed and then spoke. "All right. Just this once. But never again!"

"You ungrateful—" Stevie began, but she didn't bother to finish. Alex had hung up on her.

Stevie hung up the phone and walked out of the office to return to class. She released the knot in Comanche's lead rope but then saw the horses trotting in pairs. Class was almost over. There was no point in going back to the ring. She led Comanche back to his stall for untacking, going over her checklist of the things she needed to do before she went home. She had to give Carole her money for grooming Cobalt yesterday, but first, she had to collect it from Veronica. Then, she had to stop by Mrs. Traeger's to get paid for the job one of her classmates had done there yesterday. Then she had to go and fill in on the sitting job for Mrs. Vitelli that Betsy Cavanaugh had begged out of and then she had to—

"Stevie!" It was Max. Stevie stiffened when she heard his tone of voice; he didn't sound happy. Normally, she liked talking to Max. He was a wonderful teacher and a good rider and a nice man. But he took riding seriously and Stevie knew that she had been pretty sloppy today.

"Stevie, can you spare me a minute?" he asked sharply.

"Yes, Max," she said.

"Then please come to the office when you've untacked Comanche."

"I'll be there in a second," she said, knowing that all the other things on her list would have to wait. After all, riding was very important to her. The only reason she was working was to be able to go on the MTO. Max would understand that, she told herself. Wouldn't he?

"YOU READY TO go?" Carole asked, peering into Pepper's stall. When she saw Lisa hugging Pepper, she was glad she'd decided to be friendly. It had been tempting to ignore Lisa, with her fancy riding clothes, trying to be Veronica's friend. But something about the way Lisa was handling Pepper told Carole that although there was a lot Lisa didn't know about riding, there was little she wouldn't learn. They had a lot in common.

"Just a minute more," Lisa told her. "I just wanted to visit with Pepper a little."

"You had a good ride on him today, didn't you?" Carole asked. She'd noticed how well-behaved the horse had been in class, and it was obvious that Lisa was having fun riding him.

"Yeah. But you know, I don't understand something." Carole nodded, waiting. "The first time I rode him, he was sort of hard to handle. He didn't do anything I wanted him to. The next time, he was better, and every time since then, he's been better. Was he sick or something?"

Carole started laughing, but stopped when she saw that she was hurting Lisa's feelings. "I'm sorry," she said. "I'm not making fun of you, it's just that this almost always happens with new riders," she said. "They think they're getting better horses with every lesson, but what's actually happening is that their horses are getting better riders. You see, the more you know, the more you let the horse know who's in charge. A horse somehow senses when a rider doesn't know what she's doing. And horses will take advantage of that right away. That's why Max usually starts the newest riders on Patch. He's very gentle and sweet—"

"Except when he's frightened, right?"

"That's right. Normally, you could trust him with a two-year-old. But Pepper, on the other hand, has a mind of his own. You've just learned enough about riding to show Pepper you're the boss. You've learned a lot in just a few lessons, you know?"

Lisa's face flushed a little pink. She was both pleased and embarrassed. Carole was such a good rider that a compliment from her was almost as good as one from Max. She didn't know how to respond, so she changed the subject from riders to horses. "Are horses really that different from one another?" Lisa asked.

"You bet they are," Carole said. "As different as people are. Pepper's a nice even-tempered horse—as long as he knows what he's supposed to do. If his rider starts giving him confused signals, say kicking with the legs to go forward and pulling on the reins to stop, he'll get really stubborn. He likes things just so. Max really trusted you when he put you on Pepper."

Lisa gave the horse one final hug and pat, and when she was sure he was safe in his stall, she picked up the tack and stepped out into the hall. Carole rolled the door shut and latched it with the bolt and the key chain snap.

"What about Cobalt?" Lisa asked. "What's he like?"

"Cobalt's a high-strung Thoroughbred. His mother is a hunter-jumper and his father was a racehorse. In horse talk, that's his dam and his sire. Anyway, the result of breeding like that is that he's very competitive—always has to be at the front of the pack. He competes with horses *and* with people and he always wants to take charge. If his rider gives him his way, forget it, he's almost uncontrollable."

"Is that why Veronica has such a tough time with him?"

"Yeah, and she's scared of him, too."

"Would he hurt her?" Lisa asked.

"Probably not. Most horses never want to hurt people, but they're so big that sometimes they can't help it. Anyway, there's a greater danger that Cobalt would hurt himself than his rider if he got out of control." Carole hated the idea of an innocent horse being hurt by a thoughtless or careless rider. She was thoughtfully silent while she helped Lisa hang up Pepper's bridle. They each took the soda that Meg Durham gave them and left the stable, heading for the shopping center.

"Then there's a horse like Nero," Carole continued. "He's so laid-back that you think he's lazy. But really, he's just taking life at his own pace!"

"I know that. I was trying to hold Pepper's trot behind Nero today. It wasn't easy!"

"No, it wasn't. But you were doing a pretty good job," Carole told Lisa. "And Max noticed it, too."

"Hey, Carole, wait up!" Stevie called out. Carole stopped and turned around. Stevie was dashing after them.

"I thought you'd left already," Carole said, and then she remembered that Max had talked to Stevie after class in his office. "What did Max want?"

"Oh, he gave me the usual lecture about paying attention and how Pine Hollow was serious about developing riders and how he didn't want riders who weren't serious about learning. You know the stuff.

Anyway, I wanted to give you this." She held out her hand, offering four dollars to Carole.

"What's this for?" Carole asked.

"It's for Cobalt," Lisa said.

"So put it in his bank account—at the diAngelo Trust Company." Carole laughed at her own joke.

"No, it's not for the horse, Carole. It's for you—for grooming him yesterday."

"I groomed him because you asked me to, not for money," Carole said, a little annoyed that Stevie would think she'd have to pay her for a favor.

"Well, the reason I asked you to was because Veronica paid me to do it. So the money's for you," Stevie explained.

Carole looked at the money for a moment. "But you're the one who needs it for the MTO. You keep it."

"I did keep some of it—sort of my commission. Don't worry about me. I'll make it. You take this because you earned it. And I don't have time to argue now. Bye." She slammed the four dollars into Carole's hand and ran back up the stable's driveway, where her mother was waiting for her behind the wheel of their station wagon.

Carole shoved the money into her pocket. "You know, Lisa, I understand horses. They make sense to me. It's people who are confusing. Stevie wants to go on the MTO so badly, but she's doing absolutely everything wrong. First, all she had to do was a math project, but no, that wasn't good enough for Stevie. So then, she decided to earn money, but no, she's too good to do the work. I never saw anybody so eager to turn jobs over to other people. So then, while she isn't doing either of those things, she's busy getting Max so angry with her that he might not *let* her go on the trip. Some fix she's getting into."

"Listen, you tell me about horses, and I'll tell you about people," Lisa said.

"What do you mean?" Carole asked.

"I mean, Stevie isn't so dumb."

"What are you talking about?"

"Stevie just said she was taking commissions," Lisa said. "Look, how much money does Stevie need for the trip?"

"Fifty dollars," Carole said.

"Okay, well, she's been very busy, you know."

"Yeah, I know. She's been busy on the phone giving away all her money-earning opportunities. At the rate she's doing it, everybody in town *but* Stevie will be able to afford the trip."

"Oh, no wonder you're so worried about her! Stevie isn't giving work away, she's selling it! Don't you see, she's getting a commission on every job she lines up. Somehow, she's managed to get everyone in town to call her to do work. It's way more than she can do herself, so instead of doing it herself, she's a one-girl employment agency. See, she got you to curry Cobalt—"

"How come you know all this?" Carole asked.

"She told me about it when she called me to see if I could baby-sit for the Ziegler twins tomorrow, but I can't—"

"That's a good thing," Carole interrupted. "They are real monsters."

"See, you *do* understand people," Lisa teased, and then she and Carole laughed together. "Anyway, every time Stevie gets somebody to do a job, she takes a little bit of the money they earned. That's her commission for getting them the job. She gave you four dollars for grooming Cobalt, right?" Carole nodded, feeling the crumpled bills in her pocket. "Well, Veronica probably paid her five dollars. So you did the work, but she got a dollar."

"But that's just one dollar of fifty she needs. She could have earned *five*—"

"Right, but while you were doing that job for her, three other kids were probably doing other jobs for her. And she probably got a dollar for each of those jobs, too. Maybe more. She got to sit home and wait for the phone to ring while she earned four dollars."

And if she earned four dollars on one weekday afternoon, Carole thought, then she could certainly earn a lot more on Saturdays and Sundays. She'd be able to earn fifty dollars and go on the MTO if—and it seemed like a pretty big *if* today—Max would let her go.

"Don't worry, Carole. Stevie seems like a person who can figure out all the angles. She'll make it, I'm sure."

Carole wished she were so sure.

Carole and Lisa arrived at the shopping center and made their way past the supermarket to get to TD's.

"Guess what?" Carole asked.

"What?" Lisa said.

"This is going to be my treat because I just got four dollars I never expected to have."

"You don't have to pay for me," Lisa protested.

"Well, think of it as Stevie's treat, her way of making up for that stirrup trick your first day, okay?"

"Well, okay," Lisa said. "But then I'm going to have to find a way to make up for all those knots in her sneakers."

"You will," Carole told her. "You will." And she was sure it was true. She was glad she had invited Lisa to TD's today. She wished she'd done it sooner.

"TELL ME MORE about the horses at the stable," Lisa said to Carole. The two of them sat at a corner table inside TD's. The threat of rain had kept them from the picnic tables behind the shop. Their empty ice cream dishes sat in front of them as they chatted. For the first time since she'd started riding, Lisa was really happy about it. She was getting better at riding, but most important, she had a friend.

Carole sat across the table from her, talking animatedly about her favorite subject: horses. She smiled as she described the horses at Pine Hollow. "Well, then there's Comanche. He and Stevie are a perfect match—you know it's important to match up personalities, don't you? I mean, you can't have a flighty horse with a vague rider. A flighty horse needs to be told what to do all the time. Anyway, Comanche is very strong-willed. So is Stevie. And when they both want to do the same thing at the same time—wow!"

Lisa laughed. "And when they want to do different things?"

"Stevie's a good rider," Carole said. "Comanche follows her orders. Usually."

"You mean like when she was changing direction, and he didn't want to?" Lisa asked. Class always began with the horses going in a clockwise direction. Several times during the class, they switched to counterclockwise so that the horses didn't get too used to one direction or the other. Stevie was supposed to lead the class across the center of the oval ring to change direction. Comanche had wanted to keep on going clockwise. "I thought she'd just let him go around to the back of the line and let him follow the other horses. He'd have gone counterclockwise then, wouldn't he?"

"He probably would have," Carole agreed. "But then, he would have won the argument, and it's not a good idea to let a horse do that. So she kept turning him to the left until he finally went."

"It looked pretty silly," Lisa said.

"Sure it did, but he didn't misbehave through the rest of the class, did he?"

"No, he didn't. Horses are like little children, aren't they?"

Carole nodded. "Sometimes they can be pretty

bratty, too. But the rider can't let the horse be in charge."

"What do you like best about riding, Carole?"

Lisa watched Carole's face while she considered the answer. It seemed to take a long time. Lisa hadn't thought it was a difficult question.

"Everything," Carole said finally.

CAROLE SAT ON the bench at the bus stop. She had fifteen minutes until her bus arrived and not much to do until then. But she couldn't wander around. The last time she'd done that, she'd missed the bus and had to wait another half hour.

She didn't mind waiting, really. Sometimes she'd see friends, and if that didn't happen, she could look in the nearby store windows. She stood up to stretch her long legs and wandered over to the display window at Sights 'n' Sounds. She smiled, remembering the tape she'd bought for her father. He'd loved it. If she'd had enough money on her then, she would have bought another one.

There was a big sign in the window that read: GRAND PRIZE WINNERS. Something about that rang a bell. Then Carole remembered the contest that Stevie had entered while she was buying the tape for her father. Stevie had spun quite a fantasy about Hawaii, Carole remembered, smiling. Well, the winner had been announced now, and Stevie wasn't going to

Hawaii—at least not in *that* contest. Below the winner's name, there was a list of about twenty-five other people—second-, third-, fourth-, and fifth-prize winners and honorable mention. Something must have caught Carole's eye subconsciously because she leaned closer and peered at the small type. And right there, practically at the top of the list, was "Stevie Lake."

Carole looked again. Stevie's name really *was* there. It hadn't moved or changed. Stevie had actually won a prize. Her best friend was a winner! It took a few minutes to figure out what "Third Prize" next to Stevie's name meant: she'd won a portable cassette player. So, it wasn't a trip to Hawaii, or even a fifty-dollar cash award—which would have been perfect!—but it was a prize. Carole was so excited that she wanted to call Stevie right away.

She pulled some change out of her pocket and looked for a phone. There were phones at the shopping center, but she couldn't remember where they were. Finally, she spotted one near the supermarket. She dashed across the parking lot, barely noticing the cars. Her phone call was too important.

She dropped the change into the phone and dialed the number she knew by heart. Busy. She tried again. Same thing. To kill some time, she paced up and down in front of the supermarket. But when she had her back to the phone, a boy and a girl got into the booth to make a call. Carole tapped her foot restlessly, watching shoppers emerge from the supermarket. After the couple had made not one, but three calls, they came back out of the phone booth.

Carole picked up the phone and dialed Stevie's number again. It rang. And rang. And then, at the sixth ring, Carole spotted her bus coming into the shopping center. She slammed the phone down and ran for it.

But the bus stop was all the way across the parking lot from the telephone, and riding boots were not the best running shoes. She clunked along as fast as she could, but all Carole got for her trouble was a faceful of carbon monoxide from the rear of the receding bus.

Carole growled. Annoyed with herself, she returned to the telephone. This time, she got an answering machine, but it was the wrong number. She slammed the phone down, realizing that now she was out of change. She couldn't make another call.

She returned to the bench at the bus stop and promised herself she wouldn't move until the next bus came. She put her elbows on her knees and her chin in her cupped hands and glared at the world. The afternoon had been going so well, she thought, remembering the fun she'd had with Lisa. Why did it have to end this way?

"Hi, baby! I thought I might find you here." Her father's cheerful voice greeted her from the car that had pulled up at the bus stop. "I had an errand in town and was just hoping to see you after your riding class. I'll take you home."

One of the things Carole loved about her father was that he always seemed to be there when she needed him. She grinned happily and climbed into the front seat next to him.

"STEVIE! IT'S ANOTHER phone call for you—and if it's another woman who wants a dog named Fifi walked, get somebody else to do it!"

That's how grateful my brothers are, Stevie thought to herself in disgust. She'd been working hours every day to get them jobs so they could earn money, and all she got were complaints. She promised herself she'd get somebody *else* to do the next job. There were lots of people she could call. She just wasn't sure who they were.

Carefully, she laid aside the scraps of paper that had her notes on them. She was in the middle of transferring all the information to her notebook. She had so many customers and so many workers that she had to keep careful records about who owed her money and how much of that had to be paid to the workers. While it wasn't always clear to her how much was coming in and going out, she knew exactly how much was *staying* in. She knew what her portion of the earnings was. And the news was great. She had more than sixty-five dollars. She *would* go on the overnight camp-out after all!

When the scraps of paper were neatly piled on her desk, she stood up to answer the phone call. Maybe it would be another job. Who would she get to do it? Obviously, not her ungrateful brothers. Her mind raced as she headed for the phone. She still had a few friends left in her class, and she could borrow Chad's and Michael's class lists, too; even though she didn't know the kids, they'd probably be glad for work.

"Hello?" she said more positively than she felt. She didn't really like the idea of calling her brothers' classmates.

"Stevie, it's Carole. You won! I was at the mall next to Sights 'n' Sounds and they've got the winners in the window and you won. Remember the contest that you entered when we were there? Your name is in the window!" she finished breathlessly.

"Huh?" Stevie said blankly. She'd been so concerned with her next job that she almost hadn't recognized Carole's voice. What *was* she talking about? She didn't remember anything about a contest except—

"Hawaii? I'm going to *Hawaii?!*"

"Oh—no. Somebody else won that. But you won a portable cassette player," Carole said, rushing on. "I mean, your name's right there in the window. I've been trying to call you for hours, but your phone's been busy or else there wasn't any answer or . . . anyway, you have to go to the store to pick up your prize. Can you believe it?"

"You sure?"

"Sure I'm sure! You *won* something. Isn't that wonderful?"

Finally, it hit Stevie. "You mean I actually won something in that contest?"

"Uh-huh."

"Wow, thanks for calling. I can't believe it! That's great. I'll go over there right now and get it. Only problem is that I've got all my favorite albums on records. I don't have anything to play on a tape machine." Once Stevie's mind was focused on a problem, her concentration was total.

"Doesn't Alex have a tape deck? You could borrow some of his tapes."

"You think I want to listen to the junk he likes?"

"Well, maybe you could buy a tape for the machine," Carole suggested.

"Maybe," Stevie said vaguely. "Hey, I'd better go over there. This is fantastic. Thanks for calling, Car." She slid the phone into its cradle.

Stevie was almost shaking with excitement. She'd won a contest. She, Stevie Lake, who'd never even won a game of musical chairs at a birthday party, had now won something in a contest. She grinned so happily that her cheeks almost hurt. She couldn't believe it.

"I won a contest," she said out loud. The words sounded very strange to her. She sat on the edge of her bed and took three deep breaths. Was this really happening?

How could she be sure it was real if she didn't go over there right away to claim her prize? She had more than an hour until dinner. That would be plenty of time. Sights 'n' Sounds was a fifteen-minute walk.

She stood up to leave her room. She'd need identification, she knew. She took her wallet. It had her library card in it as well as all her saved-up money. When she was sure she had everything she needed, she left her room and practically flew down the stairs and out the door.

"I won a contest!" she repeated to herself, skipping nearly all the way to Sights 'n' Sounds.

IT TOOK ONLY a minute to identify herself and collect her cassette player. The store owner even knew her, so there was no question of her identification. They took some pictures of her smiling and holding the prize. It all seemed terribly unreal to Stevie and totally wonderful.

"This is the most exciting thing that's ever happened to me, you know?" she said to the store manager, Ms. Weiss.

"It *is* pretty exciting," she said. "Even for us. We hope you'll enjoy that machine for years to come."

That sounded like a great idea to Stevie—except for one thing. She *couldn't* enjoy it until she had something to play on it. She needed at least one tape. And there she was, at the store where she could buy it. And she had her wallet in her pocket. And she had lots of money in her wallet. Still almost too excited to think, she walked over to the rock cassette section to choose. She clutched her prize with one hand while she flipped through the cassettes with the other.

What a day this was! Stevie promised herself she'd remember it—remember the wonderful feeling of winning—for a long time. She sighed contentedly and began her selection in earnest.

"I STILL ALMOST can't believe it," Stevie told Carole at their Saturday class. "I mean, I really *did* win a contest. I've been listening to tapes all week. You should hear the sound. It's fabulous!"

"Stevie!" Max called. The tone of his voice meant trouble. "This is no place for gossip," he said sternly. "This riding ring is for riding. Now to show the class how you've been paying attention, please demonstrate how to change diagonals at the trot."

At least Stevie knew how to do that. She squeezed Comanche gently with her legs and the horse picked up a trot. She rose with the trot when his right foreleg stepped forward. It was a completely natural, comfortable movement to her. She'd seen new riders struggle with it—including Lisa—but she was an experienced rider. Changing diagonals was easy for her. As Comanche came through the center of the ring and changed directions (just the way he was supposed to this time), she sat for one extra "beat" of his trot, and rose again, this time when his left foreleg stepped forward. She'd changed diagonals.

"Nice," Max said. From him, that was a very big compliment, and it might, just *might,* make up for his being annoyed at her talking in class.

She brought Comanche to the end of the line as the entire class followed her pattern, some better than others. Stevie was glad they were doing something she was already good at. She didn't have to pay too close attention and could think more about the neat music she'd been listening to since Tuesday. It was hard having at least two things you *really* liked doing—in this case, riding and listening to rock music—when you couldn't do them both at once. Then she realized that she'd be able to bring her cassette player on the MTO so they could all listen to music at their campsite at night. But which tapes would she bring? She couldn't bring them all, could she? She decided to ask Carole to help her choose. After all, the MTO was only two weeks away.

At last, class was almost over. They paired up for their final trot—this time through the center of the ring to change directions. She brought her horse up next to Carole's.

"Come to my house this afternoon? I've got

something really important to show you," Stevie invited her friend.

"I thought you'd have work to do. I was kind of planning to go to TD's with Lisa. Can she come over, too?"

Stevie frowned. She knew Carole was becoming Lisa's friend, but she couldn't forget that Lisa was the one who had tied her sneakers into all those knots. And Lisa was the one who wouldn't sit for the Ziegler twins when she'd needed somebody to do that job. And Lisa was the one—

"You know, Stevie, she thought you were the one who slammed the door when she was on Patch that first day."

"Is she crazy? What kind of person does she think I am?"

"Well, she knows better now, and she's really sorry about the sneakers—just like I'm sure *you're* sorry about the stirrups. Remember the stirrups?"

She did, of course. She remembered them well. She remembered how funny Lisa looked while she groped for a way to get on the horse. It was so funny, in fact, that she snickered now. But she also remembered that Lisa had been near tears. And she remembered that since that day, Lisa had learned a lot about horses and riding and had stuck with it, which a lot of new riders didn't.

"Okay, she can come," she said. "But what I want to talk about is the MTO. Is she going on it?"

"She and her mother are meeting with Max on Tuesday after class to talk about it. She wants to come and Max thinks she's learned enough to ride on a trail safely. Her mother's the problem."

"That's funny," Stevie said. "Max asked me if I could stay after class on Tuesday. He was a little mysterious about it."

"You don't think—" Carole began.

But they were interrupted then by the very person they were discussing. "Girls!" Max said very sternly. "Class is not over yet and I am the only one who is allowed to talk while class is in session. I cannot have you continue to break this rule. Do you understand?"

"Yes," they said in unison.

"NOW, LISTEN TO *this* one," Stevie said, sliding a cassette into her machine and fast-forwarding it expertly to the song she wanted to hear. She pressed play.

It was a wonderful song, Lisa thought. She'd heard it on the radio, but it sounded much better on Stevie's cassette player. It was a dreamy, romantic song. She leaned back in the comfortable overstuffed chair in Stevie's room to enjoy the music. It wasn't easy to relax, though. She felt like an intruder. She could tell that Carole was trying to make her like Stevie, and make Stevie like her, but it wasn't easy. Lisa's disastrous first day at Pine Hollow hung like a dark cloud between them. Lisa felt badly about the sneakers and she thought Stevie probably felt badly about the stirrups, but those things had happened, and it was going to be hard to forget them. She was trying, though. Hard. She wished Stevie would try, too.

"If you like this song, you're really going to like the next," Stevie said to Carole.

"Boy, you sure have a lot of tapes here," Carole said, shuffling through the selection. "I thought you didn't have any. Are these Alex's?"

"No, they're mine. I told you, he's got junky taste in music. He likes heavy metal. UGH!"

"Right!" Lisa agreed. It made her feel better that she and Stevie liked the same music.

"You bought them?" Carole asked suspiciously.

"Sure, they've got a good selection at Sights 'n' Sounds."

"You *bought* them?" Carole asked again. "Like you paid for them?"

"Sure I paid for them. They gave away a cassette player, but they didn't give me any tapes to go with it!"

"Where'd you get the money?" Carole challenged her.

"It was in my wallet. Hey, what did you think I did? Shoplift? No way. I can't believe you think I'd steal the tapes!" Stevie said, extremely agitated. "Look, here's the receipt!"

"Of course I don't think you stole them," Carole

said. "I know you'd never do anything dishonest. But I *am* worried that you spent every penny you had earned for the MTO to buy tapes!"

Stevie's arms dropped to her sides and she stood up, looking at Carole. She clutched a tape in her right hand. While Lisa watched, Stevie's face turned pale.

"No, I couldn't have done that. I had *lots* of money. I couldn't have spent it all. I only bought a few tapes—just those few you see there and two more that I've loaned to Alex for the day. That's all. There has to be a lot of money left. I mean, what does one tape cost?"

Lisa thought about the tapes she'd seen in the stores. They were pretty expensive. She counted eight tapes on Stevie's bed, plus the two Alex had. She supplied the answer to Stevie's question. "Ten tapes at six or seven dollars each. It's about sixty-five dollars, plus tax—"

"You spent *all* your money!" Carole yowled.

"Not all of it," Stevie said defensively. "I have some left." She grabbed her wallet from her purse and opened it. "I have exactly—" She dumped the contents on her bed. "Four dollars and eighteen cents."

Stevie was transformed before Lisa's eyes. The scene that followed made Stevie's ranting about the knots in her sneaker laces look like a picnic. Stevie was so furious with herself that she began grabbing all the papers on her desk and tossing them up in the air.

"I don't believe I did that! Can you believe it? Do

you know how many hours I worked and how I made one *zillion* phone calls—make that two zillion—to get jobs for everybody so I could earn a measly fifty dollars to do the one thing I really care about, which is to go on the MTO? I even sat for the Ziegler twins myself when I couldn't get anybody else. And what have I got to show for it?" A dozen slips of paper flew out of her right hand into the air. "Nothing!" She flung more paper toward the ceiling with her left hand. "And look at this!" She picked up her notebook. "Night after night was ruined because of the bookkeeping I had to do. *Look* at this!" She tossed the notebook toward the overstuffed chair where Lisa was sitting. It slammed onto the floor and slid under the chair's skirt.

When the first tears appeared in Stevie's eyes, Carole grabbed a tissue and went over to comfort her, but Stevie was inconsolable. The MTO was a once-in-a-lifetime trip. She'd wanted it so much that she'd done something she absolutely hated—she'd worked. And now she wasn't going to go anyway. "And it's all my fault!" Stevie wailed.

Lisa felt very bad for Stevie, but she was also a little embarrassed. After all, they weren't exactly close friends. While Carole comforted Stevie, Lisa retrieved the notebook from under the chair. Idly, she glanced at it. On the first double page, there was a neat chart. It only took a second to realize that it was Stevie's record book of the jobs she'd taken on. Until she looked at the record book, Lisa had no idea how much work had been done by Stevie, her brothers, and her friends. But the situation became clear as she glanced at the page in front of her. Across the top of the page were headings: Date, Job, Employer, Employee, Rate, Time, Amount Paid, Amount Due Employee, Amount Paid Employee, Commission. There were four pages like this, listing everything that had been done. That meant that a lot of jobs had been done. It was a tremendous amount of data.

In the back of the book were pages with the names of all the kids who had worked for her. Stevie had made careful notes about them. On Polly Giacomin's page, for example, it said, "Orthodontist on Wednesdays. Mrs. Ellerman says she was good with the dog." There was a page with her own name on it. "Lisa Atwood," it said. "Didn't seem interested." It made her uncomfortable to read it. But it was true, of course. Stevie had asked her to sit and she wasn't interested. She'd given her an excuse about studying for a test, but Stevie had obviously known it was just an excuse. Then there was Carole's page. It said, "Will do anything for Cobalt. Natch." That was true, too, Lisa knew.

She looked up from the notebook. Stevie was sniffling. "I'll take the cassettes back," Stevie said, gathering them up, and trying to sort cassettes and cases. "I'll tell the store they were damaged and demand my money back."

"Stevie!" Carole said, a little exasperated.

Suddenly, Lisa got a wonderful idea. "Uh, Stevie?" Lisa tried to interrupt. Stevie didn't hear her.

"I'll tell them my family's fortune was wiped out by a tornado and we are desperate for cash."

"Stevie," Lisa said again. No luck.

"A hurricane, maybe—"

"Stevie! Get yourself together, girl," Carole chided.

"Listen, Carole," Lisa said, clutching the notebook. Carole didn't hear her, either, because she was so busy with Stevie.

"Stevie, you only have one choice," Carole told her in a matter-of-fact tone of voice. "You *have* to do a math project."

"No!" Stevie wailed. "I *can't*!"

It was Lisa's chance. "Yes!" she wailed, imitating Stevie's cry. "You already *have*!"

"Have what?" Stevie asked, looking bewildered.

"Have a math project," Lisa said.

"What do you mean?" Stevie asked, suddenly interested.

"Here," Lisa said, pointing to the notebook. "You have a math project. You said you did a lot of work. And you did. But you also did a math project when you started keeping this ledger."

Stevie started listening. She sat down on the bed facing Lisa and pulled her knees up to her chin. Carole sat next to her, dangling her legs over the edge of the bed.

"Look, you're supposed to do a project on percentages and decimals, right?" Lisa continued.

Stevie nodded.

"Well, what's more decimal than dollars and cents and what's more percentage than commissions?"

Stevie nodded, a slow smile spreading across her face.

"So, all you have to do is make sure you've got all the jobs entered, finish doing the arithmetic, and do some analytical percentages, like such and such percent of the employers paid on the spot. Such and such percent never paid. You got such and such percent of the money. The average job paid so much money, et cetera. The math isn't hard. You can even use a calculator. The only hard part is making sure you have all the information. Where are your records on the other jobs?"

"Other jobs?" Stevie asked.

"Yeah, this stuff only goes through Friday a week ago. I know other jobs have been done since then and there are some blanks before that. Where are your records?"

Stevie looked up to the ceiling and then down to the floor. The entire floor was scattered with the scraps of paper she'd thrown in the air when she was so angry.

"Oh, no," Stevie groaned.

"Oh, no!" Carole said.

"Well, there's just one thing to do," Lisa announced. "And that is to pick them up and start working on Stevie's math project. We can't have her at home alone while we're enjoying the MTO, can we, Carole?"

"No, we cannot," Carole agreed, lowering herself to the floor. She began picking up crumpled and torn scraps of paper.

Lisa and Stevie got onto the floor as well. There was still a lot of work ahead of them—and when a big job needed to be done, it was better if friends did it together.

CAROLE SPOTTED LISA in the main-floor hall of the school between her science and gym classes on Monday morning. She knew right away it was Lisa because of the perfectly pressed blouse and matching skirt. Lisa's mother still liked to dress her up like a doll. Carole wondered when Mrs. Atwood would start letting Lisa make her own decisions.

"Hey, Lisa, wait up!" she yelled, running down the hall. Lisa stopped and smiled when she saw her. Or maybe she was smiling because of the trail of papers Carole had dropped behind her. They picked them up together.

"How's it going?" Carole asked eagerly. She knew that Lisa had spent most of Sunday at Stevie's, working on Project Math Project, as they'd dubbed their joint effort.

"It's going okay, sort of. You wouldn't believe the amount of work Stevie did. When she said she'd made a zillion phone calls, she was only slightly exaggerating! And just during the time I was there, she had at least ten more calls—"

"Did she take the jobs?"

"No, she told people she was out of business. A lot of her customers seemed very disappointed, too, but we had a giant pile of work to do so she couldn't spend any more time on the phone getting workers."

"How big a giant pile? I mean, like it's due on Friday. Is she going to get it done on time?"

"With a little help from her friends," Lisa said. "Really, it's going to be a terrific report, someday."

"By Friday?" The question hung in the air. Lisa shrugged. "You know what I think?" Carole continued. "If Stevie could do all that work to earn the money, she can certainly account for it all so the three of us can go on the MTO."

"Well, that's another thing," Lisa said, ominously. Suddenly, Carole got the feeling that a bombshell was coming. "My mother is getting convinced that there's no way I can be trusted on a three-day trail ride. I mean, at first, she really wanted me to ride because that's what well-bred people supposedly do." Lisa grimaced. "But then, she met the sainted Veronica, who was a real jerk when she was at my house. Now Mom thinks too much riding isn't a good idea for a young lady. Besides, she thinks three days in the mountains sounds too rough. So, Stevie may be able to go. But I probably won't."

Just when Carole had thought things were looking up, she found out they weren't.

On Monday afternoon, Lisa was back at Stevie's, piecing together the scraps of information that would someday be a math project.

"Okay, then, you had three jobs going on the afternoon of the twentieth. But I don't understand how you've got 'Alex' down for all of them. I mean, I know he's terrific and all, being your twin brother, but he's not exactly Superman, is he?"

"No, he's not," Stevie said. "But he must have done the jobs if I said he did."

"Well, here, you look at these slips of paper. Isn't that what these say?" She handed Stevie the crumpled pieces of paper with notes scribbled on them. Stevie took them reluctantly. It seemed to her that in the last two days all she'd been doing was staring at crumpled notes—in her own messy handwriting.

"No, no, this isn't Alex," she said once she'd decoded her scratchings. "It's Alex*a*. That's Alexa Hammond, our neighbor. She's a demon in the kitchen. That's why I had her work with Mrs. Alcott—"

"But you said Mrs. Alcott was the one who never paid you and you've got this marked 'Paid.'"

"Well, I mean, I paid Alexa. It's just that Mrs. Alcott hasn't paid me. Or at least she hadn't then. I'm pretty sure she did pay me. I know I wrote a note about it."

Lisa sighed. "If you made a note of it, we'll find it." For now, that closed the subject. Lisa concentrated on the notebook on the desk in front of her. Stevie watched her, amazed at Lisa's ability to concentrate totally on something so dull. While Stevie watched her, Lisa reached for the pencil behind her right ear—no doubt changing "Alex" to "Alexa."

"Should I get us some sodas?" Stevie asked.

"Hmmm," was all she got in reply. Lisa was so focused on the notebook that Stevie doubted she'd heard her at all. Quietly, she left the room. As she scouted for sodas and cookies in the kitchen, she mused at the generosity of a friend—and she knew now that Lisa *was* a friend—who would spend so much time helping another girl with schoolwork.

She pulled two straws out of their box and returned to her room, determined to concentrate as hard as Lisa. Together, she was sure they could do the project—as sure as she'd been that she could earn the fifty dollars. She'd been right about that, too, she thought just a little smugly.

* * *

ON TUESDAY AFTERNOON, Carole wasn't certain whether she wanted her riding class to end or to go on forever. She was very aware of the fact that both of her friends had been summoned to Max's office after class, and she'd noted the arrival of Mrs. Atwood. According to Lisa, Mrs. Atwood was still determined that her daughter should not go on the MTO. Carole thought that was weird since it was Mrs. Atwood who had insisted Lisa take riding lessons in the first place. Lisa was equally determined to go. Carole had had one or two opportunities to see Lisa face up to her mother, especially that first day Lisa had come to Pine Hollow. She wasn't really very good at standing up to her mother, Carole thought glumly.

And then there was Stevie. If Stevie ever did finish her math project, she'd still have trouble convincing Max to let her go after the way she'd been acting in class recently. She'd even been late today, saying she'd had to stop and borrow a calculator from a friend before riding class. Being late to class was one of Max's pet peeves. But just one of them. He had loads, and these days it seemed that every time Carole turned around, Max was yelling at Stevie for one thing or another.

After class, Carole finished untacking Delilah, and then checked to see that Veronica had given Cobalt fresh water. She hadn't, of course, so Carole did it for her. Then she returned Delilah's tack to the tack room, where she'd decided to wait for the results of her friends' powwow with Max.

But just exactly *what* was going on? Why were Lisa, her mother, and Stevie in there all at once? Was Max just letting both of them know at the same time that they couldn't go on the MTO?

"Carole, what's on your mind, child?" Mrs. Reg asked gently as she poked her head through the tack-room door.

"Oh, nothing," Carole said as vaguely as she could, trying not to look toward Max's office.

"Well, I can't believe there's nothing on your mind when I see you putting Delilah's tack away upside down. And you can't convince me you're not worried about something when I watched you rinse out Cobalt's bucket six times—*after* you'd filled it once."

Carole smiled weakly. "That obvious, huh?"

"Yes, it is. Now straighten out the tack and come tell me what's bothering you so."

Carole was relieved to have a chance to talk about her worries. Probably Mrs. Reg couldn't change anything, but maybe just talking about it all would help. She turned Delilah's bridle right side up, straightened out the saddle, and went to sit on the bench near Mrs. Reg's desk.

"It's my friends," she began.

"They've been hurting your feelings?" Mrs. Reg asked. Her bright blue eyes flashed in anger on Carole's behalf.

"Oh, no. They've been hurting themselves," Carole explained, even though she knew it didn't make very much sense. "I've tried and tried to help them, but I'm just so afraid that it isn't enough. If I could just—" Carole let the words hang in the air. She didn't know how to finish the sentence. What, after all, *could* she do for her friends?

"Now, wait a minute," Mrs. Reg said. "There's only so much you can do for friends, Carole. And sometimes, the best thing you can do is to let them do something for themselves. I remember I had a horse once—a beauty, he was. The tack that came with him included a really harsh bit." Carole knew that meant that every time the rider put pressure on the reins, the horse would really feel it. Even the wildest horse would have trouble ignoring a command from a tough bit.

"Anyway," Mrs. Reg continued, "each time I rode that horse, I kept giving him firmer signals with the reins and the bit. We had a very uncomfortable relationship, you know. Then one day, the bit broke. The only extra one around was a jointed snaffle. I figured it would be a disaster to ride with it because the snaffle is so gentle. But I had to exercise the horse, so I tried it. It was like night and day, I'll tell you. That horse had known all along what it was he was supposed to do: It was just that he didn't like the way I was trying to control him. When he had a little bit of freedom, he did just exactly the right thing."

"I guess I shouldn't interfere so much in my friends' lives, huh?" Carole asked after a pause.

"No, that's not exactly what I mean, Carole. I think you should give people the help they need, but when it comes to the things they have to do by themselves, let them do it. Good friends always come through."

"Always?"

"Well, usually," Mrs. Reg corrected herself.

"Thanks, Mrs. Reg," Carole said as the older woman left the tack room. Still, she didn't feel comforted. It was one thing for her friends to do the right thing. It was another to expect either Mrs. Atwood or Max to do the right thing.

What *were* they all doing in his office for so long?

"SEE YOU LATER, Mom." Lisa's voice emerged from the silence. Carole sat up straight. She could practically hear her heart beat, she was so nervous about the outcome of this big meeting. She knew that Lisa and Stevie would be in the tack room in a minute. They had arranged to meet there before class. She stared at the door, barely able to contain her excitement. She strained to hear Lisa's and Stevie's footsteps.

The door opened and Stevie and Lisa appeared, solemn-faced. Then, as Carole watched, bewildered, the two of them exchanged glances and waited for the door to close soundly behind them. When it was shut, they both jumped up in the air and yelled "Yahoooooo!" at the same time.

It could only mean one thing—victory!

"What happened? Are you going? Both of you?" Carole could barely get the questions out fast enough.

"You bet we are," Stevie said positively. "Max was just great—he was wonderful. I'm telling you, Carole, he was fantastic. I didn't know he would do such a thing, but he was *outstanding.*"

"What happened?" Carole asked, practically dying of curiosity.

"You tell, Lisa. She's your mother," Stevie said, passing the honors on to her friend.

"Oh, Max was great," Lisa said.

"I know that. We all know that," Carole said. "Just what did he *do?*"

"He convinced my mother to let me go on the MTO on the grounds that Stevie would be my partner."

"Stevie?" Carole asked. Stevie was a good rider and all, but no doubt about it, Carole was the best rider in the class. If Lisa needed a partner, which, in Carole's opinion, she did not, Carole would have been the likely candidate.

"How come Stevie?" Carole asked, feeling a little hurt.

"Because he told her that Lisa was helping me with my math project. And then he told her I'd asked him for a chance to help Lisa with something in return. That was news to me, but it worked! Lisa's mother thought that was a great idea. So did I!"

Suddenly, Carole saw the light. Max had maneuvered Mrs. Atwood into letting Lisa come on the MTO! He was something else.

"Max did this with a straight face?" Carole asked.

"Just *barely*," Stevie admitted. Suddenly the three girls were overcome with relief and joy. Carole started giggling first, and then Stevie burst into laughter. In seconds, Lisa was laughing along with them both and then the three of them hugged each other with joy.

"Yahoooooo!" Carole cried.

That said it all.

Just at that moment, the door to the tack room opened and Veronica diAngelo sauntered in. Carole was surprised to see her there so late after class.

"I had to talk to Max about *private* jumping lessons," Veronica said, explaining her presence. She sat down on the bench to remove her riding boots. "And what are *you* doing here so late?" she asked.

"We were talking to Max about the MTO," Lisa volunteered. "And he said I could go—and Stevie will be my partner! Isn't that great?"

"Oh, sure, great," Veronica said. She didn't sound

like she meant it at all. Veronica finished changing her shoes, then stood up and left the tack room as regally as she had entered it.

As soon as the door closed, the three girls burst into giggles.

"Oh, sure, great!" Stevie mimicked Veronica. "Did you ever hear such insincerity?"

"What made you tell her?" Carole asked Lisa.

Lisa thought for a moment. "I think I wanted her to know that Max believes I'm a good enough rider to go on the MTO when she didn't think I was a good enough rider to be her friend."

"Well, I'll tell you one thing," Stevie said.

"What?"

"Not only are you a good enough rider to be *my* friend, but you're also a great math student and I think it's time to get back to work on Project Math Project—due in three days!" She paused for a second and then went on. "You know, today I feel so good, I could add up a column of fifty-six numbers and not make a mistake!"

"Let's not waste a second, then!" Lisa teased. "Let's go!"

Together, the three of them headed for Stevie's house.

"NOW, STEVIE, HERE'S how you set up the problems. If you do the math, I'll fill in your answers on the work sheet. We don't have all the information—we *know* some stuff is definitely missing, but you've got to start the calculations," Lisa told her in a very businesslike manner.

Stevie took the paper and calculator and sat at her desk to begin her work—nearly the final steps of the project.

Neither Stevie nor Lisa was aware of Carole. She was sprawled under Stevie's bed where she'd chased Stevie's cat, Madonna, who'd run off with her pen. In the dim light, Carole could see that the cat was crouched over a pile of little crumpled bits of paper. Madonna cocked her right front paw and began batting one of the pieces of balled-up paper. It skittered across the floor, and the cat pounced on it with glee.

Carole laughed at Madonna's antics. The cat attacked another ball of crumpled paper, while Carole watched, fascinated. Then it struck her! "Eureka!" she yelled.

"Don't distract me—I'm adding up a whole bunch of numbers," Stevie said irritably.

"Hold it a second," Carole said, knowing her voice was muffled under the bed. She waddled backwards to get out. As she moved, she collected Madonna's cache of paper balls and brought them with her. "You've got to stop adding that column because I think—if my eyes and brain haven't deceived me—that you have a whole bunch more to add in!" Proudly, Carole displayed her booty.

Lisa gasped. "The missing data!" She grabbed for the papers.

"Oh, no! More numbers to add!" Stevie groaned.

"But now we have everything," Lisa said, trying to comfort her. She smoothed out each scrap of paper, deciphering Stevie's scribbles—something she'd had an awful lot of practice doing over the last few days.

Stevie sighed, but she took the papers and methodically began adding them to her work sheets. There was a lot more work to do, but Stevie seemed determined to do it. Carole just hoped she could do it by bedtime tonight. The report was due first thing in the morning.

A few hours later, it was all done. The final calculation had been entered, the final analysis made, the last penny accounted for.

"I hope I get the grade I need on this. I don't think I've ever worked harder on something for school than I did on this," Stevie said, staring at the finished product.

"Me, neither," Lisa said. "Even on something of my own!"

The next morning, Stevie was out of bed early. She wanted to have one last look at her math project. That project represented not only a lot of work on her part—and her friends', as well—but it was almost as if it *were* the MTO. She reached for the cover to open it, but her hand stopped. She didn't dare look inside. What if it looked awful to her this morning? It was better not to know.

Later that Friday morning, she put it on her teacher's desk and walked to her own seat. She never looked back, but at that moment, she had the feeling she understood why her mother had behaved so strangely the first day Michael had gone off to nursery school. The project was her baby.

She crossed her fingers.

ON SATURDAY, THE three girls had riding class together. They were working on the proper way to sit in the saddle at a canter.

Lisa was really glad that it was hard to do because it

would have been impossible to concentrate on anything easy.

"Now slide in the saddle, rock with the horse, Lisa!" Max said. "And don't hold on!" Lisa let go of the front of the saddle and tried to slide. "Relax!" Max said. How could she relax? She tried it. It didn't work. She didn't feel relaxed about Stevie, but she must have been a little more relaxed about cantering. "Good, Lisa," Max said. "Much better." That was how much *he* knew.

ON MONDAY AFTER school, the call came. Carole had been waiting to hear from Stevie for so long that she was beginning to think she'd miss the waiting when it was over. But that was silly, of course.

"I got it back," Stevie said as soon as Carole answered the phone.

"And?" Carole said, the phone pressed tightly to her ear.

"I can barely say it," Stevie said.

"Say *what*?" Carole asked, fearing the worst.

Stevie cleared her throat. "A-plus. I got an A-plus on my math report."

Carole whooped with joy.

"That means that my term grade is now going to be a B-plus. That's the best I've done in math since third grade! Can you believe it? It's true!"

"Wow," Carole uttered in relief. "That's wonderful. Congratulations. Have you called Lisa?"

"I already did," Stevie said. "After all, I couldn't possibly have done it without her. And she's invited you and me to come over to her house Saturday after class for a celebration. Okay with you?"

"Great with me," Carole said, grinning broadly. "Saturday will be great. I'll see you tomorrow at class."

And when she hung up the phone, Carole shouted "Yahooooo!"

"What's got you so excited, baby?" her father called from the living room.

"Oh—just everything, Daddy. Everything's great! Say, Daddy, what's round and purple and gets A-pluses on her math projects?"

Not surprisingly, her father didn't answer.

"Stevie the Grape," Carole said, giggling to herself.

"OKAY, SO YOU don't think I should take a dress," Lisa said jokingly.

"Only if it's a designer dress and your mother insists," Stevie teased her. Lisa grinned in response. The three girls were gathered in Lisa's room, chatting happily about the MTO, deciding what to take with them.

"I guess I will be able to take my cassette player after all," Stevie said.

"Right, but don't bring along any music that will frighten the horses," Carole said. "Just something that will frighten Veronica—"

"Hey, great idea! Maybe I'll see if I can buy a tape of creepy night sounds. I still have some money left and, after all, Betsy owes me some from that job she did."

Lisa gave her a look. "If you don't mind, Stevie, I think that today should be the end of all talk about anything to do with the *math* project."

"Okay," Stevie said agreeably. "So today is the end of one thing—and the beginning of another. But what's it the beginning of?"

"The MTO," Lisa said.

"No," Stevie contradicted her. "The MTO starts next Friday afternoon and goes for the entire holiday weekend. Today is the start of something else, I think, but what?"

Both girls looked over at Carole, who was sitting in the overstuffed chair by the window. "Carole, you with us?" Lisa asked gently.

Carole nodded. "You know, I just keep thinking how lucky I am to have two friends like you," she said.

"Now, don't get sappy on me," Stevie teased.

"I wouldn't do that," Carole said, grinning. "I'm just happy, but also a little amazed. I mean, I think it would be hard for me to find two girls who are so different from me—and from each other. But we're all friends."

They all paused to think. "I mean, we've got Stevie the practical joker—" Carole continued.

"Who promises not to do any jokes at her friends' expense," Stevie said solemnly.

"Then there's Lisa, the straight-A student who—"

"Helps Stevie ace her math project," Lisa said.

"And Carole the flake who misses buses and scatters

papers. But who can find the critical piece of paper under Stevie's bed at just the right moment." Carole paused. They all looked at one another, more pleased than distressed at their differences.

"But," Carole continued, "we also have something in common. Something very important to each of us. We all love horses. We love riding them, we love training them, we love taking care of them."

"Well, I'm not crazy about mucking out stalls," Stevie corrected Carole.

"I never said you were crazy," Carole teased her. "I just said you were *horse* crazy. We all are, aren't we?"

"You bet," Lisa agreed. Stevie nodded as well.

"Okay, so how about this? Today marks the beginning of The Saddle Club. All you have to do to belong is to be a friend to the other members, which may include things like helping on math projects, or saddling difficult horses, or promising to be a partner on an overnight trip—and you have to be horse crazy, right?"

"But mostly you have to be horse crazy?" Stevie suggested. She didn't want to do another math project.

"Mostly," Carole agreed.

First, they all shook on it. And then they all hugged. Each knew that being horse crazy was going to be great.

"To The Saddle Club!" Lisa said, lifting her soda can high into the air.

"To The Saddle Club!" her friends echoed, clinking their sodas against hers.

It was a wonderful sound.

THE SADDLE CLUB

HORSE SHY

BONNIE BRYANT

A BANTAM BOOK®
TORONTO • NEW YORK • LONDON • SYDNEY • AUCKLAND

For my mother, Mary S. Bryant

"*Duck!*" Stevie Lake yelled.

Lisa Atwood leaned forward in the saddle and tucked her head low, near Pepper's shiny black mane. She could feel tree branches brushing the back of her neck. When the brushing stopped, she sat upright and drew Pepper to a halt next to Stevie and her horse, Comanche. In a minute their friend, Carole Hanson, caught up with them, breathless and smiling, riding on Delilah.

"Oh, I love this trail!" Carole exclaimed. "But I do wish somebody would trim those branches! Sometimes when you're trotting, you come up on them so fast that you can ram right into them."

"Why don't the horses know to go around them?" Lisa asked her friends. Stevie and Carole were experienced riders. Lisa had begun riding just a few weeks earlier, but already she knew she loved the sport as much as anything she'd ever done.

"Horses don't go around the hanging branches because they can tell that they'll fit under them. They just forget about their riders on top," Carole explained.

"That's just the kind of thing you've got to know before we go on the overnight trail ride," Stevie said. "Riding outdoors is really different from riding indoors."

Lisa could already tell that was true. She'd been riding Pepper since her second lesson and she'd never known the horse to be so frisky.

"Okay, now we can trot here for a while before the trail gets rocky," Stevie said. "I'll start, you wait until I'm up to that azalea bush, and then you can follow." Stevie nudged Comanche into motion. As soon as Stevie passed the bright pink-flowered bush, Lisa signaled Pepper to trot. He obeyed immediately, following Comanche.

Lisa liked to trot. It was fast enough, but not too fast—sort of like jogging. A horse's next-fastest gait, the canter, was more like running, and Lisa found that scary sometimes; it was hard to keep her balance. While Pepper trotted, Lisa looked straight ahead, watching Stevie in front of her.

Stevie's untidy dark blond hair trailed out of her riding hat. The sun was shining on her hair and on Comanche's chestnut coat, making them both gleam richly. Their personalities, stubborn but playful, were alike. Somebody who didn't know Stevie well might think that the advantages she'd been born with—a comfortably wealthy family, big house, private schools—might have made her think she was better than other people. That wasn't Stevie at all. Stevie just liked to have fun, and she usually managed to do it, too—even when fun looked a lot like hot water!

Lisa glanced back at Carole. Carole was a wonderful rider. She'd been riding horses since she was a very little girl on the Marine Corps bases where her father had been stationed. Carole was riding Delilah, a beautiful, spirited palomino. Carole used her legs and reins to signal Delilah so subtly that Lisa could never even see what she'd done. But Delilah knew. The two worked in nearly perfect unison.

Lisa suddenly felt Pepper's trot quicken. She shortened her reins and slowed the horse a bit. They were approaching Stevie and Comanche. Stevie had slowed her horse to a walk to cool him down. Since the trail was wide, Lisa drew up next to Stevie and they walked together.

"How come Pepper started going faster when we got closer to you?"

"You've seen that happen in class, haven't you?" Lisa nodded. "Well," Stevie continued, "it happens more outdoors because there's more room. See, horses are naturally competitive animals. They really love to race and show off to each other. As soon as Pepper got close to Comanche, he wanted to be *ahead* of Comanche. It's not as important to him when we're walking as when we're trotting—and wait until you see what happens when we canter!"

"You know, Stevie, I've been wondering," Carole said as she drew her horse up to Comanche and Pepper. "Why was Max so eager to have us come out on the trail today?"

Max—whose full name was Maxmillian Regnery III and who was the owner of Pine Hollow Stables—was usually reluctant to let young riders onto the trails around the stable without a chaperon or instructor.

"Oh, he didn't know we were going on the trails," Stevie said airily. "I told him we were going to check the cross-country course for him."

"The cross-country course? You're crazy!" Carole told her.

"Oh, no, I'm not," Stevie countered. "There's going to be a horse show on that course this summer, so Max was really glad I wanted us to go over it. And, you'll remember that I'm supposed to be Lisa's partner on the Mountain Trail Overnight in three days, and if she doesn't have any trail experience before we leave, it'll be hard for her, and for me," Stevie finished breathlessly. "Now, I'm in the lead, so let's get going."

"But why didn't you just tell him the truth?" Carole asked. Stevie just shrugged and then began trotting again—as if that were an answer.

Lisa followed her, laughing a little bit to herself.

Stevie wasn't usually a bossy person the way she sounded now. What Stevie usually was was in trouble. Lisa had a sneaking suspicion that she'd be in it as well if she followed Stevie's orders. But how could she resist?

Carole watched the riders in front of her. She and Stevie had been riding together for two years, as long as her father had been stationed at the Marine Corps base at Quantico. Colonel Hanson had bought a house in nearby Willow Creek, Virginia—the first time they had ever lived off a base—and Carole had started riding at Pine Hollow. Until that time, most of her friends had been "military brats" like herself. Now, her best friends, Stevie and Lisa, were riders. The three of them had formed The Saddle Club. The only requirement for membership in it was to be horse crazy. So far, they hadn't met anybody as horse crazy as they were, so there were just the three members.

Even though Lisa was a year older than twelve-year-old Carole and Stevie, she'd just started riding. But Carole could tell that Lisa had a natural feel for horses. She'd known it the first time she'd watched Lisa ride in the ring at Pine Hollow. When Lisa and her mother had shown up at the stable, Carole was sure Lisa was just another spoiled rich kid, dressed in fancy riding clothes. Then Max had put her on a gentle pinto named Patch to see if she knew anything about horses. Before she'd walked around the ring twice, Veronica diAngelo (who really *was* a spoiled rich kid) had let a door slam loudly enough to frighten Lisa's horse. Patch had bolted into a gallop. Carole had been sure Lisa was going to fly off Patch's back and break an arm, or worse. Somehow, though, Lisa had managed to stay on the horse, eventually controlling him. Carole had never seen another rider show such skill the first time out. But no matter how great Lisa's natural talents were, there was plenty she didn't know. That's why this practice at riding outdoors was so important before the three girls went on the overnight ride.

Suddenly, Carole was alert. Delilah shied, nearly rearing, as a rabbit scooted across the trail. Carole leaned forward for balance, tightening the reins automatically. As soon as Delilah felt Carole's sure grip, she seemed to relax. The rabbit was safely in the underbrush by the time Delilah was calmed down.

Just then, a second rabbit dashed out onto the trail just in front of Pepper and Lisa. To Carole's horror, Pepper practically jumped backwards. Lisa grabbed the front of the saddle for balance, dropping Pepper's reins. Pepper reared a moment later, but without the reins, there was no way Lisa could control him or calm him. The rabbit darted back and forth under the horse's feet, completely terrorized. Pepper reared a second time, and when he landed, he took off—without Lisa. She flew into the air and landed on her right side.

Carole knew that Lisa needed help, but Pepper had

to be stopped. She called ahead to Stevie to help Lisa. When Stevie turned around and saw what had happened, she rushed to Lisa's aid.

Carole urged Delilah into action. Pepper had sprinted into the woods, but Carole knew there was a hilly field just beyond the stand of trees that bordered the trail. When she broke through the trees, she could see Pepper galloping up a hill. She had to cut him off before he could gallop down the hill—that could be really dangerous!

Skillfully, Carole directed Delilah. They took a shortcut across the pasture to meet Pepper at the hill's crest. Carole could almost feel Delilah shifting gears, thrilled with the race. They arrived at the hilltop just seconds before Pepper. Carole was afraid he might dart down the other side of the hill when he saw them in front of him, but he'd had enough of his run. Almost as if he knew he'd been naughty, he hung his head and coyly began nibbling at the sweet young grass in the pasture.

Carole clucked to him soothingly. He lifted his head and looked at her with his liquid brown eyes.

"It's okay, boy," she said. "Nobody's angry with you. We'd better see how Lisa feels, though. Come on."

He wouldn't come to her, but he stood patiently while she reached down from Delilah and took his reins. He followed obediently as they returned to the trail.

* * *

"YOU OKAY?" STEVIE asked. Lisa was still lying awkwardly on the ground.

"Well, I'm alive, if that's what you mean," Lisa said.

"No, I mean is anything broken or permanently damaged?"

"Yeah," Lisa said.

Stevie's heart fell. "What?" she asked.

"My dignity," Lisa told her grumpily.

Stevie laughed. "Boy, you had me scared! Come on, get up. Carole went after Pepper. There's a place by a brook about a half hour's ride ahead where we can stop and have our lunch. You'll feel better after you eat something."

"You ride; I'll walk," Lisa said.

"You *are* hurt!" Stevie said, offering Lisa a hand to stand up.

"No, I'm okay, but that's it for me for riding. I obviously can't do it. I'm quitting."

"Of course you can do it," Stevie said. "I mean, you could do it ten minutes ago—two minutes ago, actually."

"No, I couldn't," Lisa protested. "Look at what just happened."

"Just because your horse shies and you fall off, you think you can't ride?" Stevie asked her.

"You didn't fall off, did you?" Lisa answered her.

"Not then, maybe, but I have, plenty of times before. And I will again, too, believe me!"

Standing now, Lisa just glared at Stevie. Stevie returned the glare, looking carefully at Lisa. For one thing, she wanted to make sure she *was* okay, but for another, she was looking to see how scared she was. Lisa had taken a bad tumble and she was afraid she'd do it again. It was a feeling Stevie knew well; everybody who rode felt that way sometimes. But Stevie knew you couldn't let that get you down, and she certainly couldn't let it get one of her best friends down.

"Here's Pepper," Carole said cheerfully, leading him back through the stand of trees. "And I think he's ready to ride now."

"Well, his rider isn't," Lisa said.

Carole brought the horses to an abrupt halt.

"Lisa figures she's no good at riding," Stevie explained. "She's giving it up. Here and now." Stevie winked at Carole, certain she could rely on Carole to say just the right thing.

"I know how you feel, Lisa," Carole said. "It's rough when you decide to quit. But look at your poor horse." She pointed to Pepper. The horse's head still hung low. He glanced at Lisa quickly and then looked at the ground again. "He feels even worse than you do. Why don't you get back on him so he'll have the confidence to take riders again? If you abandon him now, who knows what will happen to him as a stable horse?"

Lisa looked Carole straight in the eye until she saw a twinkle there. "You're telling me to get right back up on the horse to make *him* feel better?" she asked.

When Carole shrugged in answer, Lisa giggled. "Maybe I'm being silly," she said, "but I can't help being scared."

"Don't worry," Carole said. "We understand. We've both felt the same way before. Now, forget how scary that fall was and climb up on this poor animal!"

Lisa brushed the dirt off her pants and removed some dry leaves from Pepper's saddle. She straightened out his bridle, which had gone askew, and she patted him on the neck.

"We're some pair, huh?" she said. "Come on now, boy, how can you be afraid of a little rabbit when I'm not allowed to be afraid of a great big horse?" She slid her left foot into the stirrup and lifted herself up into the saddle. "Oooh," she said. "Nothing's broken, but something's sure bruised. I may have to stand up to eat! How far is this picnic area?" she asked Stevie.

"Oh, not far," Stevie said vaguely as she urged Comanche on.

AN HOUR LATER, the three girls were finished with their picnic, and the horses were rested and refreshed from the cool brook water.

"We'd better get back to Pine Hollow," Stevie said. "Max isn't going to believe we spent three hours just looking at the cross-country course."

"Personally, I don't think Max is going to believe we even went to the cross-country course," Carole said. "He's smarter than that, you know."

Stevie already suspected Max knew what they were up to and approved. He trusted her as a rider, and he trusted Carole even more; he knew they'd take good care of Lisa.

"Listen, I've got a different way to go back," Stevie said. "It's through pastures. The horses will love it, too, because they can canter a lot. And when horses canter together outside, they usually end up galloping. Wait'll you try that, Lisa!"

"I think I've tried enough for today," Lisa said.

"Trust me," Stevie said with a grin. Somehow, the way she said it, Lisa trusted her, even though at the very same time, she suspected it was a mistake.

The girls took off on their horses through a series of pastures to return to Pine Hollow. Stevie seemed to know her way, and she was right about the horses enjoying the freedom of the pastures. They alternately walked, trotted, and cantered across the rolling hills. The only problem was that they had to stop all the time to open and close gates.

"It's an unbreakable rule of horseback riding that you leave gates exactly as you found them," Carole explained to Lisa.

"Hey, we can take a shortcut!" Stevie shouted.

"What shortcut?" Carole asked dubiously.

"Look over to the left." Stevie pointed downhill. "I'm sure that red building at the foot of the hill is next to Pine Hollow. !f we go straight, we'll avoid about ten gates!"

"But we don't know whose farm that is!" Carole said. Another firm rule of riding was that riders only went where they had permission.

"Oh, who's going to care about three girls on horseback?" Stevie asked.

"A lot of people," Carole began to tell her, but it was too late. Stevie was already racing across the strange field, Lisa right behind. Carole sighed and followed them.

Lisa was enjoying the countryside, glad of her decision to ride Pepper again, and glad for the friends who made her do it.

The girls were about three quarters of the way across the field when they heard a strange sound.

At first, Lisa didn't know what it was. It sounded a little bit like a cow. But there weren't any cows in this small pasture. Herds of cows usually grazed together.

When she saw it, she knew it wasn't a cow, but she wished it were! A very large bull emerged from behind a stand of aspens. He snorted and bellowed, stomping at the ground with one front foot. His nostrils flared in anger. Lisa drew in her reins. All three girls began walking their horses slowly, hoping the bull would let them pass.

All at once, though, he began charging. He was perhaps fifty yards from the horses, and although his legs were short and he was stocky, he was fast. Very fast.

"Get out of here!" Stevie hollered, turning Comanche around and heading for the fence. Delilah and Pepper took off as well. Then, in horror, Lisa realized that there was no gate there! They'd be cornered! A rabbit was one thing for Pepper to contend with, but a bull? Before Lisa could figure out what the answer was, Stevie showed her. As soon as Comanche got close to the fence, Stevie leaned forward, rising in the seat. Then Comanche was airborne, lifting himself gracefully over the fence, landing smoothly on the other side. Stevie cantered on a few steps and then drew her horse to a halt, waiting for her friends.

Carole, on board Delilah, cleared the fence with a foot to spare. It looked so easy!

Terrified, Lisa rose in the saddle as she'd seen her friends do. She leaned forward, grabbing some of Pepper's mane in her sweaty hands. Just when she was afraid they would crash headfirst into the wooden fence, her friends cried "Now!" Maybe Pepper heard them. Maybe he just knew what he was supposed to do. It didn't matter to Lisa how it happened, because it happened. While she clutched the saddle and mane with all her strength, she felt Pepper lift off the ground and sail to safety on the other side of the fence.

Lisa had never been more thrilled—or more scared—in her life. Stevie and Carole cheered wildly, clapping for Pepper and for Lisa.

"Gee, I didn't know you could jump!" Stevie said.

"Neither did I," Lisa said. "Neither did I."

2

"IF ONE MORE person asks me where the extra stirrup leathers are, I'm going to scream!" Carole announced. But nobody was listening to her.

Everything around the stable and front driveway of Pine Hollow Stables was in an advanced state of confusion. It seemed to Carole that she was the only organized part of it.

The eleven people and eleven horses who were going on the Mountain Trail Overnight—or the MTO, as the girls called it—were swarming around the bus and horse vans. All the riders were trying to make sure their own things were packed. Carole clutched a clipboard tightly in her hand. She checked it one more time—a *final* time, she hoped—but she knew better.

"Need any help?" Stevie asked, hauling her own bedroll and knapsack over to the bus.

"Hey, thanks," Carole said. "Everybody else wants to know how I can help *them.*" Carole looked at the clipboard again. "Oh, here's what you can do. We're going to need hoof-picks. Joe Novick said he'd get them, but right after he promised, I saw him go in the opposite direction and I haven't seen him since. Grab a couple from the tack room, will you? And put them in with the grooming gear?"

Stevie saluted with a grin and headed for the stable's tack room. Carole put a second check mark next to "hoof-picks."

Veronica diAngelo was standing near the bus. Three of her friends—more like ladies-in-waiting, Carole thought—were gathered around her. Carole stifled a giggle when she noticed that each of them—Meg Durham, Lorraine Olsen, and Betsy Cavanaugh—was wearing the identical riding pants that Veronica had worn. Last week. They'd probably driven their mothers crazy trying to imitate Veronica's fashion-show riding habit.

As far as Carole was concerned, there was nothing about Veronica that she wanted to imitate—but Veronica did have one thing Carole longed for. Veronica's father had bought her a beautiful Thoroughbred stallion named Cobalt. Carole would have given anything to own Cobalt, and sometimes it almost seemed like she did. Veronica liked owning a prize Thoroughbred.

She didn't like taking care of him and exercising him regularly, though. She often asked Carole to help and Carole never said no. She loved that horse.

"Did we remember to bring horse blankets?" Red O'Malley, one of Pine Hollow's stableboys, asked Carole.

She checked her list and told him they were packed.

When Carole was certain everything on her clipboard had been checked twice, she helped load the horses onto the vans. Most horses learned to accept occasional van trips. Some even liked them. But a few, like Barq, whom Lorraine would ride, were van haters. He was an Arabian—named after the Arabic word for lightning—and when he got near a van, he tried to streak the other way! To avoid trouble this time, they led him up the ramp with a bucket of oats. With his nose in the feed bag, he was in the van before he knew it, and it was too late for protests.

Today, Carole saw with a sigh of relief, Barq was no trouble at all. Diablo and Harry gave Max and Red a hard time, but eventually, the horses were loaded. When Carole assured the drivers that all the horse gear was aboard, the vans took off. The bus would follow in a few minutes.

Lisa stowed her bedroll and pack in the bus and came over to chat with Carole while the last items were loaded. She was followed closely by her mother. Mrs. Atwood had originally insisted that Lisa learn to ride. She thought all nice young ladies should know something about horses. But she never expected Lisa to become horse crazy, and she was very nervous that something terrible would happen to her daughter on the MTO.

She hovered around Lisa. While the girls talked about riding, Mrs. Atwood uttered dire warnings like "Don't go too close to the edge of the mountain, now, dear," and "Don't drink any water that hasn't been boiled, will you?" Lisa just nodded sweetly, assuring her mother she'd be careful. Carole wondered at Lisa's patience, but she knew Mrs. Atwood was just being caring, in her own way.

"Mom, I think it's time for parents to go," Lisa said gently. She gave her mother a brief hug. "See you Sunday at six o'clock, okay?"

"Okay, dear," Mrs. Atwood said, backing toward her station wagon. "Have a good time!" Lisa smiled.

Lisa wasn't the only rider with a mother hanging around. Mrs. diAngelo drove up in her Mercedes and rolled down the window. "Oh, I'm so glad you're still here, dear," she said. "I brought this for you."

Mrs. diAngelo offered Veronica a set of saddlebags. Even from across the parking area, Carole could see they weren't just saddlebags. They were from Hermès, the exclusive French saddlery. Carole knew she'd probably ridden horses that cost less than that set of saddlebags.

Veronica accepted the offering as if her mother had handed her an old pair of pajamas. "Thanks, Mother," she said drily.

"Open them up," her mother said, her voice tinged with excitement. Veronica lifted up the flap and pulled out a sack of expensive Perugina candies. "I thought you'd enjoy sharing those by the campfire," she said.

Veronica smiled briefly. "Thanks, Mother. I guess it's time to go now. See you Sunday."

Mrs. diAngelo raised her push-button window and drove off.

"Isn't that something?" Stevie said, joining Carole and Lisa. "I didn't know she cared."

Carole had to agree. Mrs. diAngelo seemed to be trying very hard to please Veronica. It was too bad that Veronica was such a pain. "Doesn't matter to me, though," Carole said. "She's still a pain."

"Yeah, but now she's a pain with some wonderful treats to share at the campfire."

"You know," Lisa said, "I think I'd rather have a mother who worries too much than one who brings me five-hundred-dollar saddlebags filled with expensive candies."

"Me, too," Stevie agreed.

Carole was quiet for a moment. Her own mother had died after a long illness the previous fall. She hadn't been like either Mrs. Atwood or Mrs. diAngelo. She'd been just about perfect. Carole really missed her, but she was glad she had her memories.

"Time to board the bus!" Max announced. At once, eleven people jostled over to the minibus, which would carry them to the start of the mountain trail.

Carole stood at the door of the bus. As the riders climbed aboard one by one, Carole asked them all—even Max—if they'd remembered their bedrolls and packs. As they promised they had, Carole put checks by their names on her list.

Then it was time for Carole to climb on board. "Okay, Hanson, did you remember *your* bedroll and backpack?" Stevie teased, trying to sound like a Marine drill instructor.

Carole blushed. She knew then that she'd been impossibly bossy, but there were so many things to do, and Max was really counting on her to help.

"Of course!" she answered. She could envision the two bundles clearly. Right by her front door. Ready to be picked up and put in the car. She gasped. She knew suddenly that they were still there, right by her front door. If she didn't have her pack and bedroll, there was no way she could go on the trip! Max would probably agree to take a detour past her house to pick them up, but could she ever live it down?

She stood, frozen, on the steps of the bus. Then she heard the sound of a car horn. Startled, she turned around. Her father! He pulled up in front of the bus, then threw open the door and dragged out the two bundles Carole most wanted to see.

"Didn't think you'd want to go without these, honey," he said, handing them to Carole. She slung them into the luggage compartment and slammed its door shut.

"Thanks, Daddy," she said. And then, while everybody watched and waited, she gave him the great big hug he deserved. "You're the best."

"Yeah, I know," he told her. "You have a good time, hear?" She smiled at him.

"Hey, Colonel Hanson!" Stevie hollered out the bus window. The colonel waved a greeting to her. They were great friends, constantly trading old jokes with each other. "What has four legs and a trunk?" Stevie asked.

"An elephant going on a trip," he shot back.

"And what do you call Carole when *she* goes on a trip?" Stevie asked.

"Forgetful!" he said. When everybody was done laughing, Carole boarded the bus.

And they were off!

3

CAROLE COULDN'T BELIEVE it, but getting everything *un*loaded at the start of the trail was almost as much trouble as getting it loaded.

Delilah was unusually docile coming off the trailer, but it turned out that Barq hated getting off as much as he hated getting on. Red O'Malley got a nasty kick on his shin. He grimaced, but said it was okay. Carole thought it would be swollen and black-and-blue for a long time. Horses were big animals, and strong. If you were going to spend a lot of time with them, you had to be prepared to get hurt some of the time. Red didn't complain; he knew that, too.

Finally, the horses were unloaded, and the camping and picnic gear was loaded onto a van that would meet them at the rendezvous for lunch and then the overnight campsite.

"I hope the truck doesn't get lost," Carole joked with Lisa and Stevie.

When their horses were all off the van, the riders each fetched tack and began saddling.

"I always hate tacking up—especially when Comanche's in a bad mood," Stevie said. "But Comanche's standing still today. I think he's as eager to get going as I am!"

"I think you're right," Lisa said. "Look at Pepper. He's so busy sniffing the fresh mountain air that he didn't even notice when I tightened the girth!" Pepper had a way of taking in a big breath of air when his rider drew the girth tight. Then, after it had been fastened, he'd let out his breath and his saddle would be nice and loose, the way he liked it. From his rider's point of view, though, it was dangerous. Lisa always had to tighten the girth twice. This time, though, it wasn't necessary.

"Mount up!" Max called, and the trail ride really began.

MAX HAD TOLD the riders that their first day would be relatively easy. They would ride for an hour or so to their picnic lunch rendezvous. Then, after lunch, they would be going uphill most of the way to a meadow about halfway up the mountain. They were supposed to reach the meadow by midafternoon. The horses would spend the night in the meadow, and the campsite was just uphill from it.

Lisa couldn't believe how lucky she was. Just a month ago, she'd never ridden anything more exciting than a pony in a zoo. Now, here she was on a warm, sparkling day, riding through a beautiful mountain forest just bursting with late-spring flowers. They rode single file on the narrow path, shaded by majestic oak trees. For the first half mile, the way was lined with mountain laurel, covered with pink and white blossoms. Lisa picked a small flower and tucked it behind her ear. It made her feel exotic.

"Can you believe this place?" Stevie asked from behind her.

"No, I can't," Lisa said. "It makes me feel like I'm in a dream, or maybe a fairy tale. I sort of expect to see a little gingerbread cottage around the next bend."

Just then the trail widened in a hemlock grove. The warm sunshine seemed to bake the trees and the carpet of pine needles. There was a wonderful forest smell all around them.

"Doesn't it smell like Christmas?" Carole called back to her friends. She inhaled deeply, thinking how great the fresh evergreen scent was.

While the trail was wide, Max had the group trot and then canter, one at a time. Pepper was ready. He was frisky and full of excitement. Lisa thought maybe he was as excited as she was. She'd never known him so eager to respond to her signals. When she sat in the trot and then nudged him behind his girth with her left leg, he responded immediately, springing into a wonderful rocking canter. It had never felt so good. It had never been so much fun. She tucked her head down behind Pepper's to avoid some low-slung hemlock branches. As she reined him back down to a walk where the path narrowed again, she sighed contentedly.

"Did you like that?" Stevie asked.

"It was *wonderful*," she replied truthfully. She couldn't stop grinning, and she felt that in his own way Pepper was grinning, too.

"I'M SO HUNGRY, I could eat a—" Stevie paused. "Elephant," she said, giggling.

Lisa groaned at Stevie's joke. "I think I'll make do with the peanut butter sandwiches I saw Mrs. Reg making this morning," she said, referring to Max's mother who was well-loved by the girls.

"We'll eat soon enough," Carole told her friends. "But we'd better see to the horses first."

Lisa and Stevie obediently followed Carole to the area where the horses were tied up.

The three girls took their heavy-duty buckets to the creek and scooped the fresh, cool water for their horses.

"Not too much," Carole warned Lisa.

"That's right, you never want to give a hot horse a lot of water to drink at once," Stevie explained. "They can get terrible stomach cramps that way. Same thing can happen to people, you know."

"Yeah, I know," Lisa said. "After ballet class they only let us have sips of water, especially on hot days." Considering how heavy the bucket could be when it was full, Lisa was relieved she only had to fill it a quarter full. Pepper was glad for the water and nuzzled her neck when she brought the bucket. When he'd had a few sips, she gave him a handful of hay from the bale the van had brought. Pepper seemed totally content. Lisa and Stevie returned to the picnic area, promising to save a spot for Carole.

Carole watched Delilah drinking and patted the golden horse's neck softly. Delilah's mood seemed changed. The horse was enjoying herself, but she was more reserved than usual. She'd been happy to follow Carole's directions, but somehow the usual fight in her seemed faded. Carole supposed she should have been happy with that change, but any mood change in a horse could signal trouble. She made a mental note to talk with Max about it.

When Delilah was munching on her hay, Carole knew it was time for her PBJ and fruit punch. She was hungry and ready for them. She returned to the picnic site, grabbed two sandwiches, some carrot sticks, and a mug of juice, and looked around for Lisa and Stevie. They had just sat down under a big old hickory tree, which was surrounded by soft green ferns.

"Having a good time?" Betsy Cavanaugh asked Carole as she passed. Betsy was sitting with Veronica and the rest of her fan club.

"I sure am. How about you?"

"Oh, it's wonderful," Betsy said.

Carole smiled in acknowledgment and began to walk on. But something made her look back at Veronica, who was sitting on a rock with an empty plate and mug at her side. She had her boots off and was completely relaxed.

If Veronica was already finished with her lunch, that could only mean that she hadn't done anything about Cobalt. Carole knew that, once again, Veronica had just assumed that somebody would do her work for her. And once again, she was right. *She doesn't deserve that horse,* Carole told herself, taking her plate over to the hickory tree.

"Keep the ants out of my lunch for a few minutes, will you?" she asked her friends.

"Sure," Lisa agreed, tucking a napkin over the sandwiches.

Carole returned to the horse area. It only took a few minutes to give Cobalt some water and hay. She knew she should have made Veronica do it herself, but Carole got tremendous pleasure from everything she did with this majestic horse. She patted his sleek neck after she fed him, and he nickered with pleasure.

When she was sure he was properly fed and watered, she returned for her own lunch.

MIRACULOUSLY, THEY ARRIVED at their meadowside campsite a full half hour ahead of schedule.

"Can you believe this?" Stevie asked Carole. "We're actually early!"

"Yeah, it's great," Carole agreed. "The horses all practically pranced through the last couple of miles of trails. I guess they're glad for the chance for a good run."

"You mean they're having as much fun as we are!" Stevie teased.

Max told the boys and girls to tie up their horses outside the paddock where the horses would be penned for the night and to keep the saddles on them.

"The horses should cool down a bit and relax while we set up the campsite. Then, when we're all finished with that, I want to play some horse games. Is that okay with you all?" he asked.

He didn't have to ask twice! Carole knew that horse games were some of the most fun of all.

"ALL RIGHT," MAX told his riders a half hour later. "We're going to play a game called Around the World. There are two teams, five each, and each member is assigned a number, one to five. We make a large circle in no particular order. I'll call out a number and a pace, for example, 'Number Ones, trot.' Then, the two 'Number One' riders will trot around the circle to their right, and whoever gets back to their original position first wins a point for the team. If you break gait—either faster or slower—or go back to the wrong spot, the other rider in your pair wins a point and a point is deducted from your team's total."

"Oh, boy, this is going to be fun. I hope we get the boys on our team," Stevie said. "I certainly don't want Veronica and her shadows!" She'd seen Veronica play games before and she knew she was an incredibly bad sport.

"I have the funny feeling it's not going to work that way," Carole warned her. Much to Stevie's dismay, The Saddle Club was broken up. She and Carole were on one team, with Meg, Lorraine, and Red. Lisa was teamed up with Veronica, Joe, Betsy, and Adam Levine, one of Max's newer students. Stevie saw Lisa grimace when Max announced the teams. But she could tell that Max was trying to match skill levels on the teams.

Soon the numbers were assigned and they all formed a circle. Max and his horse, Diablo, stood in the center of the ring as Max hollered out numbers and gaits. Stevie waited anxiously for her number—three—to be called. And then it was.

"Number Threes, canter!" Max cried.

Stevie was surprised to find herself competing with Lisa. The teams had kept their number assignments secret. Lisa was such a new rider that Stevie was sure she would beat her. But Lisa pulled Pepper out of the circle and turned him to the right very quickly. He broke into a canter, and before Stevie had circled the ring, Lisa and Pepper were breathlessly pulling back into their spot.

Stevie laughed and waved at Lisa. She'd been so cocksure of herself that she hadn't even tried too hard. Lisa had won, fair and square, and she'd deserved to win. *This* time.

When the first game ended, Stevie's team, the Blues, had won, in spite of her own carelessness. In the second game, it seemed that the Reds had learned their lesson and tried much harder. The final score was close—three to two—but the Reds were victors.

"Final match!" Max announced. "Losers will collect kindling for the fire!"

It was just like Max to assign jobs by horsemanship. Usually Stevie wouldn't mind doing something like collecting kindling, but she certainly didn't want to do it if it meant that somebody had beat her at something! She glanced around at her teammates. As usual, Carole's calm, assured face revealed nothing. But Carole was matched against Adam Levine and she was eight times the rider he was. She had beat him twice. Everybody knew she'd beat him a third time.

Stevie saw the looks of determination on the faces of Meg, Lorraine, and Red. She was pretty sure they'd win.

"Number Fours, trot!" Max called to start off the final game. Lorraine and Betsy took off. It wasn't even close. Lorraine's horse didn't want to trot at all. Betsy won easily. The Reds were ahead, one to nothing.

"Number Fives, walk!" Max announced.

Red and Joe took off at a stately walk. Joe was an okay rider, but Red was better. He knew how to urge his horse, Harry, into an extended walk. Harry and Red won easily.

When Carole and Adam had to trot, it was the same story. Carole knew how to get Delilah to lengthen her strides so that, with each beat, she covered more ground. Adam got Tecumseh to a nice collected trot, but it wasn't enough and Carole won easily.

"Number Twos, canter!" Veronica and Meg were off in an instant, but not before Stevie saw the bratty look on Veronica's face. Veronica had never been particularly competitive, but Stevie suspected she'd rather do almost anything than collect twigs. And she did. While Veronica was behind Max's back, she urged Cobalt from a canter to a gallop, which was a much faster gait. Veronica would win easily. Stevie saw Meg glance across the circle. The open-mouthed look on Meg's face revealed that she'd seen Veronica break her gait. But then Meg's mouth closed into a thin line of determination. Stevie knew that if Meg tattled on Veronica, she'd be banned from Veronica's circle of friends forever. That was not a price Meg would be willing to pay.

For her own part, Stevie wasn't interested in tattling. If Max hadn't seen the gallop, well, Stevie and the Blues would take their chances. The score was tied.

Before Max called the final pair, Stevie had a moment to wonder who else had seen what Veronica had done. Maybe someone would say something after the game.

"Number Threes, trot!" Stevie and Lisa turned their horses out of the circle. Stevie nudged Comanche with her heels and he broke into a good extended trot. But when Stevie glanced across the circle it was clear that Pepper, still inspired by the great outdoors, was trotting very quickly and was beating Comanche. Stevie wanted to win—*really* wanted to win. She urged Comanche ahead and he responded with a longer stride, but Stevie wasn't at all sure it would be enough.

Every competitor knows that it's usually an awful mistake to look at your competition in a race, but Stevie kept watching Lisa. She was doing really well and Stevie couldn't help being a little proud of her. After all, who had helped her since she'd started riding!

While Stevie stole peeks at Lisa and Pepper, she saw, to her astonishment, that Lisa was pulling in on Pepper's reins. It wasn't easy to see, but she definitely moved them toward her hips. In an instant, Pepper drew to a walk. He broke his gait! That automatically meant victory for the Blues! Stevie completed her circle, pulled Comanche back into her place in the circle, and waited for Lisa to finish her round.

As Stevie watched, she expected to see embarrassment on Lisa's face. After all, breaking from a trot to a walk was really baby stuff. Lisa was better than that. But when Stevie looked at Lisa's face, what she saw instead was a sly smile, and then she understood.

Lisa had seen Veronica's stunt. If she'd tattled, it might have ruined the whole camp-out. So she'd done the only thing that would guarantee the right outcome of the game. She'd thrown it. She had intentionally pulled Pepper into a walk. Everybody would believe it was just a mistake since that was the kind of thing that happened to new riders.

Stevie was proud of the way Lisa had handled the situation. She wondered if she'd have had the guts to do the same thing.

"How could you *do* that?" Veronica wailed at Lisa.

"I dunno," Lisa said dumbly.

"Well, you're not going to be on *my* team again! Ever!" Veronica declared.

"*Fine* by me," Lisa said.

Stevie grinned over at Carole.

"CAROLE, SOMETIMES I wonder what I'd do without you," Max said.

Carole beamed. Max wasn't the kind of man who complimented people easily. In fact, he hadn't said anything nice about her riding until the third class she'd taken with him!

"I like to help," she said, straightening Patch's blanket and retying the strings at his neck. It was always cool in the mountains at night and the horses would be glad for the covers. "Besides, if I'm ever actually going to own a horse farm, I'll have to get used to the work."

"And it's a *lot* of work," Max assured her.

"It's a lot more work than it ought to be if you've got somebody like Veronica boarding her horse with you," Red said, as Max walked away to check Diablo's blanket. The disgust in his voice was clear. "She didn't even bother with grain for Cobalt's dinner—"

"I'll take care of that," Carole said eagerly.

"I did it already," Red said. "I thought you did your part at lunch."

Carole wasn't surprised that Red had also noticed Veronica's carelessness at lunchtime.

"These are really barn horses," Max told Carole when he returned. "They need extra special care when they are on the trail."

That reminded Carole of something she'd been meaning to ask him. "Gosh, Max, speaking of that, Delilah's been acting strangely. Could she be sick, do you think?"

"What do you mean?" Max snapped, instantly concerned.

"It's like she's suddenly sort of ladylike, more gentle than usual. But, then, she tried to bite me when I was feeding her tonight. She just seems unpredictable."

Max laughed. "Women," he said. "It doesn't sound to me like there's anything to worry about."

But Carole still wasn't sure.

STEVIE LEANED AGAINST a tree, scratching her tired back on its rough bark. The day had been great, and now she knew they were about to play one of the students' favorite games. It was informally called Who Was Max the First?

Maxmillian Regnery III was the current owner and operator of Pine Hollow Stables. It had been founded by his grandfather early in the century. Some people around town remembered Max's father, known as Max the Second. He was a stern, sour-faced man, known for strutting along the town's sidewalks, slapping a riding crop into the palm of his hand. Max the First had died more than 50 years earlier and it had become a Pine Hollow tradition to sort through the wild stories about what kind of man would establish such a wonderful place as Pine Hollow.

"He was a Rough Rider, you know," Stevie began.

"I always thought Max the First was a *good* rider," Meg protested.

"No, I mean a Rough Rider, like pounding up San Juan Hill with Teddy Roosevelt and the Rough Riders. Remember that stuff about the Spanish-American War?"

"Oh, yeah," Meg said. "Roosevelt was the guy who said 'Speak softly and carry a big stick'?"

"That's right!" Stevie said. "And that's why Max the Second always carried his riding crop in town!"

Everybody laughed, except Joe Novick. He was waiting for a quiet moment. "I don't think so," he said. The crowd around the campfire turned to hear *his* theory. "I mean, well, maybe he did that *before* . . ."

"Before *what*?" Betsy Cavanaugh asked eagerly.

"Well, the earthquake, of course," Joe said matter-of-factly. "See, the way I figure it, he was in San Francisco in 1906. You know those old sand buckets in the stables?" They all knew them. Fire was a constant threat in a stable and, in addition to the standard fire extinguishers, there were old leather sand buckets every few feet. "I think he was part of the horseback bucket brigade that saved the city of San Francisco—"

"Saved it?" Carole interrupted. "The whole place was burned down!"

"I just thought the buckets were mementos of the Great Fire," Joe finished.

Maybe they were.

"Oh, no, no," Lisa jumped in, entering into the spirit of the thing. "You've got this all wrong." Everybody turned to her. Even Max seemed interested in what she had to say. "A name like Maxmillian Regnery has to be a cover," she began. "I just learned in school that the Latin word for king is *rex* or *regis,* so the name *Regnery* was chosen because Max the First had royal blood, and I think it was Russian royal blood!"

The kids around the campfire burst into laughter. This was the strangest theory yet. While they listened, Lisa explained that Max the First was probably actually a son of the Russian czar Nicholas II. "He and Alexandra had so many kids, nobody could keep track of them. And when the revolution began, Max the First began spying for the revolutionaries. That's how he escaped execution. But he was always afraid the royalists would find him. So he escaped to Virginia, changed his name, and opened Pine Hollow!"

There was a great round of applause for Lisa's new, untested theory.

"Not bad," Stevie told her, grinning with amusement. At school, Lisa was a straight-A student. Now Stevie could see some use for all the knowledge Lisa had to acquire to be so good.

Adam Levine took Lisa's story about Russian history as a challenge.

"I think you're on the completely wrong track," he began, trying not to laugh. "You're ignoring the well-known fact that Mrs. Reg always keeps that broom near her desk. It was, of course, the broom Max the First's mother used to fly on Halloween. She wouldn't let *him* fly it, so he started riding horses."

Everybody burst into laughter.

"Come on, Max," Meg urged. "What's the real truth?"

The campers turned to him and waited. Max never commented on the silly stories about his grandfather, which, of course, just made the old man seem all the more mysterious. "Well, I'll tell you this," he said, and then paused. Stevie wondered if he might actually reveal something of the truth. A cricket chirped. When the last chirp had echoed in the darkness, Max continued. "I'll tell you this," he repeated. "I think you're on the right track now."

He'd sounded so serious that, for a moment, Stevie had believed him.

Later on, tucked into sleeping bags, safe in their tent, Lisa and Stevie giggled about the silly stories. Carole, tired and happy, plopped a pillow over her ears and went to sleep immediately.

"You know, there is a true answer to the question about Max the First," Lisa whispered to Stevie so she wouldn't wake Carole up.

"Sure, I know that, but there have been so many outrageous rumors that there's no way to tell the truth anymore!"

"Well, we could go back to the beginning," Lisa suggested.

"You mean travel through time?"

"No, I mean go to the library and look through the town records. The man lived in Willow Creek. He bought land, he had children. We ought to be able to find out *something* about him with a little research."

Lisa, the straight-A student, was coming through again. "That's a great idea!" Stevie said. "And I bet when we find out the truth, nobody will believe us."

"Sure, everybody knows that truth is stranger than fiction."

What a delicious idea that was. Stevie snuggled down and closed her eyes. She went to sleep dreaming of Max the First, tied to the mast of a pirate ship.

5

THE NEXT MORNING, Lisa sat on Pepper next to Max and Diablo. They were both watching the other students doing a combination jump—first over a brook, and then, a few yards farther on, over a log that lay across the forest path.

"These aren't hard jumps," Max told Lisa when Betsy Cavanaugh had cleared the log on Patch. "But you're not ready to start jumping classes. You may begin jump classes twelve months after you start your regular riding classes. Perhaps next year you could try a jump like this."

Lisa just nodded. There was no *way* she was going to tell Max she'd already jumped a four-foot fence! Max was very strict about what his students learned and when they learned it. Nobody, but nobody, began jumping until she'd been riding for at least a year. For now, Lisa had to be satisfied to watch the others.

She didn't mind a bit. Nothing could bother Lisa today. She was having such a wonderful time on the trip that even a thunderstorm wouldn't dampen her spirits. She was loving every minute. Take this morning, for instance. Lisa had awakened early. She'd crawled out of her sleeping bag and, curious to watch the horses at play, she'd walked down to the paddock near the campsite.

The sight that had greeted her was beautiful almost beyond her own imagination. In the pasture, hazy with morning mists, were eleven horses and seven deer! The deer had obviously jumped the fences, probably to eat some of the oats the horses might have missed. Lisa had held her breath. She'd been afraid that if she breathed, it would all go away, as if it were a dream.

In a moment it had gone away. From the campsite, Lisa heard a bloodcurdling shriek—unmistakably Veronica diAngelo. The second her voice pierced the silence, the deer fled, soaring over the fences. When Lisa had returned to the campsite, she learned that Veronica had discovered a daddy longlegs spider near her sleeping bag. Lisa knew they were completely harmless and was annoyed with Veronica. She had wanted to share the beautiful sight with The Saddle Club—and Veronica, true to form, had ruined it.

"Lean forward, Joe! Rise in the saddle . . . NOW!" Max called. Lisa turned her attention back to the jumping. At that instant, Dusty flew into the air over the creek. He landed smoothly, took another three strides, and then rose over the log. It was great to watch, and Lisa could really learn while she did it.

"He's got a good jump position," Max confided to her. "Keep a mental picture of it for yourself. For when the time comes, I mean."

"Okay," she assured him. "He was holding Dusty's mane. Is that a good idea?" she asked.

"Can't talk now," Max shushed her. "Here comes Veronica."

Veronica and Cobalt came galloping down the path toward the creek.

"Slow down to a canter!" Max yelled.

But Veronica didn't pull Cobalt back at all. In fact, to Lisa's eye, she seemed to rush her horse even more. Cobalt was going very fast as he neared the creek. Veronica rose in the saddle and nudged him to jump. His sleek body lifted into the air and landed on the far side of the creek. But he was off-balance. Cobalt stumbled. Veronica whacked him with her riding crop. He righted himself and took another two strides before jumping the small log. His next landing was smoother, but only a little bit.

"Veronica, come over here!" Max commanded.

Veronica's face was set with a look that said "you can't tell me anything." But she waited impatiently while Max spoke to her.

"You *are* aware that you cannot gallop a horse up to a jump like that? You *must* slow down before you jump! The horse's body has far too much weight in the front to be able to fling himself over a jump the way you expect Cobalt to be able to do it. If you care for your horse, you will not do that again."

"Yes, Max," she said, without the slightest tinge of regret in her voice. She signaled Cobalt into motion and turned him around to join the advancing riders.

Max shook his head slightly, angrily. Then, when he realized that Stevie was about to jump, he turned all his attention to her.

Lisa watched Stevie as well, but her thoughts were on Veronica. She thought Max must have enjoyed giving Veronica a lecture. After all, she was the daughter of the richest man in town—a banker who held the mortgage on Pine Hollow Stables. Veronica was a total pain, but Lisa and everybody else knew that Max had to put up with her.

"WHERE DID YOU disappear to so early this morning?" Carole asked Lisa later. The three girls were helping Red water the horses and give them lunch before their own picnic.

"It was the deer!" Lisa said, almost breathlessly. This was the first chance there had been all day for The Saddle Club members to talk. Carole and Stevie listened intently as Lisa described the scene in the pasture at dawn.

"I thought I saw some deer along the trail yesterday afternoon. But to see them grazing with the horses! That must have been outstanding!" Stevie said.

"It was," Lisa said. "Want to get up early tomorrow and see if it happens again?"

"You bet!" Carole and Stevie agreed.

"Just hope Miss Perfect diAngelo doesn't scare them away again," Stevie said.

"Oh, I don't think she'll be scaring anything," Lisa said. "Not after the bawling out Max gave her."

"About what?" Stevie asked, wickedly interested.

"About galloping Cobalt down to the jump," Lisa explained. "I think he was just having a good time because he had a good excuse to yell at her. I mean, nothing happened to her or Cobalt."

"You're kidding!" Stevie said.

"No, he really told her off," Lisa said.

"I'm sure he did!" Carole said. "Did she really gallop down that hill to the jump?"

"Uh-huh," Lisa said. "What's the big deal?"

"You're such a good rider that sometimes I forget you don't know much," Stevie said.

"Thanks," Lisa said stiffly.

"I'm sorry—that came out the wrong way," Stevie said, realizing she'd hurt Lisa's feelings. "That's a compliment." Lisa looked at her sideways. "What I meant," Stevie went on, "was that you're really a good rider, even though you're so new at it!"

Lisa nodded. "That's okay," she said.

"Well, you know the old joke about how a camel is supposed to be a horse—designed by a committee?"

Lisa smiled. Stevie was famous for telling "old" jokes. She'd heard that one. It meant that when a lot of people get together to accomplish something one person *should* do alone, the results are often goofed-up.

"See," Stevie continued seriously, "in some ways, a horse *is* a horse designed by a committee." Lisa cocked her head to listen carefully. Stevie and Carole knew so much about horses!

"A horse has two sets of legs: the big, strong ones in the back where most of the power comes from—that's the good part of the design—and then there are the weaker legs in the front. The problem is that almost two thirds of a horse's weight is carried by his front legs. Now, when the back legs push off *really* hard like they do when the horse is galloping—*especially* downhill—then when the horse lands out of a jump, his weaker front legs take one heck of a beating. And sometimes they don't make it. The horse can stumble and fall, he can throw the rider—all kinds of things can happen. Veronica should know better."

"I didn't realize it was that serious," Lisa said.

"It is," Carole told her. "Poor baby."

Carole turned to Cobalt, and gave the big black horse a hug. He nodded, as if to hug her back, and then nickered gently, nuzzling her ear.

"I think they're in love," Stevie told Lisa, joking. But as both girls watched, each knew that it wasn't really a joking matter.

"NOW, WE'RE GOING to canter in jump position," Max announced to the group. "One at a time. Carole, you begin."

One by one, the students rose out of their saddles, putting all their weight on their stirrups. Lisa lifted herself up and leaned forward the way Carole had done. Max had had her practice this position since her second lesson. It was important for learning balance, and balance was important for riding.

Pepper picked up a trot, and when his gait was rhythmic and steady, she touched his belly behind the girth with her left heel. He immediately began shifting into a canter. Twenty yards ahead of her, Stevie was doing the same thing. Almost as soon as she began cantering, Lisa got the feeling that something was wrong. First, Pepper's ears began twitching every which way, then they laid back, almost flat to his head—a very bad sign. He was listening for trouble.

Then Lisa could hear it, too. Another horse was coming up close behind her. Pepper was usually even-tempered, except when there was a horse right at his flank. If Lisa tried to slow him down, the other horse would get closer. If she tried to speed him up, she'd be in worse trouble!

"Pepper," she whispered. "It's okay—just keep going. There, there, boy." The words sounded calming to her, but Pepper wasn't in the mood for them. His ears twitched some more. Although the path was nice and wide, Pepper shifted over to the extreme right side, perhaps trying to cut off the horse behind him. Lisa glanced over her right shoulder to see who was there. Just at that moment, Pepper shifted over to the left side of the trail. If she'd been seated and balanced, it would have been no trouble, but Lisa was too far out of her saddle and her balance had been upset when she looked over her shoulder. Pepper went over to the left, all right, but Lisa stayed on the right side of the path—in the weeds!

As she tumbled off Pepper, she rolled forward, landing harmlessly on her shoulder. As soon as she landed, Pepper drew to a halt across the path. He looked at her, seeming surprised to find her on the ground. That's just the way Lisa felt, too!

Lorraine flew past her on Barq.

"Come here, boy!" Lisa said to Pepper, pulling herself to her feet.

"You okay, Lisa?" Max called along the trail.

"Oh, sure. Pepper and I just had a disagreement about which way he was going to go!"

She waited a second to be sure nothing hurt and then rambled across the trail to the waiting Pepper.

"Silly boy," she said, patting his neck, and lifting the reins back over his head. "Silly me, too, I guess, huh?" She lifted her left leg up to the stirrup.

Just then, Max arrived by her side. "Will you be able to ride now?" he asked. "I mean, are you hurt anywhere?"

Lisa paused for just a second before she mounted Pepper. She looked at Max. There was something in the way he asked the question—was he worried about her? No, that wasn't it. Lisa was almost certain he was trying to control a smile—or maybe a laugh.

"I looked pretty silly, didn't I?" she asked, suddenly getting the full impact of what a funny picture she must have made.

"Well, perhaps a little bit undigni-ni-ni—" And then, there was an unmistakable snort of Max's laughter.

Lisa lifted herself up into the saddle and burst into giggles herself. She didn't hurt anyplace. "I guess both getting back on the horse *and* laughing about it are the best cures," she said when she stopped giggling.

"Only when it's funny," he said. And then Lisa realized how fortunate she was!

"PSST! WAKE UP!" Lisa whispered, shaking the sleeping Carole from her dreams.

"Whassa matter?" Carole said. She could barely see Lisa in the darkness.

"It's almost dawn!" Lisa said excitedly. "Let's see if there are any deer in the paddock with the horses." Carole was completely awake instantly.

Stevie rubbed her eyes drowsily. "Is it really morning?" she asked.

"Not really," Lisa told her. "But it's time to get up anyway. We're having a Saddle Club meeting down by the paddock."

The three girls crept out of their tent, still wearing their warm nightclothes. They didn't want to take the time to get dressed—not just then, anyway.

They tiptoed on bare feet through the campsite, down the gentle slope to the paddock where the horses spent the night. It was still almost completely dark—the velvet sky was studded with stars. The nearly full moon hung near the horizon and looked as if it were almost resting on a mountaintop. In the east were the first streaks of dawn.

"Oh!" Stevie said, settling herself on a rock near the paddock. "It's beautiful!" She scrunched her knees up to her chest for warmth. Carole sat beside her, Lisa on the other side. Stevie took in a deep breath of the fresh, chilly air. "I can't believe I slept through this yesterday," she said, gazing at the mountains to the east.

The girls sat in a contented silence, listening only to the sounds of the night. The horses, asleep on their feet, were quiet. Here and there, a few crickets chirped. From the edge of the nearby creek, they could hear the call of a bullfrog. The silence was broken by the first whinny from the paddock. In seconds all the horses were awake. By the light of the moon and the stars, the girls watched the horses begin to munch on the sweet grass.

"No deer this morning," Lisa said sadly.

"You never know," Carole said. Suddenly, they all heard a rustling in the forest. Then, so close they could almost touch him, a deer emerged from behind the cover of a hemlock tree. Stevie gasped. Startled, the deer fled, but in a moment, he returned. This time he wasn't alone. The two deer skirted the rock where the girls sat, giving it a wide berth. Then, in unison, they jumped the fence of the paddock, joining the horses at the sweet grass.

The girls were motionless and silent. While they watched in awe, three more deer leaped into the field. The deer eyed the horses with some suspicion, but apparently sensed no harm. Each of the animals munched hungrily, as if it were the most natural thing in the world for horses and deer to breakfast together on a mountainside.

"It's *beautiful*!" Carole whispered to her friends. They nodded. Lisa was about to speak, but just then there was another rustle of leaves nearby. The girls turned to watch the newcomer.

But it wasn't just one newcomer. It was a doe and her baby! The fawn was so little! His head only reached to the top of his mother's legs. His own little legs were long and spindly, with knobby knees—just like a foal's. The doe led her baby to the edge of the field and nibbled the grass under the fence. Her baby nursed while she ate.

The next visitor was smaller—and less welcome. It was a skunk, meandering through the woods with his snout to the ground, sniffing as he went.

"Hey!" Carole exclaimed, pointing to the black-and-white intruder. The three girls pulled their legs up onto the rock to keep out of the skunk's way. The skunk barely seemed to notice them, though. He waddled toward the field and, seeing nothing of interest to his stomach, he waddled away, sniffing everything in his path.

"You know, that one's almost cute," Stevie said to her friends.

"*Almost,*" Lisa agreed. "But don't get him angry!"

"Look!" Carole said, pointing to the eastern horizon. The first of the sun's rays were now over the top of the mountain. A breeze stirred the morning air, bringing the sun's warmth. The horses lifted their heads toward the light. The deer, sensing change, stood alert. The doe fled suddenly, followed by her leggy fawn. And then all the other deer followed, abandoning the sweet grass for the safety of the mountain forest, springing over the fence.

"Did it really happen?" Stevie asked when the deer were gone.

"Yes, it really did," Carole assured her. She stood up and walked toward the paddock fence. She whistled. All the horses looked at her. Cobalt broke from the pack, trotting over for his morning greeting. Lisa and Stevie joined her, and a few of the other horses came over, looking for oats.

"Not yet, guys," Carole said. "Not time for breakfast yet. First we have to—Yipes!"

"What is it?" Stevie asked.

"We've got to get back to camp and put some clothes on before Max and the boys see us in our pajamas!"

In a split second, the girls headed back to their tent. They arrived, puffing and breathless, just an instant before they heard Max's voice call out "Morning time! Everybody up! Time for breakfast! No dawdling today!"

Quickly, Lisa, Stevie, and Carole shed their nightclothes and slipped back into their riding clothes.

"That was the best Saddle Club meeting we ever had!" Lisa said excitedly.

"I wish they could all be like that," Stevie agreed.

"So do I," Carole said. "Gee, remember how beautiful it was when the deer—"

"Stevie!" Max barked. "Your turn to get water for us. Lisa! I need some more kindling! Carole! You're on oats today!"

He almost broke the mood, but not quite. "I remember," Stevie assured Carole. "I'll always remember."

"Yeah, forever," Lisa said. And that was how they all felt.

"I CAN'T BELIEVE it's almost over," Carole said wistfully.

The bright sunshine sparkled through the early-summer leaves in the forest. The day, which had begun in the cool darkness, was now bright and hot, and it was almost time to stop for lunch. Max told the riders to dismount and walk their horses for the last half mile or so, to cool them down.

"Yeah, and to warm *us* up!" Stevie said.

They all laughed about that.

Carole sighed. Horses seemed to her to be a gift, a fabulous, wonderful, magical gift. What she wanted to do most in the world was to take care of horses. That was why she'd agreed to do extra chores for Max at the stable. Her father's salary as a Marine Corps colonel could cover riding lessons and anything else she wanted (as long as she didn't develop Veronica-like tastes). But she worked at the stable because that's what she wanted to do, forever. It's what she'd always wanted to do. Except right now, when she was having fun with the idea of running away with Delilah.

"You know, I think I could build a nice little lean-to near that bluff we passed this morning. Two lean-tos, one for me, one for Delilah. We'd live there, ride every day, and have a great view of the Blue Ridge Mountains. What do you think of that?" Carole asked.

"I think it's time to get you back to civilization," Stevie said matter-of-factly.

"I guess," Carole said. "But it's been wonderful, hasn't it?"

"I could have done without the spill I took yesterday afternoon," Lisa confided. "I'm going to have a bruise in a place I don't want to mention!"

"It's not so bad the *second* time you fall off, is it?" Stevie asked her. "I mean, you knew enough to climb right back onto Pepper, right?"

"*Very* carefully!" Lisa said, and they all giggled. "But I guess it's better than the bee sting Adam got on his arm."

"Those things happen on a camp-out," Carole said. "But—"

"Oooooh! Look!" Stevie said, cutting her off. Carole turned to see a spectacular sight. The little creek that had been running gently near the trail, crossing it several times, suddenly joined another little creek from high up on the mountain. Together they tumbled down a dramatic rocky waterfall into a small natural pond.

"It's *beautiful*!" Lisa said.

Carole stared for a moment, awestruck, then carefully walked Delilah down the incline. Of course, Max had known this was here. He had picked this spot for lunch, where the horses could drink and where the riders could swim!

It took only a few minutes to tie the horses to trees and to let them have a bit of water and some hay.

"Okay, girls, go change in the woods on the far side of the pond. The guys will stay on this side. Last one in is a rotten egg!" Max yelled.

The girls met the challenge. Even Veronica couldn't wait to jump into the cool mountain water. Clothes were flung over every branch in the heat of the race for the water. The girls grabbed their bathing suits out of their backpacks and slid into them. Stevie found a path to the pond, and the sweat and grime of two days of riding quickly disappeared as The Saddle Club plunged with the other girls into the crystal-clear pond. Cuts, bumps, bruises, and bug bites were forgotten in the cool water.

"This is *wonderful*," Lisa said. "Maybe even better than riding—" Carole shot her a mock dirty look. "Just joking," she assured Carole. Carole smiled.

When they were completely refreshed, when the splash fights had subsided (the girls swore they'd won), and when hunger overcame the riders, they emerged from the pond to find that their picnic was ready for them.

Exhausted, and totally content, everybody sat down on the soft, mossy ground, and ate.

"Except for that awful spider and the gross bee bite you got, Adam, this has been a fun trip," Veronica said.

Carole looked at her, more than a little surprised. Veronica wasn't one for roughing it. She'd seemed to be having a hard time of it without her family gardeners, cooks, and chauffeurs to ease the way for her.

"Oh, I could just live like this, couldn't you?" Carole asked her, suddenly feeling at one with everybody, even Veronica.

"Live like this?" Veronica asked, in genuine surprise. "Oh, no. I mean, I've had a good time and all, but I don't even want to look at a horse for a week."

"Mean that?" Carole asked. Veronica nodded. "Want me to exercise Cobalt for you this week?"

"If it means that much to you," Veronica said. It irked Carole that Veronica had to turn it into a favor to Carole, but she was eager to take care of Cobalt.

"I'll do it," she said.

Veronica smiled sweetly. Then she stood up and brought out the saddlebags stuffed with candies that her mother had given her in the parking lot.

"I can't drag these home," she explained as she offered them to the riders. "Mother will never forgive me. Eat all you want."

They were wonderful Italian hard candies, sweet and tart all at the same time. And, Carole was certain, as expensive as could be! What a strange girl Veronica was. Just then, Stevie and Lisa caught her eye. The three of them exchanged glances, all as confused by Veronica as ever.

No, Carole told herself. *This day, this trip—they are too wonderful to be ruined by Veronica.* Content once again, she slipped back into the chilly waters of the pond for one last swim; they'd soon be taking their final ride before they had to return to Pine Hollow.

THE WHOLE RIDE back in the van was quiet. Everyone was tired, but Carole knew it was more than that. The trip had been perfect. It was as if all of them wanted to go over every minute of it in their own minds while it was still fresh so they wouldn't forget anything. Then, quiet as the ride had been, everybody began to shriek when they arrived back at Pine Hollow.

The driveway there was filled with cars and station wagons, waiting for the kids. Everybody wanted to tell everything all at once. Mothers, fathers, brothers, and sisters wanted to know all the details, and the riders wanted to share.

Backpacks and bedrolls were unloaded and loaded, switched around, emptied, dumped. Bug bites were displayed.

"You mean you actually camped out in the woods for *two* nights?" Stevie's younger brother, Michael, demanded. He was a scout, and of the opinion that camping was for boys, not girls.

Stevie glared at him. "Yessss," she hissed. But she hugged him anyway. She'd missed him a little. And she'd missed her twin, Alex, and her older brother, Chad. Her mother and father greeted her warmly as well. While she put her things in the back of the station wagon, she was happy to see that the Atwoods were smothering Lisa with welcoming hugs, too.

Carole, she knew, had planned to help Max unload the horses. Her father would come for her later.

Happy, tired, sweaty, dirty, sore, and thrilled, the riders climbed into the waiting cars, ready to go home, but wishing that the camp-out had never ended.

WHEN THE FINAL car door slammed, and the last station wagon pulled out of the drive, Carole, Max, and Red turned to the task of unloading the horses from the trailers.

Carole put Delilah in her stall and then returned for Cobalt. He followed her down the ramp without any difficulty. There was something wonderfully familiar about the clumping of his hooves on the wide wooden boards of the stable's floor. Like the riders, the horses—especially Cobalt—seemed happy to be home. Contentedly, he walked into his stall. But then he turned around right away to look out the window. Carole knew just how he felt.

"Don't worry, boy," she said to him, patting his neck gently. "We'll go back there. One day, you and I will go back to the mountains. We'll climb the hills and canter through the valleys. We'll splash in the ponds and the waterfall. We'll ride together."

And someday they would, she was sure. Until then, at least they could ride in the ring every day this week. It wasn't everything, but it was something.

Carole sighed and then slid the door closed on Cobalt's stall. It was time to go home.

8

"THERE'S SOMETHING I don't understand," Carole told Max Thursday afternoon while she was saddling Cobalt.

"What's that?" he asked, smoothing the saddle pad for her.

"It's that Veronica always complains that Cobalt is difficult." She lifted the saddle and placed it firmly on the horse's back. Then she slid it into place and reached for the girth.

"You do understand," Max said. "You're just being polite."

"Maybe." Carole shrugged, knowing that was Max's way of saying she was a much better rider than Veronica.

"But I'll tell you this," he continued. "I never approved of Mr. diAngelo buying a stallion for Veronica to ride. A gelding or a mare would be much better for a young rider. A stallion like Cobalt has got an awful lot of spirit. It takes a very skilled rider to handle a stallion. Veronica isn't one; you are."

Carole really didn't know what to say to Max. He rarely complimented his students. Most of them—including Carole—were thrilled with an "okay" or a "that's better" from him. And that was all most of them got.

"I shouldn't complain, though," Max confided. "Cobalt is a Thoroughbred with fine bloodlines. It's an honor to have him in my stable."

Horses, Carole knew, were always evaluated by their bloodlines, meaning who their parents were, and *their* parents. It wasn't the least bit unusual to know a hundred years' worth of breeding history for the better horses, like Cobalt. And, since horses tended to pass on predictable characteristics like speed and temperament to their offspring, it could be extremely important to know that those characteristics were part of the family history carried in the bloodlines.

"I know that running fast and jumping high are in his bloodlines," Carole told Max. "But what constantly amazes me is how smart he is. You know what I got him to do yesterday? I got him to bow! Can you believe it?"

"I was watching from my office," Max said. "I was pretty impressed." There was a sly grin on his face.

"Oh, I know it's silly show-off rodeo stuff," she said. "But it was like he *wanted* to do it. After only about four tries, he just did it."

"Well, today why don't you see if you can teach him something more useful?" Max said.

"I thought we'd work on sideways movements and circles today, and then tomorrow, if it's okay with you, we'll just have a fun ride on the trail."

"And on Saturday?" Max asked.

"On Saturday, Veronica will ride him in class. I won't be here this weekend at all. Dad and I are taking a trip together. He has to go to Camp Lejeune for the Corps and I get to go along." Carole adjusted the stirrups to the right length for her lanky legs.

"You have family down there in North Carolina, don't you?"

"Yes, I'm staying at Aunt Elaine's. She's my mother's sister. We aren't coming back until Tuesday. Dad got special permission for me to miss school."

"He didn't ask me if you could miss riding school," Max said.

For a second, Carole was afraid he was serious, but when she looked at his suntanned face and saw the sparkle in his sky-blue eyes, she knew it was a joke.

"Have a good time," Max said. "But don't fall for any of those Nowth Cahalaina howses, yuh heah?!" he teased in a southern accent.

"No way!" Carole told him, laughing. "There's only one horse for me and he's right here!"

Carole led Cobalt out of his stall and over to the entrance to the ring. She slipped her left foot into the stirrup and lifted herself up. As she settled into the saddle, she saw a look of concern cross Max's face. But when she looked again, it was gone. Clucking softly to Cobalt, she brought him out into the ring, remembering to touch the stable's "good-luck horseshoe" nailed on the wall by the mounting block.

That horseshoe was one of Pine Hollow's oldest traditions. Every rider touched it before beginning a ride. As long as anybody could remember, nobody had ever been seriously hurt riding at Pine Hollow. Carole was pretty sure that the *real* reason for that safety record was because Max (and Maxes I and II) had always been very fussy about the quality of riding at Pine Hollow, but it didn't stop her from touching the horseshoe every time she mounted. It also didn't stop her from riding very carefully.

"COME ON, BOY," Carole urged Cobalt. "Over to the left. You can do it."

She knew perfectly well that Cobalt didn't understand the words, but hearing her voice seemed to give him confidence. She was working with him on lateral, or sideways, moves. Usually riders practiced moving a horse forward, and sometimes backward, but for the experienced rider, sideways could be just as important. It was often essential for shows, demonstrating the rider's ability to control the horse and the horse's ability to respond to commands.

Today Carole wanted to teach Cobalt to turn on the forehand—and she wanted to learn it herself.

Holding the reins short enough so that she knew for sure when she was putting pressure on Cobalt's mouth, she moved her right leg back a very little bit and pressed on Cobalt's side. First, he stepped forward. She drew the reins inward to stop his forward movement and held them there. Then, she pressed again with her right leg.

It worked! Cobalt's right rear leg stepped to the left, his left leg following, while his front legs remained stable, shifting only to pivot. Carole did this several more times and, before she knew it, the horse had turned completely around a circle, with his front legs at the center of it.

"Good boy!" she said, patting his neck firmly. "Good boy! I knew you could do it! Let's try it again, okay?"

Cobalt stretched his neck. Carole could have sworn he was nodding to her, but she knew better. After all, how many times had Max told her horses couldn't understand English? A lot of them learned to respond to words like "trot" and "canter" if they heard them during a class and there were other horses doing those paces already. Some days it seemed to Carole that they could tell time, too, the way they started heading for their stalls when an hour-long class was *almost* over. But those things were really the result of training, not an understanding of language or clocks. It was the same as when she got fidgety in her math class after about thirty-eight minutes—or sometimes only three minutes!

Cobalt, however, seemed to understand more. Maybe it was more than Carole's words and tone of voice. Part of it, she was sure, was how well she could feel his movements under her with her legs and with her seat. It was logical that he was as sensitive to her on top of him.

Standing still once again, she tried a turn on the forehand to the right. Cobalt executed it perfectly, as if he'd been doing it all his life.

How on earth, she wondered, could Veronica own this wonderful animal and not want to spend every waking minute with him?

"I know you're going to miss me, boy," she said, leaning forward in her saddle, stroking the horse's glistening black coat. "But I won't be gone long. I'll be back in a couple of days. We'll ride together again soon—just you and me, Cobalt."

Carole nudged Cobalt with her heels and he began a regal walk around the ring. As they passed Max's office window, it suddenly flew open. Max stuck his head out.

"Looks like you and Cobalt had a pretty good session. But how many times do I have to tell you that horses don't understand English?" he said, only half-joking.

"Don't worry, Max," she shot back. "It's not English. I'm teaching him Swahili!"

Max shook his head, then pulled it back in and shut the window firmly. Carole signaled Cobalt to pick up the pace. Soon they were cantering around the ring, smooth as glass, fast as the wind.

CAROLE'S FOUR-DAY visit with Aunt Elaine was every bit as nice as she'd thought it was going to be. While Colonel Hanson worked, Carole and her aunt chatted, gossiped, and giggled together while taking care of Elaine's three young boys. She and Aunt Elaine even spent one morning horseback riding along the beach. It was fun, but it wasn't the same as riding Cobalt. It felt wonderfully wicked to be excused from school for two days without even being sick, but when it came time to go home, Carole was ready. Saying good-bye to her aunt's family was hard, though. It seemed as if she couldn't give or get enough hugs until she thought about how much she wanted to see Cobalt again.

"So you enjoyed it, did you?" her father asked as they drove back home from the airport.

"I had a great time with Aunt Elaine," Carole said. "She's just fun to be with. So are her kids."

"I know you miss your mother," Colonel Hanson began. "I miss her, too. I try to fill in, but there are some things . . ."

The time since her mother's death the previous fall had been hard on both of them. Carole knew that her father had worried a lot about trying to be both mother and father to her, but as far as she was concerned, he was her father and that was great.

"Don't worry about that, Daddy. I had fun with Aunt Elaine, even though sometimes she reminded me of Mom. She does look like her, doesn't she? But as far as parents go, you're enough for me—at least until you meet some wonderful woman and decide to get married again," she added with a sly grin.

"Now, don't *you* start in," her father said.

"Oh, Aunt Elaine gave you a hard time, huh? She told me she thought you should get married again. Is that why she kept having all her 'friends' at the house when you were there?"

"I think so. And I had thought I'd get some relief from that when we got away from home."

Carole had to laugh. Almost every one of their friends seemed to know a single woman who would be "just perfect" for Carole's father. "You know what Marjorie Jennings—you know, the major's daughter—told me? She said that the ladies in the bridge league at the Officers' Club at Quantico call you 'Colonel Handsome.' Of course, they're right. You're the handsomest man I know. And you look so *dashing* in your uniform—especially the dress blues with the red stripe!" she teased her father.

He laughed. "And don't you think for a minute that Mrs. Jennings hasn't invited her unmarried sister down for a visit. Every time I see the woman, she tells me how wonderful her sister is and what a *marvelous* mother she'd make. See, Carole, it isn't just *me* they're after. The woman wants to be a mother to *you*. Are you ready for that?"

"Not from any sister of Mrs. Jennings's!" Carole said, laughing. "But Dad, seriously, wouldn't you like to get married again?"

"Well, hon, I'll tell you. I loved your mom. She was one in a million—no, make that two million. There just isn't anybody to replace her."

Carole was quiet for a moment. Her father was often very lonely without her mother. She knew that one day he would probably find another woman to share his life with. Until he was ready, or until the right woman came along, nothing she could say would make it happen.

"Especially Mrs. Jennings's sister," Carole said.

"And *especially* if she looks like Mrs. Jennings!"

"A fine thing for you to say, Colonel Handsome!" Carole chided him. They laughed together. Carole felt then, as she had felt many times since her mother's death, that losing her mother was the most awful thing that could have happened to her. But she still had her father, and a pretty terrific one at that. One in two million.

A HALF HOUR later, Carole's suitcase was unpacked and she was beginning to feel as if she were actually back home again. That made it time to call Stevie and Lisa. Maybe they could all get together at the Tastee Delight ice cream parlor—TD's, as the girls called their favorite meeting place. But just as she reached for the phone, it rang.

"Hello?"

"Oh, Carole, you're back!" Stevie said.

"Right on time," Carole said cheerfully. "I was just about to call you. I had a wonderful time in North Carolina. I can't wait to tell you and Lisa all about it. Saddle Club meeting tomorrow right after school? We can meet at TD's for ice cream—"

"Carole, stop!" Stevie said. "You've got to get over here."

"You missed me that badly, huh?" Carole teased. But when there was a silence, Carole began to get the awful feeling that something was wrong. Really wrong. "Where are you? What's the matter?"

"I'm at Pine Hollow. It's Cobalt—I mean, just get over here, will you?"

"*What?*" she said, but Stevie had already hung up the phone.

In a matter of minutes, Carole and her father were back in their car, this time headed for Pine Hollow. Carole was so worried she couldn't speak. Her father just squeezed her hand and said, "It's going to be all right, hon. You'll see."

As they neared the stable, Carole could hear the terrible whine of a siren. An ambulance pulled out of the driveway and turned toward the hospital, lights flashing, siren wailing. The diAngelos' Mercedes was parked carelessly in the lot, its doors left open.

But the only things Carole really saw were the veterinarian's pickup truck and the county vet's wagon. That was when Carole knew the worst. Two veterinarians always had to sign a certificate before a horse could be destroyed.

"*Cobalt!*" she screamed, jumping from the car almost before it stopped.

Lisa and Stevie came running out of the stable. Lisa reached Carole first and put her arm around her. Stevie had tears streaming down her face.

"It's too late, Carole," she said. "He was too badly hurt! They had to do it. He would never heal. It was the long bone in his foreleg—it was shattered. He just lay there. And then it was over."

"And then the ambulance came for Veronica," Lisa continued. "She's going to be okay. I guess she broke her arm. She was lucky. Luckier than Cobalt." Lisa gasped at her own words, trying to hold back tears.

Carole stared blankly at the stable, wanting to go in, wanting to go away. She remembered feeling like that once before. She stood still, unable to move, until her father came up to her and put his strong arms around her shoulders.

"Come on home, hon," he said. "There's nothing we can do here."

"*Cobalt!*" she sobbed.

Slowly, she turned, letting her father take her home.

"WE'VE GOT TO help Carole," Lisa said. "She was like a zombie at school today." She and Stevie were walking toward Carole's house the day after the accident that had cost Cobalt his life.

"I think Carole's going to have to get over this herself," Stevie warned Lisa. She wanted to comfort Carole, but she knew that sympathy and comfort could only go so far.

"Carole showed me how important it was to get back on the horse when I fell off. This is different, I know, but in some ways it's the same. We can't let her feel too sorry for herself."

"I don't think she's feeling sorry for herself. If I know Carole, she's feeling sorry for Cobalt."

"Well, just wait until we tell her what happened when we saw Veronica at the hospital, then," Lisa said.

"That may just make her feel sorrier for Cobalt," Stevie said, shaking her head. She just couldn't understand the whole diAngelo family.

Carole was in her room when her friends arrived. She'd gone to school that morning, but she didn't think she'd heard anyone or learned a single thing. As soon as she got home, she retreated to her bedroom. She was lying on her bed, staring at the ceiling, when Stevie and Lisa knocked.

"Your dad said it was okay for us to come up," Stevie said, poking her head in the room.

Carole sighed deeply. She knew her friends had come to make her feel better. She also knew that they felt badly about Cobalt's accident and maybe they needed somebody to make them feel better, too. She only wished she could have made Cobalt better. But, of course, she couldn't.

"Sure, come on in," Carole told the girls. They came in and sat on her bed with her. Stevie handed her a soda. Carole took a sip and nodded thanks. "I guess you'd better tell me exactly what happened. I really didn't want to know yesterday, but I think I'm ready now."

"It was Veronica's fault," Lisa began, confirming Carole's suspicions. "It was just exactly what Max had been telling her not to do on the camp-out. We were all there—it was a jumping class on the cross-country course. I was watching with Max. Stevie had just gone over the jump on Comanche. Veronica came barreling down the hill at a gallop and expected Cobalt to jump a high fence, landing on a downhill slope."

"He had such a big heart, you know, Carole. He just always wanted to please his rider—even when he knew it was wrong. He didn't slow down one bit. He just jumped," Stevie said.

"It was beautiful in a way," Lisa continued. "There's no horse in that stable that jumps as smoothly as Cobalt—jumped, I mean—but he didn't land right."

"I saw it then, too," Stevie said. "It was like he was flying, until his front legs landed. There was just too much of him, coming too fast. His forelegs hit the ground straight and then the right one buckled, but not at the knee. He began to stumble."

"Veronica flew off over his head. She landed five feet in front of him. She broke her arm when she landed. Cobalt broke his leg. Everybody could see it was broken. . . ."

Stevie and Lisa went on, describing the horrible scene that Carole had been reliving in her mind for the past twenty-four hours: Veronica screaming her head off; Cobalt lying quietly, bearing his pain in silence.

Sometimes when horses broke bones, they could be set, like people's bones, and they could heal and be as good as new. With the horse's cannon bone, though, it was almost impossible to keep the horse's weight off the break long enough for it to heal. A million-dollar racehorse might be suspended in a body sling long enough for the bone to knit, but even then, with a broken cannon bone, he'd probably never race again. Although Cobalt was a fine horse with good bloodlines, he was no million-dollar horse, and that kind of treatment was too expensive and not reliable enough. And, even if the bone could have healed, he'd never have been as good as new, and he'd have been in pain all his life.

"If only they could have tried something to save him," Lisa said.

"No," Carole told her. "They did the right thing. Cobalt's life was over. He was born to run with the wind, not limp."

Stevie got the feeling it was time to change the subject a little. "Say, we just saw Veronica. We visited her at St. Claire's. She's got a private room and there are nurses running all over the place."

"Was she hurt that badly? I thought it was just a broken arm."

"It was, but you know her parents," Lisa said. Carole nodded. They all knew her parents. They were the richest people in town and liked to show it off. "You'd think she'd had open-heart surgery from all the attention she was demanding—and the flowers!"

"It looked like a funeral!" Stevie said.

"It was," Carole told her friends. Stevie and Lisa exchanged looks.

"Well, Veronica was all full of talk about how Max wasn't a very good teacher and this would never have happened if it hadn't been for him."

"That's outrageous!" Carole said. "We all heard Max tell her a hundred times she was jumping the wrong way. How can she—"

"That's not even really the worst of it," Stevie said, full of indignation. "Her father was prancing around the room telling her not to worry—that they were going to get plenty of insurance money for Cobalt and she'd have another horse as soon as her arm healed. Can you believe trying to replace Cobalt?"

Carole shook her head. "That sounds like the diAngelos," she said. "They think they can solve every problem with money."

"Oh, he'll have a new horse for Veronica soon, that's for sure," Lisa said.

"Well, he won't be able to make her ride it," Carole said.

"She'll ride it for sure," Stevie said. "The trick will be to make her ride it *right.*"

"What makes you think she'll ever get on a horse again?" Carole asked.

Stevie almost laughed. "Of course she will! She said she would and we both believed her. She may not be horse crazy the way we are, but she likes riding and she knows accidents happen. She knows you have to get back on—the same way you do."

"Not me," Carole said.

Stevie was startled. Had she heard Carole right? "What?" she asked.

"I said not me. I'm done riding. For good."

Lisa and Stevie both stared at her. Was it possible? Carole was the best. Her life was riding. She was the one who was going to own a stable, was going to teach, was going to train and breed horses. Horses were everything to her. It couldn't be true, Stevie was sure.

"Oh, that's the way you feel now, I know, but you won't feel that way always. You'll start riding again. You love it too much."

"I don't expect you two to understand," Carole said. "But Cobalt was more than just a horse to me. There could never be another horse like that. With him gone, there's no point in riding. Anyway, this is kind of hard to explain, but when I was outside the stable yesterday, knowing that he was gone and he wasn't coming back, it reminded me of the day my mother died. I don't ever want to feel that way again. So I'm quitting."

"Carole!" Lisa said, her voice filled with worry.

"Lisa, I think we should get to the bus stop now," Stevie said, cutting her off.

Lisa was about to remind Stevie that her mother was picking them up at Carole's in an hour when she saw the look on Stevie's face and clammed up.

"We do?"

"Yeah, sure," she agreed. "Will you be okay, Carole? I'll see you in school tomorrow."

Carole nodded.

Lisa and Stevie backed out of her room and quickly went downstairs. Colonel Hanson was in the kitchen making dinner.

"It's bad, isn't it?" he asked the girls.

"Yeah," Stevie said. "She says she doesn't want to ride again."

"Well, if she wants to give it up, that's her choice," the colonel said.

"But it's not a choice!" Lisa protested. "It's some kind of phony escape. Horses are too important to her."

"Well, certainly *one* horse was," Stevie said.

"We'll just have to see what happens," Carole's father said. Stevie and Lisa reluctantly agreed with that.

"I DON'T UNDERSTAND Carole," Lisa said as she and Stevie waited around the corner from Carole's house for Mrs. Atwood to pick them up.

"I'm not sure I do, either. But it looks like a bad case of horse shyness, like after an accident. This time, she can't just climb back up on the horse—because the horse isn't there. I have the feeling that nothing we say or do will help. She'll have to come around on her own. Look, are we horse crazy, or what?" Stevie asked.

"We're horse crazy," Lisa agreed.

"So, our only choice is to keep riding and try to help Carole come around. After all, she's horse crazy, too, but right now, she's more crazy than she is horse. You'll be at class on Saturday, won't you?"

"Of course," Lisa told her.

"So, we'll ride and then, afterward, we have some work to do."

"We do?"

"Yeah, remember how we planned to do research on Max the First?"

"Oh, yeah, we want to find out if he really was in the Russian Revolution."

"I think we know he wasn't there, but the question is: Where was he? You said we should start in the library."

"Right! We can look at the back issues of *The Willow Creek Gazette.* That'll be fun." Lisa knew that Stevie was right. At least the two of them would continue riding and having fun together. But she wondered how long The Saddle Club would survive with just two members.

"YOU'RE REALLY LEARNING fast, Lisa!" Stevie complimented her after class on Saturday. "Your seat is much firmer, your contact is better. I mean, you're riding!"

"It seems like months ago that I didn't know anything about horses—except for which was the front end and which wasn't. But, actually, it's only weeks, right?"

"If you keep on learning at the rate you're going now, it'll seem like years when it's only weeks. And then, when school's out and summer starts, we'll be able to ride almost every day. You'll be a champion by August."

"You mean I'll be as good as you?" Lisa teased.

Stevie, who was very proud of her own hard-earned riding skills, glanced sideways at Lisa. When she saw the sly grin on the older girl's face, she knew Lisa was joking.

"Oh, that'll happen about the same day Max sprouts wings!"

"I noticed some feathers on his back today," Lisa joked.

Together, the two girls walked back into town. Each had come to riding class armed with notebook, pencil, and library card.

The sun was shining brightly off the sidewalk. It was a hot Saturday, promising an even hotter summer to come. It was a day to sit by a pool—or better yet, *in* a pool—not one to be at the library. But the unspoken agreement between Lisa and Stevie was that as long as they worked hard together on a Saddle Club project (like finding out who the *real* Max the First was), then they might not have to think so much about the death of Cobalt or how much they missed Carole at class.

"Excuse me," Lisa said politely to the woman at the information desk. "We want to do some research on history—"

"Section nine hundred, the shelves to your left," the woman said briskly.

"Specifically, American—"

"Section nine hundred seventy, the first eight shelves." The librarian rattled off the information without looking up.

"Well, really, Virginia—" Lisa continued.

"Section nine hundred seventy-three, shelves five and six."

"Actually, Willow Creek, early this century."

"Section—Willow Creek?" For the first time, the librarian looked at Lisa and Stevie. "I don't think anybody's ever actually written a book about Willow Creek."

Suddenly, the woman was interested. She took Stevie and Lisa to the card file, but it was clear that there wasn't a book.

"How about old newspapers?" Lisa asked. Stevie was very glad she had Lisa the A-student on this trip.

"Ah, yes!" the librarian exclaimed. "At the insistence of the editor of *The Willow Creek Gazette*, we have five complete sets of every newspaper ever issued in this town. Be my guest, but be careful. Some of this stuff is very old and the paper is delicate."

She led Stevie and Lisa into a small room off the main reading room. She turned on the light and showed them the big old books containing over a hundred years of news.

"If you consider Mrs. Rappaport's garden party news," Stevie said a few minutes later, glancing through a musty old volume.

Lisa took one of the volumes off the shelf. "The trouble is that not only do we not know what we're looking for, we don't even know *when* we're looking for. I'll start in 1920. You work through Mrs. Rappaport's social season of 1905. It's probably somewhere between the two. We'll work toward each other."

Stevie nodded, pulling her notebook over to where she could reach it in case something interesting showed up. Two hours later, she knew an awful lot about the sewer system the town had installed and a great deal about the Rappaports' guest lists, but she didn't know anything at all about Maxmillian Regnery the First.

"I keep seeing the same advertisement for riding lessons," Lisa said. "The ad just refers to The Stable at Pine Hollow, but I guess that's the same one. There's no address and no name. The one thing I can say is that riding lessons were a lot cheaper then than they are now!"

Stevie peered over her shoulder at the ad. It showed an old-fashioned picture of a lady—"Probably Mrs. Rappaport," Stevie said—riding sidesaddle on a fine horse. It was fun to see, but it really didn't help them at all.

"There aren't any stable ads in the 1905 papers. It took me a while to figure out that in 1905, almost everybody owned horses since that was the way most people got around. They had their own stables, same as we have our own garages. There are ads for blacksmiths, but that's as close as we get here."

"I'm still sure this is the thing to do if we want to find out about Max," Lisa said.

"Oh, I agree," Stevie told her. "But I don't think we've hit it yet. And that's all the musty old newspapers I want to read today."

"Me too," Lisa said, slipping the big volume back onto the shelf. Together, they finished tidying up, turned out the light in the little room, and left the library, thanking the surprised librarian on their way out.

"We'll be back!" Lisa promised.

"You're welcome anytime!" the woman said cheerfully. Lisa had the distinct impression that the librarian would call the editor of the *Gazette* to tell him that somebody was actually reading the back issues. It would make his day. But so far, it hadn't done anything for theirs.

"You know, that's not the only source we have," Lisa said after a moment.

"Sure, we can check with the crystal ball lady at the fair when she comes to town in August," Stevie said.

"Crystal balls are supposed to tell the future, not the past," Lisa said, giggling. "No, what I mean is that, for one thing, we could try official records at town hall and—" she paused, "*and* we can try pumping Mrs. Reg. After all, the man was her father-in-law. She might have some juicy tidbits for us."

"Hey, great idea," Stevie said. "I never thought of that. Why don't we get to the stable early on Tuesday before class and see if she'll give us some hints?"

"It's a date," Lisa agreed.

"WHAT ARE YOU two doing here?" Mrs. Reg asked when Stevie and Lisa walked into the tack room Tuesday afternoon.

Lisa felt trapped and was glad when Stevie answered the question. "Oh, we just thought we'd do some saddle-soaping before class," she said airily.

Mrs. Reg looked at her suspiciously. Lisa knew they were on thin ice. Although they'd both worked hard at the stable (all of Max's students worked hard at the stable; Max insisted that taking care of horses was an important part of riding them), it was Carole who usually wanted to clean the tack. Lisa was sure Mrs. Reg would see right through them.

The woman stood up and went to the shelf where the cleaning gear was kept. "Here you go, girls," she said, handing each of them a tin of saddle soap, sponges, and cloths. "The bridles over on that wall need cleaning today." Her voice softened. "I'm glad to see you here. I miss Carole. She's the best soaper we ever had."

"She's the best at a lot of stuff," Lisa said.

"Yeah, we miss her, too. That's why we wanted to help you today," Stevie agreed.

The girls took their gear and headed for the bridles. There sure were a lot of them. It looked like an endless job—almost as endless as Mrs. Rappaport's garden parties!

"Say, Mrs. Reg," Stevie began casually while she worked the dirt out of a throatlatch.

"Hmm?" Mrs. Reg responded.

"How about that guy, Maxmillian the First, was he something?"

"Who?" asked Mrs. Reg.

"You know, Max's grandfather—the founder of this place? He was your father-in-law, right?"

"Oh, sure," Mrs. Reg said.

Lisa could see that Stevie was trying to lay a trap for Mrs. Reg. She wanted to get her talking about the old man without her really noticing it. Lisa held her breath, hoping.

"I mean, like when he opened the stable—" Stevie paused. Lisa hoped Mrs. Reg would pick up the idea and start talking.

"Hmmm," was all the older woman said.

"It was a long time ago, right?" Stevie prompted.

"Uh, yes," Mrs. Reg told them. She was shuffling through papers on her desk. "I suppose it seems that way, if you're twelve years old."

That was a rebuff if Lisa had ever heard one!

"But were you around then?" Stevie asked.

"I'm not sure," Mrs. Reg said.

This conversation was definitely not going the way the girls wanted it to go.

"Well, what was he like?" Stevie asked. Lisa could tell she'd decided to be more direct. Being indirect was getting them exactly nowhere.

"Who?" Mrs. Reg asked. Being direct was getting them nowhere, too.

"Your father-in-law," Stevie persisted.

"Oh, he was a fine rider," Mrs. Reg told the girls.

"Where did he learn to ride?" Stevie asked.

"Everybody rode in those days," Mrs. Reg said.

And that was all they could get out of her. When Lisa and Stevie looked up from their bridles, they could see that Mrs. Reg's eyes were sparkling with mischief. They realized that they were not the first Pine Hollow students to try to pump her about the stable's founder—nor were they the only ones who weren't going to get anything from her.

"It's a conspiracy!" Stevie hissed to Lisa. "They won't tell us *any*thing. The old man was probably a bank robber—or a horse thief! We'll get to the bottom of this!"

Lisa was becoming as convinced as Stevie that the mystery was a cover-up, and she was as determined as Stevie to uncover it. The problem was that right then their curiosity had only earned them the right to clean bridles. They were stuck.

"Have you girls talked to Carole?" Mrs. Reg asked, breaking the silence.

"Yeah, we went to visit her on Saturday. She's going to quit riding, you know?" Lisa said.

"So my son told me," Mrs. Reg said. "She really loved that horse, didn't she?"

Stevie nodded. "He was a beauty," she said, thinking of how magnificent Cobalt had been. She could see him soaring over jumps with Carole in the saddle. She felt a lump in her throat. She set her jaw firmly. She didn't want to cry. She began rubbing the bridle harder to keep her mind off Cobalt.

"There'll never be another horse like that for Carole," Lisa told Mrs. Reg. "And if she can't have a horse like that, she doesn't want any horse at all. I think I can understand that." Lisa thought she *could* understand the perfect relationship Carole and Cobalt had enjoyed. She hated to think about it, but she knew it must really hurt to lose someone you loved so much.

"Nonsense!" Mrs. Reg said firmly, startling both of the girls.

"She's serious!" Stevie said, defending her friend.

"Sure she is, but she's also wrong," Mrs. Reg told them. "And she'll realize it one of these days."

"Oh, no!" Lisa said. "She's made up her mind."

"You know, if I could tell you how many fine riders decide at one time or another that they're never going to ride again—well, it would be a long list. But I'll say this: Carole has got horses in her blood. She'll be back. I don't know when, but she'll be back. Count on it."

"You really think so?" Stevie asked.

"Of course I do," Mrs. Reg said. "But I hate to see her waste so much time right now. Say, I've got an idea—"

And when she told them, Stevie and Lisa had to agree with her that it might just work. At least, they'd give it a try.

"HI, CAROLE, IT'S me," Stevie said into the phone on Wednesday night. "How've you been?" Stevie and Carole went to different schools. Usually they saw each other at riding class. Now that Carole wasn't going to classes, they weren't seeing each other at all.

"I'm okay," Carole said dully. Stevie thought she sounded anything but okay.

"We missed you at class this week," Stevie told her. "They were good classes, too. Max had us all working on paces and strides. Lisa's doing really well. I think she may be able to talk him into letting her start jumping classes in the fall. He said he'd never seen such a natural rider—since you, I mean."

"Lisa can have the honors now," Carole said.

Stevie was disappointed. She'd wanted to goad Carole into returning to Pine Hollow, but it obviously wasn't going to work. She decided to try Mrs. Reg's suggestion.

"Mrs. Reg said she was going to call you."

"I hope she doesn't want to try to convince me to come back," Carole said.

"Oh, no. She said she understands that. But she told me you'd promised to help her in the tack room. It was something about the trip—" Stevie paused, hoping Carole herself would remember.

"All those extra bits and stirrup leathers!" Carole said. "We just bunched them up and put them in bags when we left on the MTO. I promised her I'd sort them out and put them away when we got back—but can't she do that herself?"

Stevie knew she had to be very careful now. Of course Mrs. Reg could do it herself, but Carole wasn't to know that. "I'm sure she can. Don't worry about it. She'll do it when the pain goes away."

"Pain?" Carole asked. Her voice was filled with concern.

"She said her arthritis was hurting her. All this humidity, you know? She'll get better when it cools down." *Perfect,* Stevie told herself. *You're doing it perfectly.* After all, it wouldn't cool down for months!

"Oh," Carole said. Stevie was quiet for a moment. She just wanted her little bit of information to sink in. What Mrs. Reg knew about Carole was that, above all, she was a kind person. When Carole made a promise, she kept it. When somebody needed her help, she got it.

And when Carole needed help, her friends gave it to her—even if she didn't think she wanted it!

CAROLE FELT VERY awkward when she arrived at Pine Hollow on Saturday. For one thing, she was wearing overalls and a loose shirt and sneakers. She usually wore riding clothes. But she'd always been there before to ride. This time she was only coming to sort out tack. She didn't need to wear riding breeches and boots to sort out tack. In fact, she didn't need to wear breeches and boots ever again. She wasn't going to ride anymore.

She'd waited until the last of her classmates had left after Saturday's lesson. Max was busy with the adults who took a jumping class after the girls' class. Mrs. Reg was, as usual, in her office off the tack room. Carole would go to her—in a few minutes.

She let herself in the side door of the stable. It had been almost two weeks since Cobalt's death—but Carole felt as though she'd been away for months. As soon as she stepped inside, memories came flooding back to her. The smell of hay and horses was sharp and welcoming—but not to her, she told herself. She breathed deeply and waited for her eyes to adjust to the muted light.

Patch stuck his head out over the top of his stall door. Carole automatically reached for his soft nose, rubbing it gently. He nuzzled her neck, but she hadn't brought any tidbits for him. She patted him once again. Next door, Pepper's head popped out of his stall.

It was just like Pepper to want to get in on the patting, Carole laughed to herself. She scratched his forehead and patted his big strong neck.

Pepper was a big horse, almost as big as Cobalt, but he didn't have Cobalt's brilliant, shiny black coat and he didn't have the smooth trot and the wonderful rolling canter that Cobalt had had. He didn't have—Carole stopped these thoughts. They wouldn't bring Cobalt back. Nothing would bring him back. Cobalt's stall was the one just beyond Pepper's. Carole didn't want to see it. Quickly, Carole turned and retreated to the tack room.

"Hi, Mrs. Reg," she said. "I just remembered I promised you I'd straighten out the stuff we took on the MTO. Here I am."

"Oh, hi, Carole. That bag's in the corner. I haven't even opened it. Thanks for coming by."

Carole got the sack and dumped out its contents. She had to laugh at what she saw. Every time somebody had asked her about extra stirrup leathers, she'd put two in the bag. There were dozens there! And they hadn't needed any of them. She began sorting them out, as well as the stirrups, bits, and other miscellaneous items that had been stuffed in—none of which they'd needed. She knew, though, that if she hadn't brought them, stirrup leathers would have been snapping left and right.

"Be careful where you toss it over there," Mrs. Reg said after a moment.

"Why's that?" Carole asked.

"Eclipse just had a litter of kittens last week and they're bedded down in the box in the corner," Mrs. Reg explained.

"Can I look?" Carole asked.

"Sure, just be careful. They're starting to scramble and trying to get out of the box. Every time we have a litter I'm so afraid that the little ones will get hurt, you know?"

"I'll be careful," Carole promised. Quietly, cautiously, she peeked into the box. There, sleeping contentedly, were six little furry kittens. They were so tangled up with one another as they slept that it was impossible to tell where one began and the other one ended. Eclipse, their mother, was awake, watching them proudly. "Oh, Mrs. Reg, they're the cutest ever! Aren't they wonderful?"

"As long as they're good mousers, they're wonderful," Mrs. Reg said, always practical.

Pine Hollow, like all stables, had occasional problems with mice who liked oats almost as much as the horses did. For centuries, horse people had known that the best exterminator in a barn was a hungry cat. Pine Hollow usually had four or five cats, and every once in a while, that meant four or five kittens as well. This time, there were six! "What have you named them?" Carole asked.

At Pine Hollow, the tradition was to name the cats after the most distinguished horses in history. Eclipse, for example, was named after a famous Thoroughbred racehorse from the eighteenth century. The main drawback of this system of naming cats was that the most famous horses were stallions. With a name like Copperbottom, who was a famous Quarter Horse, it didn't matter. But the last litter of kittens had been born to Sir Archie!

"Oh, I haven't decided," Mrs. Reg said. "I think it's about time to use some of the Standardbreds. How about Messenger, Hambletonian, Dutchman, Yankee, Dan Patch?"

"Yes," Carole agreed. "Those are good names. The little black-and-white one has to be Dan Patch—or are those really two kittens all tangled up?" Carole was trying to figure that out when the question was answered for her. Half of the "black-and-white one" woke up. He was completely black and his eyes were barely open. He was so small, he could have sat on the palm of her hand. The kitten stretched and began walking across his brothers and sisters, heading for the side of the box. He stood on his hind feet, his forelegs straddling the rim. He tried to push himself up and over, struggling mightily. He scratched at the side of the box with his hind legs, trying to get a grasp on it to push himself up—and out.

"This black one's trying to get out," Carole said, gently lowering him back toward his sleeping littermates.

"That one's been trying to get out practically since the day he was born. He's smarter than the rest, tougher, stronger. He always feeds first, and he was the first to walk. That one's a handful of trouble, but he's a winner. You want to name him?" Mrs. Reg asked.

Carole watched the kitten a moment. His blue, blue eyes gleamed with curiosity about the world. Then the sun caught his black coat and it shone brightly, almost a blue-black. Carole had seen a coat like that before. She'd known an animal with a heart like that before. She knew what name that little kitten had earned. But she couldn't say it.

"Maybe," she told Mrs. Reg. "I'll think about it."

Carole turned to the mixed-up pile of leathers and bits she had to sort.

"You know, I was thinking the other day about a horse I once rode," Mrs. Reg said.

Mrs. Reg had ridden horses all her life until her arthritis made it impossible. She'd known horses and horse people. She had wonderful stories to tell and Carole always enjoyed listening to them. It made her work with the tack pass quickly. Carole tugged at the long leather straps, trying to untangle them, and listened with pleasure.

"She was a fine horse, that one. Her name was Lady Day. She was a Saddlebred with wonderful showy gaits, lifting her legs up high with every step, moving smooth as glass. She belonged to the real estate man in town. He used to love to take people to see property in a buggy, pulled by Lady Day. He sold a lot of houses that way, I'll tell you. But when he didn't have customers, she just stayed with us. Max would let her out in the paddock for exercise, but that wasn't enough for her. That one liked to perform. She needed an audience, riding her or watching her.

"So, I took to riding her—with Mr. Marsh's permission, of course. She was as much fun to ride as any horse I've known. She would prance across the fields, pretty and proud as could be. I always sat tall on her back, feeling as proud as she did. And, as you can imagine, when spring rolled around and Mr. Marsh's business got busier and he was using her every day, well, I missed her a lot. She was a winter horse for me, see, because he wouldn't take his customers out in the cold. We were sort of foul-weather friends."

Mrs. Reg stopped talking and Carole waited for her to go on. When she didn't, Carole urged her. "What happened to her?"

"Oh, Mr. Marsh sold her one day—said she'd stumbled pulling his buggy and he couldn't have an animal that wasn't surefooted taking his customers around."

"Was that true?"

"No, I don't think so. I think his business wasn't going so well then and he needed the money."

"But didn't you feel awful when Lady Day was gone?" Carole asked.

"Me? No, not really. But what a horse she was!"

"I never heard you talk about her before. Was she your favorite horse ever?" Carole asked.

"Favorite?" Mrs. Reg said, as if she were considering what the word meant. "I don't think so, though she made me want to own a Saddlebred myself. I nagged Max until he bought one. That one was named Jefferson. Sweetest horse, I'll tell you. Now, he used to wait for me every morning. Old Max would tell you I was crazy, but I swear that horse smiled when he saw me. When I curried him, he never budged. He even stood still for the blacksmith. You gave him a signal to do something, he did it right away. I don't think I ever touched the creature with a riding crop."

"Oh, he must have been a *dream* to ride," Carole said breathlessly.

"Not really," Mrs. Reg told her. "He spent so much time being nice that he had almost no spirit of his own. But that was nothing like old Foxfire."

"Who was Foxfire?" Carole asked.

"Foxfire was a mare we had. She was a fine horse, good to ride, gentle with the youngsters, nice jumper, too. And then we bred her. We wanted to see if we could have that nice temperament carry over another generation."

"Did it?"

"Hard to tell," Mrs. Reg said. "See, as soon as her foal was born—it was a pretty bay colt with a white star on his forehead—Foxfire completely changed personalities. She became so protective of her colt that she wouldn't let anybody near him, or her, for that matter."

"What did you do?" Carole asked.

"We sold them. We sold them both together. Some man from downstate said he was sure he could retrain the mare. Took them away in a van one day and we never heard another word from him."

Carole laughed to herself. Mrs. Reg's stories were never what she expected. People who told horse stories usually told about the unlikely undersized weakling foal who grew up to take blue ribbons at the National Horse Show. Real life, Carole knew, wasn't like that. Mrs. Reg was good at telling real-life stories about horses and riders. Her horses always had good points and bad ones the way most real-life horses did—except Cobalt. And their owners were real people, too, with good and bad mixed together.

"Come on, Mrs. Reg," Carole urged her. "Tell me. You must have had a favorite horse over all the others, didn't you?"

"Oh, let's see, now," Mrs. Reg mused. "Of course, I loved to ride Lady Day, but then I could watch a beauty like Jesse's Pride forever. What a lovely horse he was. And then, there was the jumper; Roo was what we called him, short for Kangaroo. There was a whole bunch of grays, one after the other, that Max kept for this funny old woman in town. Said she wanted horses with whiter hair than her own. And then—"

"You mean there never was a favorite?" Carole asked as she hung the final stirrup leather on the rack and tossed the bits into the bit tray.

Mrs. Reg shook her head. "Nope, never was," she said, and Carole knew she was telling the truth. Mrs. Reg loved all her horses, in one way or another.

Just then, the little black kitten succeeded in getting over the top edge of the box.

"You better catch that one!" Mrs. Reg said.

The kitten began stumbling across the tack room floor in search of adventure. He found a piece of straw and started batting it fiercely.

Carole and Mrs. Reg laughed, watching the little creature fight the straw so valiantly.

"He's something," Carole said.

"He sure is," Mrs. Reg agreed. "Let me know when you decide on a name for him, okay?"

Carole had completed putting away the sack of extra leathers, bits, and stirrups. She was done now, finished with Pine Hollow. She didn't really want to remind Mrs. Reg that she wasn't coming back.

"Okay," she said. "'Bye." Mrs. Reg told her goodnight and Carole left slowly, saying good-bye to Pine Hollow, for the night, for the week, for—ever?

"YOU KNOW, I really miss Carole," Stevie told Lisa a week later.

"Me, too," Lisa agreed. "Even seeing her at school isn't the same thing as riding with her. She waves to me in the hall and sometimes we sit together at lunch. But she won't talk about horses! Can you imagine? We spent the entire lunch period on Tuesday talking about *history.* Maybe you should call her. She's got to change her mind and start riding again, doesn't she?"

"I sure hope so," Stevie told Lisa. "But I do call her and it's the same thing. I talked to her three times this week and she wouldn't even use the word 'horse.' I'm still pretty sure she'll get over this. I just wish she'd do it right away!"

"Me, too—then she could help us on our research project about Max!"

"I don't think I can stand another afternoon looking at the town register," Stevie groaned. "We haven't even found the man's name, and that register has *everything* in it: land sales, building permits, birth, death, marriage records. Let's face it, the man was invisible."

"Maybe he never existed," Lisa said. "Should we consider that possibility?"

"No way—not until we've exhausted everything else. Besides, if our Max is Max the Third, there *had* to be a Max the First. Right?"

Lisa had to agree that it was logical. "Okay, then, back to the library. We've been reading the *Gazette* until it comes out of our ears. Today, instead of that, let's look into old books on horses. Max was some kind of star in his day—maybe he made it into the books about horses."

"Well . . . okay. But I think there might be an awful lot of books on horses in the library." Stevie sighed.

Willow Creek was in the heart of Virginia's horse country. Horses had played an important part in the lives of its citizens for a long time. Stevie knew there was a good chance that the library could have lots of books about horses, breeding, records, and ownership. She sighed again. At least she wasn't going to have to read any more about the controversial town sewers!

"And no more Mrs. Rappaport!" she said out loud. Lisa grinned at her. "Listen," Stevie continued, "I had a great idea last night. Since Max almost certainly owned some Thoroughbreds, maybe we could get some information about him from the Thoroughbred Owners and Breeders Association. They have a *million* years' worth of records about horses and owners."

"Hey, that's a great idea," Lisa told her. "I was beginning to think we'd used up all our sources. Well, congratulations! Since you had the idea, *you* get to write the letter to them while I look in the books."

The girls stepped into the library. Their newfound friend, the librarian, was at the desk, eager to help them.

"Want to look at some more newspapers?" she asked. "You know, at the turn of the century, there was a second weekly being published in town. We have some of those, too. Want to read those?"

"I don't think so," Lisa told her. "We're going to try something else first. Do you have a section on horses and breeding and ownership, that sort of thing?"

"Oh, sure we do," the librarian said. "After all, this is horse country. Come on, I'll show you."

Lisa followed the woman into the stacks while Stevie settled into a hard wooden chair in the main reading area. She hated writing letters. She especially hated writing letters to people she didn't know. And most of all, she hated writing letters when she didn't know what it was she really wanted to ask—and she was afraid that when she *did* figure out what she wanted to ask, it might sound dumb.

"Dear Sir," she wrote. She erased the comma and added "or Madam." That sounded better. She crossed that out and wrote "Dear Madam or Sir." She'd have to recopy it in ink anyway. She bit the end of her pencil, hoping that would help her think. In books and movies, people were always biting the ends of their pencils so they could think better. It didn't make Stevie think better. It just got pieces of eraser in her mouth. She picked them out carefully. Then she stared into space. Sometimes *that* helped people in books and movies. All it did for Stevie, though, was distract her.

She watched an old man come into the library. He greeted the librarian and then sat down in a comfortable chair. The librarian brought him a newspaper. It looked like something they did every day. Stevie liked that. She wondered how long the man had been coming here to read the paper. He greeted some of the people in the library as if they were old friends. He almost made a ceremony of taking out his glasses and adjusting them. He seemed to enjoy all the little steps of his ritual. She wondered if he'd enjoy writing her letter for her. It certainly wasn't going very well. All she had so far was:

~~I was~~ We were ~~wondering~~ hoping
you ~~w~~ could help us ~~maybe~~
find out ~~something~~ some things
about ~~somebody~~ a man

It wasn't going right at all. Stevie wished she'd never thought of the idea. Maybe when Lisa got back with her books, *she* could write the letter and Stevie could look up "Regnery" and "Pine Hollow" in the indexes. While she waited, she began to draw horses on the pad in front of her.

The old man finished the first section of the paper, which he had read from front to back, and picked up the second section. He seemed to be reading a little more slowly now—almost as if he didn't want his afternoon ritual to end.

He was much more interesting than the dumb letter Stevie was supposed to write. As a matter of fact, a lot of people in the library were more interesting than that. There was a lady standing outside the door of the library with a slice of pizza in her hand. She couldn't bring it inside, so she was finishing it outside. Finally, when the lady tried to jam the rest of the slice into her mouth, a big gob of cheese slid off the pizza, down her blouse, and plopped onto the sidewalk.

Stevie clapped a hand over her mouth to stifle her giggles. She wished Lisa had seen the woman, too, so they could laugh about it together. The woman chewed the last bite and stepped into the library. Stevie thought she didn't know about the stripe of tomato sauce on her blouse. It would be hard to wash. Then the woman looked up and saw Stevie staring at her. Nervously, Stevie looked away, pretending she was interested in something going on behind her.

And suddenly, she was. Because there was Veronica diAngelo sitting at a table on the other side of a bookcase. Through the open shelves, Stevie could see that she was concentrating very hard on the book in front of her. Veronica, ever the perfect little lady, was sitting backwards in her chair, with her legs straddling the seat.

"Oh, boy, have they got books about horses here!" Lisa exclaimed, dropping a stack of books on their table.

"Shhhh!" Stevie hissed, pointing through the shelves. As soon as Lisa saw Veronica, she sat down to watch, too.

"What's she doing?" Lisa asked. "It can't be homework. Her housekeeper and her gardener and her chauffeur probably does it for her!"

"I'm surprised to see her here at all," Stevie said. "I would have thought that if she needed a library, her daddy would buy her one!"

They giggled at their jokes, but they were more than a little curious. Veronica's left arm was in a cast and in a sling. She was using it to hold a book open on the table. In her right hand was a twelve-inch ruler. There was something very familiar about the way she was straddling the chair.

"It's like she's riding!" Lisa said. Veronica was sitting as if she were on a horse, and she held the ruler as if it were a riding crop. Just then, with her eyes glued to the book, Veronica leaned forward in her chair, lifted her seat out of the chair, and brought the two back legs off the floor.

"She's jumping!" Stevie said. "Look—perfect jump position!" Veronica sat forward in the chair, leaning toward the table so she could see the book. Her seat was raised slightly from the chair and she put her weight on the balls of her feet. Her back was flat, her knees bent but supple. Suddenly, her body folded forward and her head came up.

"She's watching where she's going and keeping herself perfectly centered. Up and over—" Stevie narrated.

Slowly and smoothly, Veronica rocked herself into an upright position, bringing the rear legs of the chair back to the floor. She settled back onto the chair and relaxed.

"Well!" Stevie said. "That's better than she ever did it on a horse."

"But why here?" Lisa asked. "She's had all the lessons she could want. She had the finest horse in the stable. Why is she studying riding in the library?"

"I think you and I have just seen a side of Veronica that's never been seen before—and may never be seen again," Stevie said. "What I think is that Veronica's had a zillion lessons and a fabulous horse, but she never listened and she never learned. She thought she was too good to make a mistake, but she was wrong. She knows that now. Cobalt's life was a horrible price, but at least she learned something from it."

"You could be right," Lisa agreed. "But if I know Veronica, she'd never admit that to anybody. If we let her know we saw her, she'll tell us we were wrong. But we're not. Look, there she goes again."

While Stevie and Lisa watched, Veronica went through the jumping motions several more times, improving with each try. Finally, she seemed satisfied with her efforts and stood up from the table. Furtively, she closed the book and took it back to the shelves in the riding section where Lisa had found her stack of books. Then, as Veronica left the library, Stevie and Lisa buried themselves in books so she wouldn't recognize them. The door closed behind Veronica.

"Now, that's what I call amazing," Stevie said. But Lisa didn't hear her. She was already combing through the books she'd gotten.

"Nothing," she said, slamming another book on the reject pile. "How's your letter coming?" she asked.

"Same," Stevie said noncommittally, though actually she was pleased with her progress—on the picture of the horse she was drawing. Her letter was at zero.

Fifteen minutes later, Lisa shook her head. "There's nothing at all here. Unless we get a response to your letter, I think we're going to have to give up."

"I don't think we'll get any answer to this," Stevie confessed, shoving the sketch into her pocket. She helped Lisa carry the books back to the desk for reshelving.

"You don't look very happy," the librarian said. "Perhaps if you could tell me exactly what you're looking for, I could suggest another source?"

"I don't think so," Stevie said. But Lisa gave her a look that reminded her who the A-student was.

"Maybe," Lisa said. "If it's not too much trouble."

"That's what I'm here for," the librarian said eagerly.

"Well, we're doing a report about the men who made Willow Creek what it is today. Our subject is Maxmillian Regnery, the founder of Pine Hollow Stables. All we know is that he started the stable early this century and it doesn't look like we'll learn anything else, either. Any suggestions?"

"Max? Is that what you're after?" said a gruff male voice from behind them.

Stevie and Lisa turned. It was the white-haired man who had been reading his newspaper.

"Maxmillian Regnery the First," Lisa said.

"Old Max, Senior," the man said.

"Right, him," Stevie said. "Did you know him?" The man nodded. "Really?" she persisted.

"Said so, didn't I?" he retorted.

"Well, who was he? Where did he come from? What was he like? How did he get the money to buy the stable? Was he a real wild guy?" Stevie found herself so excited to be nearing a "source," as Lisa called it, that the questions were just bubbling out of her.

"Was he at the earthquake?" Lisa asked.

"No, it was San Juan Hill, I'm sure!" Stevie cut in.

"You girls talking about Old Max who took over that stable, right?"

"Right!" they said, breathlessly.

"Dullest man I ever knew," the old man said.

"You're kidding!" Lisa exclaimed. "He was part of the Russian Revolution, wasn't he? That's not dull."

"Nope, and it's not true, either," the man said.

Finally, they were going to get answers, and Stevie had the feeling that they were going to be surprised at what they were.

"You know, Mr., uh—"

"Thompson," the man supplied.

"Mr. Thompson, we were just going over to the coffee shop for a soda. Would you like to come with us? We could buy you a soda and you could tell us about Max the First."

"Ice-cream soda?" he asked, with a twinkle in his eyes.

"Sure," Stevie said, knowing that would deplete her allowance. But if she could learn about Max the First, it would be worth every penny—even if it meant she wasn't going to like what she heard.

"You're on," he said, and they left.

Stevie, Lisa, and Mr. Thompson settled into a back booth in the coffee shop. Stevie was careful about picking their spot. She didn't want anybody else from Pine Hollow to see them. This was a Saddle Club secret.

In a few minutes, they all had their orders and Mr. Thompson began to tell the story. Lisa and Stevie sat still, absolutely astonished. The tale was so different from what they'd expected that it *had* to be the truth.

Maxmillian Regnery I, the elderly man told them, was a rather dull, totally normal human being. He was the son of Irish immigrants who had come to America in the 1850's. Max's father was a blacksmith. Max had tried smithing, but wasn't any good at it. He'd gone to school, but hadn't done well. He'd tried working at the dry goods store, but that hadn't worked either since he wasn't very good with figures. Eventually, he'd gone to work at a stable, tending horses. He had been good at that.

The stable's owner, none other than Mr. Rappaport (Stevie liked that part), thought Max showed some potential, so he'd given him a raise of ten cents a week. Old Max had put away every penny he could—including all ten cents of his raise a week—and had bought Pine Hollow after Rappaport died. Max the First had lived his entire life in Willow Creek, and, as far as the girls could tell, had never left it—not even for the San Francisco Earthquake *or* the Russian Revolution!

"What was he really like—you know, as a person?" Stevie asked.

"I told you. He was dull. Really dull. You couldn't make conversation with the man. People who learned to ride from him—and he *was* a good rider, I remember that—used to joke about him. He was so rigid, wouldn't let anybody fiddle in his classes. You couldn't talk to the other students. He used to make a big thing, too, about talking to the horses. 'They don't speak English!' he'd yell. I was one of his students, you know. My mother, bless her, invited the man and his wife for dinner one night to discuss my riding lessons. She wanted me to learn to jump right away, but he refused. 'One year,' he said sternly. He wouldn't budge. He also wouldn't let me get out of the chores at the stable. He made all the students work like stablehands! They left right after dinner. My father swore he'd never speak to my mother again if she had Old Max back in the house. 'This is *my* house,' he said. 'And I won't be bored to death in it!' She never did invite them back. I stopped riding soon after that, too."

So that was Max the First. No hero of the earthquake, San Juan Hill, or the Russian Revolution. Just an ordinary man who was extraordinarily dull. In fact, the only interesting thing about him was that his grandson, Max the Third, taught riding exactly the same way he had, seventy-five years earlier! But Max the Third wasn't dull—far from it. His students adored him.

"What are we doing to *do*?" Lisa asked Stevie, almost desperate, after Mr. Thompson had left the coffee shop.

"Do?" Stevie echoed. "What do you mean?"

"Well, now we know Max's story, and it's not worth telling."

"We're not going to tell it," Stevie said. "But now we won't have to bother with the rumors other people started. We can start our own!" Stevie's eyes lit up. "Max was kidnapped by pirates, you know. They stole everything he owned and abandoned him on a South Sea island where the only inhabitants were horses.

When he was finally rescued by the Tasmanian Navy, he refused to leave unless he could bring some of the horses—" she said, remembering a dream she'd had on the MTO.

"That's the idea!" Lisa said enthusiastically. "Now we're in business."

They drank up the last of their sodas and headed home. On the way out of the coffee shop, Stevie dropped the scribbled and scratched draft of her letter into the garbage.

14

"HONEY, I'M GOING out now. Are you sure you don't want to come with me?" Colonel Hanson asked Carole.

"No thanks, Dad. Have a good time playing tennis. Mrs. Lerner's your partner today, huh?"

"Yes, and she's got a mean backhand!" he said. "We beat the Morrisons in straight sets last week. Tennis is a great sport. Would you like to try some lessons?"

"No, but thanks anyway," Carole said. She knew her father was trying to be helpful. It was Saturday—the day she used to go horseback riding. For the last few weeks, her father had been full of suggestions for Saturday activities. Carole hadn't wanted to do any of them. "I have to read about pyramids for my term paper. I think I'll do that today."

"After tennis, Barbara and I are going out to dinner with the Morrisons."

Carole's ears perked up. "Is that a date?" she asked.

"Well, I'm not sure I'd call it a date. It's just sort of, you know, like a—well, a date, I guess."

Carole laughed at her father's stammering. "It's okay, Dad. I like the idea of you going out on a date—even with Mrs. Lerner. As long as she doesn't use her mean backhand on you!"

"Thanks for your concern," he said, giving her a hug. "We won't be late. There's a frozen pizza in the fridge and *Sands of Iwo Jima* is on TV tonight at ten. That's the John Wayne movie about the Marines in World War Two. I'll make the popcorn this time. Is it a date?" he asked slyly.

"Well, er, uh," Carole stammered, teasing her father. "I'm not, uh, exactly, well, sure I'd call it a—er—*date*."

"Okay, then *you* make the popcorn. I'll see you later, you rascal."

"Okay, it's a date," Carole told him, grinning. She and her father loved to watch old movies together and her father was never happier than when the movies were about the Marines. That would be a fun evening to look forward to.

In the meantime, Carole was very pleased that her father was spending the day with Mrs. Lerner. He'd been talking about her a lot recently, so Carole wasn't surprised they had a date.

So, that took care of her father. But what about her?

Carole didn't want to read about pyramids. She wanted to ride Cobalt. She wanted, once more, to feel the magnificent horse beneath her, flying across a field, lofting over a jump, moving surely and gracefully, responding to her every command.

Carole put her hands over her face and shook her head, but she couldn't shake the image of Cobalt from her mind.

Then, almost without thinking, Carole stood up, went to her room and changed her clothes, got her wallet and her house keys, and left the house, locking the door behind her.

In a short time, the bus drew up to the curb where she waited. She dropped her fare into the box and found a seat at the rear of the bus. It was six stops exactly. How well she knew them! Almost blindly, she descended from the bus at the shopping center and walked across the lot, down the street, across the field. To Pine Hollow.

It was still early on Saturday. People were riding already, but the class of her own friends wouldn't ride until afternoon. Carole was pretty sure she could get into the stable without anybody seeing her. She wasn't in the mood to talk and she didn't want to answer any questions. She'd come to find answers to her own questions.

She slipped into the side door of the stable. Mrs. Reg was in the tack room, but she didn't look up as Carole passed the open door. Patch and Pepper were out of their stalls—in class or on the trails, Carole thought.

And there was the third stall, the empty one. It was Cobalt's stall. It had been cleaned out completely, with fresh straw covering the floor. The clean feed and water buckets had been turned upside down to dry the last time they had been washed, and they'd been left there. It was empty, unoccupied, waiting.

Carole slid the door open and stepped inside. She breathed deeply, loving the pungent scent of the stable. For a moment, she thought that if she closed her eyes very tight and then reopened them, maybe, just maybe, Cobalt would reappear. She shut her lids, blocking out the streams of sunlight that came through the window. When she opened her eyes again, Cobalt wasn't there. And then Carole really knew for the first time that Cobalt was gone and he wasn't going to come back. No amount of wishing would change that, ever.

She leaned against the wall of the stall and slid down to sit on the clean straw. Then, for the first time since Cobalt had died, Carole cried. She sat there alone in his empty stall, her body racked with sorrow. Tears streamed down her face in silent anguish.

When all her tears were spent, she lay down in the straw and slept, exhausted by her grief.

Carole didn't know how long she slept. When she awoke, the sun was no longer coming in the window. That meant it had to be afternoon, but she didn't know what time in the afternoon. For a moment, she wondered what had awakened her, and then she heard the voices.

"No, Daddy, *no*!" the girl's voice whined. It was Veronica. Carole hated the idea that Veronica might find her in Cobalt's stall. She shifted from the side of the stall, cowering against the front wall where she couldn't be seen by somebody walking by. But she could hear everything.

"You're being silly, Ronnie," a man said. Carole realized that was Mr. diAngelo. It was a little surprising to hear him call her Ronnie. Veronica certainly wouldn't let anybody else call her that!

"Daddy, the answer is no, and I mean it."

Were Stevie and Lisa wrong? Was Veronica giving up riding, too? Was that what she was fighting with her father about?

"Delilah's a good horse!" Mr. diAngelo said. "Isn't she the mare that girl—what's her name, Carole?—rides?"

"Yes, Daddy. Carole used to ride Delilah. She's stopped coming to lessons, though."

"If Carole was the best rider in your class, then I'm sure Max gave her the best horse in the stable. And, pet, you'd look so good on her—she's got that beautiful creamy mane and the golden coat. . . ."

"That's not the point, Daddy."

"Well, if Delilah's not the right horse, I'll have my agent buy you another Thoroughbred at the auction next month. We got enough out of the insurance for Cobalt to buy you the best horse at the sale. You want one that looks like Cobalt?"

"Daddy, what a horse looks like doesn't matter," Veronica said, echoing the thought in Carole's mind.

"It's how a horse rides that's important. But even more important is how the *rider* rides."

"What are you saying, Veronica?" the man asked his daughter.

There was a long silence. Carole held her breath, waiting for Veronica's answer.

"It was my fault, Daddy," she said at last. "I caused the accident that broke my arm and that killed Cobalt."

"Nonsense!" her father protested. "You said it was Max's fault. He shouldn't have set up the jump the way he did."

"I was wrong," Veronica said. "It was a tricky jump, all right, but Max had told us how to jump it, and I decided not to pay any attention to him. If I'd had any sense, I would have told him I didn't know how to make that jump. Cobalt would never have refused the jump. But I went ahead anyway. And it cost Cobalt his life."

"Oh, don't worry about that, lamb," Mr. diAngelo said, comforting his daughter. "After all, we got the insurance money, didn't we?"

"Money doesn't have anything to do with it, Daddy! Cobalt's dead—and I don't want to own another horse until I can take care of him!"

As long as Carole had known Veronica, she'd never heard her admit that she'd made a mistake. In this case, Veronica was absolutely right. She wasn't a very good rider. She didn't deserve a horse like Cobalt.

She didn't listen to instructions. Her carelessness had cost Cobalt his life. Carole shook her head in wonder. She never would have thought that those were lessons Veronica could learn. Now, not only had she learned them, but she was trying, without success, to teach them to her father.

"You don't have to worry about taking care of your horse, Ronnie," her father said, completely missing his daughter's point. "That's why Max has all these stableboys here. *They* can take care of him for you."

"But they can't ride him for me, Daddy," she said. "Thanks for wanting to buy me a horse, but I'll keep on riding the stable horses until I've learned a lot more about riding. One day I'll own another horse. But not until I'm ready."

"I can just see you on that pretty palomino, Ronnie," Mr. diAngelo said, his voice dripping with temptation.

"*Daddy!*" Veronica said.

Stunned, Carole remained hidden in Cobalt's empty stall.

"I CAN DO it," Carole said to the empty stall, after Veronica's footsteps had faded away. "And even more important, I want to do it."

In a rush, all of her dreams came back to her. For as long as she could remember, her love of horses had been the one thing in Carole's life that had never changed. With her father in the Marines, she'd spent much of her life moving from one base to another, or living alone with her mother while her father had duty someplace they couldn't live. Her mother sometimes used to joke that they ought to "take up residence" in a moving van. But Carole hadn't minded, because wherever they lived, there were always horses.

She'd first learned to ride at the stables on the bases. When the bases didn't have stables, her parents always found a stable nearby. Then she'd found that taking classes at a private stable was a good way to make friends in a new town. Pine Hollow was the best of all, too. Max always had really good horses and he was a strict but good teacher. Max and his father and grandfather had trained quite a lot of national championship riders—and even a few Olympic riders.

Her whole life, all Carole had ever wanted to do was to ride horses, own them, breed them, train them. And yet, she had been willing to give it all up just because of Cobalt.

Now she knew that she couldn't give up on her dreams, but maybe it wasn't going to be so easy to make them come true. After all, she'd just about walked out on Max and Mrs. Reg. Max wouldn't take just anybody as a student and he required a real devotion from his riders. Carole realized that it was possible Max would tell her she wasn't welcome.

"Well, there's only one way to find out, isn't there?" she asked herself.

She stood up in the stall and brushed the straw off of her blouse. She was more than a little surprised, when she looked down, to see that she was wearing her breeches and riding boots. With a start, she understood that she'd made up her mind to ride again the moment she'd decided to come to the stable that morning. Without realizing it at all, she'd changed into her riding clothes!

She swept the straw off her breeches, plucked a final strand out of her hair, and peered over the stall door. Until she had talked to Max—and until she'd ridden again and proved to herself that she could still do it with the same commitment—she really didn't want to talk to anybody or answer anybody's questions. Fortunately, the coast was clear.

Carole stepped out into the aisle and headed for Max's office. But as she passed the tack room she saw Mrs. Reg. Mrs. Reg didn't see her, though. She was entirely too busy retrieving a little black kitten from a rafter in the tack room.

"You get down here, you rascal. How did you get up there?" she demanded furiously. Mrs. Reg stood on a chair and reached for the kitten, but he scampered along the rafter, just out of her reach.

"I'll give you a hand, Mrs. Reg," Carole said, stepping into the tack room. "You shouldn't be standing on a chair with your arthritis," she added.

"Oh, I wouldn't, believe me, if I didn't have to get this little one down. Remember him? This is the cute little newborn kitten you were playing with. Now, he's a devil—an absolute devil. He's into everything."

"Listen, you stay on the chair there, and I'll shoo him back to you, okay?"

"A devil! That's what this one is," Mrs. Reg continued, barely acknowledging Carole's presence. "Whatever you expect him to do, he doesn't. Now, you try shooing him, okay?"

Carole moved a tack box under the rafter and climbed up on it. The kitten was trapped between Carole and Mrs. Reg. Eventually, he'd get to one of them.

"Here, kitty," Mrs. Reg invited.

"Go on! Shoo!" Carole said, hustling the black furball toward Mrs. Reg.

With that, the kitten turned from Mrs. Reg and began walking precisely toward Carole. His little tail waved back and forth to preserve his balance. "You're right about him," Carole said. "He does just the opposite of what an ordinary cat would do, doesn't he?"

"Since the day he was born," Mrs. Reg agreed.

"Go away, kitty!" Carole said, looking straight into his sky-blue eyes. "Go away!"

She could hear his purring, the magical motor going full tilt. The little kitten stepped off the rafter and onto Carole's shoulder. Cradling him so that he wouldn't fall, Carole stepped off the tack box and then helped Mrs. Reg get off her chair.

"Got a name for him yet?" Mrs. Reg asked, picking up their conversation from several weeks ago, just as if no time had passed at all.

"Yeah, I do," Carole said. She sat down on the tack box and held the kitten on her lap. Within seconds, the black kitten's purring stopped. He was curled up and sound asleep.

"His name's Snowball," Carole told Mrs. Reg.

"Perfect!" Mrs. Reg said, laughing. "He's so contrary that he's truly earned a name like that. But there's a problem with that."

"What's that?" Carole asked, stroking the kitten softly.

"Our cats are named after horses. I don't know of any 'Snowball.'"

"Can't you make an exception?"

"I don't think so," Mrs. Reg said. "But I have another solution. If he's not a stable cat, he doesn't have to have a stable name. Why don't you keep him? He'll be weaned and ready to go to a new home in about two weeks. If you'd like him, ask your dad, okay?"

"Okay," Carole said. "I'd like that."

She picked up the sleeping kitten and put him back in the box where he'd been born. All his littermates were awake from their naps and were crawling out of the box.

"I'll ask Dad tonight," Carole said, sure that he'd agree. After all, who could resist a little black kitten named Snowball?

"Snowball's the right name, that's for sure," Mrs. Reg said.

Then Carole remembered that she'd once thought she should name the kitten Cobalt. That wouldn't have been right at all. Cobalt *was* a great horse, but the kitten deserved his own name. Carole glanced at the clock in the tack room. Only fifteen minutes until class!

"Gotta see Max!" she said. "'Bye!"

She ran out of the tack room and headed for Max's office, skidding to a stop as she neared the door. Then she proceeded to walk calmly. It wouldn't do to arrive huffing and puffing.

"Can I talk to you, Max?" she asked politely.

"Sure, Carole. Come on in," he said, smiling warmly. Carole hoped he meant it.

"Max, I was wondering if it would be okay for me to come back—join the class again."

Max was quiet for a minute. Was he angry with her? Had he filled her spot in the class? Did he have rules about quitters? Was she going to have to find another stable?

"Carole," he began, "I know what you've been through. I know how much you cared for Cobalt and I know how much his death hurt you—as indeed it did all of us. I am very happy to have you back. But class starts in fifteen—" he glanced at his digital watch "—thirteen minutes. Can you get saddled up by then?"

"You bet I can!" she said. "I'll get Delilah's saddle and bridle right away."

"Not Delilah," Max said.

Carole gulped. If she couldn't ride Delilah, that must mean that Mr. diAngelo had talked Veronica into letting him buy the horse! That meant that Veronica hadn't learned anything after all. Would she kill Delilah, too?

"I guess you had to do it," Carole said dully. She understood that the owner of a stable really had to go along with some of the patrons. After all, Mr. diAngelo owned the bank and he could cause trouble for Max—

"Had to do what?" he asked.

"Had to sell her," Carole said. "I heard that Mr. diAngelo wanted to buy her for Veronica. I understand that kind of thing happens." She was trying to be realistic.

"Not to me, it doesn't," Max said, surprising her. "I couldn't sell her now, anyway."

"Is she sick?" Carole asked, suddenly recalling how oddly Delilah had behaved on the MTO with her mood shifts and unpredictable appetite.

"Not exactly," Max said evasively.

"Then what, exactly?" Carole said.

"She's carrying a foal, Carole. She's due in a couple of months and until then she'll have rest and pasture time. Nobody rides her and she's not for sale."

A foal! That meant there would be a birth at the stable. It could be a beautiful palomino like Delilah—a whole new life coming to Pine Hollow.

"You mean she wasn't sick on the MTO?"

"Nope, she was just getting ready for motherhood—and sometimes mares act up a bit when their time gets nearer. She's fine and healthy. So's the foal so far. Vet says she'll be delivering at the end of the summer. So, it's time for her to stop work."

"That's wonderful!" Carole sat still in the chair across from Max's desk, too excited to move, or even to think about class.

"Carole," Max said gently. She looked up at him. "You haven't asked the question I was expecting."

"What's that?"

"You haven't asked who the sire of Delilah's foal is."

"Okay, who is—" Carole suddenly didn't have to ask. There was only one stallion at Pine Hollow, only one horse who *could* have sired a foal. "Cobalt?"

Max smiled and nodded. "See, in a way, he's going to live on." Carole was silent, taking in the good news.

Suddenly Max was his old businesslike self again. "Breeding a mare is a lot of work, Carole," he said. "From now on, we're going to have to watch Delilah carefully. We want a healthy foal. And after it's born, there's going to be even more work. We'll be doing feeding and tending and training—" he paused and looked into Carole's eyes. "You'll help, won't you?"

"*Will* I!" she said breathlessly. It was a dream come true.

"Okay, if you're going to help, you're going to have to be a better rider than you are now. What are you doing just sitting here? Why aren't you getting ready for class? You're to ride Diablo from now on, understand?"

"Yes, *sir*!" she said. She stood up and saluted Max, Marine Corps-style—just like her father taught her.

And then she floated on air back out to the stable. She didn't have a second to waste before class.

"Hi, Carole!" Betsy Cavanaugh greeted her as she tried to dash down the aisle to Diablo's stall. "Did you hear?"

"Hear what?" Carole asked suspiciously. She didn't think Max had shared the news about Delilah yet, otherwise she was certain Lisa or Stevie would have called to tell her.

"About Max—the First. He was captured by pirates!"

"Give me a break," Carole said, making her way to her horse.

"No, it's true! I think it is, anyway," Betsy said.

Carole didn't have time to listen to any more. She stepped into Diablo's stall and began putting the saddle on him.

"Max the First was a horse thief," a voice told her, coming over the door to the stall. It was Meg Durham speaking. "It seems that he rode with Billy the Kid and they were rustling horses out west. Then—"

"Meg! I'm late for class and I have to get this done in a hurry. Tell me about it after class, maybe?"

"Sure, Carole," Meg said. "Nice to see you back."

By the time Carole had the saddle and bridle on Diablo and was walking him toward the ring—and toward the good-luck horseshoe—two other people had told her two other stories about Max the First. Carole had never heard such zany stories in her whole life—and every single person who told her a tale swore it was true.

"Carole! You're back!" Stevie shrieked. She had just mounted Comanche and was walking around the ring until class started.

Lisa came up behind her on Pepper. "Oh, Carole, I knew you'd come back. I'm so glad to see you. We missed you!"

"Really?" Carole brushed the good-luck horseshoe with her right hand and then mounted Diablo. "And I think I got back just in time to see this place go crazy. What's all this stuff I hear about Max the First?"

Lisa and Stevie exchanged glances and then slapped their hands over their mouths. Carole had the distinct impression they were trying to stifle giggles.

"Are you going to tell me that Max was actually the first human being to reach the south pole—on horseback? A little-known expedition that took place at the turn of the century?"

"Hey, that's a great idea!" Stevie said, her eyes popping open.

"What is going on around here?" Carole asked.

But before either Lisa or Stevie could answer, Max entered the ring.

"Now, class begins!" he said sternly. From that moment on, talking was strictly forbidden.

"Saddle Club meeting at TD's after class!" Stevie hissed.

Carole nodded happily. Did she have news for them!

"SO YOU GUYS found this old guy at the library who actually knew Max?" Carole asked in surprise.

The three girls were seated at their favorite table in TD's, the ice cream store at the shopping center. They were each working their way through a sundae, the first Stevie had been able to afford since buying Mr. Thompson the soda!

"Oh, yeah!" Stevie said. "And Max was nothing like anyone had guessed! He was a good rider and a strict teacher—just like our Max—but apparently he was this boring old guy who could put people practically to sleep just by talking. He never left Willow Creek his whole life. He never even did anything *interesting*, so forget about exciting."

"So, why's everybody telling me about pirates and expeditions and everything?"

"See, now that we know the truth, we don't have to worry about anybody believing it!" Lisa said. "So, we tell people we've done research—and that part's true—and this is what we found. Only we tell everybody something different *and* we tell them not to tell anybody else!"

"Somehow this sounds like an idea of Stevie's," Carole said, laughing. "You're really something, you know?"

"I never could have done it without Lisa," Stevie said. "She had a lot of great research ideas. But if you ever get curious about a certain Mrs. Rappaport, or the town sewer system, just ask me, okay?"

"You'll be the first person I'll ask," Carole assured her. "What I really want to ask, though, is what's going on with Veronica?" Carole told them about the conversation Veronica had with her father. Stevie and Lisa told her about Veronica's jumping class—in the library. "Is she changing—or what?" Carole asked.

"I think she is," Lisa said solemnly. "She really learned something when Cobalt got hurt. You have to respect that, don't you?"

"I respect it," Stevie said. "But it doesn't make me like her much better. She's still a pain. Now, if she stops being a *pain*, that'll be news!" The Saddle Club members laughed together.

"Now, let me tell you *my* news." Stevie and Lisa listened eagerly, almost as thrilled as Carole when she told them about Snowball and then, best of all, about Delilah's foal.

"I can't wait!" Stevie exclaimed. "The newborns are *so* cute! Do you think it'll be black like Cobalt—or a pretty palomino like Delilah?"

They talked animatedly about the foal for a while as they finished their sundaes. Then the talk turned to Carole. She'd known it would come, and she knew that her friends deserved an answer.

"What made you decide to come back?" Lisa asked.

"There were a lot of things. I think that you were right in a way when you said I was horse shy. But not just about any horse—it was Cobalt. It hurt so much when he died that I was afraid I might get hurt again if something like that happened to another horse. But when I saw what Veronica had learned—well, I thought if there's hope for her, then there's hope for me. Anyway, the only thing worse than losing something you care about is not having something you care about at all. I learned that when Mom died."

Stevie and Lisa sat quietly. "There was something else," Carole continued. "I finally realized that no matter how much I cared about him, Cobalt wasn't mine. He belonged to somebody else."

"But you rode him more than Veronica did!" Lisa reminded her.

"I did, that's right. And I rode him better. But Mrs. Reg had the final lesson for me, though she didn't say it in so many words. There are lots of horses, some good, some bad, most mixes of good and bad. And I want to ride them all!"

"Uh-oh," Stevie said. Carole and Lisa turned to her. "With that kind of determination, Carole won't be horse shy anymore, that's for sure. But the poor horses—they'll become Carole shy!"

The three girls laughed together and it felt very, very good. The Saddle Club was now back in full operation.

THE SADDLE CLUB

HORSE SENSE

BONNIE BRYANT

A BANTAM BOOK®
TORONTO • NEW YORK • LONDON • SYDNEY • AUCKLAND

—for Neil

1

"I CAN TELL I'm really getting better at riding," Lisa Atwood announced to her two best friends with a smile. "Max is only giving me four instructions at a time now—instead of the *eight* he gave me during my first few lessons!"

Carole Hanson and Stevie Lake laughed along with Lisa. Max Regnery, their riding teacher at Pine Hollow Stables, was quite a character sometimes. But they also understood the complexity of riding well. There were always dozens of things to remember at once!

The girls were lounging contentedly in Stevie's room, talking about their favorite subject: horses. The three friends were the members of The Saddle Club, and this get-together was a "meeting." The girls had created the Club, with only two requirements: The members had to be horse crazy and they had to be willing to help one another when help was needed. At the moment, with no problems or crises in evidence, the girls were lazily talking about riding.

Lisa sat cross-legged on Stevie's bed. She twirled her long light brown hair around one finger as she and her friends talked. Lisa was petite and fine-boned, and she looked younger than her thirteen years. Also, the clothes her mother steered her into choosing—classic styles, like pleated plaid skirts and penny loafers—exaggerated her good-little-girl look. Occasionally Lisa daydreamed about having her hair cut in spikes or buying some offbeat clothes at the secondhand store at the mall, but there wasn't enough rebel in her to defy her mother—or, usually, anybody else.

Although a year older than her friends, Lisa was the newest rider of the group. She'd only begun a few months before. She'd started lessons because her mother thought every well-brought-up young girl should know how to ride ("—and dance and paint and play the piano and do needlework, and every other boring thing you could imagine!" Lisa had said in exasperation one day). Then, Lisa had surprised her mother by becoming very interested in riding—and had especially surprised herself, and even Max, by how good she had become at it.

"Well, what were the four instructions?" Stevie asked Lisa with a grin. Stevie was lying on the floor of her room, with her legs propped up on her bed, and her dark blond hair spread out dramatically on the floor. Her hazel eyes were full of mischief. Stevie lived in a comfortable, spacious home with her three brothers (Michael, eight; Alex, her twin; and Chad, fourteen) and her parents. In contrast to Lisa's stylish outfits, Stevie's usually looked like hand-me-downs. She rode in jeans and beat-up cowboy boots. Now, relaxing after riding class, she was lounging in an oversize sweatshirt and a pair of tights.

Stevie was the only rider in her family. Sometimes it was hard for her parents to understand her love of horses, but her commitment had finally convinced them Stevie was serious about riding—perhaps because it was the only thing she *was* serious about. Stevie was a practical joker and frequently in trouble. Somehow, though, Stevie always managed to come out on top. To Lisa, that was one of Stevie's most endearing qualities.

Lisa had to think for a moment to remember Max's instructions. She rolled her eyes and said in a deep, serious voice, "'Heels down, toes in, look straight ahead, and'—" she paused, laughing, then resumed sternly, "and, 'stop talking to your horse!'"

Her friends joined Lisa in a burst of laughter. Max not only taught riding but also owned Pine Hollow Stables. And he was famous for certain idiosyncrasies, among them his belief that horses couldn't understand English. He told his riders that a horse would appreciate the sound of a reassuring word now and again, but they were never to speak *instructions* such as "whoa." For instructions, the rider should always use "aids"—signals with hands, legs, and a riding crop.

"What were you saying to Pepper?" Carole asked.

"I just told him that he should stop looking at the clock—there was another half hour to go in class!"

"You're right, you know. When Pepper decides class should be over, he gets very 'barny,' doesn't he?" Any horse in a hurry to get back to his stall was called barny.

Carole was the most experienced rider of the three girls, having ridden all her life on the Marine Corps bases where her father, now a colonel, had been stationed. Lisa thought Carole was beautiful, with her wavy black hair that hung loose to her shoulders and her intense big brown eyes. Lisa knew that Carole dreamed of owning a stable one day. She wanted to breed horses, train them, and, most of all, to ride them. Riding was the most important thing in her life. So Lisa was always pleased when Carole agreed with her observations about horses.

"He sure does," Lisa said. "Every time we passed the door to the stalls, he slowed down and looked that way—just to remind me that we *could* go in there instead of around in circles."

"I rode a horse on the base at Twenty-Nine Palms once," Carole began, "who was so barny that if you took him out, you always had to keep him turned away from the barn. Once he was turned toward home, no matter how far away he was, nothing could keep him from heading back. They nicknamed him Pidge because he was like a homing pigeon!"

The girls were laughing when there was a knock at Stevie's door. "It's me, Chad," Stevie's older brother said. He opened the door. "Mom said to tell you that there are cookies in the kitchen if you're hungry. I could bring them up, if you'd like." With that, he disappeared from the door.

"What's that all about?" Carole asked.

"Beats me," Stevie said. "The last time he offered to do anything for me, it was to eat all my Halloween candy when I was six. Tried to convince me I'd get a stomachache. But he volunteered to take the risk himself!"

"I guess brothers can be weird," Carole remarked. "And speaking of weird, did you hear that new French girl shouting at Nero? She was *really* angry. You're taking French, Stevie, could you understand her?"

"I think the words Estelle used *aren't* included in the vocabulary lists that Mlle. Lebrun gives us." She shook her head and grinned wickedly.

"You shouldn't make fun of her," said Lisa, who always tried to be fair. "After all, Estelle is new to this country. I'm sure they just do things differently in France. And it can't be easy to move your entire life to a new country, you know, just because your father's job is here."

"Well, if they do things differently in France, they do them *very* differently," Carole said, almost smirking.

Before Lisa had a chance to ask Carole what she meant, there was another knock at the door. Chad was back with a snack for the girls. He brought a tray with a little plate of cookies and a glass of milk for each of them. By the time he'd finished serving them, the girls had forgotten about Estelle and had started talking about horses again.

"How's Delilah?" Stevie asked Carole. Delilah, a mare at Pine Hollow, was due to deliver a foal within the next month. The foal had been sired by Cobalt, a Thoroughbred who'd had to be put to sleep after his leg had been shattered beyond repair in a jumping accident. After the tragedy of his sudden death, Carole had wanted to give up riding. He'd been her favorite horse to ride, ever. Then she'd learned about Cobalt's foal.

"The vet says she's doing just fine." Carole's eyes lit up with excitement. "In fact, she was examining Delilah today. It's not going to be long now before Delilah delivers, and the vet promises she'll call me when the time comes. I'm so excited!"

"Wouldn't it be great if we could *all* be there?" Lisa said.

"It would probably upset Delilah," Carole said, deflating Lisa. Lisa hoped Carole didn't think that her special love for Cobalt made her the only one who could help at the foaling. Lisa and Stevie exchanged glances. Carole was very knowledgeable about horses, but there were times when she seemed maybe just a little bit *too* knowledgeable—and a bit too possessive about her knowledge.

"You know what I like best about summer?" Stevie said, changing the subject. Then, without waiting for an answer, she continued. "I like being able to ride every day."

Carole and Lisa nodded. School had let out a few weeks earlier. Now the girls were attending the stable's camp program, which ran every weekday at the stable. Then, if they wanted to, they could ride on weekends as well.

"It's like there's finally enough time to do all the riding I want," Stevie said. "And, not only do we have the foal to look forward to, but I have the feeling there's something else coming up, too."

"What's that?" Lisa asked, suddenly interested.

"Well, I'm not exactly sure, but Max said he wanted to talk to me after camp tomorrow. He sounded *very* mysterious," Stevie finished in her dramatic way.

"The last time Max wanted to talk to you it was because you were getting a C-minus in math, wasn't it?" Carole teased.

"Don't remind me," Stevie said, throwing a pillow at her.

It was a firm rule at Pine Hollow that riding came second to schoolwork. No student was allowed to ride unless school grades were satisfactory. And Max kept a sharp eye on enforcement. "But I ended the year with a B-plus—thanks to Lisa's help—and I'm not at summer school, so it can't have anything to do with that."

"Think he might have found out it was you who put the toad in Veronica's riding hat?" Carole asked.

"No way!" Stevie giggled. "Even though Veronica wanted the toad checked for fingerprints!"

"Boy, I loved the look of horror on her too-perfect face, didn't you?" Carol asked.

Veronica diAngelo was a snooty girl who was in their class at Pine Hollow. Cobalt had belonged to her, and the accident that had cost him his life had been her fault. Even though she was now trying to learn more about riding, she was still Veronica, and the girls didn't like her much.

"You know, I was thinking about trying the toad trick on Estelle, too. After all, one of Pine Hollow's traditions is playing practical jokes on new students," Stevie said.

Practical jokes were Lisa's least-favorite tradition at Pine Hollow. She was about to suggest that it wouldn't be a good idea, when Stevie discarded the notion herself.

"Nah, I don't think so. It might make Max angry and if he gets really mad then he won't tell me what it is he wants to tell me—unless, of course, he's already mad. Then a trick would make it worse. What do you think, Carole?"

"I think it's going to be a colt. . . ." Carole said dreamily.

"Huh? What's that got to do with Max?" Stevie asked.

"Oh, sorry—I was just thinking about Delilah some more."

Lisa watched as Carole and Stevie tried to carry on a conversation, but it was weird because they were talking about different things. Lisa felt a little left out of it. While they were talking back and forth, she began to think about The Saddle Club. She always had fun with Carole and Stevie, but she couldn't help wishing that their club were more official, with rules and regulations. If their meetings were more organized, then they'd all talk about the same subject. That was really the way clubs were supposed to work. Meetings were supposed to be orderly. There was supposed to be new business and old business, election of officers, budgets and motions. Lisa's mother belonged to lots of clubs. That was how it always was. Just because they *called* it The Saddle Club didn't make it a club.

To be a real club, they'd need a constitution. And who, she asked herself, suddenly inspired, was better prepared to make a constitution than the person who had gotten an A on her paper about the United States Constitution? Now Lisa was excited. She had a project too, just like Carole had Delilah and her foal, and Stevie had her mysterious meeting with Max. Lisa grinned to herself, thinking how pleased her friends would be when they found that they belonged to a *real* club.

"Stevie! It's almost time for dinner!" Mrs. Lake's voice came up the stairs. "Lisa? Carole? Isn't it time for your dinner too?" she called out.

"We'd better go," Carole said, taking the hint and tugging her riding jacket out of the soft chair where she'd been sitting. "You know, even though we can ride every day now, there are still two things there's never enough time for."

"Yeah, I know," Stevie said. "Horses and horses, right?"

"Right." Carole nodded. "Riding them and talking about them."

"Make that three things, then," Lisa said grumpily. "We never seem to have enough time for The Saddle Club, either. Or maybe it's just that we don't always use our time right."

"Could be," Carole said agreeably. She and Lisa said their good-byes to Stevie, and then Lisa trailed Carole down the stairs and out the door of Stevie's house.

Lisa was so lost in thought about the articles of the club's unwritten constitution that she barely remembered to say good-bye to Carole when they got to her bus stop.

2

THE FOLLOWING AFTERNOON, which was a Friday, Stevie headed for Max's office, more than a little bit nervous. Sometimes Max was hard to predict. She *hoped* this meeting was going to be good news, but she wasn't at all sure. Stevie thought she'd seen Max grinning to himself when Veronica discovered the toad in her riding hat, but then again, maybe that wasn't a grin. With Max, it was hard to tell.

And, two days ago, she'd been talking with Lisa during class. Max was more likely to be upset about that; no talking in class was another one of his firm rules. He usually didn't care what happened after class, as long as it didn't hurt the horses. Toads were after class; talking was *in* class.

Just to be on the safe side, Stevie detoured past the good-luck horseshoe. It was nailed next to the mounting area. It was a Pine Hollow tradition that all the riders were supposed to touch the shoe before every ride. The horseshoe had been there as long as anybody could remember, and no rider had ever been seriously hurt at Pine Hollow. Stevie brushed it with her hand on her way to Max's office. It was worn smooth with wishes. Maybe it wouldn't make any difference, she thought, but it made her feel better.

A few seconds later, Max was telling her to come in and sit down. That was when Stevie knew it was all right. One thing that was absolutely predictable about Max was that if he was going to chew you out (and Stevie had plenty of experience at that), he never asked you to sit down. She made herself comfortable in the chair that faced his desk.

"Stevie, do you know what a gymkhana is?" Max asked her.

"Well, sure I do," she told him. "It's a kind of horse show for young riders, only with games and races and things like that—right?"

"Right. In another six weeks, there's going to be a three-day event here for the stable's adult riders and other local competitors. I've been spending so much time planning the other events that I've almost forgotten about my young riders. You'll all have a good time watching the events, but I want to have something special for you as well. And I don't have one extra minute to plan it." He sat forward in his chair and looked Stevie square in the eye. "It has come to my attention that you have a certain knack for funny activities pertaining to horses, not that I approve of a lot of what you've done—we won't even talk about the recent insult to the local toad population—" Stevie giggled involuntarily. Max continued. "—but I'd like to make use of your weird sense of humor. How about it? Can you make up some events for the riders in your class, as well as the really young kids? They should be safe, of course, but fun. And they should require the use of real riding skills. Other than that, it's up to you. Can you do it?"

Could she? "You *bet* I can!" Stevie told him. This was the chance of a lifetime. Her imagination was already in high gear. "You mean things like races and games? Stuff like that?"

"Yes, and they need to be races that can be run by teams of mixed ages—you know, everybody from the six-year-olds on through fifteen. All the older riders will be involved in the three-day event. The gymkhana will take place each afternoon of the three-day event. Mrs. Reg will help you compose the teams. One of the stableboys, probably Red O'Malley, will do the setups for you and will be in charge of getting props. This is a big job, Stevie. If you need help, you can get it—from everybody but me. The success of the gymkhana will pretty much be your responsibility. Are you still game?"

"Am I ever!" she said. "But—"

"Yes?" he asked.

"Well, why *me?*" she asked.

"You're a good rider, Stevie, a really good rider. I'd like to see you take on more responsibility here at Pine Hollow. This seemed like a perfect opportunity. Besides, I really need the help. Look, we'll discuss your ideas every now and again to see where you are. In the meantime—uh-oh, I've got to remember to call Mrs.—uh . . . about the, uh . . ." Max grabbed for the phone. As soon as he'd dialed a number, he began making notes, and it was as if Stevie weren't there anymore. She decided that meant that Max was probably through with her. Quietly, so as not to disturb his concentration, she crept out of his office. He didn't seem to notice.

A gymkhana would be lots of fun and being in charge of it would be even better. She'd read about them and she had heard about one from a cousin of hers who lived in New Jersey, but she'd never actually seen one. She'd need some information about what sort of games they should have, and when it came to getting information at Pine Hollow, no one was more helpful than Mrs. Reg, Max's mother. When his father had died, Max had taken over the stable, and his mother had remained in charge of the tack room and the equipment. She was always full of great horse stories. The only drawback to getting advice from Mrs. Reg was that you had to do something in return—like clean tack.

Like the other Saddle Club members, Stevie loved to ride horses, but knew that horses were at least as much work as pleasure. For every hour spent riding horses, owners probably spent two taking care of them. Another Pine Hollow tradition—and ironclad rule—was that all the riders had to do chores around the stable. Some jobs were officially assigned and others were done as needed; all the riders were simply expected to pitch in. Carole loved horses so much that she'd do anything for them. But Stevie was not thrilled with the messy stable chores. Cleaning tack qualified as a messy stable chore in Stevie's book.

Stevie stepped into the tack room. There, along one wall, was an endless sea of saddles and bridles. One bridle hung above each saddle, adjusted for a specific horse. The first set of tack on the right-hand wall had been assigned to the first horse in the right-hand stable. Since they were cleaned methodically, there was always a marker by the next set of tack due for a saddle soaping. Stevie automatically picked up the tack and the soap can and sponge, shooing away the kitten that had pounced on the bridle she carried, and walked into Mrs. Reg's office. She sat down on the tack box near Mrs. Reg's desk and began her work.

"What can I do for you, child?" Mrs. Reg asked. She knew Stevie wouldn't submit to saddle soaping unasked unless she needed something.

"What do you know about gymkhanas?" Stevie asked.

Mrs. Reg smiled broadly. "Oh, I think we can cook something up, don't you?" she asked.

Stevie filled her sponge with saddle soap and began cleaning the saddle's flaps while she listened.

"WE'RE LOOKING FOR definite signs now," the vet, Judy Barker, told Carole. The two of them stood outside the foaling stall where Delilah was being kept until her foal was born. The foaling stall was different from the other horses' stalls; it was larger and specially designed to be completely safe for a foal. There were no slats in the walls where a tiny hoof could get stuck and no hooks to scratch or damage the unwary baby. Judy had showed Carole how even the slightest mistake could hurt a newborn.

Although she was a doctor, Judy's uniform consisted of soft blue jeans, a cool cotton blouse, and leather boots. She was a familiar sight throughout the county, driving along the country roads—sometimes at breakneck speed—in her light blue pickup truck, with a camper on the back to hold the oversize medical equipment she needed for her oversize patients.

Sometimes, Carole could picture herself in such a rig, taking emergency calls on the cellular phone in the truck's cab. She'd rush to the side of a colicky mare, or clear up a skin infection on a jumper, or calm a nervous mother-to-be, as Judy was doing now.

And sometimes Carole saw herself only as the owner of the mare, or the jumper, or the mother-to-be. Carole didn't know exactly how she was going to work with horses when she grew up—whether as an owner, trainer, breeder, or vet—but whatever she did, she knew it would always involve horses. Until she made up her mind, she wanted to learn everything she possibly could.

Delilah's foal was the most exciting thing that had ever happened to her as a rider. Not only had Cobalt been the horse of her dreams, until his tragic death, but Delilah was the stable horse she had always ridden. She knew Delilah better than she knew any other horse. Delilah trusted her. And Max had already asked her if she would help raise and train the foal. She hadn't had to think twice to answer that question.

"There are signs that she's about to deliver her foal," Judy explained.

"Is it that soon?"

"Well, maybe," Judy told her. "Mares—particularly ones foaling for the first time—can be pretty unpredictable. We have to watch them very closely. From the look of this one now, I'd say she'll deliver sometime in the next three weeks."

"How do you know?" Carole asked, fascinated.

Judy showed her where the foal lay in the mare's huge belly. Then she showed her the mare's enlarged udder, already filling with milk to be ready when her newborn was hungry for the first time. "See, these are signs that we're not far off. But she's not ready yet. I really don't expect the foal for at least two weeks, and it could be four or five."

"Should somebody be staying with her now? I mean, I could bring in my sleeping bag and stay with her, like, just in case—"

"No, not yet," Judy said, smiling at Carole. "The time will come, but it's not yet. I'll let you know—when Delilah tells me." Just then, the phone in Judy's truck rang. While Judy answered the call, Carole stood at the door to Delilah's stall, patting the horse's nose and whispering reassuring words in her big, soft ears. Delilah eyed Carole calmly. Then, because the foal inside her was growing at a tremendous rate, Delilah turned to the thing that interested her most these days—fresh hay—and began eating. Carole wandered outside and found Judy cramming the last of her equipment back in her truck.

"Emergency?" Carole asked with concern.

"The big bay mare at Cloverleaf is about to foal. She had us all in a tither with her last foal, so I want to be cautious this time. Say, you want to come along? You might even be some help. I'll drive you home afterward. You can call your dad on my phone here. . . ."

Without a second's thought, Carole yanked open the door on the passenger side of the blue pickup and jumped in.

"You *bet*!" she said. As soon as the door slammed, Judy turned on the engine and pulled out of the drive at Pine Hollow. When they roared past one of the town's police cars a few minutes later, they were going fifty in a thirty-five-mile-per-hour speed zone. Judy waved at the officer in the car.

"Isn't he going to give you a ticket?" Carole asked.

"That's Jack Miller," Judy said, as if it were an explanation. "He's got a pony for his kids. Jingles nearly died last year with a deep cut he got from a barbed-wire fence. Jack knows why I drive fast."

Carole gripped the armrest and watched the countryside fly by. She was too excited to be nervous anyway.

AT HOME IN her own room, Lisa got ready for her surprise for The Saddle Club. She expected to spend most of the weekend working on it. Her desk, almost unused since school had closed for the summer, was clear and waiting. She took out a notebook she'd bought to write the constitution in. The clean white pages and neat blue lines, edged on the left with a red vertical border, were inviting. She selected a sharp-pointed pen from the mug on her desk. She adjusted her chair. She turned on the three-way lamp.

THE SADDLE CLUB

she wrote.

But how was it to begin?

There was a familiar scratching at her door. Her dog, a golden Lhasa apso named Dolly, wanted to come in. Lisa opened the door and patted Dolly, scratching her neck just where she liked it the most. The fluffy dog scampered up onto the upholstered chair next to the window. Lisa watched while Dolly circled exactly three times and then settled down for a nap. She always circled three times and it always fascinated Lisa. Dolly was such a creature of habit. But then, so was Lisa. They were a good pair.

Lisa sat down in her chair again, adjusting the light.

Rules

she wrote.

We, the members of The Saddle Club, in order to form a more perfect union . . .

Lisa groaned at the familiarity of those words. Plagiarism was no way to start a good club! She really needed to organize her thoughts before she began making up the rules. So, she jotted down a list of subjects for the rules.

meetings
dues
officers
projects
requirements for membership
new members
purpose

That was the start she needed. Lisa began outlining the regulations under each of the categories she'd created and soon her pen was moving quickly across the page.

When Dolly scratched at the inside of the door to signal that it was time to go outside for a walk, Lisa was surprised to see that an hour had passed. She glanced at her notebook. She'd filled eight pages with outlines and rules.

Now, that was progress!

3

STEVIE DASHED UP the stairs to her room. She dumped her boots and her riding hat in the general vicinity of a chair and yanked her closet door open.

"I'm sure it's still here," she mumbled as she burrowed into the back of her less-than-perfectly-organized closet. "I *couldn't* have thrown it away." She grabbed the handle of an umbrella with four broken ribs. That wasn't what she wanted. She shoved it back into a corner. "*Could* Mom have . . . ?" Then she extracted what turned out to be a drum majorette's baton. That wasn't what she wanted at all. She tossed that next to the umbrella. But maybe it had possibilities for the games. She decided to consider it later.

Then, at last, her hand closed on the rounded object she sought. She tugged at it gently, trying not to topple the rest of the stuff in the closet. Finally, Stevie emerged triumphantly from her closet clutching a Hula-Hoop.

"Perfect!" she said proudly. Her father had bought it for her at a garage sale a year ago. He'd thought it was terribly funny to find one of those big plastic hoops that had been all the rage when her parents were kids. Stevie had thought this toy was fairly dumb until now. Now all she had to do was to figure out how to use a Hula-Hoop while riding a horse. She put it over her head and tried to get it to circle her waist. The thing quickly clattered to the floor. That didn't matter, though, because it would be impossible to hula on horseback. But could she swing it around on, say, her forearm without spooking the horse?

She got the hoop to circle her forearm. She tried to imagine being a horse, watching the spinning hoop, and decided she wasn't upset by it—even when it upset a lampshade. Then she decided that wasn't really an objective test.

"What are you doing?" asked her twin brother, Alex, opening the door. "I mean, are you into busting up furniture now?"

"No, I'm just—hey, you can help me. Come on in here." She grabbed his arm and pulled him into her room. "I really need help, see. It's for the gymkhana," she began, but he interrupted her.

"Gym-what?" he asked.

"The gymkhana. It's for Pine Hollow—a tournament of fun, silly games you play on horseback."

"Not me, Sis," Alex said. "I don't know anything about horses, you know that. And, anyway, I'm on my way over to Ron Ziegler's house. His little brothers got a Laser Tag for their birthday, but they've gone to a friend's house this afternoon, so Ron and I—"

"Laser Tag! That's perfect!" Stevie shouted. She'd never actually played it, but she knew it was an electronic game of tag with guns that shot light beams at a vest, which lit up when the beam hit its target. It seemed like a perfect gymkhana game. "I've *got* to borrow it."

"What do you mean you've got to borrow it? It belongs to Ron's little brothers, and you know what monsters they are. If you want to borrow something from them, in the first place, you're crazy, but in the second place, *you* ask them."

"Oh, come on, Alex," Stevie said in her sweetest, most appealing twin-sister voice, ignoring the phone as it began to ring. "You've just got to get them to let me use it—"

"Stevie, phone call!" her brother Chad yelled up the stairs.

She walked to the door and opened it. Looking down toward Chad at the foot of the stairs, she asked, "Who is it?"

"I dunno," he informed her.

"I'll be right there," she told Chad. "But first . . ." She turned to talk to Alex again, but he'd escaped through the other door to her room while she was talking with Chad. She stepped to her window, and saw him jogging across their lawn. She raised the sash. "Come on, Alex, you've only got to *ask* them for me!" she called after him. He continued on his way, pretending not to hear her.

Stevie sighed and picked up the phone on her bedside table—a major, long-hoped-for twelfth birthday present (though at that moment, she wished she'd gotten Laser Tag).

"Hullo?"

"Where were you? What took you so long to answer?" Carole asked her over the phone.

"Oh, it's my dumb brother," Stevie explained. "I've just got to borrow a Laser Tag set, and he won't ask his best friend—well, actually it's his little brothers—to lend it to me. I mean, it'll be fantastic. Don't you think so?"

"Well, I guess it's a pretty good game," Carole said, "but I never much wanted to play it myself."

"It's for the gymkhana!" Stevie said. "Oh, but I didn't get a chance to tell you about it, did I?"

"Nope," Carole said just a little sarcastically, but Stevie didn't notice.

"Well, that's what Max wanted to see me about. We're going to have a gymkhana and he wants me to come up with all kinds of neat games for it. Mrs. Reg just suggested an egg-in-a-spoon race and a rope race, but I want something more exciting than that stuff.

Can you think of anything better than Laser Tag on horseback?"

"I guess that would be fun," Carole told her.

"You guess? Is that all you can say? It would be the best thing in the world!"

"No, *I* just saw the best thing in the world," Carole said. "I just saw a newborn foal."

Suddenly, gymkhanas didn't seem so all-important to Stevie. "Delilah had the foal already?"

"Not yet. This was a mare at Cloverleaf. I went over there with Judy because the trainer called while Judy was visiting Delilah. By the time we got to Cloverleaf, the foal was born, but we got to watch her nursing for the first time. You can't imagine how cute she was! She's a little bay filly—you know, brown with a black mane and tail—but she's got these gigantic ears and long spindly legs with big knobby knees."

Stevie could picture the newborn foal. She knew it was a female because Carole had called it a filly. Males were called colts. Stevie had seen pictures of foals less than an hour old struggling to their feet for their first meals, short tails swishing tentatively. "Oh, she must be so cute!" Stevie said. "Hey, can we visit her tomorrow?"

"Well, I don't know about that," Carole told her. "Newborn foals are very delicate. Judy said the trainer is going to have to keep almost constant watch for the next couple of days. You can't believe the number of diseases foals can get right after they're born—"

"Well, I'm not going to give her any germs, if that's what you're scared of," Stevie said. She was hurt that Carole would think she was any less able to be careful around a newborn than Carole herself would be.

"Well, it's not just that," Carole protested. "I mean, it was sort of a special thing that I got to be there and I wouldn't want Judy to think that just anybody could crowd into the stable, you know what I mean?" Carole asked.

There was a part of Stevie that did know what Carole meant—or at least understood why she wanted to be special. But most of her was just hurt by the implication that she would upset the foal while Carole wouldn't. That was like Carole—trying to share, but winding up bragging instead. "How come you're less of a 'just anybody' than I am?" Stevie asked suspiciously.

"Oh, I didn't mean it that way, Stevie," Carole said quickly. "It's just that, well, I don't know, I sort of felt, like I was the luckiest person in the world to be there. The whole time, I was thinking how great it would be if you and Lisa could be there, too. But this wasn't our horse or our stable. I was just kind of an uninvited guest. So, I was afraid if I asked to invite somebody else, they'd tell me to go away. Does that make sense?"

"Just a little," Stevie conceded. She was sure, though, that if she had been there, she would have telephoned her best friends and told them to come right away. Carole could be a little timid. Nobody ever accused Stevie of that. "You'll be sure to let us know if Delilah gets ready to deliver, won't you?" Stevie asked.

"I mean, Lisa and I won't be uninvited guests *then*, will we?"

"Of course I'll call you. And you can bet I'll be there," Carole told her. "As soon as Judy says Delilah's getting ready to deliver, I'm moving into the stable. Dad already got me a cot from the base, and a sleeping bag and a bunch of camping stuff so I won't have to leave Delilah's side. I wouldn't miss this for the world! And since I'll be there, you'll be there. Lisa, too. It's a promise."

Stevie knew she meant that. When it came to horses, Carole could be just as stubborn and determined as Stevie was—maybe even more so.

"Okay, then in the meantime, I'm going to be very busy with this gymkhana. I've never been in one. Have you?" Stevie asked.

"Oh, sure. We had one at the last base Dad was stationed at. It was fun. We had a rope race where you had to hold a rope with your partner and go around the poles. Then in another race, you had to hold an egg on a spoon."

"Oh, those are the ordinary kinds of races Mrs. Reg told me about," Stevie said. "I'm trying to do something a little different—I want this to be the *best*! That's why I want to borrow the Laser Tag. And, you know what I found that I think will be perfect, but I'm just not exactly sure how? A Hula-Hoop! Say, your dad has all kinds of fifties stuff. Do you think he has a Hula-Hoop somewhere?"

"I'll ask him," Carole said without enthusiasm. "But I don't remember seeing anything like that. Oh, he's at the door now. Gotta go. I want to tell him about the foal."

"Don't forget to ask about the Hula-Hoop, huh?" Stevie reminded her.

"Uh, sure," Carole said, but she didn't sound sure, and that irritated Stevie. "Bye."

Stevie stared at her phone for a while after she'd hung up. It had been a peculiarly unsatisfying phone call from her best friend. Well, one of her best friends. She picked up the phone to call Lisa.

A FEW BLOCKS away, Lisa was grinning with pride. She leaned back, lifting the front legs of her chair off the floor. She held a sheaf of papers filled with her tidy handwriting in front of her. The job was almost complete now. She only had to type the rules on her mother's computer and she'd be able to make as many copies as she needed.

She had decided to make five rules for each section of the rule book. The rule book itself began with the statement of purpose. That had taken her the most time. It read: "The purpose of The Saddle Club is to increase the knowledge and enjoyment of horseback riding for its members." For a while, she'd thought of just putting, "The purpose of The Saddle Club is threefold: horses, horses, and horses," but that seemed silly. Anyway, once she knew what her purpose was, the rules were easy.

Regular meetings would be held once a week, on Thursdays from three to five o'clock. Members had to come to meetings, but if they couldn't, they could miss up to one a month. If they missed any more, they'd have to pay fines of one dollar per missed meeting. If they missed three in a row, they could be voted out by other members. If they were late to meetings, they'd be fined twenty-five cents for each quarter hour they were late. Meetings would follow the standard *Rules of Order*.

Officers would be elected by the members. There would be a president, vice president, and secretary-treasurer.

Lisa figured Carole would be the president because she was the best rider. Stevie would be the vice president because she was the next-best rider and she was too disorganized to be the secretary-treasurer. Lisa herself would be the secretary-treasurer.

There were eight more pages of rules, including sections on projects, new members, and dues, all neatly detailing every aspect of The Saddle Club. Lisa had spent a lot of time on the section on projects, since one of the things members had to do was to help others in the Club. After all, the Club had been formed when she and Carole had pitched in to help Stevie with her math project for school.

She was very proud of what she'd done. She was sure Carole and Stevie would be, too. In fact, she was about to call one of them when the phone rang. It was Stevie calling her.

"Oh, I was just going to call you," Lisa said.

"I wanted to tell you what Max said to me," Stevie explained. "He wants *me* to plan a gymkhana for every afternoon of the three-day event next month. Can you believe it?"

"What's a gymkhana?" Lisa asked. Stevie explained about the games and races she was working on.

"Oh, like relay races, huh? I know a neat race you can do carrying an egg in a spoon. I bet that would be fun on a horse."

"That's the oldest race in the book," Stevie said. "I want to come up with some new things. This time it's going to be more fun than ever. That's why Max asked *me* to do it. See, he knows he can count on me to be outrageous."

"I guess that's true," Lisa agreed, but she really didn't see anything wrong with carrying an egg in a spoon. It certainly wouldn't be easy on a horse. "Well, I've been busy, too," Lisa said, trying to change the subject to one more to her liking. "I've been working on a Saddle Club project."

"Is there one?" Stevie asked.

"Well, there's our new set of rules and regulations," Lisa said proudly. She waited for Stevie to be impressed, but she was soon disappointed.

"You mean like rules for the games I'm making up?" Stevie asked.

"No, rules for the Club," Lisa went on. "You know how frustrated we always are when we have a meeting and then it's over and we haven't really accomplished anything? Now we can accomplish things. Wait'll you see—"

"Rules aren't my strong point," Stevie told Lisa.

"Well, you just don't like the dumb rules they have at school and the strict ones Max makes up. These are *good* rules. They're just absolutely going to *make* The Saddle Club. Now, finally, we're going to be a *real* club."

"We weren't already a *real* club?" Stevie wondered.

"Not really. At least, not until now. Wait till you see," Lisa said again.

"And wait'll you see what wonderful and outrageous games I come up with!"

"See you Monday," Lisa told her.

"Right," Stevie said.

Lisa wasn't awfully surprised that Stevie was lukewarm about her project. She'd see, though, Lisa was sure, how much better and more fun it would be to have a club that really was a club. It just wasn't the sort of thing Stevie would be excited about right away. She didn't think much of rules. But Carole, on the other hand, would be excited about it all.

"OH, DAD, YOU can't imagine how wonderful it was!" Carole cooed from the couch in the living room.

"I think I can, honey," Colonel Hanson told his daughter. He peered around the corner at her from the kitchen. "Birth is probably the most exciting thing in the world."

"I was right next to Judy the whole time, too," Carole continued. "I watched her examine the mare and the filly. The little baby kept trying to nip at her hands. I think she was looking for more milk!"

Carole was practically exploding with excitment and wanted to share every detail with her father. Stevie certainly hadn't been a satisfactory audience—too involved with her games. A gymkhana would be fun, to be sure, but it wasn't in the same league as a newborn foal.

The phone rang. Carole dashed into the kitchen. Maybe it was about Delilah, she thought. She picked up the receiver from just beneath her father's hand. He stepped back, amused.

"Oh, it's you, Lisa," Carole said, disappointment in her voice.

Of course Carole had been about to call Lisa and tell her about the foal, but before she could even get into it, Lisa began telling her about rules and The Saddle Club. Carole's mind was so focused on the newborn foal that she really couldn't make much sense of Lisa's excitement. It seemed an awful lot like Stevie and the gymkhana. It was clear to Carole that this was no time to try to talk to Lisa about the foal. It would be better to tell her father the rest of the story.

"Gee, Lisa, that sounds great," Carole said, mustering all the sincerity she could find for whatever Lisa was talking about. "But I'm kind of busy with my dad now. Mind if we talk about this on Monday?"

Quickly, the phone conversation ended. For a moment Carole paused to wonder what Lisa had been talking about. Rules? The Club didn't have any rules. Right then, it didn't really matter to Carole anyway. All she could think about was the foal.

4

THE THING ABOUT being mad at Stevie and Carole was that Lisa couldn't be mad at them while they were at class. They all had too much fun together when they were riding.

As soon as the three of them were on their horses on Monday morning, all the irritations from Friday were gone. It was a new week, a fresh start.

All twelve of the stable's summer-camp students were in the class, which took place in the outdoor ring. The ring, at the back of the stable, was really a large rectangle, sixty by eighty meters. Max stood in the center and barked orders at his eager students.

"Today, we're going to try something a little different," Max began. "I'm thinking of starting a drill team. This isn't exactly a tryout, but I want to see how well each of you can follow the orders and control your horse. Both of those are extremely important for drill work."

Lisa's heart sank. She was sure she didn't have the knowledge or experience to be able to do this at all. She'd seen drill teams doing their exercises. In fact, she'd seen an exhibition of it on cable television not long ago. It had looked just about impossible, considering the skill needed for such precision, but it also had looked wonderful. Lisa's fear was so mixed up with her excitement that she wasn't sure which she should be feeling. She looked over at Stevie and Carole, paired together on the other side of the ring. The looks on their faces answered the question for her: She should be excited.

"Listen up!" Max called. "I want a single line, evenly spaced. Get your horses trotting and maintain a trot throughout this exercise."

Usually Max didn't use a riding crop when he was teaching, but today he was strutting around, slapping the riding crop against his leg and the palm of his hand. He looked very stern. It made Lisa more nervous than usual.

"Up! Down! Up! Down! Pay attention, now, Lisa. You know how to post better than that!" Max yelled as they all started trotting.

So even when Max was looking like a movie director, he was still paying attention to every single mistake Lisa could make. Her heart sank. If she couldn't keep up with his instructions, she'd never make the drill team!

"Heels down!" Lisa pushed down on her heels as hard as possible. "Much better now, Betsy," Max continued. "But you must *remember* to keep your heels down." Lisa realized that she was getting so paranoid that she assumed Max was *always* criticizing her. "Look at Lisa, Betsy," he said. "She's got her heels way down. You want yours like that, too." Lisa smiled to herself.

Quickly, however, she found that sitting properly on her horse, with her heels down, wasn't going to be her only problem. The real trick of this exercise was to keep her horse at a dead-even pace—and aligned with all the other horses. If one horse speeded up, its rider had to slow it down, or everyone *else* had to speed up. The most important thing was unison.

"Now, down to a walk," Max said. Lisa reined in on Pepper. He seemed only too happy to walk. She patted his neck, rewarding him for keeping up his trot so nicely. "We'll try this once at a walk, and then we'll be back trotting," Max said. Then he described how they were to walk their horses in a figure eight across the center of the ring, alternating sides at the crossing point in the middle of the eight. If they messed up and let more than one horse pass at a time, the figure would be uneven.

Lisa was sure she'd be the one to mess it up. That made her all the more determined to do it right.

She was following Betsy Cavanaugh, who still wasn't sitting properly on her horse, Barq. He could tell it, too, and was giving her trouble, breaking gait and sort of sidling off course.

"Look straight ahead, Betsy," Max said. Betsy turned her head and focused on her lane with determination. In response, her horse got back where she wanted him. But Lisa was still worried; if Betsy lost her concentration, it could make Lisa mess up as well.

And, of course, it happened. When Betsy got to the cross in the eight, she was so busy looking to her right to see if the other horse was coming that Barq, confused by her different signals, came to a sudden halt. Two horses went past him before she could get him back into gear and across the middle of the eight.

Lisa wasted no time in making up her mind. She urged Pepper in front of the next horse—Comanche, with Stevie on board—and hurried across after Betsy. Lisa's maneuver left Stevie groaning at her, since she was all ready to go across the path, but it kept the figure eight in balance, with six horses on each half.

"Nice work, Lisa," Max said. "When one person makes a mistake, everybody *else* has to correct it."

Did she hear it right? Max was actually praising her!

"Sorry, Lisa," Betsy called over her shoulder. "I'm just having a terrible time with Barq today—or else it's me. I don't know."

Lisa knew. It had clearly been Betsy's fault, but since Max had lavished her with praise, she didn't want to be mean to Betsy. "No problem, Betsy," Lisa said magnanimously. "Horses have bad days, too, just like people."

"Nice work," Max said to the entire class at the end of the lesson. "If you all enjoyed that, we can do more of it. Who thought it was fun?"

Lisa glanced around at her classmates. Most of them looked sort of frustrated and tired. It was true that it had been a tough lesson. Max had shouted a lot—and not just at Betsy. Still, it had been fun for Lisa, and *very* satisfying when she'd succeeded. Lisa put her hand up.

To her surprise, only two other hands went up—Stevie's and Carole's. For a second, Lisa thought Max was trying to hide a smile. Then he spoke. "Okay, if you three enjoyed it, then I think it would be a good idea for you to work on drills. We'll have additional classes Monday, Wednesday, and Friday at three. Now, pair up, walk your horses around the circle until they've cooled down, then break for lunch. At two o'clock this afternoon, we're going to work on grooming, so put your horses in their stalls for now, untack them, and give them fresh water and hay. *Dis-missed*!!"

"Wasn't that just great?" Stevie asked Carole as the two of them led their horses to their stalls. "I mean, it's like almost a perfect combination of the things I enjoy about riding—equitation and dressage. The only thing missing is jumping and, I guess, cross-country, and racing, and uh, well, check that. What I enjoy about riding is *everything*! Drill work included."

"It's neat," Carole agreed. "Since I lived on Marine Corps bases for ten years, I've seen an awful lot of drill work—mostly on foot, you know, like parades. This is really the first time I've gotten to do it, unless you count the time my Girl Scout troop marched in the Marine Corps Birthday Parade a couple of years ago."

"I don't think that's exactly the same thing," Stevie said, laughing.

"Me neither." Carole grinned. "It's much more fun on horseback. And I just knew when Max asked who had liked it that it would be the three of us."

"Yeah, I'm glad about that," Stevie agreed. "After all, we are The Saddle Club."

"You going to have lunch now?" Carole asked.

"No, I forgot my sandwich. It doesn't matter, though. I've got something I have to work on as soon as I untack Comanche."

"If you're in such a rush, I'll untack him for you," Carole offered.

"Would you?"

"Sure I would," Carole told her, reaching for the reins. Gladly, Stevie relinquished them.

"See you later," she said, dashing off to the tack room.

Carole really didn't mind at all. She'd rather spend time with horses than doing almost anything. Besides, it would make the time pass faster until Judy came to check Delilah for the day.

LATER, LISA FOUND Carole sitting on a knoll by the paddock where Delilah was being kept until she foaled. It was next to her foaling stall, in sight of the office so she could be watched all the time. Carole was eating her sandwich and drinking her soda, but one hundred percent of her attention was on Delilah.

"How's she doing?" Lisa asked as she sat down beside her friend.

"Judy says she's doing just fine. You always have to be concerned about a mare with her first foal, but Judy says Delilah seems to be a good mother. She eats her special mash and she's resting a lot. Judy says it should be just fine."

"She seems to be kind of listless," Lisa said, observing how slowly Delilah walked.

"That's just because she's gotten so big now that it's almost hard for her to walk. But Judy says she'll be back in good shape within a few weeks after the birth. She'll be running in the paddock with her foal and that'll slim her right down again. She'll be her old self in no time. Isn't that amazing?"

For a second, Lisa wondered if she was really talking to Carole—or to Judy. Then she remembered why she particularly wanted to see Carole.

"I have your set of rules," Lisa told her. She had spent hours over the weekend working on her mother's computer, inputting everything on the word processor. Her mother had helped her, and when they'd finally printed it all out, it was beautiful—as pretty as a term paper, Lisa thought.

"What rules?" Carole asked.

"The Saddle Club rules," Lisa said, containing her impatience. "Remember, I told you about them Friday when I called? I know you were busy, but I'm sure I told you about all this work I'd done so we could have a *real* club. Remember?"

"Oh, yeah," Carole said vaguely, taking the papers from Lisa's hand. "I'll read them later, okay?"

"Okay," Lisa agreed. "And we'll have a meeting on Thursday afternoon after class, at TD's, to make any changes you guys want. Then we can ratify them. That means make them official."

"Thursday," Carole echoed. "Okay. Look at the way she's eating now." Lisa realized Carole was talking about Delilah again. "It's like she's hungry all the time. And Judy says that's good. She needs fresh hay and fresh water constantly. I'm going to muck out her stall before Judy gets here. Oh, how I love doing things for that horse!"

Lisa liked to do things for horses too, but mucking out stalls wasn't high on her list. "I've got to find Stevie. Know where she is?"

"She was in an awful hurry right after class, but I don't know where she went. Try the indoor ring. She was headed in that direction."

"See you," Lisa said, but she really didn't think her friend heard her at all. Carole was already headed for Delilah's stall. Lisa made her way down the knoll and into the stable. It seemed terribly dark inside, in comparison to the bright summer sunshine. They were spending almost all of their riding time outdoors, mostly in the ring, and sometimes on the trails. It was nice to be out in the fresh air. The class only used the cramped indoor ring on rainy days. It seemed a long time since Lisa had taken her first lesson in that ring.

Lisa passed the tack room and peered into the indoor ring. There was Stevie. She'd borrowed a pony. Lisa knew that any horse less than four feet ten inches tall at the withers was called a pony. A lot of mounted games took place on ponies because the ponies were what the little kids could ride. Stevie, it seemed, was trying to determine whether a pony could do one of the games she was planning.

While Lisa watched, Stevie climbed onto Nickel, a pretty silver-colored pony. She held a Hula-Hoop in her right hand. She put the hoop around her right arm and began trying to get it to swing around her arm. It did just fine when it was *up*, but as soon as it came *down*, it smacked into the soft dirt and bounced off her arm. It wasn't working at all. The pony was just too short. She tried swinging it over her head, but right away, it got tangled in her hard hat. Angrily, Stevie threw the thing across the ring.

Next, Lisa watched her take a spoon with a marshmallow on it, climb on Nickel, and begin galloping across the ring. The marshmallow fell off right away. Stevie dismounted, picked it up, and climbed up again. This time the marshmallow fell off before she even got back in the saddle. She picked it up a third time, mashed it into the spoon so it was more of a glob than a marshmallow, climbed into the saddle, and was off. The only problem was that when she got to the end of the ring, where there was a bucket, she couldn't get the gooey marshmallow out of the spoon and into the bucket. After the third try at shaking it loose, she threw *that* across the ring as well, so it landed near the abandoned Hula-Hoop.

Something told Lisa this was no time to try to talk to Stevie. As quietly as she had come, she left, going into the tack room. There, she quickly spotted Stevie's shoes. She rolled up a copy of the rules and stuck it into one of Stevie's shoes, leaving a note about the Thursday meeting at TD's.

Stevie would find the note there and they could talk about the new rules on Thursday at TD's. She was sure Stevie would be in a better mood by then. Well, pretty sure.

Lisa fetched her own sandwich and soda from the refrigerator and looked for a place to eat. Just as she stepped into the stall area, she saw Estelle Duval, the new French girl, eating alone.

"Can I sit down?" Lisa asked.

"*Mais, oui,*" Estelle said. "Of course."

Lisa just loved the sound of her accent.

5

ON THURSDAY AFTERNOON, Lisa couldn't find Stevie and Carole after camp was over. It was time for The Saddle Club meeting at TD's—their favorite ice cream store, in the nearby shopping center—and it was an important meeting, too. It was the meeting Lisa had called so they could discuss and approve all the rules she'd written.

When she couldn't find her friends, Lisa decided they must have left for TD's, thinking *she'd* already gone. She changed into her jeans and street shoes and set out for the shopping center, a little annoyed to have been left behind.

As soon as she crossed the roadway, Lisa spotted Estelle walking in the same direction she was headed. She and Estelle had eaten lunch together two days in a row and Lisa was really getting to like her. She was so chic, so sophisticated, so nice!

It surprised Lisa that Estelle seemed to want to be her friend. After all, Estelle had told her she had been riding since she was a toddler, and most of the friends she talked about were really fancy people, like princes and counts and children of diplomats. She'd been to school in several different countries and spoke four languages. Lisa only spoke English, a few words of French, and pig latin!

"Hey, Estelle! Wait up!" Lisa called, and jogged up to the French girl. "Which way are you going?" she asked.

"I'm going to the little shopping center," Estelle told her. "I wanted to see if there is a jewelry store there. I have a necklace that needs to have a new gold chain."

"Well, I'm going that way, too, though I don't have to buy any jewelry today," Lisa joked. Then she explained she was meeting friends at TD's. "You were having some trouble today on Nero, weren't you?" she asked after a moment as they continued on their way.

"Oh?" Estelle said. She seemed to be surprised that Lisa had noticed, but the fact was that everybody had noticed. Nero had ended up doing almost exactly what he'd wanted to do all through the class. That was really bad. Lisa had been taught from her very first lesson that a rider had to be the one in control, and the horse needed to know it.

"Nero was in such a bad mood!" Estelle explained. "You see, I am much more used to my own horse,

Napoleon. He would never behave that way."

"Your own horse!" Lisa exclaimed. "And you had to leave him in France, I guess. You must miss him a lot."

"I certainly do. He's a white horse, a beautiful stallion. He was a gift to me from a friend of my father's—the ambassador," she explained. "But I have had him since my seventh birthday. I rode him for hours that day, and every day since, when I am at home. He never acted so naughty like Nero was today."

"I thought you lived in the city of Paris. Do you keep him in the city?" Lisa asked, recalling her earlier conversations with Estelle.

"Oh—uh, no, but he is kept at our country home in Normandy, northwest of Paris. We go there on weekends and for vacations. That's when I ride him. At other times, the stable manager exercises him for me, you see?"

Lisa *did* see. Her mind's eye built a spacious country estate with a large barn and rolling hills where horses frolicked gracefully through the spring flowers in the pastures. Liveried staff tended to the home while the Duvals were in Paris, and catered to their every whim when they returned to the country. It seemed so incredibly elegant that Lisa could hardly believe it was true.

"You know, Estelle, I haven't been riding very long," Lisa explained. "I just started a few months ago. I really love it, though, and every time I hear about somebody like you, who has been riding since she was really little, well, it makes me wish I'd started it a long time ago, too. I hate to think of all the wonderful rides I missed!"

"But Lisa, all the rides are *not* wonderful," Estelle corrected her.

"You mean like all the trouble you had with Nero today?"

"Well, that too, but let me tell you about the pony I had *before* Napoleon. That one was a mare. Her name was Étoile—French for 'star' because of the perfect five-pointed star on her forehead. But it was the only perfect thing about her. One day I was riding her. I was just a little girl then, of course. By mistake, I happened to tug at her mane when I was standing up in the saddle, trying to get my balance. It must have hurt her terribly, for right away, she began trying to kick at me with her hind foot. I pulled the reins to make her stop. Then I climbed down from her saddle right there in the middle of the field, and I told Maman I was never going to ride the beast again!"

Estelle laughed so hard at the story that Lisa began laughing, too. She could just see the stubborn child informing her mother she was through. But she couldn't see herself trying the same thing with Max! Max certainly wouldn't force people to ride if they didn't enjoy it. But there was no way he would let somebody quit just because one bad thing happened—even a nasty fall. Lisa decided it was a good thing for Estelle that Max wasn't her mother.

The two girls strolled across the parking lot of the little shopping center. It wasn't really a mall. It only boasted a supermarket, a few shoe stores, a drugstore, a record store, a jewelry store, and the ice cream parlor, TD's. If what you wanted after riding class was an ice-cream sundae, there was no place better than TD's. Lisa paused at TD's, but there was no sign of Stevie or Carole. Realizing they must have been delayed, she continued to walk with Estelle.

Together, the girls went into the jewelry store. Estelle spoke with the salesman for a long time, though Lisa couldn't hear what she was saying. Lisa loved jewelry and always had fun looking at it. She could imagine a day when she might have long conversations with jewelers the way Estelle was, but for now, she satisfied herself with glancing at the costume jewelry section. She looked at the pins under the glass counter. There, in the center, was a pin with the silhouette of a horse head superimposed on a horseshoe. The horse's ears were perked alertly, his mane brushed slightly by the wind. The whole effect was so pretty that it nearly took Lisa's breath away. Somehow, that pin seemed to represent everything Lisa loved about horses. If only . . .

"Oh, this man can't help me at all," Estelle whined, interrupting Lisa's thoughts. "I have wasted my time!"

"Not exactly," Lisa consoled her, turning from the showcase with the horse-head pin. "We got to walk together and have a nice talk."

"Let's get out of here," Estelle said, leading Lisa back onto the shopping center sidewalk. "You have to meet your friends now, no?"

"Oh, yes," Lisa said, heading for TD's. But even before she entered the ice cream shop, she could see through the window that neither Stevie nor Carole was there yet. She wondered what had happened. How could she have missed them at Pine Hollow? She was just about certain they'd gone by the time she left.

"What's the matter, Lisa?" Estelle asked.

"I'm looking for Stevie and Carole," she explained. "We were supposed to meet here. I'm sure they'd left Pine Hollow by the time I did, so where are they?"

"Carole Hanson and Stevie Lake?" Estelle asked. Lisa nodded. "But I saw them go," Estelle said. "Carole, she went off in the truck with that woman doctor, Judy is her name? And, then, Stevie, she saddled up the pony, Nickel, and was taking him out into the field. She had the most tremendous bag full of things, but I don't know what was in it."

Lisa got a deep sinking feeling. It was clear that both Carole and Stevie had completely forgotten The Club meeting they were supposed to have. Each was so wrapped up in her own special project that she didn't even remember *Lisa's* special project! Lisa was just about to explode with anger and hurt. How could her best friends let her down?

"So look at us now," Estelle said brightly. "You came here to meet your friends, but they're not coming. I came here to go to the jewelry store, but they did not have what I wanted! We are in the same pair of shoes!"

Lisa laughed at Estelle's joke and she was glad for it. She swallowed hard and scrunched her eyes to hide any possible tears. "Well, since neither of our plans worked out, how about some ice cream?"

"That's a great idea," Estelle agreed, and together they headed for TD's.

Within a few minutes, they'd found a table and ordered their sundaes. Lisa was surprised to learn that Estelle wasn't familiar with all the possibilities at an ice cream parlor.

"Don't you have ice cream in France?" she asked.

"Of course we do, but we don't have it so fancy as you do here—and I don't know what these things are." She lifted the menu and pointed. "Like what's this 'marshmallow fluff'?"

The way she said *fluff* made it sound more like *floof.* Lisa laughed.

Estelle seemed a little hurt. "I'm sorry," Lisa said quickly. "It's just that you make it sound so much better than it is! But it's pronounced *fluff,*" she said, emphasizing the short *u.* Estelle tried it again and got it right. Lisa told her what it was.

"But it must be marvelous—sort of like meringue, eh?"

"Want to try it? They can add it on top of your hot fudge."

Estelle's eyes sparkled at the idea. Lisa stepped over to the counter and asked the waitress to add marshmallow fluff to one of the sundaes. Then she returned and the two girls talked.

Lisa found that talking to Estelle was fun. She had done so many exciting things in her life, and lived in so many interesting places, that Lisa was almost jealous.

"Did I tell you about the princess who used to be in my class at boarding school?"

"Princess? A *real* princess?" Estelle nodded. "What country?" Lisa asked breathlessly.

"Oh, goodness, I'm not sure I remember. One of those small ones, you know?" Estelle told her.

Lisa didn't know, but she told Estelle she did. It was one thing if a person needed to know what marshmallow fluff was. Anybody could need to know about that. But it was another thing altogether to need to be told about entire countries, even small ones. Lisa decided to cling to her ignorance rather than exhibit it.

Estelle went on to tell a story about how this girl had invited everybody in the class to her parents' castle for the weekend, but it turned out that it was such a small estate that there wasn't room in the castle for all the girls to have their own rooms. As the tale unfolded, Lisa was simply swept away. To her, it was like a movie come alive, a dream come true. She just loved listening to Estelle's stories. What a life she'd lived—and how lucky Lisa was even to know her.

Before she knew it, she had an empty sundae dish in front of her, and the clock on the wall told her it was time to get home.

"I've got to go," she said. "My mom will be expecting me."

"Me too," Estelle told her. "My chauffeur is picking

me up here in a little while. Would you like a ride home?"

Lisa was tempted. Really tempted. But her house was only a short walk and she really couldn't wait any longer. "Another time," she said.

They paid their check and left TD's. Lisa set off for home at a quick pace. She'd had such a nice time with Estelle that, for an hour, she'd completely forgotten about Carole and Stevie and how much they had hurt her. She'd forgotten about how much she'd been looking forward to discussing her rules with them. Talking to Estelle was like being swept away in the fantasy land of a wonderful book. Everything about her was so different, and so exciting!

Lisa's copy of the Club's rules was in her tote bag. She hadn't even taken it out at TD's because there hadn't been a meeting.

But there *had* been, she told herself. She'd called a meeting at TD's and just because two people hadn't showed up it didn't mean there hadn't been a meeting. There was nothing in the rules that said that everybody had to be there for a meeting. So, she would simply tell Stevie and Carole that the meeting had taken place without them and the rules had been voted into effect. Unanimously.

After all, that was true, wasn't it?

6

THE NEXT MORNING, Stevie slipped into the locker area of the tack room. She was really tired. After class yesterday, she'd spent about three hours trying to teach Nickel not to shy when he saw the Hula-Hoop twirl. The only thing she accomplished was getting him to shy as soon as he saw the thing, whether it was twirling or not. A Hula-Hoop race was definitely out. Today she'd try something with the baton from her closet. She couldn't think of any use for the broken umbrella.

She took off her sneakers and pulled on her riding boots. A lot of the time Stevie liked to ride in jeans and low boots, but in the summer, when she was spending five or six hours a day on horseback, breeches and high boots, though hotter, were a lot more comfortable. The high boots protected her legs from the straps and flaps on the saddle.

When her boots were on, she tried to shove her shoes and her boot hooks into her cubby, but there was something in it at the back, blocking the way. She leaned over to look into the knee-high nook. She couldn't see anything, but she also still couldn't fit her shoes in. It wasn't until she got down on her hands and knees and peered at the back of the cubby that she saw, crumpled and torn, the papers that Lisa had left for her the other day.

She reached in and pulled them out. At the top it read:

THE SADDLE CLUB
Rules

That was when Stevie remembered that Lisa's note called for a Saddle Club meeting at TD's. She'd gotten so busy with Nickel that she'd forgotten all about the meeting! She sat on the bench, staring at the papers. There was a dull, empty feeling in her stomach. She'd let her friends down.

Just then, Carole came into the locker area.

"Oh, Carole, I'm so sorry about yesterday," Stevie began, serious for once.

"What about yesterday?" Carole asked.

"The Club meeting at TD's . . ."

Carole looked blank for a second, then gasped. "Oh, no!" she said. "I forgot all about it. What happened?"

"I don't know," Stevie said. "That's what I'm sorry about. I wasn't there."

"You weren't? I wasn't either. I went over to the stable with Judy to check on that newborn foal. She was afraid the filly was getting sick, but it turned out she was okay. I looked for you to see if you wanted to come along, but I couldn't find you."

"Yeah, well, I was pretty busy too, planning the gymkhana, but that means we left Lisa out in the cold. Unless maybe she forgot, too."

"No way, considering how excited she was about those rules. Boy, I feel like a worm! Let's see if we can find her."

"Yeah, let's."

"Oh, Stevie!" It was Mrs. Reg, calling from her office off the tack room. "Come in here a moment, will you?"

"Sure, just a sec," Stevie called back. Then she turned to Carole. "Listen, you find Lisa and tell her how sorry we are. We can have a meeting at my house after drill practice this afternoon, okay? I've got to talk to Mrs. Reg. I'll see you both in class."

"I'll tell her, but I still feel like a worm."

"Well, she knows how busy we've both been—"

"Yeah, but still . . ."

"Stevie!" Mrs. Reg called.

"Coming."

Carole went in search of Lisa. Stevie stepped into Mrs. Reg's office and sat down on the tack box in front of her desk. "So, now, tell me," Mrs. Reg began. "How're you doing in making up games and races?"

That was another thing Stevie wasn't feeling too good about at the moment. So far, this day hadn't been exactly terrific. "To tell you the truth, Mrs. Reg, not so well. I've been trying to come up with some really original ideas. I spent a lot of time trying to make up a game with a Hula-Hoop, but that just spooked Nickel, and if he spooks, most of the other ponies will too. Then I tried a marshmallow game. No luck. I was sure I could get something going by riding on the saddle backward, but that only got Nickel confused—and me bruised! Finally, I've been working on something to do with Laser Tag. It's going to be wonderful, I'm sure, but the trouble is, I don't have a Laser Tag set to use yet. So, all in all, not so hot."

"How about an egg-and-spoon race?" Mrs. Reg asked brightly.

Stevie couldn't believe it. Every time she talked to someone about the gymkhana, all anybody ever suggested was an egg-and-spoon race. "Everybody already knows about egg-and-spoon races. I want to do something different, something interesting, something *fun*! Isn't that what Max wants, too?"

"Max wants a good set of games," Mrs. Reg said. "That doesn't necessarily mean they have to be so unusual that nobody can do them! Use your horse sense, Stevie," Mrs. Reg urged.

"Don't worry, Mrs. Reg," Stevie said. "I'm working on something with a baton that will be lots of fun. You'll see."

"Yes, I'm sure I will," Mrs. Reg said. "And I put a dozen eggs in the fridge if you want to give that a try, okay?"

Just then, the bell sounded. "Hey, class is about to start and I've still got to tack up Comanche. I'll talk to you next week again, Mrs. Reg."

"Okay," Mrs. Reg agreed. "By then, you should have a pretty good idea of the games you want to include, and you and I can start to plan a schedule and figure out how much time to allow and how to award points for prizes."

Schedule? Points? Prizes? How could they possibly do all that? Stevie had a growing awareness that she was going to have to move faster and work harder to make up the games if Mrs. Reg expected to plan a schedule and point system next week. That would mean another couple of hours on Nickel over the weekend. But how could she work harder than she was already working? It seemed impossible, for her and for Nickel.

Poor pony, she thought, sighing, as she headed for Comanche's stall with his tack. *Poor me.*

LISA ALMOST ALWAYS felt happy when she was riding. She'd gotten to like just about everything to do with it. She loved her clothes, the sleek breeches, the tall boots with the rich shine. She'd even gotten over being self-conscious about the hard hat they had to wear. She had only had to fall off once to appreciate how it could really be a lifesaver. When she'd first gotten her brand-new riding outfit, she'd thought it was silly and noticed how other people, even riders, stared at her. She knew now that was because everything had been so new that it sort of stuck out. Now her riding clothes showed wear—marks on her boots, smudges on her hat. *That* showed she was a real rider and she was proud of those marks and smudges.

Today, while the more advanced riders were in the jumping class, she was taking a "flat class." Estelle rode near her on a trail through some fields near Pine Hollow. Estelle's clothes were even newer than Lisa's. At first that seemed odd to Lisa, but she realized that Estelle must have bought new clothes in America. It would hardly be worth the trouble to bring a worn outfit all the way from France.

"How come you're not taking the jumping class?" Lisa asked. "I mean, you did jump, didn't you, on Napoleon?"

"Napoleon?" Estelle echoed. "Oh, right, well, I can't jump, see. My doctor won't let me do it."

"Why not? He must be a fuddy-duddy doctor if he won't let an experienced rider like you jump! I mean, Max says it's okay for us to start jumping as soon as we've been riding for a year. I just can't wait. I mean, I know he's right, but I'm ready, believe me!"

"I had an accident, you see," Estelle explained. "When I was a little girl, I hurt my back. I was in the hospital for a long time. I spent my seventh birthday in the hospital, it was horrible. The doctor said I should never jump. The risk is too great. So, here I am. Just happy to be able to ride at all."

"Oh, that's terrible. Does it still hurt?"

"My back? Oh, no, but, you see, it *could* hurt, and then I might not be able to ride ever again." Just then, Nero headed off the trail to the other side of the field at a trot. "*Arretez!*" Estelle yelled at him. "*À gauche! Maintenant! Cheval bête!*" Lisa had had enough French in school to know that Estelle was saying, "Stop! Turn left! Now! Stupid horse!"

Red O'Malley, who was instructing the class while Max worked with the jumpers, broke out of the file of riders and cantered over to rescue Estelle. All the riders watched in astonishment while Nero bolted, dumping Estelle unceremoniously in the grass. Within a few seconds, Red had recaptured the horse and led him back to Estelle. She stood in the middle of the field, brushing dirt and grass off her stylish riding breeches. Lisa suspected she was also rubbing something that was going to be a nasty bruise.

"Up you go," Red instructed her. Estelle just glared at the horse.

"I don't think I should have to ride him anymore," Estelle said. "He is too wild."

There were snorts of laughter from some of the riders. Everybody knew that Nero wasn't a wild horse. He was usually very complacent and gentle. Lisa couldn't understand why sweet old Nero was behaving so badly for Estelle.

"Estelle," Red said politely, "Nero just needs to have you let him know who is the boss. If he starts acting up, put more leg on him. It will remind him that you're on board and you're in charge. If that doesn't work, put some pressure on the reins. As a matter of fact, here, get up, and I'll show you what to do."

Reluctantly, Estelle remounted the horse. Red gave her the reins and explained that if she squeezed her fingers on the reins, alternating hands, it would put just the smallest amount of pressure on the bit in the horse's mouth. It wouldn't be enough pressure for him to think it was a signal, but it would be enough to make him think he should pay attention.

"Watch his ears when you do that," Red suggested. "You'll see that he's alert to *you* instead of doing his own thing."

When Estelle was back in the group they all started trotting. Lisa decided to try what Red had suggested, although her own horse, Pepper, hadn't been giving her any trouble. As soon as she squeezed the reins, moving them perhaps only a half an inch, Pepper seemed more alert to her, picked up his pace, and lifted his head sharply. It was a neat trick. Once she had his attention, she stopped doing it, but if he lagged, she could try it again.

Estelle, however, didn't seem to be having the same kind of luck. For the rest of the class she was fighting with Nero, and losing. Lisa thought it very strange indeed that Estelle should have such trouble. She'd never seen an experienced rider let her horse take the lead the way Nero did that day. Estelle must be right, she told herself. There was something terribly wrong with Nero.

When the class finally ended, Lisa got the soda whip. That was another one of Pine Hollow's traditions, and one that almost everybody enjoyed. Each class member pulled a riding whip out of a bucket. One of the whips had a bottle cap attached to it. It meant that rider was in charge of getting sodas for everybody in the class and delivering them to the stalls where the other students would be untacking their horses. Lisa took Pepper to his stall, then quickly scooped eight cans out of the little refrigerator in the tack room.

She delivered the drinks to the riders, ending with Estelle. When she opened Nero's stall, she found Estelle hanging onto the horse's bridle, almost being lifted off the ground by his nodding head. His ears were almost flat back against his head and his eyes were wide open, showing white. Lisa knew those were signs that the horse was very upset.

"Steady, boy," Lisa said, reaching to pat Nero's neck. "Take it easy, now. Nobody's going to hurt you. We just want to take off the bridle and saddle; calm down." He blinked his eyes and seemed to relax a little bit. "Let go of the bridle," Lisa told Estelle. Estelle released the bridle. The reins dangled to the ground. "Not the reins. Hold those!" Lisa told her sharply. It would be very easy for Nero to get his legs tangled in the long reins and then there would be *real* trouble.

Estelle's hand darted toward the reins, but when Nero tried to push her away with his nose, she jumped back, obviously scared. Lisa picked up the reins with her left hand and gave them to Estelle, who accepted them reluctantly.

"Whatsamatter, boy?" Lisa asked, still trying to calm the big horse. "We'll take care of you—no problem. Ready for some hay, maybe some fresh water?"

Lisa knew that the horse couldn't understand her. Max had told them all many times that horses couldn't speak English. But from experience, she also knew that horses could sense fear, and that they reacted with fear of their own. She tried to speak as calmly and fearlessly as possible. Finally, Nero got the message. His ears stood straight up, his head held steady, his liquid brown eyes gazed calmly at her.

Lisa continued to pat him while she removed his bridle. She handed it to Estelle and, with dismay, saw the French girl take it by one of the cheek straps. That was a sure way to tangle it, and Lisa would have to cope with that in a minute. First, though, she needed to finish with Nero. She loosened the girth and removed the saddle. The girls took the tack out of the stall, closed the door carefully, and carried the bridle and saddle back to the tack room.

"Come, help me with Pepper," Lisa said. "I'll show you what you need to do to keep a horse calm. Then we can give them both some water, okay?"

"I know how to take care of a horse!" Estelle snapped. "I have been doing it since I was a little girl!

Do you think I have really learned nothing in all these years? *I* do not need to learn anything. It is Nero who needs a lesson. Max must see to this right away." With that, Estelle turned and stormed off to Max's office.

Lisa was confused. Estelle was an experienced rider. She'd been riding for years. She owned her own horse. Still, she didn't seem to understand the simplest things about riding. It didn't make sense. Something didn't fit at all.

While she untacked Pepper and drank her own soda, Lisa thought about Estelle and the miserable day she had had with Nero. It was possible that Nero was ill. It was even possible that he needed to be taught a lesson, though if a rider felt a horse needed punishment of any kind, it was best to administer it at the very moment it was needed. What seemed the most possible, though, was that riding in France was very different from riding in America. Obviously, Estelle simply didn't know many of the things Lisa had been taught. Riders must be taught differently and horses must be trained differently in France, Lisa reasoned.

It was as if Estelle used a different language with her horse than Lisa did. Max often told his students that they spoke to their horses with their hands and their legs because a horse's sense of communication was more physical than anything. So, how could that be different in France? Lisa asked herself.

Once again, Lisa thought about the white stallion, Napoleon, a gift on Estelle's seventh birthday. Then Lisa recalled that Estelle had also told her that was a day she had spent in a hospital with a back injury. She must have heard it wrong—or else Estelle said it wrong.

When she'd stowed Pepper's tack, she brought him water and fresh hay and then did the same for Nero. By then he was completely calmed down, his same old placid self. He welcomed Lisa's pats and dug into the fresh hay enthusiastically.

Lisa shook her head in confusion. Something seemed out of kilter in her world, but she didn't know what it was.

Having no answer, and lost in thought, she slid his door shut and locked it.

7

"CAROLE, PAY ATTENTION!" Max snapped at Carole in jump class later that Friday. "If *you're* not paying attention, how can you expect your horse to do it?"

Carole tried again to focus. Diablo's ears perked up immediately in response to her soft tug on his reins. She circled the ring until he was in a nice, smooth, rocking canter, then she aimed him straight for the jump. It was a two-foot training jump, hardly a wall, but she knew that jumping high wasn't as important as jumping well. She approached the jump on Diablo, leaning forward ever so slightly, but holding the reins taut until they were close. Smoothly, she rose in the saddle and, keeping her back nearly parallel to the horse's neck, she leaned forward, letting the motion of

Diablo's head move her hands along his neck. Diablo lifted into the air and landed gently on the other side.

"See how well it works when you pay attention?" Max asked. Carole nodded her answer, but she hadn't really heard the question. Already her mind was someplace else. She was listening for the familiar sound of Judy's truck. The vet was due for Delilah's checkup and Carole hoped she'd arrive during the lunch break. Carole had noticed some changes in Delilah, and hoped that meant the foal's birth would be soon.

Something else distracted Carole as well. Lisa stood at the edge of the ring watching the end of the jump class. Carole hadn't had a chance to talk to her yet about missing yesterday's Club meeting. She knew how she'd feel if that had happened to her. She really wanted a chance to explain, but it seemed like every single second of the day was filled, at least up through their drill practice. And if Delilah was as close to her delivery as Carole suspected, she'd be even busier soon.

Just then, the French girl, Estelle, came into the ring and stood next to Lisa. Carole cringed. Estelle gave her goose bumps. Carole had watched her ride enough to know that she was a big phony on horseback—and probably everywhere else, too. When she'd overheard Estelle telling Meg Durham about this horse she'd supposedly been riding since she was seven, Carole had barely been able to contain her snort of laughter. There was no way Estelle had been riding for so long and learned so little! So what was she doing hanging around Lisa? Carole wondered.

AS SOON AS jump class was over, Stevie dashed into the tack room hoping to find Lisa there. There was no sign of her. Stevie took her sandwich and a soda from the refrigerator and went in search of her friend. Finally, in the stable area, she found a small crowd gathered near Delilah's stall. Lisa stood there along with seven or eight other students, watching Judy examine Delilah.

"Lisa, can I talk to you?" Stevie asked. Lisa turned in surprise. "I can't believe I forgot the meeting yesterday," Stevie rushed on. "I mean, I was busy with the gymkhana stuff, but that didn't mean I had to forget the Club meeting. I'm awfully sorry, especially since Carole told me she forgot, too. It was a terrible mistake, and I hope you can forget about it."

"It's okay, Stevie," Lisa said. "I just saw Carole, and she already told me how sorry you both were. It turned out all right anyway. Estelle was with me, so I wasn't hanging around there by myself, you know?"

Stevie felt an unbelievable rush of relief. From the second she'd realized what they'd done, she'd known how she would have felt if two friends had done that to her—and she knew that she wouldn't have been at all nice about it the way Lisa was being. Sighing happily, she slung her arm across Lisa's shoulder. "Thanks for understanding. How about a Club meeting at my house this afternoon after drill?"

"That'd be great," Lisa said.

"Now, what's going on here?" Stevie asked.

"Judy's examining Delilah. Carole's helping her."

Stevie stood on tiptoe to see. Carole was holding Delilah's halter while Judy felt around the horse's large belly. It was hard to believe, Stevie thought, that there really was another whole life growing inside the mare. And it wouldn't be long now before they'd all see it.

"Everything looks fine here," Judy said. Everybody seemed relieved, though there had never been any indication that anything was wrong. "And I still think we're on schedule for a delivery in a couple of weeks. This gal's not rushing into anything!" The girls all laughed. "But I'd better go now. I got a call on the way over here—"

"Judy!" Estelle called from the fringe of the group. "Before you go, could you take a look at Nero? He has been misbehaving terribly."

Judy glanced up at Estelle. "Old Nero? What's his trouble? Max didn't say anything to me—"

"Well, I didn't have time to tell him yet," Estelle explained.

"Sure, I'll look at him now," Judy agreed. "Describe his symptoms to me, will you?" While Judy packed her medical bag, Estelle explained the problems the horse had given her.

"Sounds like he's just cranky," Judy said.

"*Le mot juste!*" Estelle declared. Then she blushed, realizing nobody had understood her. "Excuse my French," she said. "It means that that is just exactly the right word."

Judy picked up her bag and followed Estelle to Nero's stall.

Stevie and a couple of the other girls tried to stifle giggles. They'd seen Estelle riding, and they knew it wasn't Nero who had the problem. *Le mot juste* was *phony,* Stevie thought.

Living near Washington meant that there were a lot of diplomats' children of all nationalities around. Stevie usually found them interesting and fun. Estelle was definitely an exception to that, though. Stevie didn't believe a word of her fantastic stories, and the idea that she'd been riding for a long time was just laughable.

Stevie looked for Lisa to continue their talk, but, much to her surprise, Lisa was following Estelle and Judy to Nero's stall.

Now, what's that about? Stevie asked herself. Shrugging for lack of an answer, Stevie headed for Nickel's stall. Carole was still busy with Delilah, and besides, she had a full hour at lunch to work on a game with a baton. A baton couldn't frighten a pony, could it?

"Hi, boy!" Stevie greeted Nickel cheerfully. Slowly, she pulled the baton out of her bag and showed it to the horse. Without hesitating, he reached for the white rubber tip of the baton and bit. Hard.

TWENTY MINUTES LATER, Lisa and Estelle sat together near the paddocks, eating their lunches.

"Gee, I'm glad to know Nero's okay," Lisa said. "When a horse gets sick, it can be big trouble, you know?"

"Of course I know," Estelle said quickly. "I have taken care of my horse when he was sick. Sometimes it's not pretty, either. Just last year, before the vet could treat him, he even threw up on me. It was awful, but he is my horse, you know, and I care for him like a child." Suddenly, Estelle changed the subject. "What was that you were talking with Stevie and Carole about?" she asked.

"Oh, they were explaining what happened yesterday, why they missed The Club meeting at TD's."

"Club? What is The Club?" Estelle asked.

Lisa had never spoken about the Club to anybody else. It wasn't exactly a secret. It just had always been more like a name for her friendship with Stevie and Carole, and until the rules had come along, that's really all it had been. Now Estelle wanted to know about it, and suddenly Lisa was terribly afraid Estelle would think it was silly.

"Well, we call it The Saddle Club," she explained. "It's sort of silly, I guess." That's all she could think to say.

"But what do you *do?*" Estelle asked insistently.

What did they do? Lisa asked herself. Until she'd written the rules she really would not have been able to answer that question, but now that there were rules, and they had been passed—sort of—she could answer it—sort of.

"Well, we have meetings once a week or so, like yesterday afternoon, only since it was just me, it wasn't much of a meeting. But we plan projects, and help each other, and talk about horses, you know?"

"Oh, it sounds wonderful!" Estelle said. "You know, Lisa, it hasn't been easy for me, being new in America, to meet people and make friends. But a club like *that* . . . how many members are there in this club?"

"Well, just the three of us so far," Lisa told her.

"Three? Only three? Well, that's too bad, then," Estelle said.

Before Lisa could ask her why it was too bad, the bell sounded, signaling them to get ready for the next class. Estelle stood up quickly. "I must go see Max right away," she announced. "I will not ride Nero this afternoon. *Adieu.*" She walked off toward Max's office.

LATE THAT AFTERNOON, as soon as drill class was over, Lisa untacked Pepper, gave him something to eat and drink, and went in search of Stevie and Carole. Unlike the day before, she found them right away. Carole was already in Delilah's stall, carefully grooming her.

"Ready for the meeting?" Lisa asked.

"You bet," Carole said. "I still need to make up a batch of Delilah's special mash, but that'll just take me a few minutes. You and Stevie go on ahead. Don't wait for me. I'll join you at Stevie's, okay?"

"Sure," Lisa agreed. "Know where Stevie is?"

"I think she's having a serious talk with Nickel. She can't get that poor pony to do anything she wants him to."

"I'll go cheer her on," Lisa said. "See you in a little while." Lisa jogged over to Nickel's stall. There she saw Stevie holding a mangled drum majorette's baton.

"What's that for?" she asked.

"Depends on your point of view," Stevie said. "Nickel, for instance, thinks it's dinner, since he already had a piece of it for lunch."

Stevie looked so serious that Lisa couldn't help laughing. "You're funny, you know that?"

"Boy, I wish it were funny," Stevie said. "This old guy is supposed to be the backbone of the pony-game team, and I'm having a heck of a time convincing him to have any fun."

"If anybody can do it, you can," Lisa said encouragingly. "And speaking of having some fun, Carole said we should go along to your house ahead of her. She has to make the special mash for Delilah and will be a couple of minutes late."

"You all ready to go now?" Stevie asked.

"Yup."

"I've got to finish up here first. It'll be about ten minutes. I'll meet you in the tack room, okay?"

Lisa had an idea. "Since you and Carole are each working on something for a few minutes, I think I'll go on ahead. I've got an errand to run at the shopping center. It'll only take me about twenty minutes. I can meet you at your house because it's practically on the way. Okay?"

"Sounds fine to me. If you get there first, get my mom to show you where the chocolate chip cookies are, okay?"

"Deal," Lisa said.

FIFTEEN MINUTES LATER, Lisa was back in the jewelry store at the shopping center, once again looking in the case where the horse-head pin was kept. In her pocket was the birthday cash she'd gotten from her mother's sister. Aunt Elizabeth, after whom she'd been named, was her godmother, too, and a pretty generous one at that. Lisa hoped the money she had would be enough to buy a pin for every member of The Saddle Club. Maybe even more than rules, that would make it a *real* club.

"CAROLE, THAT DOESN'T look right," Max said. "Are you sure you followed the recipe that Judy gave you for Delilah's bran mash?"

"I think so, Max. Look, here, I put a scoop of concentrated grain into the boiling water, then four scoops of wheat bran—"

"No, no, that's not a one—that's a four. You have to start with four scoops of grain. You're going to have to throw this out and start again."

"But *Max*!" Carole said in exasperation.

"You wanted to know how to take care of a mare, Carole," he reminded her.

"Yes, Max," she said, dumping her mistake into the garbage. It wouldn't be at all fair to Delilah to give her a mistake when she and her foal needed wholesome, nourishing food. "But I'm supposed to be somewhere now. Can I use the phone?"

Like all good stables, Pine Hollow had phones near the stalls so someone taking care of a horse wouldn't have to leave it alone to summon help. It was a special privilege to make a call from the stable. Max agreed.

Carole thought it was odd that Stevie and Lisa hadn't gotten to Stevie's when she called, but she left the message with Stevie's brother Chad. He promised to tell Stevie and Lisa that she just couldn't make it.

"NICKEL? NICKEL? YOU didn't really swallow that, did you? Nickel?"

Stevie glared at the pony and he glared back at her dully. He swished his tail uneasily and then stomped at the floor repeatedly. She didn't like the way he was behaving. She'd seen horses with colic before and Nickel was showing signs of it. A colicky horse was one with a digestive problem, a stomachache, but in a horse it could be a very serious problem—especially when it might have been caused by the horse eating something like the rubber end of a baton!

Stevie slipped her fingers into Nickel's mouth and twisted them to make him open up. He didn't like that at all. Nickel pulled away and tried to nip at her.

There was no way she'd be able to see if the rubber was still in his mouth. This was going to take an expert, maybe even a vet. How on earth was she going to explain to Max or Judy how Nickel had eaten a piece of rubber?

But his health was a lot more important than her embarrassment. Stevie secured his stall and went into Max's office. She *had* to tell him what she'd done. He listened carefully while Stevie described Nickel's symptoms and he waited while she explained what might have caused it.

"I'm not sure, Max. I didn't actually see him swallow it. But it could be in him now."

"No time to waste," Max said. "I'll go to Nickel. You call Judy and tell her to get here right away. We'll talk about how it happened later."

Her heart thumping with worry about Nickel, Stevie sat down at the phone at Max's desk and dialed Judy's number. She was so relieved when Judy answered it herself, and even more relieved when Judy told Stevie she was only about five minutes away. She'd be right there.

Before returning to Nickel's stall, Stevie made one more call. She knew Carole and Lisa would understand. She had to stay with Nickel until he was better. It was her responsibility.

"Oh, Chad?" she said when her brother answered the phone. "Listen, I'm in a rush. There's an emergency here at the stable. Tell Carole and Lisa that Nickel's sick and I've got to stay here. I don't know when I'll be home. I'm sorry, but they'll understand. Bye."

She hung up quickly and headed back to Nickel's stall.

LISA WALKED HAPPILY up the stone stairs that led to Stevie's front door and rang the bell. She'd been able to buy four pins with her birthday money. There would be one for each member of The Saddle Club and one for the first new member they voted into the Club. And Lisa knew just who she thought that should be.

Chad Lake opened the door. "Hi there, uh, Lisa. Come on in."

"Carole and Stevie here yet?" she asked, stepping through the doorway.

"Well, not exactly," Chad began uncomfortably. "Both of them called. I mean each of them called. But they didn't know that the other wasn't coming. Say, why don't you come in anyway? I mean, I'm sure Stevie would want you to come in and anyway, if it had been me, I wouldn't have missed a meeting with you." He grinned warmly at her. Lisa was a little surprised by the way he was acting toward her, but she was more surprised by what her friends had done. Even from Chad's slightly garbled message, it was clear that neither Stevie nor Carole was going to be able to make it to *this* meeting either.

Furious, and shrugging off Chad's offer of cookies, milk, or video games, she stomped back down the stairs, shoving The Club pins deep into her pants pocket.

"They'll see," she muttered to herself as she turned toward home. "They'll see."

She barely got the door to her own room closed before the hot tears began streaming down her cheeks. *What had happened to The Saddle Club?*

8

NOBODY EVER SAID Lisa Atwood wasn't resourceful. She always managed to find a way to accomplish things—even when they seemed impossible. Lisa knew this about herself, but she was beginning to think that The Saddle Club would be her greatest challenge.

She stopped crying after a few minutes. Then she sat sullenly on her bed, glaring out at space. She could have gone on doing that for a while, but Dolly scratched at her door. One look at that cute little face with its golden fur, and she couldn't help smiling a little.

She'd worked for hours and hours on the rules for the Club, just to make it a *real* club. Now that she'd accomplished that, it was beginning to look as if it didn't matter to Carole and Stevie what she did. In her orderly mind, the possibilities began slipping into place. If Carole and Stevie wanted out of the Club, she couldn't stop them, and if they left, one of two things would happen: The Club would stop altogether, or—*or* it would continue only if there were other members.

That had to be the answer. Lisa pulled the set of rules out of her desk drawer. Right there, Rule Four in the New Members section said that new members could be voted in at any Club meeting by a majority of the members present. Well, there *was* a Club meeting, right? Just because Carole and Stevie hadn't shown up didn't mean it wasn't a Club meeting.

Lisa decided it was time for formalities. "I'd like to propose a new member for The Saddle Club," she said. Dolly's ears perked up. She lifted her head from her paws and looked at Lisa. "I'd like to propose that we admit Estelle Duval." Dolly put her head back down on her paws. "Is there any discussion?" Dolly blinked her eyes. "Shall we vote?" Lisa asked. "All in favor say 'aye.'" She waited a few seconds and then voted in favor of Estelle's admission to The Saddle Club. "All opposed?" There was no opposition. "Well, then, it's settled," Lisa told Dolly. "We now have four members in The Saddle Club."

She took out the four small pins she'd bought that afternoon and laid them in a line on her bed. She loved the regal horse head with his mane swept back by the wind. She'd be proud to wear her pin, symbol of both her friendship and her love of horses. She picked up the first pin and stepped over to her mirror. Carefully, she unlocked the clasp and slid the pin through the fabric of her blouse. There was a little fingerprint on the horse's head. She took a tissue and wiped the pin until it gleamed.

"Lisa, phone for you," her mother called up the stairs.

Lisa opened her door. "Who is it?" she asked.

"Stevie."

"Tell her I'm busy," Lisa said, and when her mother looked a little bit shocked, she added, "Please."

"Sure, hon," Mrs. Atwood agreed. "I'll tell her."

A few minutes later, there was a call from Carole. Lisa didn't speak to her either. She just wasn't in the mood to hear their excuses.

There was also a little corner of her that knew she wasn't quite ready to tell her friends about the things that had gone on at the Club meetings they'd missed.

They'd find out in time—and it would serve them right for not paying any attention to anything she was doing.

STEVIE HUNG UP the phone in a fury. Trying to talk the Zieglers into letting her borrow their Laser Tag had been a lousy idea. Absolutely nothing was working out. Well, that wasn't quite true, she reminded herself. After all, right after Judy had arrived to examine Nickel, Stevie had found the missing chunk of rubber from the baton. It had landed in the peat and straw on the floor of his stall. It had never gotten anywhere near his stomach. Nickel got a clean bill of health from Judy, and Stevie got a well-deserved lecture about horse care from Max.

What really made her angry, though, was that she'd spent more than a week trying to create new and interesting games and races for the gymkhana and she'd gotten nowhere at all. It certainly wasn't her fault, though. She'd done everything she could and nothing had worked. Now Max was angry with her, Mrs. Reg was worried that they wouldn't have any games for the young riders, Carole was too busy with Delilah to talk to her, and Lisa spent all her time with Estelle Duval. She wasn't getting help from anybody. Even her very own twin brother, Alex, had refused to help her with the Laser Tag game.

The crowning glory had come that evening at the dinner table when she'd told her family how much trouble she was having with the games. She was admitting nearly total defeat by announcing it at dinner.

"I've got an idea for a neat relay race," her father had said. "I'm pretty sure you can do it on horseback."

"What is it, Dad?" she'd asked excitedly.

"Well, it's kind of a spoon race, but, you know, carrying eggs?"

Why in the world couldn't anybody suggest something that didn't have to do with eggs?

CAROLE SLID WEARILY into the overstuffed chair in the living room, where her father sat polishing his shoes. Next in line was the brass.

"Inspection tomorrow, huh?" Carole asked.

"Yes, and if there's one thing I've learned it's that the colonel's leather and brass have to be brighter and shinier than the troops'."

"Let me do the shoes, Dad. I get so much experience at the stable with saddles and bridles that I can always make leather shine. Besides, you'll never get a shine unless it's really clean. Don't you have any saddle soap?"

"At my age—and with eighteen years in the Marine Corps—I'm getting polishing lessons from a twelve-year-old?" He laughed. "You're welcome to them." He handed Carole his shoes and belt.

Carole brought a tin of saddle soap into the living room from her room, took her father's shoes, and began cleaning them thoroughly.

"What's got you so droopy these days, hon? I thought you were excited about that mare. Isn't she going to foal any day now?"

"That's what Judy says. But it's so much work, Dad. You know Delilah has to have a special bran mash, and it's a real nuisance to make. I had to make three batches tonight before I got it right. Then I had to wait for it to cool before I could give it to her. Imagine, cooking for a horse! I thought it would take me just ten minutes, but it took me hours. It's not that I don't care about Delilah, I do. Really. But it's a *lot* of work."

"Don't your friends help you with that kind of thing?"

"I sort of expected that they would, but they're so busy with their own things . . ."

The colonel applied a small smear of brass polish to his belt buckle and began rubbing vigorously. "Sounds to me like you're too busy to help them with their projects, too, aren't you?"

"Well, yeah," Carole admitted. "Do you know that I have to clean Delilah's stable twice as often now that she's almost due? Judy says it's terribly dangerous to have a foal born in an unsanitary stall. And with all the hay she's eating these days—"

"Spare me the details," her father said, laughing. Carole grinned. She'd finished cleaning the first shoe. She picked up the second. "Oh, wait'll I tell you what General Morris's aide did today," the colonel said, chatting about his day. Carole listened, applying polish to the shoes and buffing hard until each had a deep shine.

Carole displayed the gleaming shoes proudly when he'd finished talking. "See how shiny you can get them when you use saddle soap before you polish them?"

"Hey, that's great," her father said, admiring the shine on his shoes. "So we've gotten some benefit from your horseback riding after all. Very good. And look at me. I'm all done with my brass, too. Work always goes faster and better when two people do it at once. At least, that's what I think."

"You know, I think you're right," Carole mused. Then the truth finally occurred to her. "And I think it goes even faster and better when *three* people do it at once."

"Interesting idea," her father said. "I've got to hit the rack now. Inspection's very early."

"Me too. Judy's coming to check Delilah early tomorrow, so even though it's Saturday, you can still drop me off at Pine Hollow."

"Good night, Carole."

"Night, Dad," she said, giving him the great big hug he deserved. "You're the greatest."

9

FIRST THING MONDAY morning, Carole wanted to talk to Stevie and Lisa. The talk she'd had with her father had made her understand a lot of things—first and foremost that she and her friends really needed one another. She got to the stable especially early to allow extra time, but she'd forgotten that Stevie and Lisa couldn't have known she wanted to see them. She was just pulling on her second boot when Judy's truck drove up in front of the stable. She waved at the vet through the dirty window and met her in Delilah's stall. She'd talk to her friends later, she decided.

Stevie dashed into the locker area a half hour before class started. She needed every spare moment these days. She finished dressing in a matter of minutes, then started looking for some gear for the gymkhana in the tack box outside Mrs. Reg's office.

When Lisa arrived at the stable fifteen minutes before class, she wasn't surprised to see both of her friends totally occupied. As usual, Carole was with Judy in Delilah's stall. Stevie was shuffling through boxes of stuff in the tack room. It wasn't clear what she wanted, but it was clear she wasn't finding it. Lisa left her alone.

Once she'd donned her riding clothes, Lisa sat on the fence in front of the stable, waiting for The Saddle Club's newest member. Estelle usually arrived at the last minute, so Lisa wasn't going to have much time. What she had to say would only take a moment, but it should be fun. It was always nice to share good news.

Lisa was wearing her own Saddle Club pin. She knew it was just a pin, although in her opinion, it was a very pretty pin. What was important to her—even more important than the pin itself—was what the pin represented. It told her, and the people who mattered to her, that she cared deeply about horses—that she loved them and could ride them and that, after her friends, horses were about the most important thing in the world to her. She was sure the sun gleaming off the shiny surface of her horse-head pin made it even more beautiful.

Just then, Estelle's chauffered Citroën pulled into the drive. The rear door opened slowly and Estelle emerged sedately. That was an interesting thing about Estelle, Lisa thought as she waited for her. There were only about three minutes until class. If *she* were that late, she'd be running at full speed. Estelle, however, never seemed to be in a hurry. As a result, Max was forever speaking to her about keeping other people (especially him) waiting. That didn't speed her up, though.

"Hi, Estelle," Lisa said brightly, falling in step with the French girl.

"Oh, good morning, Lisa," she replied, walking toward the stable.

"I've got some good news for you," Lisa said, hoping she sounded as cool and sophisticated as Estelle always did.

"Yes?"

"It's about The Saddle Club," Lisa said. "There was a meeting Friday night and you were voted in."

"Voted in?" Estelle repeated. "What does this mean?"

"It means you're now a member of The Saddle Club," Lisa told her, grinning proudly. "And as a member, you're entitled to wear our pin."

"Oh?"

Lisa was pleased by Estelle's obvious interest and she handed Estelle her pin. It was wrapped in tissue so it wouldn't get any fingerprints on it.

Estelle carefully unwrapped the tissue and then held the pin in her hand for a moment. "It's a horse head," she said flatly.

"Yes, and isn't it pretty? See how nice and shiny it is? We can all wear our pins on our jackets and that can show other riders that we're all friends. Here, I'll help you pin it on," Lisa offered.

"Thanks, but I can put it on myself," Estelle said. "I'll do it later. I'm late now." For once, Estelle seemed to be in a hurry. She shoved the pin in her pocket, letting the tissue fall onto the ground. "See you in class," she told Lisa, turning to the stable.

Lisa was too stunned to move. Could she be mistaken? Lisa was trying to share one of the most important things in her life with her new friend, and unless she was totally off her mark, Estelle wasn't in the least bit excited, either about the Club *or* about the beautiful pin. How could that be?

It just wasn't possible, Lisa decided. Estelle really *was* in a hurry. She'd probably have her pin on in time for class.

Once Lisa had given Estelle the pin, she felt very relieved. The deed was done. If Stevie and Carole didn't like it, that was their problem. They should have come to the meetings.

MAX WAS IN an especially strict mood that day. He had all of his students working harder than ever before. There was no fooling around at all, all day long.

"Boy, if he tells me to keep my heels down one more time, I'm going to scream," Lisa confided to Carole during the chore period. Lisa had hoped to be assigned to do something with Estelle so they could talk about the Club some more, but Estelle and Veronica were tending to the horses in the paddocks. As it turned out, Lisa, Carole, and Stevie were all assigned to cleaning tack.

"He's got a thing about heels today, that's for sure," Carole agreed, "and toes. I found myself forcing mine inward every time he was facing me!"

"*That* must be why I heard him tell you not to stick your heels out!"

"Just my luck," Carole said. "I hope he'll go a little easier during jump class."

"You always do well then, don't you?"

"Not always," Carole said.

"I wish you could be in jump class too, Lisa," Stevie said.

"Me too. I like riding on the trail, but the only students there are the babies, except for me and Estelle." Carole and Stevie exchanged glances. "Red is so worried that somebody's going to get hurt that he'll barely let us trot. You'd think he'd let us do something more daring, like cantering, more often," Lisa said.

"Well, you certainly can," Stevie began. "I don't know about Estelle, though. She seems pretty green to me."

"Oh, no," Lisa said. "She's been riding for years—since she was five."

"She has?"

"Yes, and she has her own horse and her family has this country home with a stable near Paris where they go on weekends. They're all just as horse crazy as we are. But they do things differently in France, that's all.

She has to get used to the American way of doing things."

"Girls," Mrs. Reg called from her office. "Not so much gabbing, please. There's a lot of work to be done today. All of the dressage saddles are positively dingy and we'll need them for the upcoming show. Now, see if you can finish those before your next class."

"I think it's running in the family today," Stevie whispered. The three girls burst into giggles—and then muffled them right away so Mrs. Reg wouldn't hear.

"You still talking in there?" she called out.

"No ma'am," Carole said politely. "We're not talking anymore."

"Right, we're just giggling," Stevie whispered to her friends. "That's more fun anyway."

"Which are the dressage saddles?" Lisa asked.

"Those over there," Carole said, pointing to ten saddles stored together. "See how the flap is straight on both sides and how the rider will sit back in the saddle? It gives the rider more control over the horse. Wait'll you see. When dressage is done right, it's fantastic."

"Girls!"

Lisa hung up the bridle she'd been working on and brought one of the dressage saddles over to clean. They'd each have to do three, and then whoever finished first could do the last one while the other two cleaned up. It wouldn't be so bad if they worked together, she thought.

AT THREE O'CLOCK, Stevie, Lisa, and Carole were all together again, this time for drill practice. Normally, Stevie wasn't particularly interested in things that required such precision. Her whole personality was more flamboyant. But this drill work was just plain fun as far as she was concerned.

"What we're working on now is something I call the clover leaf," Max explained. "Normally, it's a four-leaf clover, but with just three of you, a three-leafer is better. But harder."

With that, he explained how each rider was to lead off on her own "leaf" in a clockwise path, leading into the next rider's leaf.

"The whole pleasure here for the audience is seeing how you *don't* run into each other at the cross. Try it."

Carole led off on the bottom right leaf. Stevie followed, two trotting paces later, on the upright leaf. Lisa went last, two paces after Stevie. Somehow, magically, when it came to the cross, Carole passed through first, then Stevie, then Lisa.

"Wonderful, girls! That was *great*. I've seen so-called experts who couldn't manage that maneuver anywhere near as well as you can. You three work together *so* well! Now, try it again, but keep it going as long as you can."

It turned out that "as long as you can" was only three times through the exercise. By then, Carole was well ahead of the other riders, and Lisa and Stevie were practically ramming into each other at the cross.

"It's still good," Max told them. "At least you could get through it enough times so each of you could complete the clover. You should be proud of what you can do together."

Stevie was beaming with the pleasure of success, and one glance at her friends confirmed that they were feeling the same way. But was this really *Max* talking?

"What I want you to do next is to begin trotting at the edge of the ring, evenly spaced and proceeding in a circle. As I instruct you, make your circle smaller, but maintaining a uniform distance from one another. At the end, you should have your horses practically head-to-tail, at the same speed, in a very small circle at the center of the ring. Think you can do it?"

At that moment, Stevie thought they could do anything. The three girls brought their horses to a nice collected trot, as close to the pace of the horse in front as they could. Then Max had them begin the exercise.

It turned out to be much trickier than Stevie expected. If horses follow one another, they always seem to want to catch up to the horse in front. Horses are naturally competitive, and one of the ways they prove that is by racing—even when they're not supposed to, like in a drill exercise. No matter how hard Stevie tried, it seemed almost impossible to control Comanche's trot. And as soon as Comanche quickened his pace to catch up with Diablo, Pepper wanted to get into the act. Pretty soon, all three horses were trotting contentedly on one side of the ring. The girls tried it four times and each time the same thing happened.

"I think there's some work to be done here, girls," Max said. "You should have better control of your horses, you know. Perhaps we should try again next time."

"Can't we try again now?" Stevie asked.

"Not now, Stevie. I've got a private lesson to give on the trail and it's time for you all to go home now."

"One more time?" Lisa asked.

"As I said, I have to go. If you all want to work on it by yourselves, of course, you may, but only for a few minutes. The horses need a rest, too. Good night," he said. Then, as only Max could, he bowed to his students and left the ring.

"We can do better," Stevie said.

"You bet we can," Lisa agreed. "I mean, I know that clover thing was harder than this, but it seems almost impossible to keep Pepper from running up to Diablo."

"Music," Carole said suddenly. "I think that's the answer."

"Hey, great idea!" Stevie said.

"The horses can follow the beat of the music?" Lisa said in wonderment.

"I doubt it," Carole told her, "but *we* can. See, then we can maintain an even beat with our posting. If we're all going up-down at the same beat, we can use that to guide our horses to the pace we want."

"Well, we'll work this out together, won't we?" Stevie asked. The grins on her friends' faces answered the question.

"I'll go see what tapes Mrs. Reg has that she can put on the P.A. system for us, okay? Here, hold Diablo for me, will you?"

Stevie took the reins from Carole and watched while she dashed off to Mrs. Reg's office.

CAROLE WAS NEARLY breathless with excitement. She loved the drill work as much as her friends did and she was thrilled to have come up with a possible solution to a big problem.

Mrs. Reg wasn't in her office, though, and Carole suddenly remembered that she had scheduled a trip to the saddle shop for supplies for the horse show. The office was completely locked up, so although the music idea was a good one, they couldn't try it today.

Disappointed, Carole headed back to the outdoor ring. The stable was quiet. Max was on the trail with his private student; Mrs. Reg was at the shop; and except for the three of them, the camp class had all gone for the day. Even Red O'Malley was away. He'd gone along with Mrs. Reg.

Carole glanced at the horses' stalls as she passed, clucking gently, patting noses here and there, feeling very much in charge, and liking it.

She detoured around to say hello to Delilah, isolated in her foaling stall. Usually Delilah had her head out over the top of the sliding door, but there was no sign of her today.

Curious, Carole clucked, but there was no response, no familiar nodding head with its platinum forelock.

She clucked again. This time she heard a mild whinny. Carole hastened to the door of the special stall. When she looked in, what she saw made her heart jump.

Delilah was in a far corner of the stall. She was pacing back and forth, alternately pawing at the ground and kicking at her own belly. Her tail switched rapidly, flicking upward as well as sideways. There was a froth of sweat on her flanks and her chest.

There was no doubt about it. Delilah was in labor. Her foal was about to be born—and the only people in the stable were Carole, Stevie, and Lisa!

10

WITHIN SECONDS, CAROLE marshaled her troops. "Stevie, you call Judy. Tell her I'm just about certain Delilah's in labor, and find out how long it'll take her to get here. Lisa, put the horses in their stalls and untack them. Then both of you come on back to Delilah's stall. There's work to be done!"

Carole pivoted on her toes and raced back to Delilah, excited, nervous, relieved that the time had come, really come. The mare was still storming back and forth in the stall when Carole got back. Hoping to calm her, Carole reached over the tall door and tried to pat Delilah soothingly. Delilah swept her head back, obviously rejecting the affectionate pat. Once again, the horse appeared to be kicking at her belly, and then she began digging away at the clean hay in her stall, almost as if she were making a nest.

"Judy'll get here as soon as she can," Stevie reported, approaching the stall cautiously. "Her assistant told me a horse over at Ridge Farm got attacked by a group of dogs and needs a zillion stitches. She really can't leave now. It'll be at least an hour before she's done and then a half hour to get here. She won't have the foal that fast, will she?" Stevie asked.

"No way to tell," Carole said calmly. "This is Delilah's first foal. It could be a few minutes. It could be a day or more. To tell you the truth, I know she's showing early symptoms of being in labor, but I have no idea how long these last." Carole glanced at the horse and her calm quickly vanished. "Oh, no!"

"What's the matter?"

"Look at her udder," Carole said. "See the milk coming out of it? I'm sure Judy told me that meant things were moving rapidly—or did she say it was something that could happen a lot before the foal arrives? I don't know—I don't remember!" she said, nearly frantic.

"Hey, hey, calm down," Stevie said. "We're all here, and we're going to help you *and* Delilah. It's going to be okay. This horse is going to have the most beautiful foal ever born, and we'll see to it that it happens right. Besides, if I remember correctly, horses have been having baby horses a lot longer than people have been trying to help them. Isn't Delilah going to do most of the work, anyway?"

"Yeah, I guess so," Carole said, smiling bashfully. "I just care so much about this foal, and its mother—"

"And its father, right?" Stevie asked softly, reminding Carole of Cobalt, the coal-black Thoroughbred who had sired the foal. "We won't let him down, either, will we?"

"Yeah, right. I just don't want to let how much I care make me nervous."

"Nervous? Who's nervous?" Lisa asked, arriving all out of breath.

"Me," Carole confessed.

"No need to be nervous," Lisa said reassuringly. "Stevie and I are right here beside you, ready to do your bidding. What's the first thing we do?"

All of a sudden, Carole's mind was a complete blank. She couldn't remember anything Judy had ever told her about *anything*, much less about foaling. Delilah's insistent stomping only made her more confused. She felt tense knowing she would be practically useless to Delilah just when the mare needed her the very most. But without her help, would the foal make it? Carole could barely speak.

"The birthing kit—where is it?" Stevie asked, breaking through Carole's terror.

"Oh, yes, that's right. We need that. It's in the chest, right over there."

Stevie turned and opened the chest where Carole and Judy had only recently stowed the birthing kit. It was really just a cardboard carton, but it contained all the things an owner routinely needed to assist at a normal delivery. Everything was carefully arranged in the order in which it was most likely to be needed. Right on top was a big roll of three-inch gauze bandage.

That made it all come back to Carole. "I remember now. Thanks for reminding me about the birthing kit, Stevie. For a moment there, I couldn't have told you my name, much less what we'd have to do for Delilah. First thing, though, grab that roll of gauze, okay? We have to bind up Delilah's tail. I'll hold her head and see if I can keep her relatively calm and distracted while you wrap her tail. See, we don't want those long hairs to get in the way of anything or to carry any germs that could cause infections. She's better off if we just fold it up and wrap it up."

Cautiously, the two of them entered Delilah's stall. The horse eyed her visitors uncertainly. Carole grasped the mare's halter gently and began rubbing her nose and forehead. The familiar affectionate motion seemed to calm the horse.

"There, there, girl. We'll take care of you," Carole said soothingly.

"I never wrapped a tail before," Stevie said from the horse's rear. "But my mother says I'm the best in the house at Christmas presents. My biggest challenge was an umbrella. Did you ever try to wrap something so it didn't look like what's actually in the package?"

"I don't think Delilah's going to mind if her tail actually *looks* like a tail," Carole teased.

"No problem," Stevie said cheerfully, rolling the gauze carefully around the folded tail. "It's still going to look like a tail, just a well-wrapped one. There, I think that will do it. Scissors please, Lisa."

Lisa passed the scissors over. Stevie finished up her task with a flourish. "Ta-*da*!" she said.

Carole had to admit she'd never seen a more nicely wrapped tail, nor one with a prettier bow on it! "I'm sure Delilah will appreciate that," Carole said. "Okay, next, she needs to be cleansed with a disinfectant. Your turn, Lisa."

Following Carole's instructions, Lisa used the cleansing soap and disinfectant on Delilah's hindquarters. With Carole continuing her sweet talk to Delilah, the horse seemed to be almost unaware of what Lisa was doing.

"Finished," Lisa announced. "She's as clean as I can make her."

"That's great. Now come on out of the stall. I'm going to follow you. We should move carefully so as not to upset Delilah, okay?"

Smoothly and quietly the girls left Delilah alone in her stall. Carole slid the door closed and latched it.

"Well, look at Delilah," Stevie teased. "She's all squeaky clean and purtied up. What comes next?"

"We wait," Carole said. "And that's probably all we can do—that is if Delilah does what she's supposed to do. . . ."

"And where do we wait?"

"We wait where she can't see us. Judy says that mares don't like to be watched—"

"We can't *watch*? I thought that was what we've been waiting to do," Stevie complained.

"Oh, we can watch, all right. I wouldn't miss it for the world. We just can't watch where she can see us, or at least not where she's aware of us. We can hide right here in the next stall. We need to be pretty quiet, but we can see everything right through the knotholes."

"Don't tell me Delilah doesn't know we're here," Lisa said as they made their way into the empty stall.

"Oh, if she thought about it, she would," Carole said. "But Delilah's got other things on her mind right now. As long as we stay pretty much out of sight, we'll be out of mind."

"How long is this going to take?" Lisa asked.

"Psst! Delilah's lying down!" Stevie said, looking through the hole.

"What does that mean?" Lisa asked.

"It means she's tired," Carole explained.

"She's standing up again!" Stevie reported.

"What does *that* mean?" Lisa asked.

"It means she's had enough rest," Carole told her.

"She's pawing at the straw again," Stevie said.

"What does that mean?" Lisa asked.

"It means she's trying to build a sand castle, right, Carole?" Stevie joked.

"Whatever you say, Stevie," Carole said, laughing.

"I'm hungry," Stevie said a moment later.

"Well, I've got some good things to eat here," Carole said. "I put my cot and all my snacks in this stall so

I could stay here while I waited for Delilah to foal. Now it sort of looks like I won't need all that food, because something tells me Delilah isn't going to take all that long. Here." Carole reached for a large backpack. She unzipped it and began producing the goodies she'd expected to eat alone.

"I never saw such a lot of nourishing food all at once," Stevie joked, looking over the array of cupcakes, cookies, candy bars, and chips.

"Food from all the major food groups, I see," Lisa quipped.

"Yeah, the cupcake-and-cookie group, the peanut-and-popcorn group, the chips-and-crackers group, the—"

"You want it or don't you?" Carole asked.

"You bet I want it," Stevie said.

"Me too," Lisa agreed, reaching for the bag of cookies. "I usually have a snack when I get home in the afternoon and I'm usually home much earlier than this. No wonder I'm so hungry—yeah, what time is it, anyway?"

Stevie glanced at her watch. "Five-fifteen! My mother's going to be worried. I'd better give her a call."

"We all better call home," Lisa agreed.

Temporarily abandoning their snack, the girls headed for the phone and hurriedly made their calls. Stevie's mother agreed to pick up all of them when they were ready to leave. Another round of calls resolved that, and the girls returned to the empty stall next to Delilah's.

"Something's different," Stevie reported from her vantage point at the largest knothole.

"What do you mean?" Carole asked.

"Well, for one thing, Delilah's lying down, but not on her stomach. She's lying on her side, and her legs are sticking straight out. She looks weird and uncomfortable. Is she okay?" Carole was upset by the worry in Stevie's voice.

"Let me see!" Carole got onto her knees and peered through the hole. There was Delilah, just like Stevie said, lying on her side. But Stevie had forgotten to mention a few things. "She isn't just lying there—she's having contractions! See her muscles rippling? And unless I miss my guess by a mile, I can see the foal's feet! The baby's coming and it's coming *now!*"

All three girls got to their feet and climbed up on the horizontal slats that separated the two stalls. About six feet up, the wood stopped and there was only a screen. They could see more clearly there because they could see the whole stall at once.

"Look, there it is, don't you see? The little feet, now there are two of them. The foal is still in the sack—that's the white part—but you can see the outline of its pointy little hooves, and now—look, the foal's nose!"

All three girls gasped in awe at the foal's emergence. Nothing that had ever happened to any of them before could prepare them for the event that was taking place then.

"You know, I always knew in a sort of textbook way that there was a foal inside that mare, but to see it, to actually *see* it. That's not like a textbook at all. I mean—that's real," Lisa said. "And it's incredible."

"You got that right," Stevie agreed.

"Come on, girls," Carole said. "Delilah needs our help now. Where's the birthing kit?"

"Right here," Lisa announced. "What do you need?"

"I need the scissors. Judy told me how to do this when the other foal was born. I'm pretty sure I know what to do. See, we need to cut the sack—"

Just then, Delilah had another contraction and more of the foal emerged, and before Carole could enter the stall and cut the sack, there was a final contraction and the foal was completely born. Then the sack broke open by itself. The little baby lifted its head and looked at the world around it, sniffing tentatively. Delilah looked warily at her foal, then nudged the baby with her nose, sniffing, too.

"They're getting acquainted," Carole explained. "Aren't they adorable?"

Lisa and Stevie nodded, not wanting to take their eyes off the foal.

"What color is it?" Stevie asked.

"Hard to tell when it's so wet," Lisa added.

"It's black," Carole said in a daze. "Coal-black, just like its father—just like I knew it would be."

"Look!" Lisa said. "It's trying to stand up."

The foal moved its front legs forward, awkwardly pushing from the rear. It didn't work, though. As soon as its rear legs began to straighten, its front legs collapsed, sending the newborn sprawling into the straw bedding.

The girls burst into laughter.

Delilah, having rested for a few minutes, stood up and regarded her baby, sniffing it all over, looking at it from all directions. Apparently satisfied, she nudged it with her nose.

The baby looked up at its mother, its eyes focusing for the first time in its short life on its mother's face. Delilah nudged the baby again impatiently. Then she began licking it gently, until the foal renewed its efforts to rise. Once again, the foal's front legs stretched forward and its hind legs began scrambling. It stumbled, but its back legs were straight. Slowly, one at a time, the baby straightened out its forelegs, and then brought them to an upright position.

"It's standing!" Carole gasped. "Cobalt's foal is standing—and what a beauty!"

The newborn was perhaps three and a half feet tall, almost all of which appeared to be legs. The foal's small body was precariously balanced atop the spindly legs; the only parts of the baby that moved with any assurance were the ears and the tail, all flicking this way and that experimentally. The newborn lifted a foreleg and then put it back down again. The performance was repeated in turn with each leg. It seemed that once the baby was certain each of its legs worked, it was ready to try them out together. While Delilah waited patiently, licking her baby occasionally, the foal got itself turned around and, just the way it was supposed to, it began nuzzling under its mother's belly.

"It's nursing!" Carole gasped. "Can you believe it? That baby is less than fifteen minutes old and it's nursing already."

They watched in silence for a while as the foal nursed and Delilah finished licking her baby's wet coat dry. After just a few minutes, the foal and Delilah both lay down in the straw and, within seconds, both were asleep.

Just then, the girls heard the familiar sound of Judy's truck pulling up to the stable, followed almost immediately by the vet's hurried footsteps.

"How's she doing, Carole? Is she almost ready to deliver?" Judy called ahead.

"Not for at least another year," Carole said.

Stunned, Judy came to a halt by the stall and then put down her bag quietly so as not to disturb the mare and foal. "Oh," she whispered, startled. And then she stood with the girls, circling them with her arms, enjoying the moment. Her eyes sparkled with pleasure. "I've watched scenes like this hundreds of times, you know. It's always the same and it's always absolutely wonderful. Tell me about it," she said excitedly. "Did you actually see the birth?"

"Oh, yes," Stevie piped up. "We watched almost everything, and it was incredible."

Quickly, but including all the details they could recall, the girls filled the vet in on Delilah's delivery. "You were great!" Judy told the girls. "You did everything just right. You didn't need me at all."

"Actually, Judy," Lisa said, "it seemed to me that Delilah did most of the work."

"That's why they call it labor, Lisa. Now, I think I'll check our patients."

While the girls cleaned up the birthing kit and threw away the papers and wrappers from their snack, Judy finished up with Delilah and the foal. By the time they were all done, Max had returned from his trail ride.

"I had no idea she was so close to delivery, Judy," he said, somewhat embarrassed. "I never would have left her unattended."

"It appears to me, Max, that she was very well attended indeed."

"Yes, I think you're right, Judy. These girls did a fine job and I bet Delilah was pleased they were here. How else would she ever have gotten such a nice bow on her tail wrap?"

Stevie, Lisa, and Carole all giggled. Max and Judy joined in the laughter.

"Well, what's our foal, girls, a filly or a colt?"

Carole felt her face flush. "I—I don't know."

"Didn't you look?" Max asked.

"I completely forgot to," Carole said. "I guess I was just too excited that it was a foal at all—you know?"

"I know," Max said, smiling. "Well, Judy, what is it?"

"It's a colt," she told them. "Cobalt sired a son, Carole. Isn't that what you wanted?"

"More than anything in the world," she said.

"You want to name him?" Max asked. "You can have a couple of days to think about it if you'd like."

Carole didn't have to think about that at all. She'd known for months what the son of Cobalt and Delilah would be called. "His name's Samson," she said. Her friends, Max, and Judy all burst into laughter. After all, Samson was a perfect name for Delilah's son.

And Carole knew that Samson would be the finest, strongest, most wonderful horse she'd ever ride.

11

"DID YOU SEE how his little tail twitched?" Stevie asked excitedly while the three girls shared a soda in the tack room, waiting for Mrs. Lake to come for them.

"Oh, yeah," Lisa said, grinning in recollection. "And he's so cute when he nuzzles Delilah for some milk. It's almost impossible to believe that only an hour ago he wasn't there at all. I mean—well, that was fantastic. And *you* were fantastic, Carole. You really knew what to do!"

Stevie glanced at Carole. The look on her friend's face was total joy. Stevie and Lisa were excited about Delilah's foal, but to Carole, it was really the final success of Cobalt's life. The little black colt was almost a rebirth, for Cobalt and for Carole.

"I may have known some of the things to do, like wrapping her tail and cleaning her up, but I couldn't have done it single-handed. You guys were the ones who did all the work."

"We helped," Lisa said. "But sometimes doing it isn't as important as knowing what has to be done, you know?"

"Let's face it," Stevie said. "We're a team." She raised her hand victoriously. Carole and Lisa both slapped it.

"What is it when three people give 'high fives' at once?" Carole asked. "A high fifteen?"

"Sounds good to me," Stevie said, grinning. "And the really important thing here is that The Saddle Club is working together again. Look what we can accomplish when we team up—a foal! Gee, if that's what *three* of us can do, imagine what would happen if there were more. Why—"

Stevie abruptly stopped talking because she noticed that very suddenly, Lisa was looking decidedly uncomfortable.

"What's up, Lisa? What's the matter?"

Lisa put the soda can on the bench and stared at the floor. Stevie started to feel nervous. It wasn't at all like Lisa to be so awkward.

Finally, Lisa spoke. "I guess I should tell you that there *are* more than three members of The Saddle Club now."

"I just see the three of us," Carole said. "Who else is here?"

"Well, she's not here now," Lisa explained, "but she *is* in the club."

"Who is?" Stevie asked.

"Estelle," Lisa said. "She was voted in as a member at the last meeting."

One look at Carole, and Stevie knew that was news to her as well. "What last meeting?" Stevie asked.

"The one Friday night," Lisa said quickly. "The one *neither* of you came to. That was the meeting that followed the one at TD's that neither of you came to either. At *that* meeting, all the rules I wrote got passed."

"I don't believe this!" Stevie said, stunned. How could one of her best friends be so disloyal? "How could you do something like that without us?"

"Well, you were each so busy doing your thing without *me*—" Lisa began.

"Hold it," Carole said. Both Stevie and Lisa turned to her. Carole was usually the voice of reason. "I have the feeling that we all learned a lesson this afternoon. We'd all totally forgotten that the real purpose of The Saddle Club is to help each other. I mean, that's the way we started and that's the way it's got to be. There's no way I could have helped Delilah by myself. I *needed* the two of you. Over the last couple of weeks, we've all been so busy worrying about our own projects that we haven't been helping each other at all. So, I guess I'm not really surprised that you passed those rules without us, Lisa, and Stevie shouldn't be either. She's been so busy with Nickel and the gymkhana that, well, like I said, I think we all learned a lesson."

"Thanks for understanding, Carole," Lisa said.

"Wait a second, there," Stevie interrupted. "I can understand that too, but there's still a small problem remaining and her name is Estelle Duval."

"What's the problem?" Lisa said defensively. "Isn't she good enough for you?"

"The problem is that the girl has got no horse sense. She doesn't know the front end from the back or the first thing about riding."

"But she's been riding since she was very little!"

"If that's the case, she hasn't learned much in all those years," Stevie said.

"She has her own horse. She told me he's a white horse named Napoleon."

"Like I said: She hasn't learned much," Stevie repeated.

"What do you mean?" Lisa demanded.

"There's no such thing as a white horse, Lisa," Carole explained. Lisa stared at her, confused. "See, all white horses are actually gray. Most of them start out dark-colored and just turn white with age. It's actually a sign of a real beginner when they call horses white."

"But she's not a beginner. For goodness sake, she even told me something that happened when she was about six!"

"What happened?" Stevie asked.

"Well, she was standing up in the saddle, trying to get her balance and tugging at her horse's mane. The mare got angry and kicked at her."

"Lisa," Carole began, "horses don't have any feeling in their manes. There are no nerves there at all. There's no way that would make a horse 'angry.' Besides that, horses just plain don't try to kick their riders when they're on their backs. A lot of times they'll buck, sometimes they'll try to nip a rider with their teeth, every once in a while they'll rear, or just plain run away, but they only kick at something or someone on the ground."

"You mean it couldn't happen that way?" Lisa asked.

"That's what I mean."

"Well, maybe she forgot. After all, she was pretty little, but she wasn't so young when she was taking care of Napoleon when he was sick and he threw up on her. That just happened last year!"

Stevie's heart went out to Lisa. It was hard to believe anybody could have been taken in by these stories, and because Lisa was such a trusting person it seemed especially cruel of Estelle. "She's told you another tall tale," Stevie began.

"How do you know?" Lisa asked.

"Because horses don't throw up. I mean, they can't. Physically, they don't work that way. It's one of the reasons a colicky horse is such a problem. They'd be better off sometimes if they could just get rid of what's causing the stomachache, but they can't."

"Why would Estelle say something that wasn't true? She doesn't have any reason to lie to me. After all, she's the one with the glamorous life, the fancy schools and friends, the country estate. . . ."

"Oh, you think so?" Stevie asked.

"I don't think we've been fair to Lisa," Carole said to Stevie. "Both you and I knew right away that she was a phony—at least when it came to horses—because she couldn't ride very well. We assumed that Lisa would recognize that, too."

"Isn't all the trouble she's had riding just because of adjusting to American horses?" Lisa asked, defending herself.

"We joke about it, but Max is really right that horses don't speak English, you know," Carole said. "There's no difference among good riders throughout the world."

"How could I know that?" Lisa asked.

"Of course you couldn't," Carole consoled her. "You're such a good natural rider that we sometimes forget what you *don't* know. That's kind of our fault. What you have, though, is really much more important than a lot of facts—you have a real feeling for horses and for riding. Stevie said it a few minutes ago. It's horse sense. You've got it. Estelle doesn't."

"Thanks," Lisa said. "I appreciate your vote of confidence, but the fact remains that as of Friday night, Estelle Duval is a member of The Saddle Club."

"Not for long," Stevie said. "Or else I'm not."

They were just words that Stevie had spoken, but they felt like a bomb to Lisa. As sure as she'd ever known anything, she knew that Stevie meant them. She looked to Carole for consolation, but there wasn't any there.

"Lisa, I think it's up to you," Carole said. Lisa didn't know what to say then. She only knew how she felt and it was bad. She was going to have to choose between her friends and her mistake. What good was horse sense if you could still get into messes like that?

Carole started to speak. Lisa thought maybe she had a suggestion, but before she really got going, Stevie's parents and all three of her brothers bounded into the tack room.

"Can I see the baby?" asked her younger brother, Michael. "Please?"

Stevie was actually happy to see them all. She knew that what she'd said about The Saddle Club was upsetting both her friends, so a change of subject right then was a good idea. But just because she didn't want to talk about her announcement anymore didn't mean she wasn't serious about it. She didn't want any part of Estelle Duval. Ever.

"Come on, guys, let's introduce my family to Samson." She linked arms with Carole and Lisa and led everybody on tiptoe to see the newborn.

When the girls had left Samson only a half hour before, he'd been sleeping soundly. Now, just a short time later, he was back up on his feet, walking around on his spindly legs and checking out his surroundings.

Michael climbed up on the slats of the stall's wall to see better. Samson glanced up at him, his soft brown eyes decidedly curious.

"Wow!" said Michael.

Stevie couldn't have said it better.

12

LISA KNEW SHE ought to feel really excited, sharing in the fun of Samson's birth, but when the sun woke her up the next morning, all she actually felt was dread. Stevie and Carole had made their positions clear. It was Estelle or them.

At first, she thought maybe she could bring her friends around, but when she'd tried to raise the subject once again on the trip home it became clear that Carole and Stevie were totally together. Lisa had made a mistake, a bad one, and she was going to have to correct it.

Correcting mistakes was sometimes impossible and never any fun. Lisa pulled the pillow over her head to shut out the sunlight. Maybe morning would go away.

"Lisa! Breakfast is on the table, dear," her mother called up. "I made you some oatmeal. . . ."

And now she had *that* to contend with, too!

By the time she arrived at the stable, she found that she didn't feel any better at all. She didn't much want to see Carole and Stevie and she certainly didn't want to see Estelle. In fact, she didn't much want to be there at all. Lisa knew that some people would have pretended to be sick, but if she'd done that her mother would have known something was wrong and then she'd have had to answer dozens of questions from *her*.

Lisa was relieved to find that the locker area and the tack room were completely empty. Not surprisingly, everybody was hanging around by the foaling stall, looking at the new baby. Lisa would have joined them, but for three things: Stevie, Carole, and Estelle.

She stowed her lunch in the little refrigerator and lingered in the tack room.

"Aren't you going to see the foal this morning?" Mrs. Reg asked.

"I guess so, in a minute. The whole wide world is there now, aren't they?"

"Yes, they are," Mrs. Reg said, laughing. "Say, while you're waiting, will you give me a hand with something?"

"Sure," Lisa agreed, wondering quickly if maybe, just maybe, Mrs. Reg's chore might take all day.

"I seem to have a whole lot of little pieces of tack and other stable hardware that need to be sorted and stored. Can you do that while I work on the schedule for the three-day event?"

"Oh, I'd be glad to," Lisa told her. She found herself looking at a jumble of metal rings, loops, hooks, bits, and stirrups. She began sorting them into piles of like items. "This is neat stuff," Lisa said, gazing at all the hardware in front of her.

"It's a mishmash of things—harness hooks, rings, double-end snaps, S-hooks, cross-tie chains. All of those are used in the stable, but none of them can be used if we don't know what we've got."

"How do you know what all these things are and what they do?" Lisa asked.

"Oh, you learn, Lisa. After all, you've just started riding. You can't expect yourself to know everything right away."

"That's what *you* think," Lisa said. Just when she wanted to think about it the least, Mrs. Reg had reminded her how little she actually knew about horses.

"You know, there was a boy here once, a new rider . . ."

"Who was that?" Lisa asked, making a chain of S-hooks. Mrs. Reg was famous for her riding stories. This could be fun.

"He was a youngster. He came into the stable knowing almost nothing about horses or riding or anything, but he was very eager to learn. It was okay when he first began. He knew he didn't know anything, so he asked questions all the time and tried to learn as much as he could. After he'd been riding here a few months, though, he got into some trouble."

"How's that?" Lisa asked.

"Well, he started thinking he knew a lot more than he did and he stopped asking questions. One day, he wanted to ride a particular horse, nice little bay gelding we had named Hickory. My husband was watching Hickory, though. He thought he showed signs of lameness. This young rider thought he knew more than my husband and took the horse out anyway—without even asking why he'd been put in a different stall. Within fifteen minutes, the horse was so lame that the rider had to get off him. Took him hours to walk him back to the stable. Vet's bill was something awful, I'll tell you. He had a bowed tendon, and even after he'd healed, he was never as good as he had been."

"But how did that happen? Did the young rider hurt the horse?"

"In a way," Mrs. Reg said. "It turned out that all that had been wrong in the first place was that he had a stone in his shoe. My husband needed a better light to find it and that's why he'd moved him to another stall, intending to check the hoof when he had time. Then, when this young rider took poor old Hickory out on the trail, the horse favored his sore foot. He stumbled, and gave his own leg a good kick, tearing his own tendon."

"You must have been furious," Lisa said.

"Oh, we were," Mrs. Reg said. "It's awful when things go wrong with a horse."

"I bet you never let that rider back here, did you?"

"We couldn't do that," Mrs. Reg said.

"Why not?"

"It was our own son, Max, who did it!"

"Max? My teacher?"

"The very one," Mrs. Reg said. "Of course, he's learned a lot since then—and he's never stopped asking questions, either. Once he got an idea of how much he *didn't* know, and understood that it was all right not to know, things went much smoother for him."

"I think you're trying to tell me something, Mrs. Reg," Lisa said.

"You almost finished with the sorting?" Mrs. Reg asked.

"Just about."

"Max used to like to play with this stable hardware when he was a boy. He'd make chains just like the one you made with the S-hooks, and he'd put a dozen rings on a crop and ride around trying to keep them all on."

"He was a little devil, wasn't he?" Lisa asked.

Mrs. Reg chuckled. "It's almost class time now, Lisa. You'll have to saddle up. Thanks for your help."

Lisa put the sorted hardware into buckets and then stood up to leave. She looked slyly at Mrs. Reg, who was so busy jotting notes on the paper in front of her that she appeared to be unaware of Lisa at all. Lisa doubted that. In fact, Lisa strongly suspected that Mrs. Reg never missed anything at all. Not a thing.

A few minutes later, Lisa was in Pepper's stall, lifting his saddle on. She heard Estelle next to her, working with Patch. Max had let her switch from Nero to another horse. Estelle was having a terrible time with the bridle. She spoke rapidly to the horse in French, but it wasn't doing any good. Estelle was clearly getting angrier and angrier.

As soon as Lisa finished smoothing a wrinkle in the saddle pad and tightening Pepper's girth, she went to Estelle's aid—Patch's, really. Patch was happily walking backward in circles while Estelle chased him with the bridle in her hands. She'd never get the tack on that way.

"Here, Estelle, I'll give you a hand," Lisa offered.

"Oh, this dumb horse. He just wants to give me trouble."

"No, I think he's having too much fun with the game. You can't let a horse get away with that kind of stuff, you know. Here, you hold him. I'll put the bridle on. If he keeps backing up, you should just cross-tie him. Otherwise, you're just teaching him bad habits."

"This horse already knows bad habits. I never had such trouble with horses before I came here."

"Perhaps that's because you never rode before," Lisa said.

"*Moi?*" Estelle asked. "But I have been riding since I was a little girl—from before my seventh birthday."

Something about the mention of her seventh birthday rang a bell to Lisa. She began remembering two other stories Estelle had told her, and they didn't fit at all.

"Was that the seventh birthday you spent in the hospital, or the seventh birthday when you got Napoleon and rode him for hours?"

"I don't know what you mean," Estelle said.

"Estelle, what I mean is that you've been lying to me. You really don't know the first thing about horses. You've hardly ever ridden before and you didn't want to admit it, so you made up stories. You probably made up all the other stories about yourself, too. Your princess friend and your four languages, and your country estate. As a matter of fact, considering the lies I know you've told me, I've begun to suspect that you've never told me the truth at all, have you?"

Estelle looked so shocked that Lisa knew that finally she had found the absolute truth.

"You know, there's nothing wrong with being a beginner at riding. I'm a beginner myself. Sometimes I hate how much I don't know, but I'm not ashamed of it. You can't learn if you can't admit what you don't know."

"I have studied riding with the finest instructors in Europe!" Estelle proclaimed. "But riding here is very different, and not nearly as good."

"If you want to be that way, Estelle, okay," Lisa said. "But I know—"

"What do you know? You and your silly friends and your club! I don't want to be in your club and I don't want to wear that cheap pin! Here, take it back!"

Estelle fumbled in the pocket of her breeches and pulled out the silver horse head. Glaring at Lisa, she threw it into the soiled bedding in Patch's stall. Carefully, Lisa handed Patch's reins to Estelle. She turned and retrieved the pin from the straw. She wiped it off, opened the clasp, and put it on her blouse. It was just as beautiful to her now as it had been the first time she'd seen it in the jewelry store showcase. She'd wear it with pride.

She turned and walked out of Patch's stall. It was time for class and it was time to get back to her horse crazy friends, Stevie and Carole.

Lisa didn't speak to Estelle again that day. The next time she saw her, in fact, Estelle was carrying all her belongings to the car, where her mother was waiting for her. Just at the moment when she might possibly have been ready to be a beginner—an honest beginner—she was quitting. Lisa certainly wouldn't miss her and neither would her friends. It was just too bad, Lisa thought, that Estelle would never really know how much fun riding could be. That was Estelle's loss, but for now, it was The Saddle Club's gain. Lisa could hardly wait to tell Stevie and Carole.

"THAT'S GOOD NEWS," Stevie agreed as the three of them ate their sandwiches together. They were sitting on the grass by the paddocks, enjoying the fresh breeze. "But here's the bad news . . ."

"What's the matter?" Carole asked. It was unlike Stevie to be serious, but the look on her face said she was just that.

"The bad news is that Mrs. Reg and Max are going to be furious with me when I tell them that I haven't come up with one decent game for the gymkhana."

"But you had such neat ideas," Lisa said. "There's something the matter with them all?"

"None of them works, that's what's the matter. I really want this gymkhana to be new and different, and unless I get on it right away, it's not only not going to be new and different, but it's not going to be—*at all!*"

"Wait a second," Carole stopped her. "Nobody here has ever been in a gymkhana before, except maybe me. It's all new and different to all of us!"

"Don't tell me the one about the eggs," Stevie groaned.

"What's the matter with an egg race?" Lisa asked. "Boy, I bet it's funny if somebody drops an egg and it breaks."

Stevie tilted her head and looked at Lisa. "Think it would be funny?"

"Yeah, I do," Lisa said.

"Me too," Carole told her.

"Okay, I give up. We'll have an egg race. What else?"

"What about Laser Tag?"

"I can't borrow it from the Zieglers, so that's out."

"If we can't play Laser Tag, which, by the way, only two people could play at once anyway, how about shadow tag?" Lisa asked.

"Hey, shadow tag? That would be *great*! But what if it rains?"

"Well, then how about some kind of musical chairs? The riders go around a bunch of chairs and when the music stops, they dismount—you get the idea."

"I like it!" Stevie said.

"You know what makes a neat relay race?" Carole asked. "The one where people put on costumes. Everybody looks so silly."

"My mother has saved all the Halloween costumes each of us ever wore," Stevie said, suddenly very excited. "That would be just great—pirates, ghosts, all that stuff. . . ."

"I was in Mrs. Reg's office today," Lisa said. "She has buckets and buckets of hardware, like S-hooks and rings and things like that. There are zillions of things you can do with that sort of stuff. How about stacking rings on a riding crop, or keeping a chain of S-hooks from breaking up while the horse gallops. You know, two riders could be sort of attached to each other with some sort of chain and have to follow a certain course—"

"That's the old rope race," Stevie said, disappointed.

"Sounds to me like a new and different version of 'the old rope race,'" Carole said.

"It does, at that," Stevie agreed. "Listen, I've got an idea, if you don't mind."

"What's that?" Lisa asked.

"I know we were going to practice our drill exercises today, to music, but do you think we could put that off a day or two and work out the fine points of some of these races? I could really use some help with it."

Carole and Lisa exchanged grins. "What else are friends for?" Carole asked.

"What about Simon Says on horseback?" Lisa asked. "And you know what else might be fun? Like maybe as a finale or something, how about a scavenger hunt? Hey, would a horse be spooked by a bouncing ball? I mean we could have a basketball-dribbling race. Imagine how it would look with the balls bouncing all over the place. I think a blind man's bluff would be dangerous, but how about some kind of, say, Pin the Tail on the Pony? It would have to be a picture of a pony, of course. All this stuff's old hat when the kids are on the ground, but they're really different games on horseback, right?" Lisa was about to go on. She hadn't even gotten to her idea about the tennis ball on the racket, but she noticed that both Stevie and Carole were staring at her. "Is something wrong?" Lisa asked.

"Nothing at all," Stevie said reassuringly. "I just never had any idea that you were so full of ideas for horseback games."

"See what I meant?" Carole asked Stevie. "This girl's got horse sense."

"I think she just likes to have fun," Stevie joked.

"With my friends," Lisa told them. She reached up in the air with her hand. Carole's and Stevie's hands met with hers. "High fifteen!" they said together.

13

"THERE YOU GO!" Carole hollered at Lisa. "You've just about got it!"

"I know *she's* got it, but what about me?" Stevie yelled back. Her question was punctuated by the unmistakable splat of an egg hitting the ground.

"You have to go get another one, Lisa, and give that to Stevie. The important part is handing the spoon over to her while you're both on moving horses."

Lisa turned her pony, Quarter, around and signaled him to go fast. He scampered back to the bowl where spare eggs were stored. She took another, placed it in the spoon, made a U-turn, and sprinted back to the starting line, where Stevie was waiting for her.

"Now slow down—" Carole instructed from the sidelines.

Lisa reined Quarter down to a trot, then, just as Nickel began to pick up speed, Stevie took the spoon from Lisa, smooth as could be—until Nickel jerked to a stop at the far line and the egg rolled out of the spoon and onto the ground. Splat!

"Hey, this is great!" Carole said.

"If you like scrambled eggs," Stevie said, making a wry face.

"Everybody likes scrambled eggs," Lisa said. "And I never had so much fun on a horse as this. It's a great race and everybody's going to love it—except maybe Red if he has to clean the ring afterward."

"We could use hard-boiled eggs," Carole suggested.

"No way! These raw ones are much more fun," Stevie said. "Okay, now we've figured out how this one works; we can't try the costume race until tomorrow. I'll bring our whole costume box then so we can sort out things that are equally hard. I mean, it's not fair to have one team just have to slip on a sheet while another has to put on a whole lot of pirate stuff! We'll just have to see how it goes tomorrow. For now, though, what can we do with all the hardware Lisa borrowed from Mrs. Reg?"

Together, they examined the booty. Within a few minutes, they'd designed a race that involved picking up a double-end snap from one of the pillars on the course and then attaching it to a chain suspended from another pillar. When they tested it, they found it was tricky holding the pony still with one hand and trying to fasten the snap with the other.

"Perfect," Stevie announced. "It's good and devious, but it's not impossible. Just the kind of thing I wanted. Now, what were you suggesting about holding a lot of rings on a riding crop?"

"I think first the rider has to sort of scoop them up from someplace, don't you?" Lisa asked.

"Yeah, but how?" Stevie asked. It took a little longer to solve that problem, because it took a while to figure out how the rings could be scoopable, but eventually they discovered that the rings stood up nicely in a glob of bubble gum, which could be perched atop the chest-high pillar.

"Great, that's another. We've gotten more done in an hour together than I could accomplish in ten days by myself."

"It's too bad you didn't ask us for help earlier," Carole said.

"Well, that's the way Niagara Falls," Stevie said philosophically. "And speaking of Niagara Falls, how about something with water? Like maybe the riders get a cupful of water and have to race to the end with it and pass it off to a teammate—sort of a variation on the egg race, but the water's going to splash out!"

"And the winner is the team that finishes with the most water," Lisa chimed in.

"I like it," Carole said. "Let's give it a trial. I'll get some paper cups."

Fifteen minutes later, all three girls had been completely sloshed with water. Their breeches were wet, the ponies' saddles were wet, and they'd had a wonderful time.

"That was so much fun that I think we'll have to do something else with water," Stevie said.

"Water-gun target shooting?"

"Bingo!" Stevie yelled.

WHEN IT CAME time to leave, the girls reluctantly untacked the ponies. Even Nickel and Quarter seemed sorry to stop for the night.

"Don't worry, guys," Stevie consoled Nickel as she slid his stall door closed. "There's lots more work to do, and lots more fun to have. We'll be back tomorrow, okay?"

"Why are all the ponies named after money?" Lisa asked.

"It's one of those Pine Hollow traditions," Carole explained. "Max names them after 'small change,' because of their small size. Some people think ponies are young horses, but that's not true. They're small horses. These guys," she said, pointing to Nickel, Quarter, and their stablemates, Penny and Tuppence, "are all full grown. Their small size makes them perfect for the kinds of games we've been working on. Even the littlest kids can ride them and they're very agile."

"Speaking of small horses, let's go take a look at Samson," Stevie suggested. The girls stowed the pony tack and then walked softly to Samson and Delilah's stall.

"He's grown already, hasn't he?" Lisa asked.

"Oh, yes. He's already bigger and stronger," Carole said excitedly. "Look how he's sort of frisking around the stall. That's not going to be big enough for him in a few days. Just wait until the two of them get out in the paddock. Judy said they could go outside in a few days. He's going to love it. Delilah will too. Horses were born to be outside. Stalls aren't natural for them. They were invented for people's convenience. On my farm, horses will spend almost all their time in the paddocks—"

"Stop her, Lisa. If she gets going on 'her farm,' we'll *never* get out of here!" Stevie said in mock alarm.

"I know, I do talk a lot, don't I?" Carole asked.

"Only about horses," Lisa said, consolingly.

"Let's go to TD's," Stevie invited her friends. "I think we have some celebrating to do."

"We'll make it a Club meeting, then, won't we?" Lisa suggested.

"Why not?" Stevie agreed. "It's about time we all went to one together," she said, joking at her own expense.

A HALF AN hour later, tired, but happy, the three girls settled into a booth at TD's and ordered some ridiculous concoctions. Stevie asked for a pineapple sundae with marshmallow fluff. Carole slapped her hand over her mouth, pretending to gag.

"You should talk," Stevie teased. "You think I want the hot fudge on pistachio you ordered?"

"I think sundaes are very personal," Lisa interrupted. "And personally, I want hot fudge too." The waitress jotted that down. "On bubble gum crunch."

"I'm not saying a thing," Stevie announced. "Lisa's right. Sundaes *are* very personal, and personally, I don't want what either of you ordered."

"Agreed," Carole said sensibly. "Now, to the first piece of business at this official meeting of The Saddle Club . . ."

"About the rules," Lisa began.

"Yes, about the rules—" Stevie said.

"No, let me talk," Lisa interrupted. Carole and Stevie were quiet. Lisa continued, "I had this idea, see, that if we didn't have rules, and purposes, and dues, that we couldn't be a real club."

"How could—" Stevie started to speak, but Carole's slight frown made her halt.

"But I've been thinking about it," Lisa went on, "and it seems to me that every club should be what all its members want it to be. Rules have a place in the world—we all need them. But we don't need them all the time, and not everything is ruled by rules. Some things are ruled by—"

She stopped because she was looking for the right word. Stevie supplied it. "Horse sense, you mean?"

"Yes, that's exactly what I mean," Lisa said, grinning. "Some people might call it common sense, but in The Saddle Club, it *ought* to be known as horse sense. Okay, so we don't need a lot of new rules. Mostly, we just need the ones we already had, like we have to help each other—the way we've been helping Stevie with making up gymkhana races."

"And members have to be horse crazy," Carole added.

"And they have to have horse sense," Stevie continued.

"And that's it," Carole finished.

"Not quite," Lisa said. "There's one thing I did that I didn't even put in the rules, but I think we should use it anyway." Lisa could feel her friends shift nervously. They really didn't want any rules at all. Their friendship and love of horses were enough.

"What's that?" Stevie asked hesitantly.

"Well, real clubs—and I know now that this is a *real* club—usually have symbols like shirts and ties and banners, stuff like that. The Saddle Club now has an official Club pin—and this is it."

She pointed to the shiny horse-head pin on her blouse.

"Hey, that's neat," Stevie said. "I didn't notice it before, but I like it."

"Me too," Carole added. "Where did you get it? Can we buy them too?"

"You don't have to," Lisa said, feeling terribly excited now that her nice secret was going to be shared. "I have one for each of you, too. Here they are." Proudly, she handed the identical pins to her friends. Proudly, they pinned them on their blouses just as Lisa had.

"That's cool," Stevie said. "I never would have thought of something like that, but I like it a lot."

"Actually," Lisa confessed, "I bought four of them. So now we have a spare pin, just in case it should ever happen that we find a person who deserves it."

"I've seen lots of horse pins, but this is the prettiest," Carole told Lisa. "Only you would think of something neat like this, Lisa. You've got a special kind of, oh, I don't know—"

"Horse sense?" Lisa suggested.

"That's exactly right," Carole said. "Dare I call it *le mot juste?*"

For a moment, just a moment, Lisa held her breath. Was Carole teasing her about Estelle? Yes, she was, Lisa decided, and moreover, she deserved it! Her solemn face broke into a grin and then she burst into giggles. Stevie and Carole joined in. They were still laughing when their sundaes arrived.

THE SADDLE CLUB

by Bonnie Bryant

Don't miss the latest titles in this super series:

PLEASURE HORSE
RIDING CLASS
HORSE SITTERS
GOLD MEDAL HORSE
GOLD MEDAL RIDER
CUTTING HORSE
TIGHT REIN
WILD HORSES
PHANTOM HORSE
HOBBYHORSE
BROKEN HORSE
HORSE BLUES
STABLE HEARTS
HORSE CAPADES
SILVER STIRRUPS
SADDLE SORE

Coming soon:

SUMMER HORSE
SUMMER RIDER